THE SILENT MARCH

C.M. KLYNE

Copyright © 2013 by C.M. Klyne
First Edition – March 2013

ISBN
978-1-77097-413-5 (Hardcover)
978-1-77097-414-2 (Paperback)
978-1-77097-415-9 (eBook)

Produced by:

FriesenPress
Suite 300 – 852 Fort Street
Victoria, BC, Canada V8W 1H8

www.friesenpress.com

Distributed to the trade by The Ingram Book Company

DEDICATION

This book is for my wife Patsy, who typed it, edited and believed that it was important enough to publish.

PART I
MAY 1919

CHAPTER ONE

When she first awoke, Anna knew she had slept badly again. She had to get up. Mrs. Jablinka would have breakfast ready soon. Anna could picture her buzzing around in her kitchen like a worker bee, preparing breakfast for her three tenants. Maybe four now, Anna thought. Hadn't she heard a new arrival the night before? A man she thought by the voice, but not an immigrant like the other tenants. She could detect no accent in the little she'd heard late last evening.

Anna had drifted off finally. Twelve to fourteen hours a day in the lab had been taking their toll and still she felt no closer to an answer. There was a huge void in her knowledge, in the structures and functions she needed to understand to proceed towards a solution. Only the certainty that she'd find it kept her going. The answer was there, just beyond the grey area of her mind, just past the tentacles of her thinking.

Then she heard Mary Jablinka's shout that breakfast was ready. When Anna sat down to eat, she was the only one at the table. The others had already set out for jobs that took most of them to the industrial area in the north end of the city. Anna knew them only slightly—a passing hello in late evening, a quick nod of acknowledgement as someone hurried out the door.

"Well, Dr. Williams, we've a new one in last night." Mary Jablinka placed two fresh coffees on the table for herself and Anna.

"I thought I heard someone late in the evening."

"You're not sleeping, Doctor. I can see it in your face. You're getting those raccoon eyes."

Anna smiled half-heartedly. "Yes, well sometimes we don't get choices in things, Mrs. Jablinka. As you well know. The work's the important thing. Else how are we to fix all the ills?"

"Hmph! Fix the ills indeed. We both know there's some things that don't get fixed and won't be, no matter how much time you spend in that lab." Mary attempted mightily to open a jar of preserves but finally gave up and handed it across to Anna.

"Your hands are bad again today, Mrs. Jablinka." She opened the jar and placed it on the table. "Let me see them, please." She took hold of the arthritic fingers gently. Mary's knuckles were horribly swollen and the knobby joints looked painful. The large, burled fingers were almost impossible to close and prevented her at times from doing even simple tasks.

Anna looked at her over the rims of her spectacles. "You're still using that snake oil you purchased. It's making your skin brittle. Is it doing any good?"

"As good as anything I guess, Doctor. They're really bad this week but who knows, maybe next week will be better." That was her, Anna thought. She wouldn't complain about it but wouldn't listen to reason about the things she might try. She'd just keep going until the inflammation subsided. As much to distract her as anything, Anna asked, "So. Tell me about the new fellow, Mrs. Jablinka. What d'you think of him? First impressions?"

"Oh, not very forthcoming that one. After eleven when he finally showed. Young fellow. Mid-twenties, I'd say. Said he was late 'cause he was out job-huntin'. But who goes job-huntin' in the late night, I ask you? Well, none of my business. Paid cash two months in advance so at least I got my money. Not like one or two o' the others, skulkin' around, tryin'to avoid me. I know it's hard for them but I can't run this house on nothing, Doctor."

"It's hard for everyone right now I guess. Jobs are scarce and now this flu. Scaring everyone I think, and maybe with good reason. Where's our new fellow come from?"

Mary rubbed her hands together. At times the throbbing pain was unceasing and made her feel like crying out. "Didn't talk that much. Seemed sorta quiet. Had cash though, which is kinda unusual. Didn't look like he's been sufferin' too much. Not like some of these other poor devils."

Anna knew she was talking about the other tenants, Karol Yablonski and Ike Stavros. Both immigrants, they struggled to put enough pennies together to both send money home and pay Mary for their living expenses. Both had jobs with the city but wages were low and their positions precarious. Layoffs were a daily occurrence and either one could find himself out of a job without notice.

The city was fermenting. Daily labour unrest. Conflict just barely below the surface, bubbling hot oil splashing and burning on both sides of the issue. *The Manitoba Free Press* ran reports on how alien subversives and socialist organizations were attempting to undermine the economy by threatening strike action.

The Winnipeg Trades and Labour Council was pushing hard for negotiations between management and labour. Short-tempered and out of sorts with all the strike talk, the business side was threatening to "run the alien bastards out of Canada and ship them back to their European homelands". Anna had heard that one of the city-councillor's favourite lines was something about "no red Bolshevik sons of bitches are gonna come in here and destroy our good prairie life". While none of this touched Anna in her current situation, it was unsettling to see the street gatherings, the gang mentality, and the malignant growth of intentions on both sides.

She was startled from her reverie by Mary Jablinka's voice. "And this, Mr. Devons, is Doctor Anna Williams." Mary apparently was waiting for her to say something.

"Oh, I'm sorry. I wasn't paying attention. Did you say your first name?"

A man stepped forward and took Anna's raised hand to shake. "It's Alvin, but people just call me Al. Good to meet you, Doctor. Must be nice to have a doctor residing in your home, Mrs. Jablinka. In case anyone gets sick I mean."

Anna was flustered. "Oh, I'm not a medical doctor, Mr. Devons. I'm a researcher. I work in a lab, studying a variety of diseases and trying to develop vaccines. Things like that."

Al sat down as Mary gripped the coffee pot in two hands, wincing all the time she was pouring. "That must be fascinating, Doctor. I wonder how one goes about doing such work?"

Anna saw that Mrs. Jablinka was right. He was quite a bit younger than she. His blue eyes met hers easily and were quite startling in their penetration. A blond mop of hair strayed about untidily on top of his head. At first she thought the question was just his way to keep the conversation afloat. But no, he was serious, genuinely interested. "Also, I haven't heard of a lot of females doing this kind of work."

She listened for a deprecatory tone in the statement but decided he was just stating it as a fact. "Indeed, Mr. Devons, all too true I'm afraid. Female bacteriologists are difficult to come by. The schools, of course, prefer males. It's unfortunate because there are many talented women out there and in this work, we need all the help we can get." Anna was somewhat astonished with herself. In the course of a few minutes, she'd spoken more words than she usually did in a whole day.

"But you've managed, Doctor Williams." Devons launched into the breakfast prepared by Mary. "I wonder how that came about?"

Anna did not have time for this. She'd be late to the lab and Stanley Parkes would wonder where she'd got to. She had never been late and was well aware that to maintain her position and be taken seriously she had to work harder by far than any male counterpart.

She smiled briefly. "Well, that's a story for another day, Mr. Devons. Right now I have to go or I'll miss my streetcar for downtown. Perhaps we'll get an opportunity to speak later."

Al stood up as she prepared to depart. "Yes, I should like that, Doctor. I too have to get moving. A lot of business to do today."

***

When Earle Nelson finally opened his eyes, the first thing he saw was Hawkins. The little man was crouched down on his haunches, staring through the tent flap at him. The melancholy face with the down-turned mouth, as always, showed nothing. Earle tried to raise his head to speak, but an electrical bolt slashed through his optic nerve and for a moment his stomach revolved as though he'd heave.

Earle closed his eyes and waited it out. When the spinning subsided and he felt some semblance of control, he moved his head slowly and experimentally back and forth. When the pain did not return, he dry-swallowed and managed a hoarse whisper. "Hawkshaw. How long I been out?"

The gnome-like figure of J.T. Hawkins—or Hawkshaw, as he much preferred—peered in at him more closely, his head cocked to one side so that it looked as if his cap might drop off. "Oh, you's awake. 'Bout time. Thought you were gonna die and never come aroun'."

Nelson tried again. "How long?"

"Don' know. Long time. Got some water. Nothin' else. Ya wan' it?"

Earle nodded and Hawkins passed it inside. He was parched, dry. He'd dehydrated badly then. He could tell. His clothes were damp and he stank. The pain in his head moved menacingly from front to back. That was from the dehydration too, he knew. Always it happened in the same way and always it took him unawares. Or almost unawares, at any rate. There was always the smell for a few moments before, like singed duck. The smell of damp, burned duck down. He drank more from the glass jar of water.

"What day is it?"

Hawkins regarded him dully, grappling with the question and finally counting on his fingers. "Uh, Tuesday...I think. Not sure."

Nelson considered this. Tuesday. At least four days, then. The last thing he remembered was Friday afternoon, returning to the tent with Hawkins. After they'd lifted the money off the drunk and bought the supplies. Yes. They'd come back to tent city. Cooked up some food. Hawkins had that pint and they each had some. That was the last thing. No! There was the singed duck. Like someone was cooking the down off a duck. He'd recognize that smell anywhere.

"You been here all this time, Hawkshaw?"

"Mostly, 'cept when I had to get stuff."

"Where are the others?"

"Oh, they's 'round. Fer a long time nobody else knew you was in here. When some o' the boys foun' out they was...uh... gonna...you know...do ya over."

Nelson gazed at him. "You stop them?"

"I tried, but well...ya know. It was mostly the smell."

"Yeah. I can smell it. I have to get cleaned up."

"An' I think they was scairt too. You was yelling. Screamin' too. They thought ya had sompin'. Some kinda disease. I guess!"

"Alright. Never mind. Help me out of here can you? I need to get down to the river. I have to get out of these clothes and wash." Hawkins pulled at Nelson until the latter had finally extracted himself from the tent and then steadied him when he was upright.

"Lucky for me," Hawkins said, "my sniffer don't work worth a damn." He added, "I thought you was gonna die, Earle. Die there in that tent."

Nelson considered this for awhile as they moved gingerly down the bank toward the water. "Better for many folks if I had, Hawkshaw."

Even if he could have known it, Earle would never have accepted that these long blackouts were a result of childhood trauma. He was very young when he first became ill. The neurons of the precentral gyrus had shut down and he'd been in a state of semi-stasis for a long time. Like some great blind primitive monster, the neuron pathways retreated, leaving the brain's electric activity devoid of movement.

For days, his neurological functions had been crippled, demobilized, incapacitated. His brain could not so much as move him to right or left.

As the hypothalamus muscled its way to the forefront, he'd slept. Huge periods of unconsciousness. The lesion creeping along the axon implanted itself with particular murderous accuracy. Cunningly it caused a misfire at the dendrite and elevated his body temperature. It spiked higher and then higher again and fanned flame-like into a storm of blue fire, crossing the muscles in painful sensory receptor patterns. It crept to his skin. His brain convulsed in self-strangulation.

He remained that way for days, alternating between the furnace of his over-heated skin cells and the diabolical drop in his body's core temperature that left him alternately freezing and overheating. In between there were periods of lucidity, but even then he was incapable of action and reaction.

In his normal waking state he also became incapable of empathy, remorse, guilt, or love. The cerebral blood flow hindrance left him oddly narcissistic while dependent upon others during these debilitating attacks. It also left him with a remarkable lack of ethical judgment and social responsibility. He was devoid of the somatic markers that otherwise worked to inhibit behaviours. Emotional connections were beyond him and the exhilaration of another's fear and pain were as close as he came to human feelings.

After he'd stripped, washed in the Red River, and cleaned himself as well as he could, Earle bundled up his clothes and moved up the embankment. He surveyed the surroundings carefully. *My Lord! What a mess!* Smoke curled gently upward in front of some of the dilapidated tents and shacks. *Hell must look like this*, Earle thought.

It crawled with vermin, the human kind as well as the rodents. Recently returned soldiers, down on their luck. The rejected, those with missing limbs, and any number with missing minds, shell-shocked into a state of sensory deprivation. And they were not the worst. Before he got sick, Earle had encountered thieves, perverts, the diseased, and the drunks.

He stood there, naked after his river bath, as if at the abyss of some camp of the itinerant dead and gazed about in melancholy. He glanced at Hawkins. "Lord, I've got to get out of here. This is no place for a human being like me. This is depressing,

Hawkshaw. Most of these poor beggars are on their way out. And soon."

Hawkins nodded. The sad, down-turned mouth groped for words. "Yeh. Well. Figured you'd go soon. But I can't. Bin here a long time. Cops'll clean us out again I s'pose. Then we'll all scatter awhile before we come back. Last time they kilt three. Saw it myself. Said we was rioting. Don't matter though. Nobody gives a shit."

Earle nodded in agreement. "That's true. But most of these would be better off dead. Maybe the cops did those three a favour. At least they never have to worry about the damned perverts after them again!" The Bible was clear. Homosexuality was a crime against God. It was a choice that only a follower of Satan could accept.

One must not suffer such deviance in a community of God! *Thou shalt not lie with mankind as with womankind: it is abomination. Leviticus 19:22.* "Deviants, Hawkshaw! Miscreants and devil's imps!"

Hawkins shuffled nervously from one foot to the other. He gazed mournfully at Nelson. "Earle. You ain't gonna do nothin' crazy, are you? Nothin' like what happened last week?"

"Like what happened last week?"

"You know, with them two guys."

Earle gazed steadily at him, "Those two got exactly what they deserved, Hawkshaw. They won't ever try out their perversions on anybody again."

The picture flashed before Hawkins's eyes. The drinking. The campfire casting a glow. Nelson's calm, watchful, demeanour. The tramp's hand reaching out and moving stealthily up the leg. The flash of the knife blade briefly as Earle plunged it up under the ribcage, then slashed across the upper abdomen. The other tramp jumping up and turning to flee. Tripping. Nelson on top of him quickly, lithe as a cat. The man opening his mouth to call out and the knife cutting across his windpipe. And then no sound, nothing. Hawkins helping Earle Nelson to drag the two bodies down the embankment. Floating them quietly, silently into the river. Peering into the darkness as the current caught them momentarily, nudging them away from the bank, pulling them off into the night.

"Just keep your mouth shut, Hawkshaw, and you won't end up like them."

Hawkins looked away. "Sure, Earle. Sure. I get you."

***

When Anna walked into the lab that day her boss, Dr. Stanley Parkes, was already at his desk recording notes. This in itself was unusual. It was a rare day that Anna was not the first one in to work. Anna knew though that this was mostly due to the fact that Stanley was married and his wife required—or demanded— at least a little of his time.

Parkes was an interesting man with an even more interest- ing mind. He was a somewhat morose person and inclined to keep things to himself—except the lab work, which he delegated enthusiastically to Anna and the rest of the research team. As always, he dressed immaculately, with tie-pin clipped in place. His soft, graying hair was neatly trimmed, including his small Charlie Chaplin style moustache. The wire-rimmed glasses gave him a scholarly look which Anna knew was accurate. He was a fine and capable administrator, but his abilities as a sci- entist were limited. Stanley Parkes was responsible for the lab's funding and he made sure he looked the part. Behind those wire-rimmed glasses glowed a rigorous and self-disciplined mind.

Parkes had hired Anna straight out of graduate school. With the massive reorganization of the health care system in the last two decades, quality researchers were more and more difficult to come by. The lab had pressing needs, and while it was small,

Parkes's total dedication to it and its production techniques had caught Anna's interest and so she left Toronto for the opportunity to do her own work in Winnipeg. She'd never regretted the choice.

Here she could work on her first love: the development of new vaccines. Only a few researchers worked the lab, and while that was tiny compared to what was happening in the huge metropolitan east and in the United States, it afforded Anna the perfect environment. She could deal in serums, vaccines, and cultures of toxic organisms.

"Good morning, Stanley. You're starting early today."

Parkes glanced up from his notes. "Anna, the new samples I'd asked for arrived. Harold is getting them set up now. Can you have a look please? And let me know your impressions by the end of the day. This Spanish flu seems to be taking off. The death rates in the army camps have been appalling. The government has asked that all laboratories and research be directed towards this epidemic. I don't have to tell you what it would mean if we can develop a solution."

Anna smiled at him. "No indeed, Stanley. You don't have to remind me." It could lead to the saving of thousands of lives, Anna knew. But she also knew that's not what Dr. Parkes meant entirely. It meant prestige. It meant reputation. It meant money.

Parkes glanced up to see her smiling. He pursed his lips. "We must stop this pathogen, Anna. If we can't, the consequences will be disastrous."

"Then I'd better get to work." Anna changed into her lab coat, stepped into the lab, spoke a quick greeting to her technician Harold, and went straight to her microscope.

People were beginning to die at an alarming rate. Young people. Not the elderly or the infirm. Not those compromised by weakened immune systems. Not even the poor, who perhaps were most susceptible when cholera was still able to rage, unchecked, across the planet. A young man in his mid-twenties could rise in the morning feeling fine and fit. A few hours later, the flu symptoms showed themselves, and within six short hours the man was dead, the Spanish flu having consumed his lungs until the life-force gurgled, spit, and choked itself to death.

Anna switched on the powerful light and bent over her Leitz Wetzlar microscope. She knew about the plight of the crew of the "City of Exeter". Almost a year previously the British freighter had docked at Philadelphia. A majority of the crew was deathly ill. The head of Public Health Services was so alarmed at the gravity of the illness aboard that only ambulance drivers were allowed to attend to the sailors, and only then to trans-port them to a medical facility. The dozens of crew members quickly overwhelmed the hospital's capacity to care for them. A special sealed-off unit was constructed by the army, where a veritable "tent city" of containment was erected. Each patient was enclosed by white canvas on four sides so that it made it almost impossible to breathe on one another.

Within weeks, the isolation tent filled up with well over a hundred catastrophically ill patients. The mortality rate was alarming. By July 30 of the previous year, over three-hundred people under forty years of age had died. All who came into the quarantined tent reception from the Exeter had perished, along with hundreds who'd been placed in with them because of having the same symptoms. This is what had alerted Anna. These people had not come into contact with the Exeter sailors but were already ill when they got there. They'd become sick elsewhere, and that meant the flu virus was also out there, drift-ing slowly, slug-style across the country, enveloping its victims. It was grasping, invading, perambulating its way through mucous membrane, almost without obstacle, and travelling inexorably toward the lungs.

And then it stopped. Burned itself out. Dead itself after killing its victims. Why? The answer was what Parkes had sent Anna and the other scientists to discover. As she bent over more slides and then more, Anna searched for clues. Something changed with the disease at some point, but what was it? At what point did the change happen? And what was the causative agent that facilitated this?

All of this passed through her mind as Anna searched the collection of samples through the microscope. This particular batch was from U.S. army Camp Fulston, just outside of Boston. When it emerged in a second wave it started with four soldiers admitted to the army hospital; in six days, there were twenty-two more. Within five more days, 179 soldiers were ill and the symptoms were nearly identical. If you touched them to offer help, they screeched in agony. Temperatures rose to the point of delirium.

September of the previous fall was devastating to the camp. Over fifteen hundred fell ill and the medical staff was exhausted. The government poured in hundreds of doctors, nurses, and medical caregivers, hoping to contain the outbreak.

Medical personnel began work at 5 A.M. and concluded a shift at 9 P.M. They ate, slept, and went back to work again. In spite of their massive effort, the patients continued to die at an atrocious rate. Then the caregivers themselves became ill and began to die. Finally, no more admissions were allowed, no matter how ill. Camp Fulston was dying, strangling just as surely as its patients were.

By the five o'clock staff meeting, Anna had checked hundreds of samples and compiled her notes. Stanley Parkes was expecting results but she had nothing to show. She hoped others had fared better. Perhaps Johnstone or McAlister had picked up something at their end. If not, they'd all be back the next day, pushing at it again and driving themselves to solve this intractable disease.

"We can't locate the virus," Parkes complained. "And yet it has to be there. Nothing else makes sense."

He glanced around at the scientists. "None of you has found anything?" His gaze landed on Carl McAlister, who looked away as if reproached.

Hugh Johnstone piped, "It's B. influenzae. It has to be, Stanley. I have no idea what else it could be."

Anna was not so sure. B. influenzae was difficult to cultivate and even more difficult to identify. It was not like others, wouldn't grow in nice, neat colonies. She thought they should consider looking elsewhere, but if she suggested this the others would only negate it. And the cost! If they changed direction and deserted the B. influenzae and she was wrong, it was unthinkable. She could not afford to be wrong—it would end her career, finish her within the scientific community. McAlister and Johnstone would make sure of that. They'd made it clear from the start that having Anna Williams in the lab with them was not to be tolerated. They'd never worked with a female and were not prepared to do so now. No matter what Stanley Parkes thought, bringing in a female research bacteriologist could only lead to trouble. And when it did, her two senior colleagues would be all too ready to see her fail. The luxury of a mistake as a professional female was disallowed and that fact hung over her like a poised scythe. But still, the doubt sat there and gnawed at the back of her mind. All of them were working on B. influenzae. Maybe that was a mistake.

She spoke before she realized she was even going to. "I want to change directions, Stanley."

"What do you mean?"

She looked around at the others. "We're all working along the same lines. Moving along in the same direction and getting similar results."

"But we agreed that we needed a common starting point. That B. influenzae was our best opportunity."

Anna grew more insistent. "I know. But what if we're all going in the wrong direction? What if it's not B. influenzae at all? What if it's something entirely new?" She stopped and looked about her at the doubting faces.

Johnstone voiced the concerns for all. "We can't go running off plowing brand new ground. If we don't focus into one area, we're doomed. It's futile to pursue so many different directions."

Anna thought this over then spoke more to Parkes than the others. "Alright, I'll offer a compromise. In the regular working hours I'll work like everybody else. On B. influenzae. But after hours I want to be free to pursue different avenues." They couldn't argue; her after hours time was her own business.

Parkes smiled and nodded in assent.

It was 6 P.M. The others changed out of their work clothes and left for home and family. Anna returned to the lab to set up more experiments. As usual, it would be 10 P.M. or later when she got back to her room at the boarding house.

***

When Alvin Devons stepped into the Winnipeg Labour Council's offices on Broadway on May 3, he was not prepared for the activity he saw. Men and women were moving about everywhere, offices spilling over with activity. A group at a long table was busy preparing posters and what looked like a huge banner.

He cast about for someone to speak with and finally lighted upon a young woman interviewing two men off in a corner, seemingly oblivious to the ant-like activity around them. When he crossed over and stood in front of them, all three stopped and stared at him.

The woman asked, "Can we help you?"

"I hope so. I'm supposed to see Sam Seigalman."

She glanced at the other two. "I don't believe he's here actually. Do you fellows know?" She addressed the two men in front of her, and they shook their heads in response.

Alvin sized up the two men with her. Working men. Neither had shaved for several days and they looked weary from lack of sleep. They eyed Devons quietly and waited.

The woman asked, "Who are you?"

"I'm Alvin Devons. I'm here from Minneapolis. The Machinists Union sent me. I'm in the right place, am I not? The Winnipeg Labour Council?"

At this, the girl broke into a smile and extended her hand. "You're in the right place, Mr. Devons. I'm Kathleen Johns. I write for the *Western Labour News*. Sam's not here. There's a rally this afternoon at the legislature." She moved her hands about, indicating the activity. "That's what this is all about. Sam's out getting things ready. Bob Russell's going to speak, so it'll be interesting."

"It's important I see Sam. I have some papers for him. He needs to see them as soon as possible."

"I might be able to help you with that, Mr. Devons, and if I can't, these men will be able to help you find your way to him. They're from the Building Trades Union. We're at a stalemate with the builders—they're refusing to negotiate."

Al studied her more closely. Very young for a journalist. Reddish hair and deep almond eyes. She was confident, pretty, and obviously well informed. Al needed a contact. Perhaps she'd be suitable. "Seems the whole world's at a stalemate, Miss Johns. Since the war ended it's like we're all busy holding our breath."

Kathleen became intrigued. Her paper was interested in anything that smacked of labour and she was always on the lookout for fresh angles and fresh faces. Like a bloodhound, she sniffed potential in Alvin Devons and decided to pursue it.

"The coffee pot's on, Alvin. Let's have a cup and talk a bit. I'd like to know more." She'd switched from her business voice to a first-name, casual basis easily and smoothly. She turned back to the carpenters. "Don't run off, fellows. I still want to finish the interview."

After pouring them each coffee, Kathleen led Al to the back of the offices where they could talk with some degree of privacy.

"So what's your part in all this, Al? Where do you fit in and what's so critical about seeing Sam Seigalman?" She sat behind a tiny desk scattered with papers and sipped at her coffee.

Her invitation to talk was meant to put him at ease. To disarm him, he thought. And those brown eyes were meant to do the same thing.

He also prodded for information. "You're a reporter I guess. But you need to know that anything we talk about can't be published. It's better if people don't notice that I'm here. It's just because of the work I do."

Kathleen could feel a potential labour story drifting away from her and was disappointed. "Oh. Okay. Well then, let's just declare everything off the record then and talk about what's happening in Winnipeg." She cocked her head to one side suspiciously. "By the way, how do I know that you are who you say you are? The so-called Citizen's Committee has been spying on us lately. Twice they've tried to infiltrate the council. You understand, part of what I'm doing right now is checking your credentials."

Devons considered this momentarily, thinking about how to respond. "And how do I know who you are, Miss Johns? And what is the Citizen's Committee? Perhaps you could fill me in for a bit."

Kathleen laughed. "Good point. And I think you better call me Kathleen. Here's how you'll know who I am." She picked up a copy of the *Western Labour News* and handed it across the desk.

Al glanced at the headline with her byline underneath. "Labour Leaders meet in their Annual Congress." His eyes moved up the page to the banner in large block letters, *The Western Labour News*, and underneath it, in tiny bold type, a long subtitle: "A Weekly Newspaper Published in the Interests of the Labouring Classes. Endorsed by the Winnipeg Trades and Labour Council."

"Alright, I'm thoroughly impressed. Now what's the "Citizen's Committee" and what do they do?"

"Actually, they're officially known as the Citizen's Committee of One Thousand. They're business people, industrialists, and local politicians. They're supposed to be the group that supplies essential services in the event of a strike. You know, transportation, food, water, that sort of thing."

Kathleen Johns sipped her coffee and lit a cigarette. Devons did not react, though he'd never seen a female smoke in public. "What they really are of course is a bunch of so-called law-abiding, self-appointed hypocrites who want to shut us down. They want iron control of the city, but our leaders are not about to just turn things over to them.

They use the North West Mounted Police to try to intimidate us. And they have their own private bully boys. You have to watch out for them. More than once they've cracked the heads of our people."

"Well, that can happen in both directions Kathleen. No need to sit back and just let ourselves take it on the chin."

She smiled at him. "Well, we don't advocate violence of course. But we have to defend ourselves too, I guess"

"How's this committee set up?"

"E.K. Atwater's their chairman. He's a grain merchant. Lots of lawyers on their side. Don't underestimate them. They're well connected, with a really powerful propaganda force. They publish *The Citizen*, which is a misnomer if there ever was one. And they have a big appetite for hating Bolshevists."

"They try to tie us to Communism, then?"

"Exactly! If they can show us as Bolsheviks trying to overthrow the elected government, then they can use force against us. Arrest our leaders, put them in jail, and put down strikes."

Devons acknowledged the severity of the situation. "So we need to be active but not violent. If things get out of hand, we play right into what they expect and what they want."

"That's why I said I needed to know who you are. The Committee's been trying to plant agents in our group. They're supposed to stir things up. Get people angry. See if they can provoke us into action and make it easier for the Committee to break us."

Alvin stood up. "Alright, Miss Kathleen Johns. I think I get the layout of things. It's time for me to go to work. How do I find Sam?"

She hesitated a moment, finished the last of her cigarette and ground it out. "You and I will attend the protest at the legislature. That's our new provincial building. Officially it won't be open until sometime next year, but it's the ideal place for us to march. I'll introduce you to Sam and you'll hear R.B. Russell speak. I think you'll find him particularly interesting."

CHAPTER TWO

When Earle Nelson extricated himself from the tent city camp by the Red River, he made his way to Main Street. His destination was Union Station. To remain any longer by the riverbank was a danger. He had to mainstream himself for a while. Regain respectability. Rebuild his life once more as he'd done so many times previously. He knew how, he just had to find the right connector, the place where he could function. He would know it when he saw it. In this way, he'd never failed. Well, except for the one time in the Dakotas and that hadn't been his fault.

How could he have foreseen that the girl was like a panther? How could he have known of her power? She had disarmed him completely and he had let his normal defenses down. That had been costly and messy. All the time he thought he was beguiling her, it was just the opposite. And she was so good at it! She even introduced him to her parents, only to find out later that they were complete fakes. All the money he'd spent on her to set it up. And she'd almost gotten away with it completely. They'd taken him for cash, clothes, liquor...how could he not have seen it?

Never again. He'd been a lot more careful since then. Not that he'd let himself become emotionally involved. He was incapable of that. But she'd seemed so soft, so genuine. And so, so vulnerable. But up until the last moment, she'd played him like a beautiful harp. Plucked his strings so very gently, unraveling his tune with tiny, melodic calibrations. Until then, he hadn't even known he'd been susceptible. As always, he'd believed himself to be fully in charge.

Right up until he'd smelled the singed duck down. When he finally awoke, she was gone, along with everything else: the cash, the furniture, the clothing, and the fake parents. That had been five years ago and it had taken Earle that long to rebuild himself, to gain a foothold, and then to solidify his position. But never again would he slip up. Only a fool didn't learn and Nelson was no fool. Now he secreted things. Kept a stash. Protected himself. Always he built in back-up.

He stood before Union Station and still felt some awe towards the building. A monument to a fast-expanding, modern industrial society. Its grand cupola arced across the horizon. Before he entered the train station, he rummaged in an adjoining storage shed and retrieved his suitcase. He knew his rundown appearance would cause second looks. There was nothing he could do about that, except to use the lower level where only the foreign immigrants congregated. He made his way to the washroom, and when it was empty he felt that first twinge of euphoria that always told him when things would go well.

He used his knife to cut the twine holding the suitcase shut. He took time to use the toilet and then to wash his hands carefully. He hated being dirty. Grime under his fingernails always revolted him and caused him to scrub at it with ferocity. He opened the small suitcase, removed clothing and a shaving kit, and retied the suitcase. Thirty minutes later, when he emerged, no one would have recognized him as the same person. His face was freshly shaved, his clothes neat and trim. The attractive, broad-brimmed hat was encircled with a black band that set it off wonderfully. His high white collar looked new and a tie peeked out above his buttoned vest. The fine cloth of his jacket spoke of a prosperous individual. He could have been a businessman of repute, an academic or a highly placed civil servant. Earle looked confident and comfortable as he moved up to the next level of Union Station, where only English-speaking immigrants were allowed. He left the building and moved out into the throng on Main Street.

First thing he needed was a good meal. He headed north on Main, crossed the street at Graham, and made his way west. At Fort, he turned north again until he came to Henry's Bar and Grille. He stepped inside, surveyed the room carefully, and satisfied, he took a window seat so he could look out onto the sidewalk. Across the street he read the business signs: a tailor shop, shoe repair, and beside it a building with a sign proclaiming "Versatile Medical Laboratories Inc.".

The waitress delivered coffee and Earle ordered bacon and eggs, a double order of toast, and orange juice. He was hungry—immensely hungry—which told him his recovery was imminent. He felt revitalized, energetic. The lethargy and fog of the last week was lifting and he felt ready to move on, to leave Winnipeg for fresh territory. He'd head east perhaps. Toronto might fit his plans well, or perhaps west to Regina. Smaller, easier to work, but also he'd be easier to find. Maybe too small.

He had no particular plan of action except that he knew it was time. He always knew when it was time.

Time was on Earle's side. It had conferred its blessings upon him as surely as had his Maker. There was so little in life that was not foreordained, so little that the single human could control and manipulate. But time was one of them.

One had to be aware, of course. Time was constantly at work, moving to and fro in a human life; she could bite like some carnivorous ogre in one guise, and in another, cradle-rock you to sleep.

But he also knew that time was capricious. It both arrived too soon and left too soon. It was a façade; fake. But having created it so very carefully, humans had been left little choice but to accept its validity. This, thought Earle, in spite of the fact that it owed no loyalties, embraced no values, and conferred no favoritism.

Except upon him.

And so it was that time brought Earle Nelson to Henry's Bar & Grille that May morning.

It was also time that brought Dr. Anna Williams out of her lab on Fort Street and led her to cross over to the restaurant to take a break from her work. Rarely did Anna leave the lab, but this morning she had to think. Had to contemplate what she believed was under her microscope lens. She had to put this new finding into a context. What did it mean? What was the best way to proceed? How much of it should she let out to others? If what she perceived was accurate, then she had to be careful. To reveal too much could send everyone off in a wrong direction with disastrous results and the blame would be entirely hers. Stanley Parkes would not understand and certainly would not be forgiving. She needed to be certain and could not leave any doubt.

So many thoughts filled her brain as she slid into the booth at the end of the room. She did not take notice of the warm Manitoba sunshine reflecting off the street. She did not notice the weary looking waitress who placed coffee before her and took out pencil and paper to write an order. She did not notice the well-dressed man sitting by the window who was studying her intently, noting the wave of her hair, the firm curve of her mouth, the attractive eyes behind the glasses, the ample breasts... And Earle Nelson knew that she did not notice.

***

There were tens of thousands of people spread across the sidewalks and streets when Al and Kathleen arrived at the rally. A raised wooden platform stood before the massive concrete steps that led up to the Manitoba Legislature Building. The crowd was quiet and calm, with no jostling or pushing for favored positions. Al looked about, impressed with the signs, placards, and banners hoisted above the heads of the crowd.

WE DEMAND DECENT WAGES
IWW SUPPORTS LABOUR UNIONS
NO BUDGET BALANCE ON OUR BACKS

It was a marvelous day for this event. Spring was arriving in Winnipeg and the resplendent trees and shrubbery were showing new buds. Assiniboine Park attracted visitors every day. In Victoria Park only a week previously, labour had held a successful rally. Activists berated the city fathers, the councillors, industrialists, the Canadian Pacific Railway executives, and the provincial and federal government leaders.

The CPR employed painters in its railway yard and paid them thirty-six cents per hour. With luck and no loss of days, the painter could make sixty dollars per month. But his expenses were astronomical. One dollar and ninety-seven cents for lights, two dollars and ten cents for three months for water, eleven dollars a ton for coal in the good months and twice as much in winter. Three dollars per cord for wood. Twenty to twenty-five dollars a month for groceries and another ten dollars for meat. The painter paid ten dollars a year for a sick benefit and union fees of eighty-five cents a month.

The painter is a hardworking man. He doesn't drink and is in no way extravagant. But he has seven children and cannot provide for the family. They live in a house by the CPR yards so he can walk to work. Twenty-three dollars a month for a house in poor condition and in a terrible location. Doomed to poverty.

Al watched a man working the crowd. The man pulled out a penknife from a breast pocket. "How about a penknife, fella? Check out this knife. It's great." He ran his thumb back and forth across the blade. He opened and closed it rapidly and then tried to bend the blade. "Won't break, see. Unbreakable. Greatest penknife in the world. This little knife is guaranteed! It won't break! Check this out!" He tried to bend the blade again. "No matter how rough you treat it, this knife won't break. And if it does you get your money back. Mind you it's no Opinel, but it gets the job done. Watch this."

He removed a small, freshly cut poplar branch about the size of his little finger and about three inches long. In a flash, he inserted the blade between the bark and meat of the branch and turned the knife in a circular pattern. He withdrew the blade and did the same thing at the other end. He slipped the tube of bark off the branch and about half way down he cut a notch. He took the white, solid piece of poplar and cut a larger notch halfway down, then planed from the notch to the tip of the wood. When he slipped the bark tube back over the branch, there was an air passage created from the notch to the nib. He held the whistle end to his lips and blew a clear single note.

Delighted faces lit up when he blew the note again. He laughed, handed the whistle to a small boy, and cried, "Here son, you try it!" He turned his attention back to the crowd. "100% guaranteed. No gimmicks! No tricks! You can see for yourself how well it works. And let's say you're goin' out with the girl you love and you check your hands and lo and behold, yer nails are dirty." The crowd laughed when he began using the blade to clean his nails.

Al nudged Kathleen in the ribs and nodded towards the man. She followed his gaze for awhile and smiled. "That's Howard Spack. Watch him work this crowd over. He's setting them up, getting them ready. Watch him, but don't buy a pen knife from him."

Spack went on to another person in the crowd. "Hey, how about a little penknife, fella? Check this out. This is such a great knife; look what I can do." He took a single dollar bill from his wallet, folded it in half and sliced it into two sheets. He held up both pieces over his head and shouted, "See, this knife can turn one dollar into two!" The men laughed and Howard Spack laughed with them. "C'mon fellas! Only thirty-five cents for this great knife! Maybe you'll be able to double your own money."

Several men reached into their pockets and Howard handed out several of the tiny knives before he moved on happily through the group. He targeted a new group a few hundred feet away, taking a new penknife out of his breast pocket.

A brass band struck up behind them and began to march. When they got closer, Al realized it was the Salvation Army. The band leader was in front, keeping everyone in tune and in step. Uniformed members who were not in the band walked alongside, holding containers for a silver collection. When they passed close by, Alvin took quarters and dimes from his pocket and dropped them into the container closest to him. The middle-aged man holding it thanked him and moved on.

Hawkers had caught wind of the rally and moved from their usual locations in places like Market Square, parading their wares through the crowd. A strongman went through his routine up by the main platform. He stripped down to show off immaculate musculature and posed for the crowd. He possessed a huge handlebar moustache, waxed to perfection at the tips, while his hair contrasted sharply by being cut back almost to nothing. He popped his muscles as he clenched his arms, fists balanced on each side of his head, and exhorted the crowd to admire his physique.

He called two men forward, and as he held his hands high over his head, he collapsed his chest as he breathed out, making it as small as he could. Quickly, the two men tied a rope around his chest, making sure they pulled it tight across his nipples. With a huge intake of air into his lungs and a fierce bunching of his arms and chest muscles, he strained the rope until it frayed and then popped. The crowd roared its approval as he took the rope and held it high over his head in his right hand, then bowed to the crowd around him.

Kathleen glanced at Al. "Very impressive I must say. Makes one wonder what other tricks he can do."

Devons laughed good-naturedly. "Yes it does, Kathleen. Not someone a person would want to tangle with, I'm certain."

"That depends entirely upon the nature of the tangling, Mr. Devons."

Al laughed even harder and looked at her with a new appreciation. "I suppose that's true, Miss Johns. It always depends upon one's perspective, does it not?"

For another thirty minutes they watched a variety of musicians, magicians, jugglers, and singers, all designed to pull in an even bigger crowd and prepare them to hear the speeches from labour leaders.

At last a man stepped forward from the back of the platform and held up both hands to get the attention of the crowd and to quiet the hawkers. "Ok, folks. Great to see all of you out here today. If you were at last week's rally then you know a little bit about what you're in for. As you know, we've got Bob Russell with us."

Many in the crowd raised their hands and shouted approval. Still others nodded their heads and spoke quietly to their neighbours. Kathleen said, "That's Sam Seigalman. He's sort of the M.C. for the rallies. It's his job to make sure things go right."

Seigalman was not at all what Al had pictured. For one thing, he was no more than five-feet-six-inches tall. He had a ring of hair around the fringe of his head that came up just above his ears. The top of his shiny pate glistened in the sun. He was also rotund, with short, spindly legs. This humpty-dumpty look was countered by a deep bass voice, which was probably, Al thought, the biggest thing about Seigalman.

Al said, "I guess he's a Jew, is he?"

Kathleen looked at him keenly before deciding how to reply. "Yes, he is actually. Is that a problem for you?"

Al shrugged. "No. Course not. It was just a question, not a judgment."

"Good. I'm glad. Because if you were an anti-Semite, then I wouldn't be able to let you kiss me."

His mouth dropped open momentarily, then snapped shut quickly and he started to laugh. "Honestly, Kathleen Johns, why do I feel as if I'm about three steps behind you?"

She put her hand on his shoulder. "It's okay. You're a male. It's expected you'd be three steps behind."

Al shook his head and continued to grin. "I think I'll just shut my mouth now and listen to the speeches."

Sam Seigalman had finished the preliminaries and waited again for the crowd to quiet. "Now, before we go on, I want to bring up to the front someone that a few of you might already have met. His name's Howard Spack and he sells penknives."

Kathleen nudged Al. "Now listen to this. This guy is outrageous."

Sure enough, the man Al had seen previously working the crowd stepped forward and removed one of the knives from a breast pocket. He held it up over his head for all to see. "Now then, how many of you fellas were good enough to buy a little penknife from me? Hold them up. Let's see 'em."

Hands went up throughout the crowd. Pockets of grinning men waved their penknives overhead.

Spack shouted, "Well! You're a bunch of suckers!" The hands began to drop. "Let me tell you something. I paid ten cents for that knife. Then I came here and sold it to you for thirty-five cents. That's a 250 percent profit. An' that's not all. Look at this!" He held his knife up over his head and snapped it in half. "It breaks like a tooth-pick. I sold you guys a bill of goods and you practically lined up to buy it." By now all the hands had dropped and a few shuffled their feet back and forth uncomfortably. Those who hadn't bought penknives grinned and waited.

"Yes, it's true. I exploited you men. After all, I'm just trying to make a living, right? But this isn't where you're really exploited is it? Every time we go to the grocery store we're exploited. Every time we buy clothing or furniture we're exploited. Every time we buy cow's milk for our children we're exploited. But we know that. We accept that. It's capitalism at work. When we buy, someone else is making a buck and that's okay. After all, we're all of us just trying to make a living, right? And you didn't have to buy the penknives. You had a choice.

But when you go to work in the foundry you don't have a choice. It's for your labour that you're really being exploited. When the company makes massive profits and the owners get fat and happy, that's when you're really being exploited.

What are they afraid of? Why are they trying to break your unions? Why do they not want you to organize? The answer's obvious. They want to exploit you even more. They want your labour at a cheaper rate. They want your sweat to make them even more rich.

But it doesn't have to be that way. We can change things. We can make a difference. We don't have to let the E.K. Atwaters of the world run things. There is nothing that makes Mayor Charles Ross better than you or me. Nothing, that is, except that he's got the money and the power of the exploiters on his side. But he only has power over us if we let him have it. Remember, he's an elected official, and if he can be elected, then he can be unelected."

Now there was a low rumble of agreement in the crowd. Those who'd bought the penknives forgot about them. A few cried out, "Let's throw the bastard out!" Spack held his hands up again for quiet.

"I don't know Mayor Ross. I've never met him. We don't run in the same circles." There were several guffaws from the crowd at this. "For all I know he's a good Christian man. Probably he has children that go to a private school. Probably he's a hard worker. Probably he makes contributions to charities and to his church. No, I don't know the man directly. Maybe he doesn't drink or gamble. Probably he doesn't even smoke or spend his social time down in the pool hall. Hell, for all I know he doesn't even show his face down at Miss Ruby's in the red light district." At this there were gales of laughter from many, and men were seen to slap one another on the back.

Spack continued. "Oh, I see many of you are already acquainted with Miss Ruby." Again, laughter rose from the crowd. "Perhaps some of you are making too much money then!" Howls of laughter from some quarters went up and howls of derision from others.

Spack's voice deepened and he roared, "But I do know this!" He held a hand up in front of him with his forefinger pointing imperiously at the crowd. "Mayor Ross thinks you're low-life scum. He despises you. He believes you've come from hell and that's where he'd like to send you back to!" Hundreds of men in the crowd raised their fists in anger and shouted protests. Several more brazen ones screamed epithets and still others pumped their protest signs into the air.

"If Mayor Ross and his cronies have their way, there'll be no unions, we'll be kept in economic slavery, and your children will become ill and very likely die because you can't afford doctors. You can't take your kid down to King Edward Hospital, and even if you could, you sure as hell can't afford the medicine."

He waited for the low rumble across the crowd to subside. "That's why we're here today. We need to teach these bastards that they have to listen to us. They have to negotiate with us. They have to recognize the legitimacy of the unions. And the only way we can do this is through strike action!" Thousands of people shouted support. Al and Kathleen glanced around them and applauded. The line of men on the back of the stage responded with the clapping of hands and pumping of fists. Howard Spack gave the crowd a full minute to vent, then raised his hands for quiet.

"Now there's a lot more important people for you to listen to today than me, my friends. But first, before I turn this stage over to the next speaker, I want to say one last thing. I'll be here at the next rally. And guess what? I'll be sellin' some of my pen-knives. And after I get some of you to buy 'em—and you will—I'll give you a little bit of a talk about the Citizen's Committee of a Thousand assholes. And what they're planning for you."

Spack was cheered off the stage with much hooting and hollering. And those who'd bought knives from him were heard to cheer the loudest. He never gave them their money back.

Once more, Seigalman moved to the front of the stage to take control of the agenda. "Now you know and I know that all of us here today are not part of the brotherhood, and in some cases the sisterhood. All of us know that in our ranks here today there are members of the North West Mounted Police, and I see a contingent of our local constabulary in the back. We know that the mayor's office has people here, and of course there are you folks from *The Manitoba Free Press*, *The Trib*, and *The Telegram*. No doubt the things being said here will get back to the appropriate ears. Well that's good. We aren't trying to hide anything. We want open and frank discussion so that when you go back to your bosses to report, you need to get it straight. The general strike committee is hard at work. Don't have any doubt in your mind. We will shut this city down if the owners and the city government don't come to the table. They've left us no other option. We will strike and we will win!"

Another roar of approval from the crowd. They were listening now, tuning in to every word. Seigalman moved things forward. "Okay, folks. I'm introducing Bob Russell. Here's a man who makes it very plain where he stands: clearly upon the side of the working man and woman. And beyond that, he doesn't really need an introduction. You know him. You know why he's here. Bob Russell!" Sam raised his hands in applause and the crowd joined in enthusiastically. Russell stepped forward, took in the crowd, and waved. He waited them out, until the last person quieted and he took time to survey them, as if weighing his options.

"In union there is strength! Without it, we are doomed to preserve the status quo. My friends, we stand here today, still less than two decades into the 20th century. It's been more or less one-hundred years since the Industrial Revolution changed the way we live. But in those same hundred years, the thinking of the bosses of industry has changed not one iota.

Still they insist that the working man and woman exist in a state of virtual slavery. They continue not only to think that our labour is worth a pittance, but to also demonize us, to negate our collective bargaining rights, to destroy our capacity to organize, and to insist that the only right and power working people have—the right to strike—is illegal and anti-democratic. I say to hell with them!" Bob Russell punched the air with a forefinger as he raised his voice. Thousands of voices shouted agreement. More shook their heads in reaction. Men and women cupped their hands around their mouths and shouted back, "Strike! Strike! Strike!"

He waited for calm and modulated his voice to a normal speaking range. "I know Arthur Meighen for the man he is. And I know Senator James M. Robinson for what he is. Do not be fooled by these men. Justice Minister Meighen wants justice, alright. But not for you and not for me. He wants justice for the factory owners, for the industrialists, for government, for the railroad barons, but not for us. He wants one-sided justice.

And Labour Minister Robinson is no better. He'll tell you he's a labour man. He can probably even show you a union card. But I'm here to tell you that Robinson is a traitor. He's in the pockets of the capitalists. To put our trust in him is to sell out the labour movement. To listen to him is to lose our cause before we've even begun.

I know that our country is being run by fools. I recognize that the heartless bastards who own our factories do not have a conscience. I realize that the government of the City of Winnipeg is made up entirely of crooks, stooges, liars, cheats and racists. They will rob you of your sweat, defy your right to support your family, hound you to death if you so much as whisper the word union. They will beat you with clubs, throw you in jail, fire you from your job and, if you're an immigrant they'll try to have you deported.

This is not work that we have, friends. It's not honourable work. This is just another form of serfdom and if we're not willing to stand up and fight them, our children and grandchildren will continue to be slaves. Is that what we want for them? Do we really want them to be condemned to being insensible, mindless drudges used to keep the economic machine of capitalism running?"

The crowd was hanging on his words now, straining to hear. They leaned forward, eager. Al watched Kathleen. Her pretty, oval-shaped face shone, the curve of the nose a gentle slope, her nostrils flared slightly as she breathed quickly, determined to hear every word. Her eyes glistened. She stood on the precipice as would a convert, completely absorbed.

Russell let his words sink in a moment longer, then dropped his voice and continued. "And now I want to tell you about Vladimir Kaminski. Twelve months ago, Kaminski was a White Russian in Crimea. He was fighting with Wrangel against the Red Army. He was captured and barely escaped execution. He was anti-Bolshevik you see, and ended up on the wrong side. He saw that there was no hope for his cause and so, in an attempt to find a better life for his family he brought them to Canada. And that's why I'm telling you about him.

I visited Vlad's home in the North End last night and I think you need to know about him. He has a job. He works at Vorox Iron Works. His home is a hovel. It's more a shack than anything, with a lean-to attached. He speaks no English, nor does his wife, who I'm sorry to say was busy trying to care for five children. These children were dirty, shoeless, and hungry. An old coal heater and a woodstove are provided by the landlord. This place is a fire-trap. It had two beds for the entire family, two chairs, and a table. And Mr. Kaminski is one of the lucky ones. He has electricity: a single light bulb hangs down from the middle of his ceiling. Should I mention the smoky, grimy walls because the chimney pipes are old, rusty, and falling apart? Should I mention the fact that there's no access to potable water? How about the rats? The lice? The vermin that infest the children?

Mr. Kaminski's smallest child is still a baby. When I was there, the child was lying in a cradle lined with old potato sacks, hung from the ceiling and suspended by some rope. There was no food in this house. Mrs. Kaminski was no better off than her children. Barefoot, unkempt, half-clothed, beaten-down. And remember, Vladimir Kaminski and his family had come to Canada so they could partake in the good life.

But E.K. Atwater owns the Vorox Iron Works and he also owns the home that the Kaminskis live in. Now I ask you, is this the Canada of which you dreamed? Is Vorox Iron Works supposed to be a shining example of how private enterprise lifts us up and makes us a better people? Because if it is, it's not my vision of Canada, my friends. I'm telling you that if we can't make things better than this for the Kaminskis, then we can't make it better for anyone. E.K. Atwater and his ilk will continue to use us, to make fools of us, to harm our families, and undermine our rights!"

A roar rose from the crowd and thousands of fists pounded skyward in anger and frustration. Kathleen placed her hands on each side of her mouth and shouted with the rest. Al Devons kept his hands in his pockets but looked around at the rising tumult. It was impossible not to feel the electrical impulses leaping across the crowd like tiny bolts of lightning.

Russell began to move towards the end of his speech. "And these so-called leaders of industry, trade, commerce, and government have the audacity to call themselves Christians. I say it is most un-Christian to obtain obscene profits when the labouring Kaminskis in our midst cannot receive even a living wage. When capital in our economy is so disproportionate, then something is very, very wrong. There is no justice in this. This is out and out profiteering.

We need legislation, my friends. We need laws that can secure a fair wage for our labour so that all Canadians—including our immigrants—can have a standard of living. So that the common citizen can live alongside the wealthy. It seems to me that this is the foundation of democracy."

Two men down in front of the stage were screaming at each other while others stood around them jeering. Bob Russell recognized this immediately. He'd been through it a dozen times before. A troublemaker—probably from the mayor's office—trying to fight with a union worker. Trying to get the crowd into it. Cause a fight to start. A riot to break out. Then the whole thing could be shut down.

Russell stood his ground, his feet planted shoulder-width apart. Very slowly, he rolled up each of his sleeves. The troublemaker swung on the union man and knocked him down. Several bystanders moved into the fray. They jostled the man about and finally subdued him alongside the stage and almost in front of Russell, who stood with his hands planted firmly on his hips.

"Don't be afraid folks! It's always like this. This fellow has been sent to us compliments of the bosses. If he can start us fighting, then they have cause to arrest us and break up this peaceful demonstration."

He turned to face the man being held against the stage and scoffed at him. "So it's a fight you want? Well, we'll give you a damn good fight, my friend." Several in the crowd clapped and there were hoots of derision aimed at the man being held. "But you'll find out. And your employers will find out that we fight in a different way out here in Winnipeg. If you want it rough and tumble then we can give you that. But you need to know, mister, and your bosses need to know that we fight even better with our tongues and with our brains!" Several hustled the man away from the stage and escorted him back towards where the North West Mounted Police waited for the order to intervene.

The crowd howled approval for Bob Russell and applauded as the man was removed. Russell held up his hands for quiet.

"And so we've come to a point of crossing over, friends. Do not be frightened. It's impossible for things to be worse. Whatever our course of action, it can only lead to things being better. When you're finally pushed to your limit, there's little left to do but fight. Even now as I stand before you, the Union's Central Committee is moving us toward a general strike. There is no room left for compromise. But we need you behind us. We are in it together. And we have to win, because if we cannot, the consequences are unimaginable. If we cannot succeed, then Vladimir Kaminski and all people like him are doomed to deportation. The union movement itself will be bludgeoned into silence and every one of you will be subjected to life-long servitude!"

The crowd surged toward the stage. The men behind Bob Russell clapped enthusiastically and pressed forward in a semi-circle around him.

Sam Seigalman stepped up beside Russell, grasped his wrist, and held his arm high for all to see. He shouted out to the crowd, "No more defeats! No more defeats!"

They took up the chant and carried it forward. Throughout the crowd, in an act akin to collective hysteria, thousands sang out in a roar.

No more defeats!
No more defeats!
No more defeats!

CHAPTER THREE

Earle Nelson stood at the back of the crowd. As the swarm worked itself to a higher and higher level, he disengaged himself and headed toward Henry's Bar & Grille. He needed to retreat, to find himself a place to nest awhile and to get away from this army of labour. He needed to develop his thoughts a bit more and find the door he would access to move his life forward.

By the time he walked to the restaurant, the evening was coming on. Earle ordered a full-course dinner and while he waited he sipped his tea and contemplated. He was not a person to make headlong, hurried decisions. From childhood he'd recognized the importance of figuring out the angles, seeing all the alternatives, and increasing the chances of success.

He'd had to learn. Aunt Lillian had insisted upon it. He had to learn what God had intended for him. After his mother died and his father had left him with his aunt, the indoctrination of learning became a vital component of Earle's life. She taught him to read but only so that he could read the Bible from cover to cover. For hours while Lillian toiled away at her crochet, Earle read Biblical verses and they would discuss them. Or rather, she would fire questions and Earle would have to examine all the possible answers to avoid her unpredictable temper.

Hosea Chapter 9 Verses 11-16

As for Ephraim, their glory shall fly away like a bird, from the birth, and from the womb, and from the conception...Ephraim shall bring forth his children to the murderer. Give them, O Lord: What wilt thou give? Give them a miscarrying womb and dry breasts. ...for the wickedness of their doings I will drive them out of mine house...Ephraim is smitten, their root is dried up, they shall bear no fruit: Yea, though they bring forth, yet will I slay even the beloved fruit of their womb.

"What does it mean, Earley? Tell us what it means." Aunt Lillian stared over her crochet at him. Her small, black eyes gleamed like some stealthy rodent eyeing its prey in the moonlight.

Earle considered carefully. It was important to get this right. He knew how—he'd performed this miracle on many occasions. He just had to maintain the line of reasoning and read her as he spun the answer. "Well, Auntie, the tribe of Ephraim became one of the lost tribes. Ephraim became jealous and angry because previously it had been powerful and fruitful, but it looked and saw that Judah was attempting to take its place in God's eyes.

Ephraim broke with Judah and God saw that as a kind of personal rejection and He became angry with Ephraim and punished them. Ephraim was at first favoured. They had fertile land, access to rivers, and were a warlike people."

Earle checked with Aunt Lillian. She rocked back and forth in her chair, focused on her crochet hook but listening intently. Good. So far, he was getting it right.

"Ephraim argued with its neighbours and even great battles took place. But when Ephraim seceded, God saw it as rebellion. And it was not the first time. The Ehraimites left Egypt on their own long before the time appointed by God. And for that they were slaughtered by the Philistines."

Again, Earle stopped and checked in with his aunt. She continued to nod and work the crochet hook. The history, he knew, was the easy part. Those were just facts, things to be memorized and recited. It was the next part that was a little more of a quagmire. To fail the interpretation was to be punished. Like Ephraim, he would be rejected and in being rejected would be cursed.

"Go on, Earley. Tell us what else it means."

He cleared his throat and plunged ahead. "Well, the children of the tribe will die. They cannot be allowed to grow and produce more children because then the tribe would multiply and would go against God's will. God will cause the women to be unable to bear their babies and even if they could they wouldn't be able to feed them. Because they have been wicked they cannot be allowed to be a part of God's master plan."

Earle stole a glance and was relieved to see the nodding of Aunt Lillian's head. This gave him the courage to broaden his analysis and to update. "And it means that we cannot allow the Godless to gain power and authority the way the Ephraimites did. Today, the wickedness of Ephraim continues. There are people who curse God, and the communists deny Him. There are married women who have lovers. But God tells us in Hosea that these people will die. If the women become pregnant they will miscarry. And even if they do have babies, these children have to be killed. God tells us this."

Earle looked again. He'd got it right. He could tell. His aunt responded, "Amen. Amen. Very good, Earley. You go outside now and play and I'll call you when your lunch is ready. And remember, Earley! God loves you. Never be an Ephraimite. Always look to do what God wants you to do."

Earle placed the Bible on the coffee table in front of him and left the room. After lunch, he knew, there'd be another lesson and at least one more in the evening.

***

It was the arrival of his supper that interrupted the reverie. Hungry, he savoured the meal and ordered pie for dessert. While he was working his way through the pie, he looked up and saw that dusk was coming down. He glanced across the street and watched as Anna Williams emerged from the lab and headed toward Broadway Avenue.

And Earle finally knew the next thing he had to do. Quickly, he took out his wallet and laid money on the table, making sure there was a substantial tip. He stood up, shrugged himself into his jacket and hat, and proceeded into the street. He got outside just in time to follow the woman.

He remained at a good distance. Earle had long known how to make himself invisible, and so when he strolled up behind Anna at the streetcar stop at Broadway she had no reason to even pay attention as he passed her seat and took one several rows behind her. The car turned west on Broadway for several blocks, then followed Portage Avenue, and eventually came to Home Street. At the corner, Anna got off and walked down Home until she came to the rooming house. When she turned in at the gate, Earle Nelson was almost a full block behind her, and when he came abreast of the house he recognized it immediately. Though he barely glanced at 614 Home, he knew that it was an apartment building. An old one. Probably not more than four or five apartments in total. Tomorrow, Earle would return to rent a room. And if there was no room it didn't matter—there would be soon, Earle knew. He whistled softly as he continued down Home Street into the gathering darkness.

***

On May 6 at nine A.M., E.K. Atwater sat in a large leather chair in his office, looking at the dozen faces staring back at him. All except one was a member of the Citizen's Committee of One Thousand. As he looked out the window, he gazed upon one of those exquisite golden Manitoba mornings.

The warmth poured through the window and lit up the tiny dust motes floating in the air. Outside, Winnipeggers were scurrying about, awakening to the promise of spring and the renewal of life. Already the buds were forming on the elms as the city awaited the burst of nature on its doorstep.

At this time of year, the mornings went on for an eternity. Atwater had been up for four hours already and three of them had been spent in his office preparing for this meeting. It was time for action. The Committee could wait no longer. If something wasn't done, the labour unrest would lead to violence and upheaval. The legitimately elected government was weak and paralyzed. It was up to people like him and the Committee to show the leadership required to face down the labour forces. He turned back to the faces sitting around the enormous oak table.

He sipped from his coffee cup, wiped his lips with a napkin, and cleared his throat to begin. "Alright, gentlemen, by now all of you know about the labour rally. More strikes to come. And bigger ones. If we have a general strike, it will shut the city down. We can't have that. We can't allow it."

Mayor Charles Ross piped in. "E.K, we really need to talk about these private police. It's intolerable. They're nothing but thugs—a motley collection of ex-soldiers, anti-unionists, and downright bullies. That's not even the worst. They're probably illegal. You can't just put an unruly mob together and call them special constables. We have our own police to look after things."

Financier, banker and coal baron Julius Archibald spoke up. "Your so-called police, Mayor, are in the pockets of the goddamn strike committee. How much do you think they're going to do when it comes to arresting and prosecuting these bastards?"

While Atwater had never particularly cared for the banker, he recognized the accuracy of what the man was saying. They could not have rioting in the streets. It was true that the local police force sympathized with the strike committee and might even walk out with them.

Mayor Ross shot back, "Even so, we still have the North West Mounted Police. I tell you, gentlemen, there's no provision in the city's charter for a private police force. We can't turn them loose against our own citizens. People would never forget it."

Archibald shouted, "We aren't turning them loose on citizens, Charles. Goddamit! We're turning them loose on these Reds. Goddamn Bolsheviks! We need to run the godless bastards out of Winnipeg, and we can send the whole goddamn strike committee along with them. What the hell are they, Mayor, except a police force for the other side? And you're sitting here whining about our tactics?"

Sir Joseph Flavelle of the meat packers' fame held up a newspaper. "Anybody see this yet? *The Western Labour News* had this on their front page." He held it up for everyone to see.

Bread by permission of the likes of Ed Parnell
Bacon by permission of Sir Joe Flavelle
Coal by permission of Nanton the August
Milk by permission of the Creamery Trust
Shelter by permission of the Lumber Rings
Clothing by permission of the Cotton Kings
Land by permission of the CPR and Peers
Life by permission of the Profiteers

Charles Ross grinned. "Well, Augustus Nanton made the headlines again I see. Wonder how he'll take to that?"

E.K. stepped in tactfully, "Look, there's no point in our getting into arguments. That won't solve anything. We're in trouble here. This is going to come to a head, and sooner, not later. We'd better be ready." He checked the room to see if anyone wanted to respond. Ross opened his mouth to speak, then closed it and sat back in his chair.

Atwater continued. "Charles, I get your point, but we are going to need the specials. When this strike comes down—and it will—we have to have a way to fight back. We have to maintain law and order. This is not just a strike. It's a revolution. And when people revolt, you've got to bring them under control. We all know these people are communists. What are we supposed to do? Let them just take over like Russia? I don't think even you are prepared to let that happen, Mayor Ross. Am I right?"

All eyes turned to focus on Charles Ross, until he squirmed in his chair and looked flustered. "Of course. That's not what I meant. We can't just let things break down. We have to, to... uh." He trailed off and stared disconsolately at the centrepiece on the table.

Julius Archibald turned to a young man. "And what have you found out?" He was half their ages and in a few cases, one-third at most. A handsome face with a somewhat boyish charm. Until now he'd said nothing, preferring to wait until called upon.

"Oh, there'll be a strike alright. And soon. The Committee has everything ready. They're just waiting for the right time."

Archibald exploded again. "Well, Jesus Christ! We know that! What the hell are we paying you for? You're supposed to find out the time. The details. That's why we've sent you in there!"

The young man's eyes remained calm. He wasn't about to allow an old, pig-headed son of a bitch like Julius Archibald to intimidate him. He peered back and in a very soft voice said,

"You know, Julius, you might think you scare a lot of people. And maybe you do. But you don't scare me one goddamn bit."

He stood up and stared at each of them in turn. "Nobody knows better than I do why I'm here. You'll get the information you need. But you men better start listening." Archibald opened his mouth to respond, but E.K. held up his hand to stop him.

"You, Ed. And you, Julius and Bill." He smiled. He knew they detested it when he called them by their first names. "And the rest of you. You need to change some of the things you do. In spite of the labour acts being passed, we've still got employers who won't listen. I know that one of you has fourteen-year-old girls working up to seventy-two hours a week in a factory. Thomas, you've had two men die in the last six weeks. Both in exactly the same way. In your plant, the circular saws throw off big splinters of wood. These pieces come straight off the saw and are just like arrows. Both men died when the splinters shot through their chests. And you, E.K. Haven't you been prosecuted twice for violating the Labour Act? And if I recall, you were convicted. Course, that doesn't mean the act has any teeth, does it?"

The members of the Citizen's Committee sat in brooding silence. Many were uncomfortable to have this pointed out. Others remained unperturbed.

E.K. finally spoke. "Well, it's obvious you've been gathering a lot of data—a good deal of it on us. I wonder if you've done as well at gathering information on them—the job we hired you to do."

"I'm not telling you these things to make you out to be villains. I'm just saying you need to start listening to others besides each other. The unions didn't get to this point all on their own, you know. You're not innocent in all of this. You're not even in the right. But neither are they, and that's why you've been able to hire me. To find things out for you. And I have.

Some of it you already know. Bob Russell, Fred Dixon, Bill Ford are the people who are driving this. The strike will happen as I said. We're past the point of being able to contain it. But you think it's just a small pot of disturbers and Reds and that if you can get at them then you can break the unions. And maybe you can. But it's not just them."

He gave them time to let this sink in.

"What do you mean?" asked Ross.

"The Social Gospel Church is in this too. Salem Bland is urging the Church to attack the commercial enterprises of the city. Financiers, he claims, are nothing but a bunch of exploiters, and you, Mayor Ross, apparently are an abomination of the political system. His words, gentlemen, not mine. And the Church is not the only one you're up against. There are all kinds of leagues with their own agendas. The Single Tax League, the Free Speech League, the Worker's Independence League, the League for Labour Unity, the League for Justice and Equality. And now they've got something else going. They call it the Winnipeg Labour Church. They even have their own motto: IF ANY MAN WILL NOT WORK, HE SHALL NOT EAT."

Thomas Bulgar offered an opinion. "Well that sounds good to me. What's wrong with that?"

The young man turned his soft blue eyes to him. "Nothing. Nothing at all. Except what the Church preaches. They're saying that you people are the reasons why every man can't work. This Church is packed with workers. They're so full that the pastor, Bill Ford, has had to up the number of services that are being held. And it's always the same message: the evils of capitalism, rallies, the right to strike. They've got different speakers coming in every week and they're being listened to. I'm telling you men, that this strike will make last year's civil service strike look very small. And you won't be able to fire them all the way the city council did last year. Very poorly handled I might add, Mr. Mayor."

Charles Ross wriggled uncomfortably in his seat and reached for a glass of water.

"You want specifics from me? Okay, I'll give you some. The strike will happen in less than a week. And when one union goes, they'll all go. You can count on easily fifty-thousand people walking off their jobs. Your plants, factories, the power company, the whole city will shut down. You know that big fancy new legislature you've got sitting there? It's to become the site of the new Labour Church. The police will go out with the strikers, so don't think you'll have support there. The strike committee will dictate what happens, which services are provided, who'll get water and food, who'll be able to get medical help. They intend to dictate the terms and the outcomes of the strike. They already have the organization and the structure to do it."

He stopped abruptly and gazed about at the Committee. He saw expressions of anger, fear, and guilt. He picked his hat off the table. "And now, I leave it to you to plan your strategy. As for me, I must return to my real work: to sniff out what else I can find on behalf of you honourable gentlemen."

***

Dr. Anna Williams sat before her microscope in the Versatile Medical Laboratory, peering intently to discover if she saw any changes from the previous day. She'd completely given up on her promise to Stanley Parkes to continue the research on B. influenzae. Her notes were now filled with an assortment of completely new observations. If indeed what she believed was a fact then all of them were chasing a fairytale and were in fact helping to promote the ever-fiery, increasing pandemic.

As always when she worked this closely her mind locked onto the problem and questions raced in her brain. What connection was there between Pfeiffer's bacillus and influenza? How would it change things if the bacillus was not the same as the flu or indeed did not result in the flu at all? By what means will the influenza virus communicate with its human hosts, slip past our natural defenses and invade us? And as she asked the questions her extraordinary capacity for observation slipped down the microscope lens until she stood on the periphery of this world of miniscule bacteria.

The fluff-topped membrane scuds around under the microscopic slide. Its spike-shaped protuberances graze about carefully, slyly searching for prey. The hemogglutinen tendrils, arising from the virus's surface, examine the particles of the epithelial cells carefully, minutely, searching to lock in to the perfect opening to gain access.

Soon, it uncovers sialic acid and, like a climber hooking to the side of a mountain with grappling spikes, welding to the rock face, so does the hemogglutinen's sleathy proboscis. Once hooked into the cell, the virus slides itself smoothly and completely into the body of the cell and wears it as a disguise. Finding another influenza virus already present it sets out to manipulate a change. Carefully, it goes to work inside, adapting to its new environment. In a motion to reinvent itself, it splits in two and recombines its eight genes into a new life form. These genes probe the invaded epithelial cell and, finding the nucleus, strike it as with a battering ram. Upon acquisition, the virus's new genes overrun the cell's own natural genome and formulate new commands.

Immediately the cell begins to produce protein structures to protect the viral gene. The new gene begins to pattern copies of itself. In an act of monstrous and traitorous proportions, it prepares to devour its host.

Meanwhile, the neuraminidase runs a salient action to aid the hemogglutinen. From outside the host cell, the sharp cutters attached to the head of the neuraminidase work with the efficiency of a farmer slicing grain stalks with a scythe. It chops at bars of the sialic acid and renders the outer part of the cell neutral. This allows the newly commandeered viral cells to emerge and begin their deadly hunt for new healthy host cells.

In this way, a million new virally infected cells are propagated and delivered into the body. Because of its special abilities to hide, and to change its shape and form, the influenza virus gains the utilitarian advantage of being able to replicate itself. The existing antibodies, unable to recognize the virus as an enemy, search back and forth, blind benign guardians who leave the rapacious newcomer to its insidious work. The protective enzymes of the immune system, betrayed into submission, fumble about in their hopeless inability to respond. The antigens are emasculated and become useless.

The human machine begins to break down. The illness symptoms appear. In a tumultuous, riotous series of paroxysms, it begins a revolution of self-destruction. It devours itself in a frenzy of self-copulation, rendering itself out of existence and leaving behind a sterile, insular island of death.

Anna was astounded by her new-found conceptualization of the mechanism by which influenza might enter and affect the human system. This organism had the capacity to adapt. It didn't just attach itself to the outside of a cell and let itself be destroyed by the body's natural defenses. It could change, reform itself, and inoculate itself against the natural predation forces of the body. Which meant that scientists were playing in a brand-new ballgame and unaware of the new rules. But this could explain so much! It meant shifting everything they thought and moving into new possibilities, sending out new expeditions and refocusing their efforts.

If she was right, then the things they were doing were useless. And if she was right, she had to broaden her work. She had to find someone infected with the organism and watch its progression. It was time for a private meeting with Dr. Stanley Parkes. It was time to put her case forward and advocate for a deliberate shift in the lab's energies.

When she took her morning coffee, she approached Parkes's office. Of all times of the day, this was when he was most receptive. The morning was his productive time. By now he'd have gotten rid of much of the daily grind of the paperwork that kept the lab running. He would have read the researchers' reports, written letters, accepted or rejected purchase orders, and made the decisions necessary for the day-to-day occupation to proceed.

When she knocked on his door, she felt positive given the quick, bright response to enter.

"Good morning, Stanley. I have something that we need to talk about. It can't wait or be put off to the next staff meeting. Maybe shouldn't even be brought up there."

"And good morning to you, Anna. My, you're brimming with mystery this morning. What can be so very important?"

Anna moved forward to perch on a chair next to the desk. "As you know, in my spare time I've been working on the flu virus."

"Ah, yes. Your spare evening time." He looked over his glasses at her casually. "Of course, only in your spare time, Anna. During the rest of the day you're focusing on B. influenzae, right?"

Anna could feel the red creeping up her neck and into her face. She'd never been great at lying. Always got caught out; always gave herself away with the blushing.

She hesitated. "Yes...well...at any rate. I found something a few nights ago that you need to know about. It could be critical."

Parkes held up his hand to stop her. "Just before you go on, Anna, I think you should see this." He handed a folder across the desk and she studied the title: *Public Health Reports*, a weekly document published by the U.S. Public Health Service. Anna began reading.

A second wave of the deadly influenza virus
has been verified by the Public Health Service.
An outbreak has been confirmed in France,

where 5 percent of new recruits at an army camp have been infected. Another outbreak has happened in Switzerland, as well as several new ones in the United States. The lethality of the outbreaks has increased markedly.

Epidemiological studies have confirmed the presence of the flu in a variety of locales including steamships, ports of call, inland cities, army barracks, isolated communities, and as far away as Sierra Leone.

The Red Cross reports an alarming number of new cases in the population it services. They report hundreds of young people entering hospitals with the same intense symptoms. Corridors have been packed tight. All spare rooms, reception areas, and even closets for supplies have been crammed full of the sick and the dying.

Morgues have been so overrun that they cannot possibly keep up. Their own staff have become exhausted and ill. Corpses are piling up faster than they can be disposed of.

Autopsies have revealed astounding results. Fluids have been pouring from nostrils of corpses that are so much as touched. Lungs that have been removed show abnormalities, including oxygen starvation.

One of the most startling aspects of the "pneumonia" is the rapidity of the mortality. Males who appeared healthy in the A.M.

contract the disease and can be dead a mere six hours later. In one day, in one Boston hospital five doctors and fourteen nurses collapsed suddenly, all due to influenza. There were no prior symptoms. One moment they were fine, and in the next they were being carried off to hospital beds. In the Philadelphia General Hospital, fourteen flu victims died in a single day. The following day there were twenty more deaths.

Clearly, we in Public Health must concentrate our efforts on containment. Currently we are recommending that the public avoid large crowds, cover the face with fabric when coughing or sneezing, and go to bed at the first signs or symptoms of a cold.

Anna finished reading and looked back to Stanley. "I'm convinced that we're on the wrong trail. This is a different disease. It's not your regular, old-fashioned, week to ten days thing. And it's definitely not B. influenzae!"

Parkes listened intently while Anna described her work of the past week. When she finished, he stroked his small moustache with a forefinger as he pondered the information. "Anna, if you're wrong about this then you've wasted a lot of precious time. Time that we can't get back. If you're wrong, many, many more people are going to die. The disease is already here. In Winnipeg. I received reports from King Edward Hospital this morning. They had to admit fifteen cases this morning. Two have already died." He turned and looked at her for a long time before continuing. "Don't be wrong about this, Anna. Continue your work but don't you dare be mistaken. Now tell me, what's your next step?"

"I'll have to go over to the hospital. I need to see an autopsy. I need to collect some samples. Then I go to work on the serum."

"I can't turn the others loose to help you. You know I would if I could but it's impossible. They must continue to work on the B. influenzae." He looked at her as if to detect any resistance to this.

But Anna was elated. "That's alright. As long as I have Harold I can continue the work. He's become invaluable to me—he knows how I work and he just goes ahead and gets things done. I must have him."

Parkes's troubled face gave way to a slight smile. "Of course, and if you are correct in this I don't have to remind you of its importance. It would be the making of the lab." He paused momentarily. "And the saving of thousands of lives as well."

Anna stood, indicating that she understood her time was up. "Yes, I'm well aware of the outcomes, Stanley. I'd have to write a paper later for publication, and it would only be right that you were credited as co-author."

Parkes only nodded slightly in agreement.

Anna finished her coffee and started back for the lab.

***

When Al Devons walked into Kathleen's office at *The Western Labour News* on May 9, it had been six days since he'd left her after the rally at the legislature building. She didn't notice him right away. She pecked at her typewriter, paused, thought, pecked again, paused, thought.

When he spoke, she looked up, somewhat startled. "And how goes everything in the labour news business I wonder?"

"Al! Where have you been? I've been looking for you but nobody seems to know where you disappeared to."

"Ah, well, you know. We all have our jobs to do. And mine keeps me very busy." He leaned over towards the typewriter to catch a glimpse of the paper. "And what are you working at so diligently that you're completely lost in it?"

Kathleen laughed. "Well as a matter of fact, it's all fodder for the cause. In this case, though it's something near and dear to the hearts of those of us who work for *The Western Labour News*. If it's good enough, Bill Ford says he'll run it in next week's edition." She pulled the paper from the machine and handed it over. "Tell me what you think."

As he glanced at the copy she removed a cigarette from a small, silver-coloured cigarette case, lit one, and drew in with satisfaction.

LIFE IN THE NEW JERUSALEM

It's not only men and immigrants who are suffering at the hands of today's labour bosses. Indeed, women are thought of as second-class citizens who neither make a significant contribution to our society nor have the rights and responsibilities of their male counterparts.

Women have been able to gain employment in the communications industry as telephone operators because they are "dexterous, patient, and willing to take less for their work than males". Of course, it's the men who are also the managers in the workplace.

The fact of the matter is that thousands of women work in poorly ventilated, poorly run, ill-lit work houses. They perform tasks that are repetitive, tedious, heavy, and noisy. And this is if they find employment at all.

If they are single and get married, they lose
their jobs. If they become pregnant, they lose
their jobs. There is no opportunity for advance-
ment because

She had stopped at this point. Al had a fairly good idea about
what it would say when she finished. He put the paper down on
her desk.

"Why did you call it 'The New Jerusalem'?"

She picked up the coffee cup and drank from it. She inhaled
deeply from the cigarette and smiled softly, thoughtfully. She
looked up and locked her eyes to his. "And I John, saw the holy
city, New Jerusalem, coming down from God out of heaven
prepared as a bride adorned for her husband. And God shall
wipe away all tears from their eyes, and there shall be no more
death, neither sorrow, nor crying, neither shall there be any
more pain."

Al nodded. Neither spoke. Kathleen rubbed at the tip of her
nose with her index finger. When she spoke again her voice was
barely above a whisper, "When I spoke to Bill Ford about what
I wanted to write in this column, he suggested I look this up
in the book of revelations." She shook her head disconsolately.
"Can you imagine anything further from The New Jerusalem
than the north end of Winnipeg? Can you?"

He shrugged. "I guess not. Plenty of sorrow, tears, and death
to go around. Everybody will be able to get a fair helping."

Kathleen nodded. "Yes, everybody except Julius Archibald,
E.K. Atwater, Sir Joe Flavelle—and we can't just sit by and let
them have it all...let them gobble up everybody else and everything else..."

Al picked up the thread of where she was going. "And in
The New Jerusalem all that's supposed to disappear. I mean the
greed, the intolerance, the exploitation."

"Precisely! That's when we all become the classless society. Finally. Or at least according to Revelations."

"And what do you think?"

Kathleen paused, cocked her head to one side, and took time responding. "I'm not sure." Her brows wrinkled in concentration. "But I'm glad Bill suggested I read it. It got me to thinking about something."

He nodded and waited her out, until finally she went on. "Bill's a smart man. Very smart. New Jerusalem is supposed to be the celestial city. The big reward. The pot of gold. What if that's just a dream? What if there's no truth in it? What if that promise is just another way of keeping all the New Jerusalems in line? Not letting them out of their place?"

She picked a pencil off her desk and repeatedly thumped it gently upon her bottom lip, deep in thought.

After a minute, Al said, "Do you think he'll actually publish it?"

Kathleen looked at him through the cigarette smoke. "Oh yes, he'll do that. One thing about Bill Ford is that he understands this is a class struggle. And he also realizes that females are way at the back of the class. Bill knows that in this society we never ask ourselves the right questions."

"What do you mean?"

She sat up straighter in her chair, brushed back strands of the auburn hair that had fallen across her eyes. Al found himself becoming more and more attracted to those eyes and he knew this was not a good thing.

"You know who Charles Darwin was?" Kathleen cocked an eye at him and dropped her head a bit to one side.

Those eyes. Those eyes.

"Yeah, theory of evolution and all that."

"Exactly. And Darwin got it right, Alvin. Not because he knew the answer. Because he asked himself the right question."

"And that question is?"

"Well it's not a 'why' question. It's not even a 'how' question. He didn't ask 'Why does God exist?' or even 'Why does God not exist?' He didn't even ask 'How did the world come to be?'"

Al crossed his arms and leaned back in his chair. "Alright, Miss Kathleen Johns. What exactly then did Darwin ask himself? 'Would you please pass the salt?'"

"Oh very funny, Mr. Devons. Here I am trying to educate you and here you are passing off bad humour."

He shrugged his shoulders helplessly. "Sorry. Okay seriously, what was it that he asked?"

She paused, looked at him, put out the cigarette in her ashtray, and sipped her coffee. "It was a 'what if' question, and once he asked it, it changed his thinking and eventually the thinking of the world. It went something like this: what if species are mutable rather than immutable? Or it could have been something like this: what if all living things on the planet are related to each other or arose from a common ancestor?"

"How do you know that the question was framed like that? It could have been framed in many different ways."

She stood up, walked around the desk, and placed herself in front of him. "You're right of course. It could have been asked in a hundred different ways. But to answer your question: I know because if he hadn't asked the question in the first place, he would never have come up with the theory of evolution as the answer."

He folded his arms, sat, and looked up at her, grinning and shaking his head as might a diamond cutter who'd been privileged to view a perfect stone. Once more he admired her flawless looks, and for the briefest moment she opened her mouth to say more, then licked her lips lightly and fell back into rumination.

He cleared his throat. "Listen, I've come to see you for another reason. It's really important that I learn Winnipeg's downtown business district quickly. I thought perhaps...you could see your way clear to helping me with that?"

She'd gone back to her desk and was about to start typing again. She tilted her head to one side, "You mean that you'd like a tour sort of thing?"

Al nodded. "Yeah...something like that. If you could do that—I don't want to steal your time or anything."

She looked at him directly. "Yes you do."

He leaned forward and stretched his arms out in a helpless plea. "Oh, alright. Yes, I intended to steal your time." He smiled. "As much of it as I can get."

Kathleen's face spread into a beautiful smile. "You're in luck, Alvin Devons. It just happens that I am the best guide in Winnipeg. We'll do it tomorrow."

Al got up and walked to the door. When he reached it he turned back. His grin stopped and he said, "It is done. I am Alpha and Omega, the beginning and the end. I will give unto him that is a thirst of the fountain of the water of life freely."

Kathleen's eyebrows shot up as he winked at her and walked out the door. Thoughts collided as if they were atomic particles, and bounded about in chaotic uncertainty. She moved back to her typewriter and wrote furiously. It was hours later when she noticed the folded note on the edge of her desk. She picked it up and read.

What would happen if we were to have supper together?

CHAPTER FOUR

In the history of humankind, the answers to questions have, too often, been blind fumblings, deliberate obfuscation, monstrous economic enterprises, and the pursuit of unworthy ideologies. Asking oneself the right question opens doors and those doors open unto others and each allows the human to peer into the abyss of unknowledge. And because we can, we adjust or adapt and it is by the adaptation that we promulgate the self. Asking the right question allows for exploration and because of this we are able to touch the future. The gate opens, the first tentative steps are taken, the obstacles seized and grappled and set aside.

Miniscule thought is born. Monstrous thought has its genesis, and out of the muck progression and regression intertwine, gain and loss is weighed, alteration and maintenance exist in a pugnacious contest, seeking to grasp hold on the building blocks of existence.

So it was true and so it will always be. It was true in the lives of our forbearers. It was true in the lives of those curious minds who wrote the first human words, for those who contracted the world's first diseases, and for those who sought the first cures.

It was true at Ypres, at Waterloo, at the birth of capitalism and socialism. It was true as the guillotine fell upon the necks of the perplexed gentry and for those who swung by the neck over Salem town.

Appeasement is the death sentence. Inaction is the symptom. Subjugation is the final tally.

Asking the right question: it is both our birth and our death. For herein lie the seeds that, grown to fruit, displace the parent and, of necessity, annihilate it. And even in doing so set forth the events, the ideas, the plots, and the surgeries. The children of its own demise. The dichotomy of self is that in its infancy it is nurtured and in age it is denied.

***

On the morning of May 10, Earle Nelson was spending his fourth successive morning opposite 614 Home Street. He knew that soon he would see a sign go up in the window: "Room to Let". He must be the one to rent this room. During the last four days, he'd been able to search out a lot of information and that gave him a huge advantage. He knew the landlady was Mary Jablinka. He also knew of the intense difficulty she had with her hands because of arthritis.

He knew of Dr. Anna Williams, of her work as a bacteriologist, of the long, long hours of work she put in at her lab. He knew of the other two tenants: Karol Yablonski and Ike Stavros. He also knew that Karol Yablonski's room was going to be rented out. The visit to tent city had gone well, and thanks to Hawkshaw, the whole business of destroying Yablonski had been quiet, efficient, and competent.

The sign was placed in the window at 10 A.M. Earle could move downtown now and bide his time until 3 P. M., when he would return and take a room with landlady Jablinka. He decided to walk. Walking was healthful and it was a beautiful day. A day when a man could think clear-headed thoughts and remember.

"Earley, it's time for a lesson. Timothy I think is important today. Read from Timothy, Chapter 2."

"Yes, Aunt Lily." Sixteen-year-old Earle picked up the book and turned immediately to the right place. The two of them had spent a lot of time with this book. It was well-thumbed, and many passages seemed to open automatically to the right place, as did this one.

Timothy Chapter 2 vs. 8-14

> I will therefore that men pray everywhere, Lifting up holy hands, without wrath and doubting. In like manner also, that women adorn themselves, In modest apparel, with shamefacedness and sobriety; Not with braided hair, or gold, or pearls, or costly array; But (which becometh women professing godliness) with good works. Let the woman learn in silence with all subjection. But I suffer not a woman to teach, nor to usurp Authority over the man, but to be in silence. For Adam was first formed, then Eve And Adam was not deceived, but the woman Being deceived was in the transgression.

Aunt Lillian sat upon her kitchen chair, rocking herself back and forth as he read. "And what does it mean, Earley? Tell us what it means."

Earle looked down and away so as not to lock eyes with Aunt Lily. He knew he had to get it correct, otherwise there would be no supper and he would be sent down into the cellar for hours to contemplate his own sin of erroneous transmission. Earle hated the cellar. There was no light and the air was fetid with musk. There were spiders and crawling bugs, and in the darkness Earle could hear the rustling of tiny rodents.

When he was allowed to emerge, there'd be yet another lesson, and if he got that one right he might be allowed his now-cold supper. Or he might just be sent off to bed with the dull thud of hunger gnawing at him.

Which direction to take? The momentary pause settled his mind and with confidence he began. "Well, Auntie, it means that women should not be allowed to think they are important." He glanced up enough to see the furrowed crease deepening between her eyes. "What I mean is, women should not think they are more important than men."

The furrowed brow lessened.

"It was Adam who was created first and then Eve came later. And it was not Adam who was tempted by the serpent. It was Eve. She thought herself smarter and that she knew better than Adam, but really it was her. She believed in Satan more than in God and so she was punished for this."

"And women have been punished ever since, Earley. They will be punished even more. Why will there be punishment, Earley?"

Earle picked up on the theme and bounded forth. "Because women are supposed to be silent and also they cannot be teachers of God's word. Women are supposed to look after their homes. They cannot teach the gospel because of Eve. In case they become tempted again and receive even more pain from God. Women don't have the type of mind needed to lead the people in prayer and to spread the gospel. And women are supposed to dress properly and not show off their...bodies. And they should not drink alcohol because that is evil. And they should not wear things just meant to attract men. Like wearing gold or silver in their braided hair. They are not supposed to flirt with men."

Aunt Lily looked at him with disdain. Earle could feel the sweat creeping into his armpits and along his hairline. She waited for a long time before she spoke. "Earley, have you noticed that girl next door? That Eloise Jacobs?"

Earle shook his head back and forth vigorously. Too vigorously. He felt the trap door on the cellar closing. He felt his knees begin to shake.

Aunt Lily said, "That girl is trash, Earley. She's exactly the kind that this lesson is about. Of course you've seen her. I know what young men see and even worse what they think about. That girl, walking around with her hair done up and putting pins on her clothes and wearing gold and silver. The Bible says that girl is a harlot, Earley. The Bible says she should be shamefaced. She has transgressed against the Lord. When Eve ate of the fruit, she lost her ability to think properly and so she came to know that she could tempt the male. And when girls dress like Eloise, that's what they're trying to do— tempt you. That girl is bad, Earley, and punishment awaits her. You mark my word."

Earle nodded. "Yes ma'm. I think I understand. I can't let her fool me the way Adam got fooled by Eve. I have to resist. I have to ask God to help me."

She studied him closely to see if he really comprehended. "Go eat your supper now, Earley."

***

Al hoped fervently that the note he'd left for Kathleen would be accepted. In the meantime, he had a lot of work to do and he had to get down to the warehouse to do it. If things had gone right, Hugo would be there and would have the equipment. Alvin had received his orders: it was time to move the agenda forward. The signs were all present. The city had the Committee of One Thousand in place. The returning veterans had become the enforcement arm and were ready to displace the police. The unions were ripe with tension, straining to the bursting point, awaiting the moment when the general strike would set them loose upon the bosses. *The Manitoba Free Press* and *The Tribune* were cobbling together stories of factory mutinies, communist sympathizers, and the destruction of democracy. All that remained was for Alvin Devons to step into the situation and precipitate the action.

At the warehouse he found Hugo Heinz uncrating the boxes and preparing the dynamite. Hugo was only a technician. His job was to put the bombs together. Alvin had located and targeted the locales. It would be up to him to plant the device and to make sure that it detonated. He knew what to do. He'd done it a dozen times before. Still it was disconcerting to know that his life depended upon Hugo's technical skills and know-how. It always made him nervous how Heinz would work over the dynamite with the cigarette dangling from his mouth.

Al watched the man carefully. Hugo was slow, patient, and paid attention to each detail of the task. Al thought he had to be in his fifties now, maybe even sixty plus. The years of a dissolute life had settled around the substantial paunch that hung over his belt. The belt wasn't enough though, and for insurance against losing his pants, a pair of broad, striped suspenders looped over each shoulder. He'd also stopped shaving again and the grizzled double chin flapped about as Hugo coughed periodically; the great shoulders shook as he fought for a breath. The cigarette never moved from the side of his mouth.

The smoke curled up and Hugo squinted and leaned his forehead back in an attempt to keep the curls of smoke out of his eyes. The man's glasses lay propped high on his forehead as he manipulated the dynamite packs.

Al had asked him once about that, assuming that he propped the glasses up because he didn't need them for close work. Not at all. Hugo explained that when the glasses sat on the bridge of his nose, the cigarette smoke crept under them and into his eyes. In fact, he could see very little up close without them.

Hugo became aware of Al gazing at him. The older man looked up and grinned. "Don't worry, son. It won't blow us to kingdom come. Has Uncle Hugo ever made a mistake, Al? I ask you, haven't I always done right by you? Haven't I?" He giggled brightly as he put several sticks of dynamite together into a package and taped them tightly.

Al watched him closely. "I guess you have, Hugo. I'm still around to talk about it, so I guess you have!"

Hugo belched. "Heh! I guess so. After all, if I blew you up, the organization wouldn't like it would they? And I'd end up without a paycheck wouldn' I? So don't you be concerned. So long as Uncle Hugo is building'em, you'll be just fine. Course I can't be held responsible if you fuck things up when yer inside now, can I?" He glanced slyly at Al out of the corner of his eye.

Al knew what he was talking about. That very first time in the office of the meat plant manager in Chicago. In spite of his background in munitions in the American army during the war, Al had made a basic mistake and the thing had misfired. Or, more to the point, had not fired at all. He'd almost compounded the problem by thinking of returning to reset it. But then his training had kicked in and he'd forced himself to walk away. To leave it behind.

When it had been found the next day, the newspapers had a field day with it. Al had been called up on the carpet. He tried to point out that perhaps it was not him, that it might have been the technician, but nobody was having any of it.

His bosses had wanted to remove him, but remarkably it was Hugo Heinz who decided he should have a second chance and persuaded the others that they should try one more time.

But as he later told Al, "You fuck this up again and nothing's going to keep them from burning your ass."

They rehearsed it for weeks. Each step was plotted. Each move accounted for, predetermined. Al picked the place, cased it, and knew exactly where the device had to go for maximum damage. When all was ready, he entered the factory on the given night and spent only thirty minutes inside. Five minutes after he'd left, the explosion was enormous. The blast took out walls, machines, equipment, and the accelerant had started a massive inferno that kept the fire brigade busy for two days. He'd done his job and regained the confidence of his associates and bosses. He owed Hugo Heinz and he knew it.

"You don't need to remind me," Al answered. "Everything's been great since that first one. Right?"

Hugo nodded and continued work on the package. "You got yer place picked out? You checked it out yet?"

Alvin thought of Julius Archibald, of the man's epithets and his massive and monstrous ego. Archibald hated the unions deep in his core. Even to an unreasonable degree that turned him into a demonic creature who believed that if the world was to be saved, then the enemy had to be crushed utterly. It was people like Julius Archibald who, through their unstilted devotion to a capitalist ideal, had forced the very creation of the unions. It was Archibald and his cronies who had been responsible for the Citizen's Committee of a Thousand and who had created the illegal police force using the veterans and their sympathizers.

The problem for Alvin was it wasn't easy to get into a bank. It wasn't the same thing as a factory or a packing plant. There was security and some even had night watchmen. He had to find a way around these and into Julius's office.

"Yeah, I've picked the place. I know where to place it."

"Goin' to be tonight? Tomorrow night?"

Al thought of Kathleen. "No, but soon. Very soon. Not tomorrow—I've got something important to do."

Hugo grinned at him. "Hmmm. Now what could be more important than doin' yer job I wonder? You meetin' with Seigalman or something?"

"No. No, I've already talked to him and shown him the new orders. He'll do what he's told. He knows where his money is coming from."

Hugo Heinz looked at Al more closely, studied him until Al started to get uncomfortable. "Okay, good. You're not lettin' yourself in for some kinda trouble, are you son? You need to keep yer head straight. Not get distracted. Distraction causes mistakes. Mistakes are for amateurs. And mistakes get the wrong people dead, Al."

Al shrugged and tried to pass off his momentary lapse. "I'll get the job done. Just like always. I'll be ready. In two days—maybe three."

But he was thinking about the guided tour ahead. And he was thinking about those eyes and how they so often disarmed him without him even knowing it. Darwin, for Christ's sake!

***

Eloise Jacobs's mother worked two jobs to keep her household together. With the disappearance of Eloise's father years before and no one to help her, she hired on at a local sewing factory, but that was not enough to support the two of them and pay for the house as well.

Because there were no other family members to turn to, her mother did what she had to do and got an evening job as well. Luckily, the evening job only required her to work the front desk at the Altamont hotel. It was not the backbreaking piecemeal work that she had to perform in the sewing factory. With the extra job, she could get by and even earn enough money to keep her daughter in school and to buy her a nice (if second-hand) dress or some inexpensive jewelry or a kerchief. Once in awhile, a pair of earrings showed up, or a shiny brooch she could wear on a sweater or on her dress.

Eloise loved the dress with the lace sleeves and the lace around the collar that dropped down gently over her breasts. Because the sleeves sat just below her elbows, she was able to wear a gold-coloured piece of costume jewelry on her left arm and a variety of bangles and clasps on her right wrist. Her blond hair dropped to shoulder length. Off to one side of her head, she liked to tie a colourful red ribbon with a bow. Eloise loved the print dress that was a part of her look. She knew that it showed the lower part of her calves and her ankles, and she'd not been unaware of the boys at school who eyed her with delight.

Eloise was pretty, but she was also hard-working and conscientious. In the evenings, after she'd cleared away the supper dishes and washed them up and finished her chores, she would sit in the kitchen under the electric light and pore over her lessons. As a junior high school student, she knew the importance of education. Her mother was perpetual in her insistence that Eloise had to become an educated female, because it was only through that avenue that she could avoid living her mother's mistakes.

By nine o'clock in the evening it was growing dark, but Eloise paid no attention. Periodically she would reach down and pull up her dress to her knee, whereupon she would scratch at her kneecap thoughtfully as she sought to untangle meaning in Shakespeare's sonnet.

As Earle stood and looked through the window at her, he knew she was doing this for him so he could get a better view of her leg. He had no compunction about looking through her window. That's why she left the window curtains open—so he could watch. He waited, holding his breath whenever she lifted the skirt and scratched her knee.

He could feel his excitement rising and realized it was as much from the prospect of being discovered as it was from Eloise's body. Standing there was a dangerous practice. He could be seen by neighbours or even by Aunt Lillian. As he watched Eloise studying, the pupils of his eyes dilated, his heart rate increased significantly, his breathing rose and fell rapidly. Adrenaline charged through his body as he stood in the growing darkness, his right hand clenched on his crotch. Soon he knew, Eloise would leave her studies and turn out the light. She would make her way to her bedroom, turn on the lamp by her bed, and close the curtains on the single window of the room. After that, he would not be able to see her again. He knew the growing anger would come over him after that. The irritability and annoyance would rise up in him like bitter, acidic fruit. He would work to beat down the irrational fear and the frustration that confounded his life.

Within the next few days he would perform some highly rash, irresponsible act. He'd cover it up of course. He always did. It would come upon him suddenly. Stealing something from Woolworth's, lying to his teacher about how he was unwell, abusing one of the younger children, or worst of all, killing someone's pet.

If Eloise had not denied him by closing her curtains, none of this would have happened.

***

On May 10 Anna left work early: a rare day for her. She'd made arrangements to observe for herself the rising impact of the flu at The King Edward hospital. At 5 P.M. when she went outside, the blue sky of the early morning and its promise of a beautiful spring day had been replaced. The clouds were delivering a fine mist and caused Anna to draw her coat more tightly around her. She'd left her umbrella at the boarding house, and so it was with some chagrin that she headed down Fort towards Broadway to catch the streetcar to the hospital.

The screeching of the wheels on the tracks was a cacophony of badly played instruments. No one noticed. Winnipeggers had long ago gotten used to the high-pitched squeals, the honking of motor car horns, and the general din of this city on the prairie. The price of progress was noise.

The grid system of cables and wires overhead was barely noticeable to Anna anymore. Without it, the streetcars couldn't run and the city would be forced to a standstill. Without it, Anna would be unable to get back and forth to work. She accepted this as one of these inevitable, necessary evils that allowed her work at Versatile Medical Laboratories to continue.

When she arrived at the hospital, Anna was met by an attendant who was to ensure that she was properly garbed to enter the flu patients' ward. The long, white, smock-style gown was requisite for anyone who attended. Along with that came the white mask covering the chin, mouth, and nose, and tied at the back with strings.

After she was gowned, the attendant led her down a long hallway to a ward separated by large doors from the rest of the building. When he opened the door and Anna entered, she was momentarily so taken aback that she stopped and stared.

The hallway was packed, both sides with beds down its entire length. Each contained a body in various stages of distress. Doctors, nurses, and attendants moved from person to person monitoring vital signs, recording data, and administering medications.

As Anna walked the hallway, she peeked into the rooms. Every one was full. Wherever a bed or cot could be stuck, there was a patient. There were hundreds of them. As much as Anna was well-aware of the situation in American hospitals, she was not prepared for the devastation before her eyes.

A man garbed from top to toe in white approached her. "Dr. Williams?"

Anna started from the mesmerizing sight to focus on him. "Yes. Are you Doctor Renaud then?" The man nodded. "Thank you for allowing me to observe."

"After Dr. Parkes told me about your work, I decided you should see this for yourself. As you can see, Doctor, we are desperate here." He moved Anna off behind a counter and into a small backroom out of earshot. "Most of these people are going to die, Doctor. It's the same all over. We seem to be well into a second wave of this infection. And it seems that when it comes back it's stronger, more virulent, and more resistant to anything we can use for treatment. But the worst thing is the speed. In a few minutes I'm going to take you to see a young man who was admitted this morning. When he first arrived he had classic symptoms, but he was able to walk and converse with us."

Anna was still shaken by the amount of illness around her. "I knew it was bad. But this...this is terrifying. I hardly know what to say, Dr. Renaud."

He grasped her elbow with some urgency. "Is anything happening in the labs? Any progress? Anything at all you can tell me?"

"We're working very hard at it of course, but as you know, these things take time and it's pretty much all speculation and experimentation. We could be months, even years away from a treatment."

Renaud grew impatient. "Excuse me, Doctor, but as I impressed upon Dr. Parkes, those are luxuries we do not have. I'll show you why. Come along with me please." He led her back into the hallway and toward a room at the end. Before they entered the room he said, "Remember, this young man was strong and healthy yesterday. His name is Andrew."

Anna entered the room with reticence. Andrew lay on a cot beside a regular hospital bed. His forehead, face, and neck were covered by large, dark splotches. His breathing was laboured and hoarse. His chest rose and fell as he struggled to force air into his lungs. Already the blue cyanotic tinge of oxygen starvation was showing around his ears and spreading outward across his cheeks. The blood travelling through the veins was becoming oxygen depleted, and this resulted in the ever-darkening hue of his skin. His face was haggard and drawn as the brain demanded more and more of the blood-delivery system.

Andrew began a wracking cough. It soon turned into huge gargling, gagging, choking sounds as his lungs sought to express the phlegm. The spots became ever darker as the oxygen withdrew from around the skin cells. Finally, after what seemed to Anna an enormously long time, a large ball of blood-soaked sputum rolled from between his lips and slid down the side of his neck. The on-duty attendant used a towel in a vain attempt to wipe up as much of it as possible.

Horrified, Anna watched as the young man struggled for each breath between coughs. She had to fight with her mind to keep on the task at hand and not be totally overcome by his suffering. She sat on the edge of the cot, took his hand, and held it tightly as his body arced in a spasm of agony.

"That's typical of the symptoms, Doctor," explained the attendant. "If you touch them, it seems to be extremely painful. Sometimes they'll scream the roof down."

Anna let go of the hand and turned to the attendant. "Please, can you get me a few sterile vials? I will have to take some samples from him."

When the man had left to do this, Anna looked at Renaud and shook her head in wonderment. Her nostrils were being bludgeoned by the smell on the ward. The sheets from the beds, the hospital gowns of the patients, and even the floors were stained from the urine and feces spilling out of human orifices. Workers scrubbing up and changing bedding could not begin to keep up.

As Anna perched on the edge of Andrew's bed, blood began to run from his nostrils and then from his ears. She felt an onslaught of fear creeping across her mind and she pushed it back with an iron will. It would not do anyone any good for her to let go and to panic, though she was hard-pressed to calm herself enough to stay seated.

When the attendant returned, Anna took the vials and steeled herself to collect specimens. All of this was too real for her. Up to now, secreted in her lab she was able to work with objectivity. The samples she'd studied came to her from far away: from Pittsburgh, New York, and even Texas. She'd not had to deal with them first-hand. The collecting was now so tangible as to be a blow to her psyche.

The sick and the dying around her were alarmingly real. Their pain was unbearable. Even as she sat by Andrew, the patient in the bed beside him ceased breathing and two orderlies moved him to a stretcher and carted him off. An attendant moved in, stripped the bed, gave it a quick wash with an antiseptic, and remade it with fresh linen. No sooner was she finished than the orderlies rushed in with a new arrival and placed her in the bed. An intern arrived to check the patient's vitals.

Anna thought to herself that all they were doing here was processing the dead. She looked back at Andrew. The blue colour was creeping down his neck to his chest, and his breathing became even more futile.

"He won't be long now, Doctor Williams. Perhaps an hour, maybe two," whispered Renaud. "You'll excuse me please—I've many others to attend to."

Anna shook her head. "Of course."

Renaud disappeared just as Andrew convulsed into another choking paroxysm. When he ejected the ball of sputum this time, Anna carefully collected enough to have a substantial sample, and also swabbed his mouth. She could have left at that point. She had what she needed, but she could not bring herself to leave him to just lie there and die alone.

Instead, she pulled the bedding from him and tossed it into a huge hamper at the foot of the bed. As he shouted in a delirium of agony, she rolled him to one side and then the other, pulling the blood-soaked sheet from beneath him. She got cool water and a basin and sponged the excrement and blood from him as well as she could, changing the water several times as she proceeded.

When she'd cleaned him and the bed, she replaced the bottom sheet. Once again, as she rolled him back and forth to replace the sheet, touching his overheated body seemed to result in an agonizing flow of pain for him.

Anna covered him as gently as possible with a dry sheet and continued to pat his head and neck with the cool cloth. She hadn't tried to get him into a clean gown—it was too painful. The blue colouring was turning deeper to a shade of black even as she'd finally finished washing him. There was nothing else to do. She waited.

Dr. Renaud was wrong—Andrew lived close to three more hours. He endured more coughing bouts until at the end, his lungs filled with viscous fluid. As more blood poured from his nostrils, his ears, and his rectum, he stopped breathing and remained still at last. Anna removed the top sheet. His entire body had turned a deep hue of blue, almost black in colour. Anna didn't know it, but Andrew was just twenty-four years old and was the forty-eighth patient to die on the ward that day.

***

"You need to understand, Al," Kathleen waved her hand to indicate the impressive Grain Exchange Building, "the elite of Winnipeg are mostly Anglo-Saxon and mostly Protestant. They love to build things because then they can see their money. I know because my father was one of them—and I am too, I guess."

They'd been standing on the sidewalk while Kathleen pointed out the architecture: the steel frame resistant to fire, the Pilazzo-style renaissance aspect of it.

She continued. "It's something, is it not? Only the Grain Exchange in Chicago is bigger."

Al offered, "It's the same everywhere I guess. You're right—for some reason, the money people love to see something concrete for their cash."

"I think it has to do with permanence. They want to know that after they're gone there'll still be something of them."

They moved off to continue the tour. Al watched attentively and listened carefully to Kathleen's explanations.

"You know, there's a mythology around our city. The last forty years mostly have been a boom period. A lot of the very wealthy like to preserve a fabrication that they started out with nothing and turned themselves into something. But not, by any means, all of them. For some, it's true, but there's old money here. Augustus Nanton, Jim Ashdown, Allen & Bridges Company. They had lots of wealth and power behind them."

Al offered, "You're trying to make a point, but I guess I'm missing it."

"They're a small, closed society, Al. They sit on boards of directors together. They belong to the Manitoba Club or the Canadian Club—very exclusive, very upper class—you have to be recommended into the clubs, and no women allowed!"

Kathleen stopped walking and turned to face him. "I despise tradition. And that's what these people are about. They marry into each other's families. They play golf at the St. Charles Country Club. Good God, even their wives have an equivalent women's club. They go there and discuss the important social issues of the day, such as why it's not a good idea to let too many non-English speaking immigrants into the country—wouldn't want to pollute the pool you know."

"What's that building?" Al put a hand on her shoulder and left it there too long. He pointed across the street.

"Ah! That's the bank of our good friend of labour, Julius Archibald. The Merchants Bank of Canada. It's invested with status, class, culture, education, and privilege." She laughed as she continued, "But not with any philanthropy."

Al took her by the hand and dashed into the street. "Come on, I need to see it more closely!" He forced her into the street, dodging horses and cars as they raced for the opposite sidewalk. When they finally stood before the bank, Al continued to hold her hand and she continued to let him.

Hours later, he'd had a thorough history and education of Winnipeg's downtown and had visited the Royal Bank on Main Street and the Imperial Bank of Commerce, with its high columns and incredible fourteen-foot, semi-circular ceilings and heavy brass doors. They ended the tour at the James Street Pumping Station, with its massive machinery used to protect expensive Winnipeg business enterprises.

Later, they sat in a café and continued their conversation. Kathleen was matter of fact. "They've had forty years of wealth-building and business growth. But it's the way it happened that gives me difficulty. Land speculators who got rich off Metis Scrip. Railways that got tax breaks and cheap labour, civic politics that politicize everyone's lives because they get to use public funds to help finance their private businesses."

They sipped coffee and finally Kathleen blurted, "So why are you really here Al? What's in this for you? And who sent you?"

He looked steadily over the rim of his cup and finally put it down without drinking. "Fair enough questions. Winnipeg's like a lot of places. There's the wealth club and then there's everyone else. I can tell you something about these people, even though I've never met them and wouldn't really want to."

He paused and let Kathleen light a cigarette and drink from her coffee before continuing. He watched her steadily as the smoke curled around her hair and her lips puckered slightly over her cup. She gazed back, smiled, and nodded for him to go on.

"These business owners, they're not much different from feudal landlords, in spite of all our progress with democracy. They really do believe they own their workers. They want unquestioning loyalty, and they want it at no cost to themselves. But the truth is that they actually despise the very people they employ. They're uncultured, ill spoken. They lack self-control and they have no appreciation for the opportunities they've been given."

Kathleen said nothing. She looked at him with interest and paid attention to the sound of his voice, how he leaned forward as he grew more intense about his topic.

"But there's really only one thing that drives them. They have to increase capital. Their interests, their partnerships, their politics, even down to their hobbies and recreations are about capital. So here's what they've done for maintenance: they've created the North End for people like the Kaminskis. They've created a banking system that changes money for East Europeans who have to send money home to Poland and the Ukraine, and they charge them a good fee to do that. They've set up newspapers that are not really free because they're locked into the wealthy class that feeds them. They've even created political parties that they control and elect the people they want to run things!"

Kathleen nodded. "You're right of course. And as long as that goes on, this inequality won't change. People outside the sphere of influence will continue to die."

"So what's in it for me? Change I hope. Why am I here? To make sure the changes happen. I can't talk to you about who sent me here, but I can say that they too have some power and some influence and more than anything they want to support the people that you work with and for."

She butted her cigarette and finished her coffee. "Okay, Al. For now we'll leave it at that. I think we're on the same side. But I also think we're in for a rough ride in the coming months. I know these people—like I said, I'm one of them—they won't go down without a fight."

He grinned at her. "That's my hope."

It was late and becoming dark as they strolled toward a street-car stop. Al changed the conversation. "Alright, Kathleen Johns. Ever since we met you've been catching me by surprise. Mostly because you're so forthright, so interesting, and so darned good-looking. So it's time for me to be straightforward also." Al hesitated momentarily. "The other day, you said I could kiss you."

Kathleen grinned at him. "Yes, I suppose I did at that." She took his hand and led him to the shadows of the building they were next to. He turned her and put a hand on each side of her waist. At first the kiss was tentative and exploratory, but as they held it, he became more insistent and pulled her closer. She pressed in to him and responded readily.

When they broke away, he was shaking and tried to make his voice strong and sure. "You'll not catch me unawares again, Kathleen."

She laughed softly. "We'll see about that."

If either had bothered to look up, they would have seen that they were firmly in the shadow of the Merchants Bank of Canada.

They moved back to await the arrival of the streetcar and stood there, content in the moment. After a few minutes, Kathleen reached up and ran the back of her fingers down his cheek. "By the way, Al. Yes, we can have supper. My house. Tomorrow night. I'll expect you about eight o'clock."

***

By 10 A.M. the anti-strike demonstration was ready to go. Thousands of veterans gathered at the corner of Portage and Main with signs held high, preparing for their march on the legislature.

Mayor Charles Ross, E.K. Atwater, Julius Archibald, and Sir Joseph Flavelle walked amongst them, shaking hands and thanking them for turning out. Another grey, misty day had descended upon the city. A very light rain fell as the organizers scurried about, getting the various groups into positions. Some of the vets had donned the uniform of their former units. Others, unemployed and angry, stood off to one side and awaited the order to march.

The leaders of the anti-strike demonstration were businessmen, city hall administrators, and political hacks. They stood in suits, ties, and attractive broad-brimmed hats. Several carried walking sticks or umbrellas. Still others wore medals of bravery pinned to their lapels as if to proclaim that nobody should try to intimidate them.

Two men unfurled a twenty-foot-long banner attached to two poles. They hoisted the banner high and stretched it out for all to see. Large block letters in black paint blared the position of the group.

WE WILL MAINTAIN
CONSTITUTED AUTHORITY, LAW, AND ORDER.
DOWN WITH THE HIGH COST OF LIVING.
TO HELL WITH THE ALIEN ENEMY
GOD SAVE THE KING

Julius Archibald cast his eyes about him with glee. He looked at Ross and with malice shouted, "Goddamn unions think they're the only ones that can organize marches. We'll show those bastards who gets things done!"

Ross gazed back at him nervously. "I'm not so sure this is a great idea, Julius. Seems to me that all we're doing is provoking them. There's sure to be a backlash to this."

Archibald laughed. "Course there is. That's the whole point, Mayor. The union comes after these boys and they'll get some Christly sense knocked into their empty heads. And that's just exactly what they need."

Ross shrugged noncommittally. It was hopeless talking to the man. Archibald seemed to have no idea of the desperation of the union men and women. Unless a compromise could be struck, the mayor feared for the worst. The demonstrations on each side would lead inevitably to violence. People were going to get hurt—or worse. Why couldn't anyone else see this? Or did they just not care?

Ross looked up as other signs propagated throughout the crowd.

DEPORT THE UNDESIRABLE ALIEN
DOWN WITH BOLSHEVISM
WE STAND BY OUR ELECTED GOVERNMENT

Another held the Union Jack high overhead and waved it back and forth.

Julius Archibald pointed across the street and Ross looked. Archibald smiled broadly. "You see those boys over there with the clubs and baseball bats? They're specials. The Committee hired them. We know we can't depend on the city police, so these fellas will take care of things if need be."

Ross said pointedly, "I don't think we can scare the strike leaders if it comes to that. It's too late for those kinds of tactics.

They're going to fight back, Julius. They feel like they're trapped and they'll force us to negotiate."

Archibald turned to Ross. He glared at him. He made sure that a number of nearby marchers could hear him. "Now you listen to me. There'll be no negotiation. We won't be talking to them. We won't even be sitting down with them. We'll bust any goddamn strike that happens. We'll fire every son of a bitch that tries to picket. We'll crack the heads of people like Bob Russell and anybody who supports him. We are not gonna let the union dictate what happens in our own businesses!" He paused and looked around him, daring anyone to say anything to contradict him. Julius Archibald was breathing hard. His face was red and his hands clenched and unclenched.

The others said nothing.

Archibald forced himself to become composed. He adjusted his tie, lifted his hat, and brushed his hair back with his hand. Replacing his hat, he reached into his pocket and removed a stogie from a package. He proffered them to those around him in a gesture of conciliation. No one except E.K. Atwater accepted the offer.

He took matches from his pocket and took his time to light up. When he drew in and exhaled, he managed to paste an awkward, half-formed smile on his face. He spoke in a calm voice. "After all, gentlemen, these people are breaking the law. Remember that last year it was the firemen, the waterworks department, even the telephone operators. That was bad enough, but now we got these Bolsheviks trying to overthrow the government. That's sedition. And we've laws about that. There'll be no revolution in Canada, not as long as I'm breathing."

Suddenly, as if on signal, the mob moved forward down Portage Avenue. Whistles blew and shouting started. The demobilized former soldiers raised their voices and shouted anti-union slogans. A few on horseback urged the crowd forward and cheered them on.

Ross recognized several members of the Committee of One Thousand. They had brought along workers from their factories and warehouses: family people who could not afford to lose their jobs and so were pressed into service. There were so many that they stretched right across Portage Avenue and spilled over onto the sidewalks. Like some mighty army of the righteous, they shouted anti-union, anti-strike obscenities and paraded their nationalist feelings for all to see.

They passed street after street and surged onward. A woman stumbled and fell and was in danger of being trampled before two men reached down and plucked her to safety. Men brandished clubs and baseball bats and screamed for blood. In particular, they called for the blood of Bob Russell, John Queen, Bill Ford, and I.A. Heaps, all tied closely to the union movement.

As the last of the crowd moved past, Charles Ross stood alone at the Main Street corner. He watched the retreating backs of the crowd as they pushed their way up Portage Avenue. He felt desolate. His stomach was upset and he badly needed a bathroom. His mouth was dry; he flicked his tongue in a vain attempt to bring some moisture to his lips.

He had an empty feeling of distress. A nauseating thudding wracked against his ribs. In his incapacity to articulate his doubts to these men lay his fearful and blossoming knowledge that what the Committee itself was doing was fraudulent and immoral.

CHAPTER FIVE

That afternoon, Earle Wilson knocked on the front door of 614 Home Street. Mary Jablinka opened the door to a broad smile and pleasant face. Earle tipped his hat and graciously addressed her. "Good afternoon, ma'am. I saw your sign in the window and wondered if you might consider allowing me to see the room. My name is Roger Wilson and when I asked at the employment centre downtown, your home was recommended as a clean, safe place with reasonable rent and a respectable Christian name."

Mary Jablinka was flattered and opened the door wider. "Why thank you, Mr. Wilson. Goodness, I only placed the rental sign this morning so you may be in luck."

"Indeed, dear lady. My fortune has been very positive of late, so perhaps it continues."

"I haven't even cleaned all of the previous tenant's things, Mr. Wilson. My hands, you see." Mary Jablinka covered one hand with the other. "The arthritis, it sometimes doesn't let me..." she trailed off.

Roger held up a hand as if to stop her. "Mrs. Jablinka, I have a perfectly capable pair of hands and I am blessed with good health. Indeed, if I like the room I'll pay you two months in advance, and if you'll give me a box, I'll pack the previous tenant's property so that you need not suffer with your affliction."

Mary opened the door wider and admitted him into her home. As she led him to Karol Yablonski's room, she was enchanted by his light, constant, charming chatter. The man seemed possessed of a huge amount of knowledge, which he willingly dished out in a musical, lilting voice. In the minutes that it took to get to the room, he'd spoken with comical authority on politics, romance, economics, fashion, and the advantages of the internal combustion engine.

Mary opened the door and motioned him inside. He made a show of surveying the room, opened the closet door, and closed it again. He crossed over to the single window and lifted it with ease. It let in a rush of air. He turned and beamed at Mary.

He tested the bed by pressing down on the centre of it several times with an open hand. He looked at Mary suddenly with concern on his face. "Forgive me for asking, dear lady, but are there spiders in here?" He motioned towards the mattress. "May I?"

She was confused by what he was indicating and was disconcerted when he raised the corner of the mattress to check the bottom of it. She felt a quick flush of anger. "I always clean and disinfect between tenants, Mr. Wilson. This room's already been done; I just haven't packed up all of Mr. Yablonski's things. I was intending to do it later today, when you caught me kind of unawares."

"Of course. Please forgive my inexcusable behavior, madam. It was never my intention to insult you. I've a dreadful fear of bugs and spiders." He moved across the room and pulled the switch on the overhead hanging light. The bulb flared briefly and then went dark.

"I'll change that right away, Mr. Wilson."

"What a wonderful room, Mrs. Jablinka. So attractive, and as I was told, so very, very clean." He removed his wallet from an inside pocket and removed two ten dollar bills. "I would be honoured to become a guest in your home, dear lady. Please accept this as two months' rent, and if you'll be kind enough to provide me with breakfast each morning I will make it very worthwhile to you."

Mary grasped the bills eagerly, though it barely made up for the rent that Karol Yablonski had skipped out on. "Of course, Mr. Wilson. I feed some of the other tenants already, so it's no more trouble to prepare yours as well."

Mary turned to leave and closed the door gently behind her. Earle spent a long time standing where he was. He turned and gazed about the sparsely furnished room. This was a rare experience for him. It hadn't happened for an extraordinarily long time. He was standing in the room of a victim, with the man's personal possessions still there. It was an amazing feeling of exhilaration and he still didn't quite know what to do with it.

On a small round bedside table, a black and white photograph stood propped against a book. He sat at the edge of the bed and examined it carefully. In it, a short, nondescript woman stood looking into a camera. She cradled a baby in her left arm. A plain kerchief covered her hair and a good part of her forehead. Her face was a weatherworn, scarred, and chipped chunk of granite. Shoulder-length dark hair peeked out just behind her ears. Her eyes were black, shadowed hollows under heavy beetle brows. Her nose seemed her finest feature. It was small, raised gently as if in defiance. She wore a dark-coloured, full-length dress. The sleeves came all the way down to her wrists, and the folds of the skirt fell to her ankles. Her only adornment was a crucifix that lay in the gentle hollow of her throat.

The downturn of her mouth gave her a forlorn look, and the baby resting in the crook of her arm caused her to lean a bit to one side. Beside her stood four other children, ranging in ages from probably eight years to four years. The oldest, a boy, stood closest to her. All were dressed in identical outfits. Their large-brimmed, peaked hats served to cover their hair and to keep off the sun. Long coats covered their white shirts so that only the collars were showing. Baggy pants were stuffed into calf-high open boots. None of the children smiled but all stared bleakly into the camera, holding poses of inexorable waiting.

The family was standing on what appeared to be a railroad platform. A variety of bags and suitcases stood off to one side, and in the top left-hand corner of the photograph, attached to the wall of the train station, perched a sign in hand lettered black on white: NO ADMITTANCE.

Earle took the photograph and tore it into two, then four, then eight. He dropped the pieces into a box and cast about for other objects. From the round table, he picked up what appeared to be a copy of the Holy Bible in some foreign language. Inside the front cover was a list of names. He recognized Karol Yablonski's name among them. Several names were above and below Karol, though Earle would have been hard-pressed to have pronounced several of them. This too, he dropped into the box.

He crossed to an old dresser and opened a top drawer. He found several pairs of socks rolled up and stuffed into a corner. When he picked them up, he found several small packs of cigarette papers. Everything went into the box.

The second drawer proved more fruitful. Earle discovered a straight razor and a shaving mug. He opened the razor, tested the edge, and satisfied that it was sharp, he closed and pocketed it. The shaving mug he took over to the box. For a while he admired the scene painted on the glass mug: a winter scene, with a horse pulling an open sleigh. A driver and two children, bundled in scarves, winter coats, and mittens appeared to be enjoying a ride. The foreign words on the cup Earle read as Merry Christmas. He carried the cup to the box and laid it on the bottom.

With the heel of his shoe, he crunched down on the cup until the handle snapped off and the sides collapsed. He went back to the sideboard. Reaching into the back, Earle felt along until his hand brushed against something. He pulled out a folded envelope and opened it. He counted out two tens, three fives, and three one-dollar bills. He pocketed the money and tore up the envelope. So Yablonski couldn't pay his rent, but had money stashed away for emergency. Always the same—damned immigrants. Squirreling away Canadian dough and no doubt sending it home for their whelps. Damn Polacks and Jews. Somebody oughta run them back to wherever they came from.

Earle scrutinized the rest of the room with fastidious compulsion. When he was satisfied that all belongings of the former tenant were in the box, he retrieved string from his coat pocket, closed the flaps on the box, and secured it tightly. When he was sure that Mary Jablinka was busy in another part of the house, he descended the steps quietly and used the back door to let himself into the alley.

He carried the box fully fifteen city blocks and then, satisfied that he was far enough removed from Home Street, he moved into a back alley. He looked for a large garbage can and deposited the box as he strolled by. He glanced about briefly but seeing no one, he continued down the alley and made his way toward his newly cleaned room.

***

The supper was delicious. Kathleen and Al had nearly finished a bottle of wine and the long, long Manitoba evening was finally beginning to lose its light. He'd been surprised when he'd arrived at her home four hours earlier. This was a mansion, left to her by her parents. Kenneth Johns had been a man of some means and his import/export business had thrived before the war. The fact that his exports during the war consisted mostly of armaments dovetailed nicely with his other interests.

Kathleen had been an only child. While her mother spent a good deal of time with her, it was Mrs. Edwards, the house-keeper and cook, who really raised her during those early years. Her father's business required him to be away, and during the pre-war years her mother spent a lot of time at her club with her friends, toiling industriously on behalf of the arts.

It was true that she loved Kathleen and spoiled her with gifts, treats, dolls, and toys. She just didn't have a lot of time for her. Kathleen wasn't angry about it. She accepted that this was the way life was and she adapted to whatever situations presented themselves. She was enrolled in a private school that focused on top marks, high standards, and development of the mind. Her math, reading, and writing skills were well above average because she willingly and easily applied herself to her studies.

Then one day when she was in grade ten, the Flett sisters paid a visit to the Arbuthnott School for Girls. Winona Flett and Lynn Flett were members of the Political Equality League, which advocated for women's suffrage, better working conditions, and the instituting of a minimum wage. Until then, Kathleen had never given a second thought to politics. But on that day she learned that she could not vote and was not even considered to be a person.

The Flett girls handed out a pamphlet entitled "The Role of Women in the New Industrialist Society". Winona talked of the suppression of females, that only traditional jobs were open to them, and that expectations for females revolved around giving birth, taking care of hearth and home, raising children, cleaning, cooking, and providing themselves as "sexual vassals" for males.

Kathleen never forgot the term "sexual vassals". She was not entirely sure what it meant, but she didn't think she'd like it. The Fletts urged the girls in Kathleen's class to resist this definition of what it meant to be female. They said there was no reason women could not be leaders. No reason why they should not be managers, newspaper writers, industrialists, and yes, ministers of the gospel and the government.

Kathleen forever remembered another line from that day. When the Fletts were concluding their talk, Lynn said, "The women's struggle is linked to you, young ladies, whether you want it to be or not. You will have to fight to break free of economic bondage and in doing so you'll have to fight the additional burden of male domination."

She never forgot the Flett girls' visit and was stirred by their presentation. She began to read voraciously from a variety of books that included topics such as political theory, art and literature, history, and current events. She went out of her way to find and listen to a wide range of women, from Ella Cora Hind to Lillian Beynon Thomas to Nellie McClung.

One day two years later in the midst of her graduation year, she listened to Dr. Mary Crawford, an obstetrician, lecture on something she called "social medicine". Dr. Crawford claimed there was a direct connection between poverty and disease. Immigrant families she said were living in abject poverty in Winnipeg's North End. Poor housing, no sanitation services, no plumbing, and often no jobs. They could neither feed themselves nor clothe their children. This cycle of poverty led to abuse, misery, despair, and family break-ups, creating an environment ripe for infectious diseases.

Mary Crawford advocated for better housing, better wages, free health care, and better treatment for the poor overall. It was the first time Kathleen ever heard anyone say that education about birth control needed to move to the forefront of discussion if these problems were to be addressed.

Kathleen's awareness and thinking grew, and she even began to learn, in a purposeful way, the ignominy of Winnipeg's North End.

"And that's how I came to be doing what I'm doing: writing for *The Western Labour News*." She reached for the wine and topped up her own glass and Al's. They sat in her dining room and finished up the remains of dinner. "It hasn't escaped my attention, Alvin Devons, that I've spent all this time talking about myself and that you haven't said a word about yourself."

He smiled at her, raised his glass, and gestured towards her as if proposing a toast. He sipped at it. "I'm afraid my story's not nearly as interesting as yours. Certainly no wealthy parents and no private school. No great epiphanies for that matter. I'm a labourer, Kathleen, as were my parents and my grandparents." He held out both hands so she could see the callouses on the fingers and on the palms of his hands.

She reached out and took hold of his wrists, pulling his hands closer. She bent and examined them closely, staring at them for a long time. She let go of his left hand and with her index finger, traced the tip down each of the digits of his right hand. She followed the lifeline down his palm and spent time rubbing the callous at the base of the thumb. She turned the hand over and one by one she examined the nails. They were clean and nicely trimmed. No hangnails and the white half-moons were healthy and prominent. She ran the tip of her finger down the thumbnail to the knuckle and rubbed back and forth across the creases there. From the base of the thumb she traced her way up toward the knuckle of the first finger.

"You have wonderful hands," she said, "That's actually unusual in a male. A lot of hands—especially in men—are not so nice. In spite of how important they are, it's amazing how they abuse and misuse them."

As she continued to examine, Al felt the blood rushing into his groin. With his free hand he reached out and touched the hair at the side of her face. When he ran his fingertips alongside her cheek, she finally looked up, but continued to hold his hand with both of hers.

She smiled and the magical eyes twinkled. "What do I look like to you, Al?"

"Are you kidding me? You're beautiful. You're an angel. You're—"

"No, that's not what I mean." She stood up, came around the table, and stood before him. "I mean physically. What do I look like to you?"

"You mean, like describe you to you?"

"Yes, something like that."

"Well, let me see. You've got this kind of chestnut hair. And your eyes are a sort of really interesting colour— a shade of brown, but not really when you look at them—"

She shook her head gently back and forth to stop him. "No, that's not exactly what I mean either. I bet you could do wondrous things with these hands. On your palms you've got identical dimples. You must have inherited them. Did your mom or dad have them?"

Al swallowed and gazed at her. He was getting very hard. His voice was husky. "I don't know. I never looked."

"Exactly," she said, and traced the palm of his hand with her fingertip.

"While your hands are big, your fingers are quite long and narrow. They look like it would be easy for you to play the piano. Tapered and with the ability to touch the keys so lightly, so gently. To stroke the keys with just exactly the right amount of pressure.

And look how steady they are. There's nothing nervous or tight about them. These hands could paint a beautiful painting or they could perform the tiniest surgical procedure. They could easily insert themselves into crevices and gently stroke and soothe oil wherever something hurt."

She looked at him. He stood, moved his hands from her grasp, and cupped her cheeks. He kissed her long and gently and she returned it, standing on her tiptoes and leaning into him, straining to get closer.

When their mouths parted, she whispered, "What does the back of you look like, Al?"

The moment almost disappeared when he replied, "Huh?"

"None of us knows what we look like from the back. We never get to see that. But I want to know. The only way I can though is if somebody tells me—and describes it. You see what I mean?"

He nodded. "Yes, I do."

"Come with me," she said. She turned out the light and led him in the gathering darkness to her bedroom.

***

The room was lit with four candles, two on each side of the bed on small mahogany tables. She lay naked, face down on top of the bedspread, her hands resting on either side of her head. Her forehead lay on the edge of a pillow.

A bottle of oil glimmered in the candlelight and Al picked it up, opened it, and poured a generous amount into his cupped palm. After he replaced the bottle, he covered the oil with his other hand to warm it before he applied any to her skin.

She was perfectly symmetrical. The auburn hair spilled down each side of her head. It shone in the light and its lush thickness rested in waves of soft tendrils, leaving the back of her neck bare. Her hairline dropped down to a V along the back of her neck and became very fine, short and soft. It was here that he located the first mole. As small as an ink dot and almost black in colour, it sat by itself just right of the spine.

The back of both shoulders were clean and soft white in the candlelight. His hands followed the backs of her shoulders and massaged the muscles of her neck. At the tip of her right shoulder, he found the second mole-like blemish. He stroked it gently and followed the muscles and skin of her upper arms. He straddled her back and leaned forward, the heat from his scrotum and penis forcing a deep, guttural moan from her.

Her forearms were surprisingly well-muscled and strong, the skin dark and freckled. He pinned her wrists to the mattress and saw the soft rise of knuckles, the sculpted nails trimmed back far enough to avoid the typewriter keys. The skin on her hands was almost translucent and even in the candlelight he could see the webbed blue veins running up and down. He leaned atop the small of her back, laying his engorged penis along the spine while his testicles pressed tightly into the small of her back. He spent some minutes this way, rocking gently back and forth and she responded with an undulating motion. She breathed more rapidly as the blood rushed to the surface of her skin.

The slope downward from her buttocks formed a delightful curvature. The expanse across the upper buttocks fit his hands perfectly and he kneaded and oiled the space, working it to a deep flush.

Her buttocks responded with upward pressure as he slid his body back over her ankles. Toward the base of the left he saw the lightest-coloured birthmark, barely visible. He placed a hand on each side and applied exactly the right amount of pressure. He travelled across every inch of her posterior, rubbing and squeezing the rounded mounds of flesh. Each time he moved he felt the response as she pressed upwards against his fingers, her hips moving in a circular arcing pattern before relaxing back to stillness.

The ivory marble of the backs of her thighs was well-muscled from walking. Using both hands, he rubbed from the top of one leg to the back of the knee then repeated the procedure on the other. He oiled the insides of the thighs, up and down, up and down. The sheath of skin on the back of her legs smoothed out to a silky, satin sheen closer to the lower thigh.

Her calves were a deeper hue of brown. Their curves diminished gradually down to small ankles. Like the thighs, the calves were well-muscled, strong, and taut. He oiled and pressed each, picking up each leg and cradling it in one hand as he rubbed the flesh at the back with the other. He did this until he could feel the muscles relaxing and giving way. Her calves were beautiful.

He placed the bottoms of her feet just below his chin and touched them tentatively, waiting for a ticklish reaction. He traced his fingertips down the soft curvature in the centre of the foot and the toes curled and strained. He soaked his hands with fresh oil, and cupping his palms below the toes of each foot, he splayed them apart. He slid his fingers about, oiling and caressing between the toes until they were well lubricated and relaxed in his hands.

When they made love, both were so on edge that they reached climax almost immediately. Shortly, they began again and two more times in the night they awoke and moved into a now-familiar pattern of rhythmic motion.

The night moved on, cradling them in darkness, buffering them from the morning.

***

Dr. Anna Williams had a dreadful night. When she did sleep for short stints, the death dreams were remarkably vivid and painful. She'd awake sweating, thinking she'd surely caught the flu, and then return to another dream sequence. The accompanying howling and screaming of the dying rebounded off the walls and ceiling of the ward of her nightmare hospital.

She worked over and over a familiar pattern of removing a dead body, stripping a bed, cleaning up blood and vomit, and putting on fresh linen, only to have another patient placed in it, already well into his death journey. At one point she had two patients in a bed at one time, then three, then four. She was finally reduced to dropping to the floor on all fours and screeching as loud as she could in an attempt to drown out the sounds of hundreds of dying throats.

In her dreams, death visited her as a rampaging, disguised, shadowy figure. It was a monumental absurdity, striking with deadly accuracy and intensity. She felt herself melting away before its monolingual mantra: obliteration.

When dawn finally showed itself, she rose to bathe and prepare herself for the day. The autopsy she'd see later today, she thought, could not possibly be worse than what she'd endured the previous evening. When she looked into the mirror, the dark rings around her eyes startled her and she thought first about the flu. Then she remembered that the telltale signs of stress were always there but looked worse from her lack of sleep.

After she was dressed for the day, Anna descended the stairs, hoping to have a quick bite to eat and to talk with Mary Jablinka before she caught her streetcar to the lab. She was quite surprised when she entered the kitchen to discover Alvin Devons and some man she'd never met before.

Mary poured coffee and set it in front of her. "Good morning, Doctor. Going to be a lovely day out there. Might even have to get myself out into the yard today. Still have a bit of cleaning up to do you know."

"Do you think your hands will be up for that? Shouldn't you get the Schmidt boy to come over and do that for you?"

"Ordinarily I would, but you know what? This new tenant Mr. Wilson brought me the most marvelous pills and they're quite wonderful. Far better than that oil I've been trying. The pain is nearly gone."

Anna stared across the table at the new tenant, who smiled back at her brightly and then acknowledged Mary with a nod of his head. "I'm only too pleased that I could help. I was just telling Mr. Devons here that I have something of a background in medicines. My father was quite a well-known alchemist in his time."

Anna greeted Alvin. "Good morning, Mr. Devons. Has your job search shown results yet?"

"Not entirely successful, Doctor. But I must say, I've certainly met some interesting people since I got here."

Anna sipped at her coffee, not knowing entirely how to respond. A silence came over the room until Mary Jablinka said, "Oh, I forgot introductions. Dr. Williams, this is Roger Wilson. He rented Mr. Yablonski's room yesterday."

"Mr. Yablonski's room?"

Mary fretted. "Yes I'm afraid Mr. Yablonski's skipped out and sneaked away, leaving me stuck for his rent."

"Oh, well hello, Mr. Wilson, and welcome to our home. I'm sure you'll find everything to your liking. Our Mary is a wonderful landlady and a good cook as well."

Mary Jablinka beamed at Anna in appreciation. "You know, it's a funny thing. I've had tenants sneak out before, owing rent. But they always go in the middle of the night. And they always take their belongings."

Anna thought about this. "What do you mean?"

Roger Wilson smiled ingratiatingly. "The gentleman left his things in the room. It does seem rather odd."

Alvin frowned and offered, "That is strange. Men like Yablonski don't have much. You'd think if he was just going to skip out that he wouldn't leave his things behind."

Mary chipped in, "Well, Mr. Wilson was kind enough to pack those few things of his. We'll hold onto the box for awhile in case he returns for it." She turned to Roger Wilson. "You don't mind keeping that in your room?"

Wilson held out his arms in an expansive gesture. "Of course not, dear lady. I'm happy to be of some service. Perhaps Mr. Yablonski was forced to leave town or something like that. After all, there appears to be a lot of unrest right now."

Al Devons and Anna Williams looked at each other. Anna was thinking that Mary Jablinka was quite taken with her newest boarder, and Al felt the tiny hairs on the back of his neck tingle. He wondered why.

"Dr. Williams," he said, focusing on Anna. "When we last met, you mentioned that you might tell me how you came to be in your particular line of work."

"And you said that most people call you Al. So you'd better call me Anna."

"Alright Anna, what exactly does a bacteriologist do?" Al dug into the bacon and eggs Mary had set out. He slathered his toast with extra butter and scooped up some of her home-made preserves.

"Right now actually I'm working on the influenza that's been such a problem."

Roger Wilson said matter-of-factly, "Yes, dreadful disease. I've been reading about it in the press. A vile disease by all accounts and spreading quite rapidly, though I've had no personal experience with it of course, nor has anyone in the family. I predict though that a disease such as this is a visitation from God himself. It's a warning for all of us."

Al decided he liked the man even less.

Anna said, "Whatever the source, Mr. Wilson, this is a terrible way for people to die. They literally contract a pneumonia and choke to death. My lab is working overtime at it."

Roger shifted course as if tacking a sailboat in a wind. "Of course, Doctor. I only meant that in such times of extreme stress, one should not forget about our Lord and Master."

Mary Jablinka smiled at Roger with kind eyes and an appreciative nod. Al and Anna both picked up on this and the man's apparently guileless return smile.

Al pressed Anna. "Doctor, if this influenza is that powerful then an entire population could be at risk."

Anna pushed her chair back in preparation to leave. "That's true, Al. But we don't want to panic people. To some extent the flu is very..." she searched for the right word. "...destructive."

"But if it's that destructive, surely the public health department is involved or they will be getting involved."

"Yes, I suppose that must be. My boss is in daily contact with them. They're well aware of the situation if that's what you mean."

Al thought this over a moment. "I wasn't thinking of that. More that if the flu is bad enough, there could be things like quarantines. People might not be able to go out. Public places could close—even workplaces. Mass gatherings might be forbidden, to keep people from infecting each other."

Anna nodded. "I understand that such things have already happened in the U.S.A. There's no reason that they couldn't happen here."

Suddenly Al forgot about Roger Wilson and Mary Jablinka. He stood up and walked over to the door, where he recovered his cap and jacket from a hook and went out without further word.

Wilson said, "Well, you appear to have put a burr under his saddle, Doctor."

Anna gathered her own things together and went out to catch her streetcar to work.

***

I had a little bird/and his name was Enza
I opened up the window/and in-flu-enza.

The public health response was in fact mixed, confused, and at times contrary. The biggest reason for this was the lack of agreement about how to proceed. In cities south of the border, many wanted to employ the old methods of avoiding large crowds, cancelling school classes, wearing masks, avoiding getting wet, staying warm, and ensuring a good diet. For the most part, the advice was sound.

But scientists like Anna Williams believed that there was only one real way to fight the epidemic. The answer lay in the production of mass inoculations with a vaccine, but the American Public Health Authority chose to close saloons, dance halls, and cinemas. In France, students exposed to the flu were restricted from attending school, and if too many became ill the school closed. In New York State, the reaction by a very strong public health authority declared that anyone showing symptoms was to be quarantined. For those victims, isolation became a way of life. Even whole institutions such as military camps, colleges, and asylums for the insane became targets for the public health manifesto.

By every means possible there was a movement to better educate the public. Flu posters were plastered everywhere encouraging hand washing, general cleanliness, and disposal of handkerchiefs after nasal discharges. "Antiseptics" became the watchword of the day. In some cities it became illegal to be outside without wearing the gauze mask.

Obey the laws
And wear the gauze
Protect your jaws
From septic paws.

Still other doctors and health authorities attacked the infection with a proactive attempt to destroy the invader in its home: the human nose. Combinations such as boric acid and sodium bicarbonate were blown up the nostrils, dissolved, and induced large quantities of mucus flow. The membranes became awash and—hopefully—cleansed.

There were almost as many treatments as there were patients. Anna knew the answer had to be in a vaccine, but the problem with that was partly logistical. It took time to develop a vaccine, run clinical trials, educate all involved, get the medicine into the field, and inoculate the populace. In the meantime, the human-stalking flu continued its conflagration.

She read through all of the facts, data, conjecture, and analysis in Stanley Parkes's reports regarding the global situation. They rattled around in her brain when she bent over the microscope to examine the slides of Andrew's sample that had been prepared by Harold.

CHAPTER SIX

On May 11 at eleven A.M. Alvin Devons walked into the Merchants Bank of Canada on Main Street downtown. The stately columns that adorned the outside door were an impressive tyndall stone. Two huge doors with big brass doorknobs opened onto a lobby that would have done any free-enterprise structure proud.

Al was dressed in a smart business suit. His matching hat dropped close to his eyebrows and his black silk tie was pinned to his shirt with a shiny silver tie-clip. He was every bit the successful businessman. The briefcase he carried bulged with its load and he set it down gingerly at a side counter, where he proceeded to take papers from his breast pocket and examine them carefully.

There were six cashiers, all busy with customers. As he scrutinized the papers he'd taken from his pocket, his eyes also scanned the room meticulously. Three offices were opposite the cashier tellers with names embossed on the doors. Behind the tellers was a much larger office with a closed door. The name "Julius Archibald" with the title MANAGER in large capital letters was painted on the glass covering the upper half of the door. Through the door, Al had a clear view of the upper half of the financier himself. He was talking assiduously at some unseen figure and was holding a large stogie and pointing with it, jabbing occasionally towards the figure as if to drive home an important point.

Al watched and found himself staring through the door at the man's outline. He was reminded of a giant silent puppet, talking with nothing important to say. He was engrossed with the up-and-down movement of the flapping jaw with the snake-like tongue tip that protruded now and then as if sensing or probing the air before slipping back behind the lips. The ponderous head moved about and lolled from side to side periodically as if it was too heavily weighted for the neck. Even in profile Al could see that Archibald's eyes were quite tiny, but they bulged behind his spectacles, which only served to make them appear larger and so to protrude even more. He was a barrel-chested man and the jacket covering his white shirt and suspenders, while expensive, could not hide the ridge of fat that ran across the back of his neck and sat on his shoulders.

The voice startled Al. "Can I help you, sir?" A uniformed guard was standing in front of him. He hadn't even spotted the man when he came in. A mistake—he'd brought attention to himself.

The cover story kicked into gear. "My company has transferred me here. We have an office close by. I need to open an account and my manager recommended your bank. I'd like to speak with someone."

"Of course, sir," the uniform said, "come right this way. I'm sure one of the assistants can help you."

Al was escorted to a counter and was soon filling out forms under his pseudonym John Marshall. He took his time to do this and was required to make a one-dollar deposit into his new account. He was sent to one of the tellers and lined up behind two other customers. He gripped the oversized briefcase in his left hand and held the papers in his right. After what seemed an interminable wait, Al put the briefcase down very gently on the floor beside him and waited while the cashier finished up his account.

When all was done he enquired, "Oh, by the way, do you have a washroom?"

The cashier smiled. "Certainly, Mr. Marshall. It's right back there." She pointed off to one side to where a corridor ran between the offices he'd first noticed.

As he picked up the briefcase and moved to the washroom, he also checked out the guard, who was busy helping out another new customer. Good—he was less likely to remember every new customer.

Inside the bathroom, Al took his time to use the facility and wash his hands. He couldn't stay here all day, of course. Too many people in and out and at closing time it was almost sure to be checked. But on his way down the corridor he'd seen what he was looking for. Next to the bathroom was another door, and when he exited, Al made his way to it. As expected, it was locked, but this would prove no difficulty. He pulled a set of keys from his coat pocket and selecting one, he tried it. The door opened easily and he slipped inside carrying the briefcase. It was a small closet with brooms, mops, and cleaning supplies: it was perfect. He pulled up a small footstool and prepared to wait. When the bank closed, he could go to work.

To while away the time, he checked and rechecked in his mind the plan he'd made to set the charges and then escape.

Hugo Heinz. Or as he preferred to call himself, Uncle Hugo. The man's knowledge of explosives and their components was astounding. Al recalled their initial meeting, when he'd been sent to Hugo to work out the details of his first botched attempt to blow up the meat-packing plant.

Hugo sat at a large carpenter table, a variety of opened packages and chemicals arrayed before him. To Al he looked odd, slouched over the table with a cigarette drooping from his lower lip. Hugo's rimless glasses pinched the end of his nose, and his substantial paunch rested over the waistband of his trousers, held up by a pair of wide-banded suspenders. His open-necked white shirt had already been abused by several droppings of cigarette ash, which had fallen from previous smokes.

"I guess you're the new guy." Hugo glanced at him suspiciously and continued, "Good Christ. They're sendin' me kids now." He beckoned Al over to the table. "Well, watch and listen. Learn the things you need to know. Uncle Hugo will reveal the secrets of destruction."

Al said, "I already know about explosives. I was in munitions in the war."

Hugo grinned. "Well I guess you don't need me then. Just collect up what you need here and go do your job."

Al stared at the paraphernalia on the table. He didn't have any idea what to pick up and take away. Hugo waited for a long time and puffed on his cigarette, never actually removing it from his lips.

Finally Al shrugged and said, "Okay. I guess you better take me through what you're doing."

Hugo turned back to the bench and continued to work as he talked, the proverbial trail of smoke drifting up his cheek, across his left eye which blinked constantly to keep it out, and then disappeared into the air over his forehead.

"Ten years ago I worked at the Pittsburgh Testing Station for the U.S. Geological Survey. We made the first explosives that were safe for coal mines. Then the Bureau of Mines took us over and I got moved to Bruceton. Jus' a little way out of Pittsburgh."

Heinz, one of the few times he was to do so, took the cigarette from between his lips and pointed it toward Al.

"Schlagwettersichere Sting-Stoffe!" He grinned and his stomach jiggled about over the trousers. "Safe explosives, my young friend. Ya see, when you have methane in the air between five an' fourteen percent, it'll explode an' burn. Now if I mix nine and a half percent methane, I easily get an explosion of about seven-hundred degrees. That's lots to set a building on fire. But it takes about ten seconds for the mixture to actually explode. In ten seconds a lot can go wrong, so we need a faster ignition—not so much delay. A thousand degrees is much better. Only about a second of delay before it explodes. That's better—a lot faster. But if I can get a temperature of around twenty-two-hundred degrees, it's BANG! Instantaneous."

Hugo grinned again and took the time to remove a packet of tobacco and papers from his white shirt pocket. Al gazed over the contents of the table in a growing appreciation of the knowledge contained in this brain.

"We don' need it to be quite that high though. Fifteen-hundred to sixteen-hundred degrees will do us nicely. Almost no delay between the detonator an' the explosion. What's more important is that we get total detonation." He tapped two packages on the table with yellowed fingertips, "This here's ammonium nitrate an' dinitrobenzene. When I put 'em together, they're called bellite an' from this we can build a nice little explosion."

Hugo reached further across the table and tapped several more containers with an index and middle finger. With his other hand he continued to manipulate the tobacco and paper, expertly and single-handedly rolling a perfectly uniformed cigarette.

"But we don' want just any old, ordinary explosion, Al. Might just explode an' then poof—it's over with. So we do some things to help the process." He pointed out each of the boxes and explained. "This here's resin, this one's sulfur, an' this is charcoal, sugar, an' oil. They burn, so they make extra heat so the explosion is bigger an' better."

Hugo took the time to light the new cigarette off the butt of the old before tossing it aside. Al glanced at the glowing butt and shuffled his feet.

Hugo caught the nervous tension. "Not to worry, son. Won't start anything. Haven't set any detonators yet. There's lots of other ways we could mix the explosives, Al. Liquid oxygen works really good an' they make good detonators too. Lots of heat when it explodes an' the flame lasts a lot longer too. Very dependable, but you got to leave it in a soaking box for awhile before you use it so it wouldn't be so great for you in a building: just complicates things. Heh!"

Hugo gave a little grunt of humour and a smile stretched across the flabby lips. The cigarette smoke curled up under his eyes.

"You'll have enough things to worry about without having to get the dynamite right. So we use a fulminate cap. All you got to do is put the cap into the charge and light. Make sure you got them all lit before you leave. If they're burnin' you'll get results."

Al's Adam's apple bobbed up and down as he took in everything Hugo said. Munitions background or not, he came to the realization that his knowledge was superficial and limited at best.

"And I'll have time to get out safely?"

Heinz nodded. "Oh yeah, couple of minutes for sure. You can be blocks away if you don't waste time." Hugo tapped two small jugs beside him. "These here contain alcohol. Burns nicely and they'll fit in a small case. Pour it around before you light the fuses. It'll act as an accelerant. Prompts the fire along, you see." Hugo smiled wistfully. "I'd love to use Rack-a-Rock. They used two-hundred-thousand pounds of it to make Hell Gate Channel in New York Harbor. They combined twenty-one parts nitrobenzene to seventy-nine parts potassium chlorate. Single blast. Can you just picture it? Must have been a beauty. Wish I coulda been there." He'd stopped working on the charges and stared dreamily into the wall as he imagined it.

Al waited for what seemed like a long time. "Hugo, when'll the stuff be ready? How soon can I pick it up?"

The huge frame shook itself back to the moment. "Oh, let's see. Give me a couple of hours to get the fuses ready. Plenty of time before tonight. Come back about seven."

And then Al had messed it up anyway and the charges had been found in the morning. Hugo had bailed him out, but before he'd agreed to work with Al again he watched him practice on an old abandoned ice house far removed from any population. Hugo guided him as he would a child through each step of the process, and they watched from a distance as the ancient structure rolled up in a ball of flame and smoke.

Al emerged from the closet at eight P.M. and as he worked, he waited for the telltale sign that would announce the arrival of the nighttime cleaning person. To his knowledge, none of the bombs he'd set had ever harmed a person. Killing was not what this was about. If that was the case, he'd have waited around for Julius Archibald to arrive in the morning and then blown him to hell. In fact, it was almost eleven P.M. and he was placing a package of dynamite in Archibald's office when he heard the unlocking of the door and the rattling about of someone coming into the building. There were some things that he already knew about whoever it was.

The individual worked for a cleaning contractor. The person also lived close by, or at least somewhere in the North End in order to be able to walk to work. It was almost certainly someone middle-aged and female. She would be an immigrant and might even be in the country illegally. She would not want to talk to the local police about herself and about her job. If he was really fortunate, she would speak poor English at best. All in all she would be a very poor witness, and any information she did give out—if she did not simply disappear altogether—would be scant and unreliable.

And even if none of this fit the profile, it didn't really matter. Everything Al did was pretty much in the dark, and at any rate, he would never see the woman again and he would never be interviewed by the police.

He had placed a comfortable wooden chair in the middle of the room. As the woman entered, she turned on the electric lights. As she turned to lock the door behind her, Al reached around and cupped his left hand over her mouth. With his right, he pulled her back to restrain her. She was very small and he easily lifted her off her feet. He held her firmly until she ceased to struggle and whispered to shush her so she would not scream. At the same time, he reached for the light switch and plunged the room back into darkness.

When he was satisfied that her initial panic had settled, he slowly eased the pressure from her mouth and from her body.

"Hush now, I won't hurt you. But don't scream and don't try to run away. Can you do that?" There was no response. "I'm sorry to scare you like this but there was no other way. I need you to be quiet and to be still. I'm going to let go of you now. If I do, can you keep silent?"

He felt the head nod up and down slowly and so he relieved the pressure a bit more. Satisfied that she had composed herself as much as possible, Al turned her towards him and asked, "What's your name?"

She answered so softly he could barely hear. "Olga."

"Good. Now Olga, I won't harm you. I just need you to do what I tell you for awhile. You're here to clean the building, yes?"

She nodded again and he asked, "Do you have a last name, Olga?"

Again, so softly he could almost not hear. "Herzagorovich."

"Ok, good. Now Mrs. Herzagorovich, please come over here and sit down." Al took her gently by the wrist and sat her in the chair in the centre of the room. Her body was rigid with tension. He stood before her for some time and gave instructions in a soft voice so as to try to put aside her fear.

"I've got about another ten or fifteen minutes of work left here, Mrs. Herzagorovich, and you and I will both be leaving. Can you sit here for that time and not try to escape? Just so that I can get finished?"

She stared into the darkness searching for a face, and when she spoke; her voice now had built some confidence. "Are you trying to rob this place then?"

He could pick up the accent now and realized her English was far better than he'd hoped. "No, Mrs. Herzagorovich. But when I'm finished, you won't be able to come back here. In fact, the police probably will question you later. It'll make things easier if you just tell them that it was already on fire when you arrived. Don't worry, they won't think it was you. There'll be plenty of evidence that it could not have been you."

"Why do you do this thing? Why you want to hurt this bank? I do not understand."

Al did not answer. He went back into Archibald's office and took his time finishing the placement of the last charge. He worked deliberately but not quickly, checking and rechecking his work and ensuring, as any good blaster would, that he'd not overlooked anything. All the while he kept a series of questions going for Olga. Where did she live? Who was her employer? Where were her people from? What other kinds of work did she do? Did she have children and a husband? What was his work?

The questions were to get her to relax even more, but also so that he knew she'd not moved from the chair. At last, satisfied that everything was correct, he lit the timed fuse and watched momentarily as it began to burn outwards toward connecting fuses.

He moved toward the middle of the room, took her gently by the wrist, and led her to the door. He retrieved the key from her, let them both out, and relocked the door. He took Olga by the elbow and moved her down Main Street at a steady pace without seeming to hurry her along.

As he did this, he continued to talk to her in a soft voice. "Of course, if you wish to, Mrs. Herzagorovich, there's nothing wrong with you telling the police the truth. That I was there when you came to work, that I made you sit in the chair while I prepared the bomb. That you and I discussed all kinds of things including your family. And then I escorted you down the street and away from the building so you would not be harmed."

She peered at Alvin in the darkness. "The police would not believe such a tale," she said.

"Exactly."

When they were several blocks away, Al stopped and turned them back toward the bank. The explosion was enormous. The fireball momentarily lit up the inside of the building before the glass in the windows showered out in a rain of deadly splinters. Instantly, flames shot out the destroyed windows and doors. The outside air rushed in and fed the inferno. The sound that suddenly burst upon them caused Olga to jump back and stare in disbelief as the rising, roaring tide of combustible blaze leaped upward. Her mouth dropped as she turned toward Al.

Briefly, she was able to look into his calm, blue eyes. The cap on his head was pulled low. Then he turned on his heel and walked away from her.

For awhile she watched his retreating back, then turned again to the roaring fire. Already, several people were on the sidewalks but standing a good distance back. Men shouted frantically to each other to call the fire department while others simply stared, completely enthralled with the sight of the Merchants Bank of Canada going up in flames.

Huge black clouds of smoke rolled into the May sky. A police car pulled up some distance from the fire and four officers moved in to secure the situation. Within a few more minutes, Olga could hear the distant clanging of fire trucks. More and more people poured onto the streets, some running past her. Finally, she turned and fled into the darkness.

***

Aunt Lillian held the duck carcass by one wing-tip while Earle held the other. Together they stretched it wide and held it over the cast-iron stove. Aunt Lillian lit the rolled-up newspaper and as it burned, she moved it back and forth beneath the plucked bird. In this way, they rid the carcass of its last downy feathers. This was their fourth and final bird and Earle could still feel his gorge rising at the smell. He hated this annual ritual. He despised the plucking and drawing of the insides. He was revolted by the chopping off of the heads and webbed feet. But the thing that always overcame him was the singeing of the down.

The curling wafts of the tendrils of smoke invaded his nostrils and assaulted his tear ducts. The fact that Aunt Lillian's church friends provided them sustenance from this annual slaughter meant nothing to him. He dreaded this time of year, knowing that these bloody ducks would be showing up and that he would be expected to help in the preparation.

Now that he was in his senior year of high school, he swore to himself that once he was gone he would never, ever eat duck again. Aunt Lillian knew of his predilection to avoid wild game and each year admonished him regarding his reluctance to partake of the Lord's bounty, as she called it. No matter, he could not stomach the smell, and on occasion had even gone so far as to refuse the revolting duck stew she so carefully prepared or the roast duck and apple dishes she provided.

It was in fact during just such a meal the previous fall that Earle was visited by an attack. It scared Aunt Lillian badly. One moment he was sitting at the table contemplating the nauseating bird, and the next he was on the floor convulsing, his arms and legs thrashing about, his eyes rolled back in his head, and his mouth hanging open as he made short, snorting, guttural sounds.

This went on for several minutes while she attempted to restrain his thrashing about. At first she tried to get him up, then yelled at him frantically. "Earley, what's wrong with you? Earley?"

He stopped making the noises as his jaws clenched tightly together and blood began to flow from his mouth. Lillian tried to pry the jaws apart but to no avail. She was sure the blood was because he was chewing on his tongue and she pulled a spoon from off the table and tried to force it between the upper and lower teeth.

Earle continued to jerk and spasm as she worked over him. His hands clenched and the muscles in his neck strained as if they would burst. As she tried desperately to force the spoon in and pry the jaws open, she inadvertently did the right thing for him: she turned him over onto his side so he was three-quarters prone. Eventually his jaw muscles relaxed and let go of his tongue and cheeks. The blood flowed freely but now his breathing became deep and ragged. He was sweating profusely, his dark hair soaked as she rubbed her hands around his temples in an effort to assuage his torment. He was burning up with a temperature and she knew she had to get him cooled down. Finally, he recovered himself enough that she could help him to her downstairs bedroom. She opened his shirt and got cool water to bathe his face, neck, and chest.

For awhile he alternated between a state of consciousness and delirium. Once she was satisfied that he would continue to breathe, she was able to fetch a doctor. Upon examination, the doctor removed Earle immediately to a hospital. He would have to run tests and try for an accurate diagnosis.

Earle was two days in a coma before he awoke to find himself in a hospital bed with absolutely no idea of how he'd gotten there or why he'd been admitted. He told the doctor that the last thing he remembered was the smell of singed duck.

The doctor said it was a medical condition in his brain that would have to be watched. Aunt Lillian knew it was something much worse: a visitation from Satan. An attempt to wrest Earley's soul from him. They would pray. Pray for a cure. She would take him to a man of God, someone who would lay hands on him and remove the evil spirit. Lillian knew all about exorcism. She'd seen it before with her own eyes. The falling-down sickness that Earle displayed. The agony of the black imps entering the brain, taking possession, squatting. It had happened to her own sister and to her cousin Arlene, but both had found peace before their untimely deaths. Both had been ministered to by agents of the Almighty and so had been cleansed and made whole.

And that could happen for Earle also. Lillian had checked him out of the hospital and placed him into the hands of Brother Sylvester, a gentle, loving man who spent much of his time with the poor souls in the state asylum. She would not allow Earle to be placed into the asylum, of course. No, that had happened to Cousin Arlene and it had not been a good experience. Still, Arlene was redeemed now and her ranting and raving had ceased at the end.

Arlene accepted both the prayers of Brother Sylvester and the drugs forced upon her by the nurses. Eventually the seizures lessened, the fire in her brain seemed to dampen, she stopped eating and drinking, and then just seemed to fade away. Her struggling body rested and one night she died in her sleep while Sylvester, Lillian, and several ladies of the church prayed over her.

It was shortly after that when Lillians's sister committed suicide. That was never talked about. Lillian always claimed that her sister, ready to meet her maker, had simply willed herself to stop living. She'd taken Earle in, and true to her sister's last wishes had brought Earley up to be God-fearing, humble, and chaste.

To Lillian's knowledge, that had been Earle's first visitation by the black imps of Satan, and it had changed his personality. He became morose. Even worse in Lillian's opinion, he became horridly enamoured of females.

A year later, an event happened that had never before taken place in Earle's life. Aunt Lillian announced after breakfast that she was going away.

"Away?" Earle lifted his head from his morning prayer and looked across the room at his aunt. She was getting old now. Grey hairs crept through her dark hair like slivers of light. The glasses perched at the end of her nose could not hide the tired eyes. Crow's feet ran away from her eyes toward her temples. The skin on her face was sallow and bagged down into the beginning of jowls. As far as Earle could remember she'd never been an attractive woman and age was grinding her away.

"Not for long. Just four or five days. Brother Sylvester is sending several of the ladies on a retreat. You're old enough to fend for yourself for a few days now. And if you need anything, there's always Brother Sylvester."

"Where's this retreat?" An image of Eloise Jacobs popped into his brain.

"In Niagara. We'll go by train tomorrow and return on Sunday. There's one thing I worry about Earley. You could have an attack while I'm gone and there'd be nobody here."

Earle's burgeoning freedom could be endangered unless he could pacify her right away. "No need to worry, Auntie. I've a friend at school."

Lillian's brows furrowed. "Friend?" She'd never heard Earley use the word "friend".

"Yes, he's a senior also. Actually, he's new here. His father's a new pastor at the Grace Lutheran across town. You don't know them."

"No. I didn't even know the Grace had a new pastor."

"I could ask William to come over and stay if you like. I'm sure his parents wouldn't mind." The image of Eloise became clearer: she smiled at Earle and pursed her lips as if for a kiss.

"Perhaps I should speak with his parents first, Earley. Although there's not much time and I've a lot to do before tomorrow morning...a pastor's son you say?"

"Yes, he's very nice. Sometimes we have really interesting discussions about theology." *Careful. Don't oversell it.*

Lillian pondered this momentarily, thinking about how much this could relieve her preparations and her mind. "Still, since I've never met him, and since you could have an attack—"

Earle interrupted to reassure her. "William already knows about them. We talk a lot actually and I've told him about them and even what I have to do to recover."

Lillian beamed at him. "So nice for you to have a friend, Earley."

He beamed back at his aunt. Eloise's generous breasts were swaying back and forth as she blew a kiss at him.

CHAPTER SEVEN

Promptly at 10 P.M. the following evening, Earle stepped onto the stoop of the Jacobs' home, the Holy Bible tucked confidently beneath his arm. Things had changed for him since the "fit" and hospitalization of the previous year. Gone were Earle's ponderous doubts and cares. He was a man now and this manifested itself in his ability to control his environment and focus in an unswerving way upon a goal, manipulating elements to his advantage.

He was his own guide now through a troubled and troublesome world. In an irony of some proportions, Earle's illness had set him free rather than confined him. He no longer wrestled with worry about his soul. He knew his place in life. Through Brother Sylvester's interventions and counseling, he'd come to understand the truth.

God had special plans for Earle. He was an emissary bearing the onerous task of enlightening the world. He must take the word to the people. As a person of superior intelligence, it was Earle's obligation to set himself as an example to others. And if he could be set free by the great revelation, then surely others could as well.

It was only through Brother Sylvester's help and prayers that he'd been saved from the Satanic, raging betrayal of his body. Earle had been able to stop masturbating, though he'd been able to do little about the imposition of spilling his seed in his sleep. A nasty little complication that he'd tried to deal with by sleeping with a handkerchief in his pajama front.

He'd also been able to resist the peer pressure that led others to smoking, alcohol, and swearing. And the more he was able to resist, the more powerful he became. On the night that he stood upon the boards of Eloise Jacobs's veranda, he was intractable. His ability to reason was superb, his intellect operated at a superior level, his social skills were as powerful as they'd ever be.

He didn't even knock on the door. When he opened it and entered, he was in total control of all that he encountered.

***

"Read it again, Eloise. Read the title also." Earle smiled across the kitchen table at her. She was so very, very pretty.

Eloise stared down at the Bible he'd placed in front of her. When he'd first come in unannounced she was frightened, then angry. She had ordered him out of the house, but Earle acted as if he hadn't even heard.

Instead, he'd opened the Bible, sat her down, and then placed himself opposite her. He ordered her to read the underlined parts and she'd stumbled over much of it.

"You know, my mother will be home any minute and she won't be happy to find you here." She tried to keep the trace of fear from creeping into her voice.

Earle was growing impatient. "No, your mother will not be here until at least 4 A.M. Read it again, Eloise, and more smoothly, dear." An edge had crept into his voice.

Eloise glanced down.

Hosea Chapter 22 - 5
Plead with your mother, plead: for she is not
my wife, neither am I her mother: let her therefore
put away her whoredoms out of her sight, and her
adulteries from between her breasts;
Lest I strip her naked and set her as in the day
she was born, and make her as a wilderness,
and set her like a dry land, and slay her with thirst.
And I will not have mercy upon her children;
for they be the children of whoredoms.
For their mother hath played the harlot:
she that conceived them hath done shamefully:

"And what does it mean?" Earle's voice was confident, soft, and steady. He would broach no opposition to his task.

Eloise looked at him, uncomprehending. "What?"

With despair he gazed across the table. "What does it mean? Tell us what it means, Eloise."

She stared at the text and tried to make her mind read it again. "I don't know. I have no idea. How am I supposed to know?"

This was totally unsatisfactory. She was not even trying. Surely she could see what was as plain as the nose on her beautiful face. Earle stared at her across the table for a long time, let his eyes drop down her neck and slide to her breasts.

"Listen, Earle. You have to get out of here. My mother wouldn't like it if she knew you were here. She'd be mad."

"She's a whore."

"What? Who?"

"Your mother."

For the first time, Eloise felt like she might lose her composure. She took a deep breath, settled herself, and made herself look across the table at Earle. She forced herself to look into his gaze. "You don't know my mother. And you don't know me.

You've lived next door with that crazy aunt of yours all these years and you still don't know anything about us. But I know lots about you. You don't have any friends at school. You don't do anything. You don't get invited any place. And even if you did, you wouldn't go. In fact, all you do is sit around and read this Bible."

Eloise felt stronger now. She wasn't afraid of Earle Nelson. Why should she be? He was a pariah alright, but for the most part she saw a frightened, insecure, silly boy who did not have the nerve to stand up to his domineering aunt.

And if she had stopped at this point she might still have avoided later events, but she made the critical mistake of believing Earle's silence was acquiescence.

"And I know lots more, Earle Nelson. You think I don't know about how you sneak around at night? You think I don't know about how you peek through the window at me? Why do you think I never go to school at the same time as you? Why do you think nobody talks to you, Earle? It's because you're just as crazy as your aunt."

As he listened, the sweat broke out on his forehead. He could feel it trickle down his temples. His mouth grew dry and a bright scarlet red crept across his face.

Earle stood up. His hands curled into fists at his sides. His shoulders hunched up tightly and he leaned forward onto the balls of his feet.

His voice was matter-of-fact, delivering the message calmly and with reason. "She's a whore, Eloise, and she's turning you into a whore. She's abominable and cannot live. She must be separated from this whoredom. Or else you'll turn into her. You'll be stripped naked so that everyone can see you for what you are. And you'll be cast into the wilderness and slain with thirst."

Eloise came around the table and stood in front of him. "Get out! Get out of my house! You're crazy!" Her right hand flashed out and crashed down hard across his face.

When Earle reached out and seized her throat, she froze momentarily, then uttered a strangulated sound of contempt. Her hands flew up and her nails raked down across his eyes and then his cheeks. He was briefly aware of the stinging sensation and then his own blood began to run into his eyes.

His free hand went up and closed over his other. He squeezed tightly and when he lifted her into the air, he was amazed that she was so light. She continued to flail at him, her hands striking out. A small fist landed on his nose and the blood spurted forth.

He shouted. "I will not have mercy upon her children, for they are the children of whoredom!" Earle dropped her and she fell into a pile on the floor.

She struggled to breathe, to force the air down the intake tube to her lungs. He seized her by an arm and forced her to her feet. He dragged her to her bedroom and threw her beside the bed. When he began to tear at the front of her dress she lashed out, but this time considerably more weakly. He grabbed her hair and with one hand lifted her back onto her feet. She landed a blow on his left eye and this time he felt the pain. Almost immediately, the eye began to puff. Now his anger swelled and a black curtain closed on his mind. His right fist lashed out and smashed down on her jaw, driving her backwards onto the bed. She lay still, her breath coming in short, shallow gasps and blood running from the broken skin along her jaw line.

Earle took time to compose himself. He crossed the bedroom and closed the frilly curtains to her window. When he returned to the bed, he continued to undress her. She offered no resistance. He didn't take off his own clothes but just dropped his pants and climbed on top of her.

***

When she got to work that morning, Anna was called to an emergency meeting in Stanley Parkes's office. When she arrived, Hugh Johnstone was there as was McAlister. The meeting also included Dr. Montague Hennessey, the chief of Public Health; and one of his assistants, Dr. Mary Pownall. Anna smiled and greeted each person. She knew why the meeting was happening: decisions had to be made about protection of the public.

Parkes turned to her. "Good morning, Anna. Monty was just updating us. Apparently, the influenza is reaching dangerous levels in Manitoba. Not just Winnipeg now. We have other outbreaks in other places. Brandon for one. We think it may be time for other action to be taken. The mayor and a few councillors will be in shortly. They'll want to know from us the science side. What we can do if anything and what kinds of recommendations we have for protection of the public. You're all here because we need to have common ground. One of the problems in other places is that there's no common approach. We all have to be on board here. How will we respond? What information will we release and what, if any, will we hold back? Keeping in mind that we don't want to create a panic response. Whatever we decide has to be calm and reasonable. If things need to be shut down, what will they be and when? What's our best approach?"

Mary Pownall passed around several sheets of paper. "These are confidential. They don't go outside this office. They're data generated by us based upon the reports we've been receiving from different points around the world."

Monty Hennessey chimed in, "The influenza is becoming increasingly aggressive. It's very likely it's mutating and if it is, that makes it an even bigger problem for us to determine an appropriate response. At all costs, we must not make recommendations that could make things worse."

Stanley Parkes volunteered, "As far as we know, we're no closer to a vaccine. And even if we get one, we don't know how much we'll be able to contain this thing. We have to come at this I believe from the perspective that for now at least, the scientific community will only be able to contribute with advice. Of course, who knows? That could change at any time."

Anna knew that this last statement was meant for her. She felt rather than knew that Stanley Parkes was looking at her.

Later that morning after much discussion with the politicians, a standard plan of action was agreed upon. Public meetings would be banned; indoor concerts and theatres could be shut down. Mass entertainment vehicles such as circus acts would not be issued performance licenses. Educating the citizenry through mass communication would be at the forefront of public health's response. Newspapers, handbills, posters, and word of mouth would fan out across the province to make the populace heed the warnings: do not place yourself, your family, or your friends at risk of infection.

When Anna returned to the lab, it was not yet noon and already she was feeling very tired. The long hours and the experience of the autopsies had taken a toll. Harold had more specimens ready for observation, and wearily she turned to the Leitz Wetzlar microscope and pulled her notepad toward her to begin recording.

The answer had to lie in the nature of the pathogen. Anna was conscious at the same time of how much science knew and how little it knew. Turn a page of science history and a problem was solved, turn another and new problems showed themselves. And the more the pages were turned, the more encumbrances were identified with their resulting mysteries.

The people in the lab could identify bacteria. They could grow it, stain it, manipulate it, and even develop treatments. Their capacity to neutralize specific pathogens was enormous and at the same time it was infantile. In dealing with this influenza, the laboratory was a dumb beast, a forlorn, inadequate creature locked in by its own inertia and inability to solve the puzzle.

A quarter century before, Richard Pfeiffer had discovered bacillus influenza and this allowed Erlich to produce the world's first drug to cure infection. But Anna was well aware of the time elements involved. Even if she worked day and night to combine all the compounds that were possible for a vaccine, the task was overwhelming. She really needed the entire team to focus upon this and that was impossible. Doubts and fears reared themselves. Had she set an impossible task? And even if she could convince Stanley Parkes to have everyone focus on her project, what if she was proven to be wrong? Could her experiments be repeated elsewhere? Would there be any reliability and validity?

But Anna hadn't gotten where she was by being overly cautious. Parkes had hired her because he saw her inquisitive nature and her willingness to take a chance when others might have tended to back away. Her instincts had led her to confound others with her ability and it was her instinct now that was causing her to look at this pathogen in a whole new light.

There were times when she looked at a normal life as intriguing and perhaps even had a wistful longing for that. But every day her search for precise knowledge drew her mind back to the intricacies of science. And so she turned to the only thing she really had faith in: vaccine therapy.

To a large extent Anna realized that she was going to have to guess. Guess right and she could produce a vaccine that would render influenza no more than a nuisance that would last for two or three weeks. Guess wrong and tens of thousands or even hundreds of thousands would lose their lives.

She began to do some procedures as an automatic response. All of the old samples garnered from cities, provinces, and states were discarded and destroyed. She focused only upon the most immediate sputum available. Having established that anything older than several hours was too long, Anna had Harold collect samples himself from King Edward Hospital and began the process of immediate investigation.

Within minutes, the mucus was placed into sterile water, treated with platinum, and moved into a test tube. Each growing colony of bacteria had to be isolated so that it could be grown within its required culture. Every form of the pathogen had to be created because only in that way could she discover the mechanism that could destroy it.

Time. It always took too much time. It was time that Anna did not have. It was that false construct that worked against her and sought to subdue her efforts, to subvert her procedures and to hold her at bay long enough for the influenza to engage itself in an evil date with the human bronchial system.

Agglutination proved to Anna that she was on the right track. She had plenty of evidence of it in front of her own eyes. The antibodies she was placing into the cultures were binding to the antigen. That proved absolutely that the influenza was present in the samples, but it said nothing about the weapon she'd need to eradicate it.

This is what could prove to be calamitous. She had to isolate the pathogen, inject it into a test animal to give it the flu, then go through the whole process of isolating the new pathogen in the animal. A variety of vaccines could then be created and tested.

When she gazed into the microscope, recorded her notes, then turned back to a new sample, a feeling of helplessness and hopelessness overcame her. She felt like crying, like walking away from it all, but she could not.

And so she continued her work. Work which had already been at twelve to thirteen hours a day became fourteen, then fifteen, then sixteen, and still this did not seem to be enough.

***

Kathleen sat and stared at *The Manitoba Free Press* headline for May 12, 1919. MERCHANTS BANK OF CANADA BOMBED. A subheading proclaimed "Communists Suspected". Bill Ford and Sam Siegalman sat across the desk from her in the Labour Council office. Ford looked tired. He removed his glasses and pinched the bridge of his nose between thumb and forefinger. He took out a handkerchief and rubbed his eyes vigorously, as if to clear them so he could see better.

He glanced up at Kathleen. "The *Western Labour News* needs to respond to this *Free Press* article, Kathleen. It's very important that we disassociate ourselves from this bombing. The Committee will try to tie this to us and if they succeed, then everything is at risk. E. K. Atwater will use this against us. He'll try to get an injunction to shut us down."

Siegalman joined in. "But nobody can tie this to us. We don't know who did this. How can it come back on us?"

"They'll find a way, Sam," said Ford. "And if they can't, they'll manufacture something. I'm telling you, this is bad business. It's exactly the kind of thing that can subvert years of work. It's this sort of fringe group that hurts the union movement. And thank God no one was killed. If there'd have been a death, they'd be out for our blood right now."

Siegalman shook his head back and forth. "I don't know. It seems to me that anything that hurts the bosses can only help us."

Kathleen responded. "Sam, this isn't really an 'us versus them' issue. In some ways we're both on the same side. We don't want to kill business and industry. These people are how we make a living. We want a better deal. We don't want them to go away or disappear. We want wages and benefits. We want to support business in our own way because when they succeed then we do also. But we want better wages, benefits, pensions. We want to have our own homes and for our children to be able to live. We just want what everyone deserves to have. This kind of thing can only set us back."

Bill Ford piped in, "Exactly. And the things you're saying right now need to go into your newspaper article, Kathleen. We need this out in the next edition."

At that moment, Al knocked on the already open door and entered. He nodded at Bill Ford and Sam Siegalman. He smiled at Kathleen and handed her the morning edition of *The Tribune*, with its own blaring headline decrying the bank bombing.

Kathleen glanced at it and handed it back. "Yes, we've just been talking about it and how bad it looks for us. We've been trying to think of how we can avoid the blame for this. People need to know that there's no connection between the bombing and the impending strike. We need to keep a distance from this whole event."

Al shrugged. "We can't. And we shouldn't try to. This can work greatly to our advantage. It's important to send a message to the Committee of One Thousand and to the local government. Even to the provincial government. They need to know they can be got at. They have to come to understand that we're serious and that we expect things to happen now, not later."

William Ford stood up. "I think they already understand that, Mr. Devons. And if they didn't before, they certainly do now. If you'll excuse me, I've plenty of work to do." He glanced over the desk at Kathleen. "You know the position we're taking on this. Show me your article before the end of the day please."

He walked out and left Sam Siegalman and Alvin Devons looking at each other.

"Well gentlemen, I guess I've got my orders, so perhaps you'll excuse me." She picked up a sheet of paper and inserted it into the typewriter. "Mr. Devons, can I see you later this morning? There are some things I have to check with you."

"Of course."

Al and Sam got up and left the office, talking to each other as they did so. Kathleen worked through the first two paragraphs of the article then stopped, deciding she needed another coffee. Picking up her cup, she left the office and turned to head toward the lobby that held the coffee pot. What was it that made her look to her right?

Al and Sam were in another room with the door closed. She could see them through the glass in the door but could not hear what was said. She admired Alvin's blond hair and nicely shaped profile. Even from the side, his mouth looked attractive. He was vibrant and alive. She watched a moment longer and that's when she noticed the shift in both men.

Siegalman's rotund little body was planted firmly and he had to look up into Al's face. He looked grim. He was talking very earnestly and vociferously. Al nodded his head in apparent agreement.

There was a tension now in Al Devons. His head was cocked a little to one side and she could see the clenched jaws and the muscles along his cheek contracting tightly into a small knot. His head jutted forward a bit as he stared down at the shorter man, focusing on each word he was saying. She could see the upper part of Al's body bunch up as Siegalman continued. His shoulders came up and a small ridge formed near the base of his neck. He barked something in response to Sam, and though she couldn't hear it, Kathleen recognized that the tone was caustic. Al was in the process of turning away when Siegalman reached out and grabbed him by the forearm. Al shook him off in anger and turned on his heel to leave. Kathleen proceeded into the lobby to her coffee.

She did not look up as Al approached. She gave him time. He was composing himself she knew and she wanted to give him the chance to do so. When she finally turned as if to head back to her office, she smiled. "Hi. I wasn't sure when I'd see you again."

"I'm sorry I haven't been around. I've been really busy this last while."

"Oh? With what?"

He felt awkward, as if he'd been caught out. "Uh. Well, just trying to get some things done."

Kathleen sipped at the coffee and gazed steadily at him over her cup. "Al, what's going on? What does Sam Seigalman have to do with you?"

"What do you mean?"

"I saw the two of you talking. You looked angry."

Al considered for a moment, thinking about how to respond. "Ah, well. He just seems to believe that his agenda is more important than anyone else's."

"I see," she said. But she didn't. Instead, she was thinking about what an odd thing that was for him to say.

"Well. I'll see you later then." She slipped by him and returned to her newspaper article.

***

The Citizen's Committee of One Thousand met in an emergency meeting in E.K. Atwater's office. It was always the same dozen or so people. Mayor Ross and two of the city councillors were at the table, as were Julius Archibald, Thomas Bulgar, Sir Joseph Flavelle, and Ed Konyk. The city's Chief of Police Henry Hebert was in attendance, along with Commissioner Stone of the Royal North West Mounted Police. Again at the end of the table sat the young man, whom the committee employed to infiltrate the unions and collect information for them.

Atwater was listening to Julius Archibald, who was in fine form this morning. "These sons of bitches want to kill me, I'm telling you. They'll stop at nothing to destroy or overthrow us. It was my bank last night, but tonight it'll be your business or maybe your house with your family in it. Or the CPR yards. Or maybe even the police station, Chief Hebert. Did you ever think of that?"

Henry Hebert was a sensible man who'd been with the Winnipeg Police for over thirty years and had been chief now for six years. Because of his ability to stay calm, others took their cues from him and were confident in his abilities. He addressed them now with assurance. "Nobody was trying to kill you, Julius. If that's what they'd wanted, the dynamite would have gone off in broad daylight when you were there. It didn't. We do think though that at least one of the charges was placed in your office. More of a personal statement than anything else is my guess."

Atwater smiled at the quip. Julius stared back at Hebert to see if he was trying to make a joke.

Chief Hebert continued, "And we don't know if this was someone from the union. Certainly it's not what I'd expect from Bob Russell or Heaps or Bill Ford. This isn't their style. I'd be very surprised if we found that any of them was behind this."

Julius Archibald shot back, "So what are you saying, Chief? Do you think I blew up my own bank just to blame it on the union?"

Stone joined the conversation. "Nobody thinks that, Mr. Archibald. We believe the Reds blew up your building, alright. But these are hardcore communists, probably a small fringe group trying to make a statement."

"Well if that's what they're trying to do Commissioner," offered E.K. Atwater, "then we've certainly heard them. And we'll certainly respond. This isn't just marching and protesting anymore. They've gone beyond that."

Thomas Bulgar waded in. "Exactly. This is a seditious act, Commissioner. It's an attempt to promote anarchy. Wouldn't you two agree?" All eyes around the table landed on the two officers.

Henry Hebert stepped in again with reassuring calm. "That's one way it can be read, certainly. But let's not go off half-cocked here. Even if it is sedition, we still have to prove it. We still have to find the suspects, get confessions. There'd have to be a trial."

Bulgar pressed, "It seems to me, Chief, that if we have reason to believe this is an attempt to overthrow duly-elected government, then we can move on the union organizers and their sympathizers. It's not about proving who did what, it's about maintaining peace and order and good government. We can have these bastards thrown in jail even before it gets to a strike."

"He's right!" Julius Archibald's voice began to rise again. "It seems to me we can cancel their goddamn meetings and marches. We can show them that we're in control in this city. And if this is an emergency, we can call in the Mounted Police and even the army! What the hell are we waiting for? Let's get this done!"

People started talking all at once. E.K. tried to restore calm and order. He hated it when Julius did this and it was clear that Ross was disturbed and feeling a lot of pressure. Finally, Atwater was able to make himself heard. "Alright! Let's remain calm about this. Chief Hebert is right. A knee-jerk reaction can only cause more problems. We have to weigh the pros and cons here. Even if we arrest the leaders, it doesn't mean a strike won't come off. We could just end up playing into the strike committee's hands and compounding the problem instead of solving anything. As you know, the police themselves are not entirely satisfied. I think you are all aware that the policeman on the beat is not unsympathetic to the strike committee. Is that accurate, Chief Hebert?"

The police chief nodded. "Quite so, Mr. Atwater. I can order the men into the streets to control the strikers, but that doesn't mean they'll go. They have their own issues."

Julius Archibald hammered a fist on the table. "I knew it! We all knew it! If the police won't do their jobs, then the whole damn lot should be fired! They're hired to maintain the peace and stop crime. And this is crime, plain and simple. If the police can't handle it, we've got people who can. The police can be replaced, Chief."

Hebert stared at him. "Yes, I've seen some of your replacements, Mr. Archibald. I'm not impressed. You turn them loose on the citizens and we could have a bloodbath on our hands. They could cause far more problems than they'd solve."

The blond young man with the blue eyes spoke for the first time since the meeting was convened. "There is another way."

All the others stopped talking and looked to him.

E.K. Atwater asked, "What do you mean?"

He waited till he was sure he had their attention. "The influenza. It's a better way and it would be hard to argue with it. Your public health people could do the job for you, Mayor Ross. And save all of you a whole lot of trouble."

Ross nodded. "How do you know about that?"

The young man shook his head. "Doesn't matter how I know, only that I do. You could have much bigger problems on your hands than a possible strike. The Spanish flu is already in the city. Down where I come from, people are dying by the bushel full. The morgues are so overloaded that they are stacking up corpses one on top of the other. In Philadelphia, people are dying so fast that steam shovels are digging mass graves. People are being buried together. They don't even make coffins for them. And now it's on your doorstep. If you declare a health emergency, it gives you certain powers, Mayor. You can curtail meetings, both large and small ones. You can close buildings, keep people off the streets, impose isolation, and quarantine if necessary. You could lock down this city and there wouldn't be anything anybody could do about it. It's a public health issue after all."

Nobody said anything. Nobody moved. The silence around the table settled like a blanket. At first they just looked at each other and weighed the possibilities.

Finally E.K. Atwater said, "You're sure of your information?"

The young man looked around. "Oh yes. I'm very sure. And you can check with the mayor here. I'm right am I not, Mayor Ross?"

Charles Ross looked around the table. He felt hot and uncomfortable. The heat of the day was beginning to build and the office suddenly felt closed in and oppressive. He licked his lips, drank from his glass of water. "There is a problem developing. It could turn into a crisis very quickly. The hospitals are already feeling overrun. We may have to shut the city down and close it to traffic. We are very likely into an epidemic. Our young friend here is right I'm afraid. The influenza has been found here. There have been many deaths already."

Thomas Bulgar said softly, "I've been hearing rumours. I guess we all have."

Ed Konyk replied, "I received a telegram yesterday from New York. I've some cousins there. Two of them died from this flu."

Julius Archibald lit a cigar and leaned back in his chair. "That's unfortunate, Ed. My condolences to your family. But it seems to me, Mayor Ross, that you've a responsibility here to protect the public's health. Perhaps you need to declare an emergency and put a plan into place that includes closing some things down. Mass gatherings might be a good place to start."

Mayor Ross said uncertainly, "Yes. I guess it means that we'll have to take certain steps. I'll meet with Dr. Hennessey and Dr. Pownall and see what kind of recommendations they come up with."

Atwater smiled. "You do that, Charles. And as soon as you have something concrete, we'll convene another meeting. Thank you all for coming."

***

Kathleen was almost finished the first draft of her article when she heard the commotion coming from the lobby at the front door. She jumped up from her desk and ran down the hall. When she burst into the lobby area, the scene before her was a melee. Two men had Bill Ford pinned to a wall and were punching him as his knees buckled and he slumped down.

Others were smashing the furniture with clubs. Pictures were ripped from the walls and tromped on. A man swung a baseball bat and the coffee urn lifted off its stand and sailed across the lobby.

Kathleen shouted and ran across the room to where the men continued to rain down blows on Bill Ford's head. She yelled at them to stop and when they did not, she forced herself between them and Bill and ended up taking several blows herself.

She could see that Sam Seigalman and others from the Labour Council had entered the fray. She was somewhat amazed that Sam, short and rotund as he was, handled himself very well. He flung off one of the attackers and was wrestling another to the floor when Kathleen turned her attention back to Bill Ford. She was trying to get him to his feet, but he was groggy. His eyes had a bleak, glassy look and he was very heavy in her hands.

More men poured through the front door carrying clubs and bats. Windows were smashed and several men were back in the offices now breaking more furniture. Others began to carry out boxes of papers and dumped them into the lobby area.

By now blood was flowing freely and a few of the Labour Council workers had been knocked to the floor and were being kicked unmercifully. Two men came in carrying gallon-size canisters of fuel oil. They poured the contents over the papers and some of the piled-up broken furniture. Another struck a match and set the room alight in a bonfire.

Kathleen shouted at Bill Ford, "We've got to get out of here. Come with me!" She supported him as best she could and moved toward the front door, carefully avoiding the flames which were mostly concentrated in the pile in the centre of the room.

Just before she got him to the front door, Kathleen looked back. The general fighting had ceased and the men with the clubs were moving out of the building through windows while others headed towards an exit door in the back. Labour Council members were helping their wounded up and trying to evacuate. One man had a jagged cut across his forehead that bled profusely. Another's foot projected out at an odd angle. He was being helped by two others who themselves were bleeding from scalp and facial wounds.

When Kathleen had finally backed out the door almost dragging Bill Ford, someone helped her to get him away from the building. Vaguely, she could hear a voice shouting. She turned to see a man standing in the street, a club in one hand which he occasionally raised and pointed toward the Labour Council workers as he spoke. Now he was pointing it at her.

"Now you know. If you continue to fuck around with us, you'll pay a heavy price. This is for the bank bombing. You union bastards are causing everyone a lot of trouble. You're a bunch of goddamn Reds and we didn't fight the war to let you sons of bitches take over and ruin things. If you want a fight, you've found it. You bomb any more buildings and we'll crack your goddamn heads open and see that you never set up operations in Winnipeg again. Best thing for all of you to do is get the hell out of here. This is a warning: don't make us come back here for you!"

Kathleen looked at him, then looked at Bill Ford and the others slumped on the ground. She looked back into the bonfire blooming inside the Labour Council Building. In the distance, the clanging of fire bells rang. She touched her fingers to her nose. Up until then she hadn't even been aware that she was bleeding. Or maybe it was Bill Ford's blood.

She looked back to the club-wielding man. "Who are you people? What are you doing here? Why are you attacking us like this?"

The man glared back at her. "We don't mind telling you, most of us are veterans. We know that you goddamn aliens are the cause of the problems. Too many of you bohunks coming here and causing all kinds of shit. Go back to wherever the hell you came from. We don't need you here. We don't want you here! Get out!"

He turned on his heel and walked away. When he did so, the rest of the invaders followed, leaving the wounded in the street and on the sidewalks.

When the fire department and police arrived, the Labour Council members looked like a small band of rag-tag soldiers who'd suffered major casualties. They were able to contain the fire to the lobby and put it out. They patched up the bleeding and the dazed and removed a few to the hospital for further treatment, including the man whose foot was almost turned backwards.

CHAPTER EIGHT

Earle was sure that she was dead, but he checked two more times just to make sure. He adjusted her underclothes and did the buttons up on her dress. Blood ran from scratch marks on his face and dropped onto her. His eye was really swollen now so that he could barely see out of it. He touched it tenderly with his fingertips and winced at the pain.

He had to decide what to do. What was the next best step? Should he get rid of her body? No. Too difficult and too complicated. Her mother would come home. She'd panic when she couldn't find Eloise. There'd be police. They'd check the neighbourhood, knock on his door. They'd see the scratches and the black eye. They'd arrest him. And so his only path became clear to him.

He wrapped the bedspread from Eloise's bed around her and then pulled her body off the bed. He pushed her under the bed and then he got right down to stuff her as far back to the wall as she would go.

Satisfied that she was stowed away as well as he could, Earle checked around the room carefully to make sure he'd left nothing behind. No missing buttons. No handkerchief. Nothing from his pants pockets. He returned to the kitchen and checked it carefully. He picked up the Bible from the table and tucked it under his arm. He crossed the room and flicked off the electric light. When he stepped outside into the darkness, the air was moist but pleasant. He could smell the fragrance of flowers from the plant box under the kitchen window. He crossed the yard and returned to his own house.

Now that the decision was made, Earle moved quite easily and confidently. He took a carpetbag out of his closet and packed several pairs of pants, shirts, socks, and underwear. He threw in his good shoes and an extra pair of suspenders. He placed the Bible on top of these.

Next he went to his aunt's room and into her overly large closet. He reached up onto the shelf and felt along the back of it. When he felt the shoebox, he lifted it down, removed the ribbon that kept it closed, and discarded the lid. Under the pictures, clippings of birth and death notices, and old personal letters, he found the money. He took it and placed it into his pocket without counting it. He tossed the box upside down on the floor and the contents spilled around.

He went to his aunt's bedside table and opened the second drawer. He scooped out a variety of rings, bracelets, necklaces, and several watches. He put these into his other pocket and closed the drawer. He opened a third drawer and took it right out, dumping the contents onto her bed. He sifted through the envelopes and papers until he finally found what he was looking for. It was a photograph of his mother and Lillian. They were younger than he was now and outside, posing beneath an arbor. Both had serious looks on their faces as they stared into the camera.

Earle tore the picture so that Aunt Lillian separated from his mother. The half with his mother he put into his shirt pocket. He dropped Aunt Lillian on the floor beside the bed.

When he felt ready, he went into the bathroom and poured cool water from the large pitcher into the basin. He washed the scratches on his face to take away some of the sting. He wet a facecloth and dabbed gently at his swollen eye. When he checked in the mirror, he was satisfied that he was already looking somewhat better. Finally, he returned to his room and changed into a fresh set of clothes. He picked up the carpetbag and went to the kitchen to retrieve a few food items to take along.

It was then that he spotted the trap door to the cellar. He walked over and flipped it open. He put down the carpetbag so that he could unbutton his fly. When he urinated into the darkness of the cellar, he had a gratified smile on his face. He did his fly back up, and just before he left he turned out the light.

When Earle left home, Eloise Jacobs was the first woman he'd killed. Before he arrived in Winnipeg many years later, there would be twenty-two more.

***

By the late afternoon of May 12, Anna had processed four dozen more samples that Harold had been able to prepare. He was getting tired also; she could see that clearly. She had to be careful not to overwork him. If he got sick, she would not be able to keep up the workload and it would put her way behind. Stanley was unlikely to supply her with another lab assistant. Whether she liked it or not, this might have to be a shorter workday. Harold needed some long-overdue sleep. If he didn't get it, it would lead to mistakes and the work would become compromised. They could not afford that.

He had enough samples ready to carry her at least through to the supper hour. She'd send him home now and would carry on until she'd used them all up and they could start again tomorrow.

Daily reports were being dropped on her desk with a variety of treatment modes being attempted. Some of them Anna recognized as possibly having some validity, but others seemed positively outrageous and some even more dangerous than the influenza itself. A doctor was reported to have used an intravenous injection of mercuric chloride into the lymph nodes of patients, using creosote as a disinfectant. Supposedly, the white corpuscles parading just below the skin would pick it up and use it as a combat tool to wage war on the flu.

Other doctors had returned to the old practice of bleeding the patient, but Anna was utterly confounded as to how any of these treatments could render the disease sterile. The answer had to be in the pathogen, isolating it and introducing the medium that would kill it.

She was no further ahead when she returned to 614 Home Street for a rare early evening and sat down to supper at Mary Jablinka's table.

Tonight there was a surprising number on hand. Both the new tenants Al Devons and Roger Wilson were present. Even Ike Stavros for goodness sake. Anna hadn't seen his ghostly apparition for months. The quiet, reserved Stavros generally was up and gone well before morning and most times did not return until well after dark. How many jobs he actually worked Anna didn't know and she'd never had a conversation with him that lasted longer than two minutes.

"How unusual," Anna said. "It's a rare day when we're all here at the same time."

Mary Jablinka was busy putting the remainder of the food on the table. Two pot roasts, potatoes, carrots, gravy, and a large pile of homemade sliced bread. Wilson was already busy piling a load onto his plate.

"This smells wonderful, Mrs. Jablinka." Anna continued "I don't know how you do it. Are your hands better then?"

"Oh, much improved Doctor." She beamed at Roger Wilson. "Since Mr. Wilson's magic pills, I've been able to even go back to my needlepoint."

Roger smiled back at her fondly. "None of God's creatures should have to suffer if it can be prevented. Wouldn't you agree, Doctor?"

Anna helped herself to some vegetables. "Indeed. There's enough suffering in the world."

Al Devons shifted the focus of the conversation. "And how does your work go, Doctor? Are you having any success with the research?"

"It goes slowly, I'm afraid. Much too slowly to respond to such a rapid spread of disease."

"So this flu is going to be with us for quite some time?"

Anna waited for a refill of tea from Mary. "I'm afraid so, Al, unless there's a breakthrough in another lab. I know that New York, Toronto, and other places are working overtime as well. Everything else has been put aside for the moment while everyone works on this."

Mary Jablinka interrupted, "Well, for my money it's not the flu we need to worry about so much as these other things. That bank bombing caused a reaction. A mob attacked the Labour Council Building last night. They set it on fire and there were several people beaten. A man had to go to hospital with a broken leg."

Al said, "Thankfully, the fire department was able to contain the blaze and no one else was injured as badly as that man."

"I hadn't heard about any of this," Anna interjected, "I suppose it has to do with all the strike talk."

Roger Wilson snorted derisively. "Ah yes. The other great evil of our time. First the flu and now the unions. Difficult to say which is the bigger problem."

Stavros contributed to the conversation for the first time. He stopped eating and gazed at Roger. "Eh?"

"Think about it, Mr. Stavros. The influenza arises from the evil germs that Dr. Williams is trying so hard to combat. Well, Unionism is just another flu arising from the germ of Communism."

Al was looking at Wilson with scorn. "Not according to a man I listened to the other day, Wilson. Bob Russell would say it's just the other way around. He'd say that it's capitalist greed that's caused the problems. The strikers don't have a choice. They've been pushed to this and now they have to fight back."

Roger Wilson turned on his charm and smiled broadly at everyone. "Of course. I only meant that if God can send the flu to us, then he can also send the unions. And no doubt in His grand plan there's room for both."

"But you're right about one thing, Wilson," affirmed Al. "The unions have come about because of a disease and the nucleus of that germ is people. E.K. Atwater is the germ. Julius Archibald is the germ. People like Thomas Bulgar. It's these people who have caused unions to come about. It's how we fight back against the disease."

"We?" Anna said. "I had no idea that you felt so strongly, Al. I guess there are things about you we don't know."

***

The hydra-headed monster. The Canadian Pacific Railway switching yard cleaved the city in two and birthed the right side of the tracks and the wrong side. The WASP business and industry giants took up residence in the South and the massive East European immigrant population settled the infamous North End. In the South End, the unnecessary half-breeds were pushed out as squatters as the city stretched its tentacle hands and sniffed out prime real estate to promote new development.

Large lots with beautiful homes, tree-lined streets, and modern sewage and water services were meticulously planned and arranged. Large parks and schools flourished.

In the North End, developers placed row upon row of tiny houses on small, cramped lots. City ghettoization was an active ingredient in the recipe of poverty.

By 1905, 80 percent of the homes in Winnipeg's South End had been hooked into the city's artesian well water system. In the North, fewer than half the buildings had any water services. Outdoor toilets were left to drain into large ditches. Typhoid deaths were as commonplace as colds.

Private verses public turned into a war. Private contractors erected telephone poles to carry power to the city's homes. The publicly owned City Hydro competed to deliver power to the same homes. The private company refused to let City Hydro use its poles, and in response City Hydro erected its own hydro poles right beside the private company's poles. The two sets of lines were put up, dangerously, side by side.

City Hydro lineman Fred Keeley was badly burned, losing a finger and a good part of his thigh. His heart was damaged by the resulting electricity passing through his body.

He and his family nearly starved to death on the meager food allowance from social welfare. Fred was declared unfit to work as a lineman and was reduced to a floorman at the substation. The response to his injury was that it was all a part of the dangers of the job. Workers accepted the possibility of such accidents whenever they accepted the position.

The South End of Winnipeg was concerned about the depraved North End. The immigrants who provided Winnipeg's cheap labour were spurious ignoramuses. They were unclean, ill-bred, and ill-conceived. Worse, they were immoral, and the traditions and customs of the homeland were curious and strange.

Why, the Ukrainian weddings often turned into wild, drunken brawls and one could readily expect a member of the wedding party to be stabbed or shot. Murder was an accepted practice in settling disputes and their families were vast and complicated. Dirty children ran amok throughout their neighbourhoods. Common decency seemed to be a concept beyond their grasping.

It was not unusual to find four or even five families crammed into a single tiny house. These houses often had multiple stoves with cooking going on constantly. No wonder so many of them burned down. All in all, the North End was a plague of dirt, grime, squalor and disease. The perfect breeding ground to foment socialist and communist ideals.

Wobblies lined up for work that didn't exist. They had to wait until the farmer sold the product in order to be paid. They left and moved on to find other work. Some never did receive pay and those lucky few who did often found themselves short-changed. There was little they could do but go back to Winnipeg's North End for the winter. Crowd into a tiny home with family. Try to survive the mind-deadening cold, influenza, joblessness, poverty, and pain.

***

"I'm sorry you were there for that." Al was holding Kathleen that evening after arriving at her home. She was still shaken from the encounter in the Labour Council Building.

"Poor Bill. It was so horrible. These men were vile. Revolting. They would have killed us, Al. I'm sure of it. They actually do believe that we're some kind of lower life form. If you could have seen them. The looks on their faces. They were enjoying themselves."

Al rocked her back and forth, "Bill will be alright. I saw him earlier and he's fairly banged up, but considering what happened he's well off. No broken bones or anything like that."

Kathleen sat up suddenly. "Al, where did you go? The last time I saw you was after you talked to Sam. You just disappeared."

He looked at her for a long time as if he was trying to make a decision. "Listen, love, there are things I can't tell you. I'm not trying to be mysterious, but I guess it must seem that way. I had to go and see someone. That's where I was when this fight happened. I'm sorry I missed it actually. I'd like to have gotten a few licks in myself." He drew her head gently back to his shoulder and brushed the auburn hair lightly with his fingers. "You must have been very frightened."

"Yes, I was. But you know what?" She sat up again. "I realize now that this was supposed to frighten us, to make us scared so that we'd quit our work or turn tail and run."

"But you're not going to are you?"

Her teeth set grimly. "No, I'm not. And I don't believe the others will either. This won't scare us into stopping. In fact, it will only make us fight harder."

"Kathleen, you have to be careful. You're fairly high profile in the Labour Movement. It's not just the labouring folks who read what you write. Others read it too. They know who you are and where you stand on things. They collect information on people. It's not just Bob Russell and Bill Ford that they target. I'm not trying to scare you, but you can bet there's a file on you. You haven't escaped notice." Al kissed her and hugged her and said playfully, "Especially by me."

She pushed him away. "I confess I'd never thought of it quite like that. But doing this work isn't some sort of game I'm in for the fun of it, Alvin. And if things are to change—and they have to—then everyone has to help out."

He grew very serious as he gazed at her. "Nobody knows that better than I do, Kathleen. Believe me. I'm not saying you should quit. I'm just saying that there are people involved who play for keeps. And you need to know that. You have to understand what you are involved in here."

She placed her hands around his neck and kissed him. "Perhaps you should enlighten me, Mr. Devons."

"I come from a very different background from yours. My father was a miner in British Columbia. When I was ten years old, my mother became pregnant with her second child. This was an unintentional thing. It shouldn't have happened. After she had me, the doctor told my parents they wouldn't conceive again, but apparently the doctor was wrong.

In those days, there was no concern for safety in the mines. You went and did the job and if you didn't you got the pink slip and somebody else did it instead. I remember my father talking about darkness. He said that the darkness at night wasn't really darkness at all. Darkness was when you were fifteen-hundred feet underground and your light failed. That was real darkness. So black that your eyes couldn't actually adjust to it. You couldn't see the rock face. You couldn't so much as see your hand one foot in front of your face. He used to carry extra matches on him because in that kind of blackness you couldn't go anywhere unless you felt your way along the wall of the drift. Funny thing how my dad grew to hate the dark. After a while, he wanted light around him all the time. Even those few times when he was at home during the nighttime I'd wake up and there'd be a light shining in my parents' bedroom. Like he couldn't tolerate the dark.

Now, those mines weren't like others, where you dug a tunnel from the surface straight down and then had shafts running off in different directions at different levels. This mine was in a mountain so it was just the reverse. You ran a tunnel straight into the base of the mountain and then, when you were a mile or so inside, the shaft ran upwards towards the top of the mountain. Every so often there'd be drifts that ran off horizontally and that's where the miners worked. There was another opening at the very top of the mountain. It was for safety and ventilation they said. If there was an accident and you couldn't get in from the bottom, there was another way into and out of the mine from the top. He drew a picture of it for me one time." Al reached to the little table beside them and took a pencil and sheet of paper to show her.

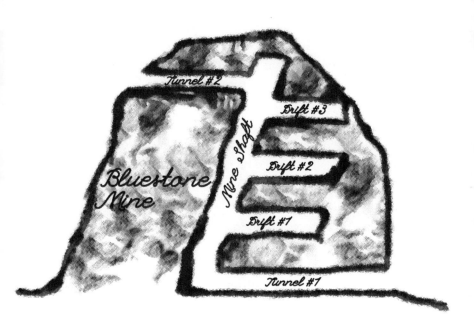

"One day there was an accident in Drift One and some miners were trapped. A mountain mine can be really unstable. The ground shifts easily and causes rockslides and cave-ins. My dad wasn't one of the miners trapped. He wasn't on shift actually, but they called him in. My mother told him to refuse because they wanted miners to go into the lower tunnel and clear away the rock and timber to see if they could get to the trapped crew. He said they'd just fire him if he didn't go. When he got there though, they already had a crew in the lower tunnel, but they got pulled back out because the ground was still moving and the main shaft was plugging up.

The mine owners ordered the mine captain to take four men up the outside of the mountain to the second tunnel. They wanted to find out if maybe they could reach the men and bring them up instead of down. It took them a long time to get to the top of the mountain, but when they did Tunnel Two was open. They went in because they needed to get to the shaft and find out if it was clear and if they could make contact with anybody. My dad was one of those four men who went in with the captain.

Later on they figured those men were probably five-hundred feet inside the tunnel when it happened. The whole top of the mountain just fell in, and when it did the pressure blew everything back out the tunnel. When the next crew got up there the following day, they found everything outside. Coal cars, timbers, jacks, steel, even huge chunks of loose rock. The men were there too—or what was left of them.

They were up in the trees that were growing just outside the mine tunnel. The pressure from the mountain caving in just picked them up and threw them back outside. They said there wasn't a bone in their bodies that wasn't broken, splintered, or protruding from the skin. Two of them were decapitated. They never found their heads.

Two days later we had their funerals. Everyone turned up for that. Everyone except my mother. She was at the doctor's. She gave birth to my sister that day.

There was an inquiry of sorts. They never did get the trapped men out. It was suggested by the government that the company should have an eye to safety in their operations. There were no laws passed though requiring them to do so. My mother received nothing. She got a small amount from the miners passing the hat around and that was it. When she was well enough after my sister's birth for us to leave, she returned to her people in the United States and that's where I grew up. In Minneapolis. My sister's still there. So's my mother."

When they went to bed that night they made love several times. They became more and more practiced. The orgasms became even more intense, electrical, shattering. Kathleen had her first multiple climaxes which left her limp, exhausted, and deeply satisfied.

The spectre of the ugly band of ferocious, club-wielding invaders left her and she slipped into a deep, deep, dreamless sleep. She had no idea that Al stared wide awake, into the darkness as he lay beside her. A darkness so profound, so black, so unremitting that light could not penetrate even the most miniscule corner. A blackness that enveloped the world, casting it into a chaos of unseen particles and hurling it through time and space.

***

The Red Scare flashed across the United States and leaped the border into Canada like a grass-fire. When the mayor of Seattle fought the strikers to a standstill and received a bomb in the mail for his efforts, the government fought back with arrests and deportations. More bombs resulted in destruction of government buildings and the homes of business leaders. When Attorney General Palmer's veranda blew up, the resulting backlash was a series of arrests of the radical elements in the Labour Movement.

In Winnipeg, the Wellington Crescent citizens kept an uneasy watch as tensions grew. For them, the expected Bolshevik bloodbath crept along the Red and Assiniboine Rivers as surely as the Spanish flu crept from town to town.

Prior to May 13, at least twenty-five unions had already voted to support a strike action. All that was needed was for the right tinder to be struck. The Winnipeg Labour Council was busy twisting the arms of the non-union workers to support a general strike. The government and the North West Mounted Police countered with a plan to suppress violence with violence if necessary.

***

Her back aching and her eyes straining to maintain focus, Dr. Anna Williams bent over her microscope to examine Harold's latest centrifuged bacterium growths. She was confused and frustrated. Johnstone and McAlister went long periods of time when they would find Pfeiffer's B. influenzae in their samples. Then in patients that they knew had died of influenza, it would disappear. At least it seemed to disappear. Was that possible? What if it was only hiding? Or what if it mutated to a new form for which they couldn't yet test?

At times, the microscopic colonies of Pfeiffer's bacillus showed up densely and easily in victims. At other times it was accompanied by hemolytic streptococci or pneumococci. This made it even more challenging, for how did one develop a vaccine that would cover all these situations? The variables were immense. The causative agents covered so many possibilities.

Anna had already succeeded in isolating the bacillus and was able to grow pure cultures from it. These she injected into test animals and waited for an immune response. When she believed she had that, she drew blood from the test cases and prepared a serum. The serum was then added back into the pure culture and there she could see agglutination forming. The serum was attaching itself to the influenza.

But when she tried it on the next culture, the binding failed and the serum did not produce antibodies. It was so frustrating! She pondered how this could be. There was no logical explanation for it. If the serum worked on one, then it should work on another and then on another. It should continue to repeat itself. Not just stop cold like this.

If it just stopped, then that must mean... And then it hit her in a flash of clarity. It must mean that there was more there than just the influenza organism! It wasn't the influenza itself that she had to look at; it was the bacterial strains that came along with it! It was the streptococcus or the pneumococcus! Everyone knew there was type I, II, and III pneumococci, but what if there was also type IV, V, VI, or twenty different types? That's why the serum wouldn't work consistently: it might work with one or two types of pneumococci, but not with others.

Anna snapped up her notebook and began to write furiously. When Harold entered the lab to deposit more samples, she didn't even notice.

When he said, "Dr. Williams?" she didn't notice. A moment later he tried again. "Dr. Williams?"

Anna's head flew up. "What?" Then impatiently, "What is it? What do you want, Harold?"

He shuffled uncomfortably, avoiding eye contact.

"I'm very, very busy Harold. What is it?"

"There's a man, Doctor. A man in the reception area. He's rather upset and he insists it's important that he speak with you."

Anna took some time to absorb this. She glanced at her notes, looked back at Harold, looked at her microscope, and a frown creased her forehead.

She removed her glasses and pinched the bridge of her nose between thumb and forefinger. She tried to clear her racing mind. "What man, Harold? Do you know him?"

"No. Never seen him before. But he's quite agitated and the receptionist is having a difficult time with him."

Anna stood up from the stool and stretched her back. "Oh, very well. I'm right in the middle of something important. This had better be something that's just as important." She left the lab and went down the hallway past offices and other laboratories.

When she emerged into reception, a man with his back to her was gesticulating wildly and talking in a very loud voice to Mr. Connors, the secretary, who was looking about with desperation for someone to help him.

Anna exclaimed, "Why Mr. Wilson! What on earth are you doing here?"

Quickly the man turned, calmed noticeably, and although he sweated profusely from his antics, he froze a smile to his face and his shining, bright-blue eyes lost some of their wildness. "Oh, Doctor. Thank goodness. I'm so sorry to just show up like this, but you need to come with me for a bit. You need to see this. Please!"

"I'm extremely busy. I can't just leave. I've got to..."

"You must see this. You really must!" His insistence was compelling, and before Anna could reply, he took her by the elbow and steered her toward the door. When they stepped outside, Anna opened her mouth in amazement. Fort Street was crammed with thousands of people. Horses and carts were standing about. The throng had totally blocked all traffic movement.

As Anna watched, a city vehicle tried in vain to move through the crowd. Pulled by two heavy draft horses with two workers perched on the seat, the driver attempted to steer the horses but they flicked their ears back and refused to move with all the people in front of them. Anna read the sign attached to the side of the wagon.

Anti-Mosquito Campaign
Oiling Cart
What are you doing to help us?
Headquarters YMCA

Anna looked to Roger Wilson and asked anxiously, "What is happening here?"

Wilson gazed grimly over the heads in front of them. "It's what I was trying to explain to you and the others at the house! This is the disaster, Dr. Williams! It's the revolution. It's the revolution!"

She looked down the street towards the Broadway intersection. Men were standing on a makeshift platform and appeared to be shouting into the crowd. Anna attempted to pull away from his grip. "I have to get back. My work is very ..."

"First you need to see this. To hear what they're saying." He gripped her arm more tightly. "We should try to get closer so we can hear better."

Around them, signs and banners popped up or hung from the buildings along both sides of the street.

IBEW SUPPORTS STRIKERS
FIREFIGHTERS DEMAND WAGE HIKES
TEAMSTERS WANT A FAIR DEAL
WOMEN'S LABOUR LEAGUE FOR EQUALITY

He forced her forward and into the crowd even as she tried to pull back. "Let me go. I have to get back to the lab. I have to ..."

Anna could hear Wilson chattering at her as she tried to make sense of the scenario before her. "There's talk of the city workers striking; the streetcars might not be running. I'll make sure you can get back and forth to work. Damnable workers. Who do they think they are? Can't just bring the entire city to a standstill like this. It's not right. The government will not permit..."

"Earle?"

Roger Wilson froze.

Anna had stopped also because he still had hold of her elbow. She could feel the sudden, tightening pressure.

"Earle. I need to talk to ya, Earle." The high sing-song voice of Hawkshaw penetrated his mind and engulfed him to such a degree that momentarily Roger wondered who the tramp was addressing.

"Earle, I got to talk to ya. It's really important. I bin lookin' all over for ya!" The sing-song voice was now standing directly in front of them, blocking their path.

Roger Wilson reached out with his free hand to brush aside the annoyance. "My good man, I've no idea who you think I am, but clearly you've mistaken me for someone else. Please move aside so the lady and I can proceed."

"But Earle! We gotta talk! Things are bad at camp and the cops are nosin' around. They keep askin' questions, Earle!"

Roger shoved the indigent forcefully. "Get out of our way, man! Can't you see you've mistaken me for someone else?"

He pushed past Hawkshaw and led a totally bewildered Anna Williams into the street, plunging through the crowd towards the speakers. Anna resisted but his grip tightened and she was forced to let herself be moved along. As they got closer, people around Anna were shouting, pushing, and milling about. A man on a small platform was shouting something about legal strike action. Others were cheering him on while still others shouted in anger. A chorus of cheers went up when a melee broke out close by the speaker. Anna felt herself physically separated from

Wilson when the crowd surged forward to get a better look at the combatants.

Anna was spun about. Her glasses came off and slipped somewhere towards the ground. She lost control of her body as someone pushed her from behind. She could feel herself starting to fall when a pair of hands grabbed her and stood her back on her feet. "Anna, what are you doing out here? You can get trampled in this crowd. You could be injured."

She looked up at Alvin Devons's blond hair. He was holding her by her upper arms, supporting her in the crush. He held her and pushed through the crowd at the same time, forcing them back towards the sidewalk. She was only partly aware that another pair of hands was behind her, firmly but gently planted on her waist and guiding her forward as she leaned in closer to Al, trying to get by the press of people.

When they reached the sidewalk, Al forced a passage through a group of men and into an alleyway. Here they had some room to move. Al drew them further in and Anna was finally able to take some breaths.

"That's no place for you to be, Doctor." Al grinned at her. Now that they were out of the maelstrom, he relaxed and let go of Anna. "Why are you out here?"

"I don't even know what happened." She was still flustered. "Mr. Wilson showed up at the lab. He was quite agitated. We went outside and then there were all these people...and then a man in front of us...." Anna trailed off, looking dazed.

A very pretty young girl was holding her hand now and brushing back Anna's disheveled hair with a handkerchief.

Al said, "Dr. Williams, this is Kathleen Johns. She works for the *Western Labour News*. She was here covering the demonstration, trying to get a story and then we saw you."

Anna felt herself recovering now. She took in the auburn hair and the most remarkable eyes she'd ever seen. She let the young lady continue to hold her hand and brush her hair back into place.

"Mr. Wilson said something about a revolution. I don't know where he went. We became separated in the crush."

Kathleen laughed. "Not a revolution, Dr. Williams. But a whole lot of people exercising their rights. Still, it's not a comfortable place to be and it can be dangerous. You need to be careful out here." Kathleen smiled at her and had taken to patting her hand.

Anna said, "Of course. I'm not even sure how I managed to be out here. I really need to get back to the laboratory."

"I think we can help with that. But there's no use in trying to fight back through this crowd. Al, let's take her back through the alley and we'll come down Smith Street. It'll be a whole lot easier." They turned and made their way as the noise receded in Anna's ears.

It was when Al and Kathleen had her safely stowed back in the laboratory that she thought a little more about these strange events. She wondered then about how Roger Wilson knew where she worked.

***

Pownall was confident, but Hennessey was terrified. As further reports poured into their offices, the numbers at first were startling and then became alarming. By now the press had hold of the story and spread its own virus of anxiety, trepidation, and falsehood.

The influenza could be prevented by drinking an elixir. It could be stopped with camphor oil. A sure cure was the Dr. Skully footbath salts. The Keyhoe Company offered the special filtering gas masks as the most effective method to avoid the pathogen.

Newspapers reported how in some cities special police were assigned to ensure that local ordinances to prevent the spread of influenza were being followed. Masked people appeared in the streets. Spitting and coughing in public were disallowed. Traffic into cities was kept to a minimum and in some instances not allowed at all.

Charles Ross was a very uncomfortable man as he sat in the afternoon meeting. Dr. Pownall stuck to the facts: 412 victims had died directly from the flu. Another seventy-eight were dead from complications arising from the flu. They had pre-existing conditions that may have killed them anyway.

Fourteen nurses and six doctors were themselves down with flu-like symptoms. Three of them had perished. As early as that day, the King Edward might have to stop admitting patients. Other hospitals were considering the same actions.

In spite of this, Pownall remained positive. Vaccines were now being tried in Toronto, Montreal, and in larger American cities. True, they'd been of limited success, but at the same time she was convinced that an effective vaccine would surface.

In the meantime, the public health service was getting the word out to the citizenry to protect themselves.

Keep your mouth clean.
Eat fresh vegetables and fruit.
Exercise moderately.
Go to bed at the first symptoms.
Do not go visiting in the homes of others.
Wear a gauze mask in public.
Don't panic.

Pownall had two sample posters to hand around as a preventative measure.

**SPITTING SPREADS DEATH Board of Health
KEEP YOUR BEDROOM WINDOWS OPEN
PREVENT INFLUENZA Board of Health**

Monty Hennessey was barely able to contain the fear. He could feel it deep in the pit of his stomach. He was afraid to speak for fear of giving himself away. He'd been to the morgues and witnessed the ever-growing stacks of bodies. In his thirty-five years of practice, nothing like this had ever come close to him and he was at a loss to explain it or even to respond. Thank God for Mary Pownall! She could be trusted to keep the lid on things, to put the best face on it. How could he reassure others when it was all he could do to keep from taking his family and bolting from the city? As it was, he still might have to send them, even if he was forced to stay.

Charles Ross asked, "What do you think, Doctor? Is it time for us to close up the city? Nobody in and nobody out?"

Hennessey thought again about his wife and three children. His sister and her family. His poor, dear, elderly mother. His throat was dry and although he knew Ross was directing the question at him, he was unable to speak.

Pownall stepped in. "That might be premature, Mr. Mayor. There are places that have done that and it still didn't stop the epidemic."

Ross said, "So are you calling it an epidemic then?"

Pownall shook her head and tried to sound reassuring. "No, no. Not at all. I'm talking about other places where it was declared an epidemic. We need to be careful about the steps we take. Shutting down the city would be a last resort. It's too soon for that."

E.K. Atwater broke in. "Look, Doctors! This public health stuff is all well and good but it seems to me it's very little in the face of this flu. You said yourself that bodies are piling up by the hundreds. The city can't be seen to be just sitting idly by while this disease overruns us. Surely you can see that at least public functions need to be curtailed."

Hennessey coughed and drank from the water glass that had been placed before him. When he spoke, he forced his voice to come out with some semblance of authority.

"It's not quite as simple as all that. Even if we declare a health emergency, remember that people still need to be able to move about. Essential service people have to get to their jobs. People need to shop for groceries. And what about the schools? Do we just close them up as well? Children still need to be educated. You realize that if we ban gatherings like demonstrations or public meetings then we also have to ban funerals, weddings, sports events, and theatre performances. What I'm saying is there's more than one side to this and we have to consider that. And remember, just because we ban it doesn't mean people won't do it anyway."

Julius Archibald said pointedly, "That's true. But it does mean we could break their goddamn heads more easily—" He stopped when E.K. held up his hand toward him, palm out.

Mary Pownall looked around the room at the dozen faces. "Even if we do agree to these extraordinary measures, we aren't doing it for political reasons, gentlemen. The only reason this city would be 'shut down' as you call it would be for health protection. Nothing else."

Ross needed to take some control of the meeting. "Of course, Doctor. We understand that. Some of us are a little frustrated by some of the labour events lately and the implications of that. The city council would realize that closing the city up is an extremely serious step to take."

When the two doctors left the room, the mix of city government officials, provincial mandarins, and business leaders sat in a brooding silence.

At last Julius Archibald spoke. "Christ, Charles, can't you just fire those two?"

Ross objected. "Like the doctor said, Julius. Things aren't quite as simple as that. The province has to be involved in this decision as well. And if we could just fire them, what then? Who'd head up public health? How would firing them help us?"

Archibald chewed on his cigar and sat back gloomily. Again a silence fell across the table and enveloped the group. Atwater and Bulgar sipped at their coffees. Henry Hebert chewed on his lower lip.

Commissioner Palmer Stone stroked his tidy moustache and considered carefully before he spoke. "You all know what needs to happen here. Something really big. The flu's not big enough to stir people into action yet and it's action we need. Because it's true that action causes reaction and that's when things really get done."

Charles Ross blinked at him and wondered what he was talking about. E.K. Atwater and Julius Archibald were looking at Stone and nodding. The young blond man rose from his chair, collected his hat and coat, and left the room.

CHAPTER NINE

When the Labour Council Building exploded in a blast just after midnight, Charles Ross would think about the conversation from that afternoon. The destruction was incredible. The fireball that exploded into the sky could be seen for miles. For blocks around, the city lit up as in daylight as gigantic flames leaped into the dark sky.

One passerby who got there only minutes after the blast described how it was impossible to get near the flames. The searing heat drove the firefighters back so that the only thing they could do was work for containment.

Surrounding buildings were in danger of catching fire and causing the conflagration to spread. It was only through an extraordinary and heroic effort that the fire department kept a damper on the blaze.

Later, the passerby would remember something else about that night, but he'd neglected to tell the police. He'd spotted a young man and a young woman when the blaze went up. They looked like they were arguing, or at least shouting at each other. She was trying to cross the street and get to the building and he was holding her back and seemed to be urging her to come away. After a brief struggle, the man took her by the wrist and dragged her off down the street and into the night.

***

The fuse that ignited the dynamite and destroyed the Labour Council Building became the fuse that triggered the strike. On Thursday, May 15 at 11 A.M. the strike committee called for a general strike by its members. Thirty-five thousand workers walked off the job and the best part for the strike committee was that a mere twelve thousand were union members. Non-members were very supportive of the strike! Plant workers, city workers, trade workers, and garment workers refused to show up for work. Daily services were suspended: no milk, no bread, no telegraph, no freight, no fire prevention. Without these, the city could not function for long.

The Citizen's Committee of One Thousand set themselves up as the champions of business, industry, free enterprise, and law and order. They had one objective: to crush the strike. This was revolution plain and simple and one's duty was clear. The nest of the viper Bolshevism must be cleaned out, annihilated, liquidated. Nothing less than that would be acceptable.

The *Western Labour News* shifted into overdrive. Kathleen became a daily columnist as the paper geared up production. The daily paper urged good conduct and orderly manner among the union members, reminding everyone that the right to bargain and the right to strike were at the heart of the process.

They also reminded supporters of the strike that the Committee of One Thousand had placed spies in their midst. People whose job it was to provoke violence and thereby allow the Committee to arrest and jail the participants. Be careful. Avoid these secret agents. Do not be fooled. Do not allow yourself to respond.

Some of the veterans became pro-strike and went so far as to pass resolutions supporting the strikers. They petitioned the city and the province to recognize the rights of the workers and to bargain with them. The strike leaders courted the alien workers in the North End to swell their ranks. It was important to have the unskilled Ukrainian, Polish, and Russian immigrants in their corner. If they were not union members, there was a very good chance they could become scabs for the other side. The rise of such an event could give way to the breaking of the strike.

***

Julius Archibald roared out across the room, "Did you see this? Did you?" He held a slip of paper high over his head for all to see. "Do you see what the goddamn strike committee has done? They think they're in charge. They believe they can do any damn thing they like."

Charles Ross also held one of the sheets. He was perplexed. Exactly what was the strike committee trying to do? He reread the handbill for a fourth time.

PERMITTED BY AUTHORITY OF STRIKE COMMITTEE

The strike committee had no authority. At least, as far as Ross knew they had no legally constituted jurisdiction. Any principal governance they believed they had came only from their own illegal actions. And yet, Ross knew that the strike had the support of at least half the citizenry and perhaps that in itself constituted some sort of sanctioning influence. Certainly it gave them a significant amount of power.

Chief Henry Hebert spoke in that deep, calming voice that always seemed to have an effect on people. "You shouldn't let yourself get upset, Julius. They aren't trying to rub your face in it you know. I've been told that it's to protect the workers. The strike committee has asked some of the workers to provide essential services, but the workers are afraid they'll be seen as scabs. The strike committee issues these 'passes' so that they don't get attacked by other strikers. Perhaps we should be grateful that the strike committee is working hard to keep the peace."

Archibald was opening his mouth to reply when Atwater cut him off. "Thank you, Chief. That makes a good deal of sense. However, there is no doubt that this strike has to be broken. If we let them win, then freedom and justice are destroyed. Capitalism steps aside and the communists take over. We can't have that. We won't ever allow it."

Commissioner Palmer Stone replied, "That's true. Sooner or later there will have to be a confrontation. That's what is going to end this. These people have to be rounded up and prosecuted. The aliens among them have to be deported. As long as we've got these Russians and Ukrainians among us, they'll always be a threat. Better to deal with them now than deal with them later."

"We don't disagree with you, Commissioner," acknowledged Atwater. "We're all on the same side here. But it's important that the Committee of One Thousand not be seen as some sort of lynch mob. There'll be enough of that in the streets. No one knows what will happen in the days to come, but there are some things we know for sure. Whatever happens, we have to win but also we must be seen to be on the right side of the law."

Bulgar offered, "Our agents tell us that the strike committee's biggest fear is that if violence breaks out the strike could be curtailed. It might run off the rails, so to speak. Perhaps that's something Hebert and Stone could make use of in a legal way."

Hebert said, "We'll take all things into consideration of course, including the fact that this flu might still be our best agent, Mr. Bulgar. It could end up being the death knell of the strike. It could still be our best weapon."

Julius Archibald scoffed. "Yes, some weapon, Chief. Especially with those two Pownall and Hennessey making the decisions. Or should I say the indecisions. If they had acted in the first place we might not be looking at this strike right now."

Atwater was calm. "Yes. But we are, Julius. And since we are, let's look to control the thing so we can best see how to bring it about to our advantage. It'll be the Committee of One Thousand who decides how this strike will be governed in spite of the strike committee." He held up a sample of the strike committee's handbill. "This won't mean anything unless we decide that it will. Russell and his lot only think they're running this show, but I tell you all, before it's over they'll discover that's not the case."

***

When Anna finally got in to work on the first morning of the strike, she was met by an angry Dr. Stanley Parkes. It had taken her a full two hours to come from Mary Jablinka's boarding house. The streets were filled with a crush of people and not a single trolley-car was running. Local taxis—if one could catch one—had extreme difficulty making their way through crowded streets.

Anna had finally decided to just walk, but at Broadway the crowd was so thick that she found it impossible to press through. She watched as a bread delivery cart was stopped by strikers. The driver was pushed aside and the horses unhitched and turned loose. The cart was then pushed onto its side by the crowd. The hapless driver stood waving his permission form from the strike committee over his head. The last she saw of him was someone grabbing the form from his hand and crushing it. The man pleaded in vain with the crowd as people plucked the bread from his overturned vehicle and threw it about.

She pressed on, hoping to find a crevice that would let her negotiate her way down the street. But for every step she tried, she was shuffled off into a new direction by the shoulders and arms of men and women shouting and waving. After what seemed like a very long time she was pushed to the fringe, where more space opened up for her to creep alongside the buildings that crowded the sidewalk.

Finally, after what felt like hours in a war zone, she arrived at the lab to find that both Harold and McAlister had not yet shown up.

Stanley Parkes was flustered. "Stupid damned thing. A strike. And what for? So a group of tiny-minded men could prove a point. How inconsequential! Interfering with really important work. Don't they realize that if the lab can't produce, they're endangering not only themselves but their own families?"

Anna took the time to calm herself. She went to the bathroom to straighten herself out and comb her hair. The whole thing had unsettled her and it didn't help that Stanley Parkes was in such a foul mood about it. As far as she could tell, the whole strike thing was none of their affair. They had work to be done and she needed to get to it.

When she felt calm enough and had recaptured her hair, she checked in at Stanley's office. He said pointedly, "We've had several people not make it in. And the damned telegraph is not working though the telephone still seems fine. Flu reports stopped coming in almost immediately. This is not acceptable! Does this strike committee not understand that we can't operate under these sorts of conditions?" He stopped abruptly, as if seeing Anna for the first time. "I'm sorry. Are you alright, Anna? Did you get hurt trying to get in? How did you get here anyway?"

She assured him that she was not injured and explained the fight she had to get to her workplace. "Very likely the others had difficulty also. How is it that you managed to get here, Stanley? You live even further away than I do."

He confessed, "I've been here all night. I haven't been home for several nights. But that's for personal reasons Anna and I'd like you to not mention this to anyone else."

"Of course." If he had reasons not to go home, they must be good ones.

"Look," he said as if making up his mind. "You go to work if you can. I'm going out to see if I can contact these so-called strike leaders. Apparently there is some sort of form one can get that allows people to go back and forth more easily. I'm going to try to get one for everyone in the lab. We really can't go on having these delays. It will set us too far behind."

"Alright, you do that. I'll start getting the samples together that we have left. Hopefully Harold will arrive with the latest ones sometime this morning." She turned to start work, then as an afterthought turned back. "Stanley, be very careful when you go out there. An angry crowd like this can get really ugly. You can't tell what they might do."

He nodded as he put on his coat and hat. "Thank you, Anna. I'm sure I'll be fine, but thanks for the warning."

She turned and headed towards her laboratory.

***

Earle Nelson knelt in the church pew and thought. Nowadays Earle did much more thinking than praying. The church was such a good place for thinking. Here his mind seemed to clear and he was able to see all of the avenues to pursue.

Running into Hawkins had been bad luck and bad timing. And then losing Anna Williams in the crowd. How had he managed to do that? He must be more careful. Would Anna remember the Hawkins encounter? If so, how could he offer a plausible explanation? Mistaken identity seemed to be the best bet.

And what about Hawkins? Perhaps he was becoming a liability. Earle thought of the skinning knife hidden under the mattress in Mary's boarding house. Perhaps it was time to pay a visit to tent city. To ensure one's safety, one's environment must be controlled. To do otherwise could invite disaster.

On the other hand, Hawkshaw was Earle's most direct line into that other world. The defeat of satanic forces could only be accomplished if one was to mix with the great enemy. Earle had proven that to his satisfaction over and over again. Satan's minions could be conquered only through one-on-one confrontation. And they were everywhere. They lived in tent city down by the river. They lived in the New Jerusalem of the North End. They lived in the strikers and in the bosses. They lived along Wellington Crescent in Winnipeg's South Side.

It was a one-by-one fight and if Earle Nelson was to do his part, then he needed people like Hawkshaw. They were his pipeline to the underworld. Yes, even to cross the mighty river Styx one must use a boat.

His time in Winnipeg would not be much longer. A mere few months at best, but in that time there was much work to do. If Hawkins was Earle's passage into the culture of the underworld, then Anna Williams was his cultural agent to move into the world of disease and modern medicine and Al Devons could be a cultural agent to introduce him into the diseased world of communist plotters, strikers, and the anti-religious. Socialism, the last great fortress of the non-believer, must also hearken to the bell of its own doom.

From his kneeling position in the pew, Earle plucked a copy of the Holy Bible from the holder on the seatback before him. He thumbed through until he found the applicable passage.

Zephaniah Chapter 1 vs. 17

And I will bring distress upon men, that they shall walk like blind men because they have sinned against the Lord: and their blood shall be poured out as dust, and their flesh as the dung. Neither their silver nor their gold shall be able to deliver them in the day of the Lord's wrath; but the whole land shall be devoured by the fire of his jealousy: for he shall make even a speedy riddance of all them that dwell in the land.

It was clear to Earle. As he had stated to the other renters at the boarding house, the influenza was foretold in the Bible. Although he had a dread of contracting it himself, he knew God's day was at hand!

The flu was the distress brought upon man. It was the agent of their demise. God's wrath visited upon the Earth. And no one was exempt. It visited all classes of people. The wealthy were destroyed along with everyone else. God commanded that their money could not spare them.

All in the land would be destroyed with rapidity. Nothing could stop what God had commanded be put into motion. Earle thought of Dr. Anna Williams and her work. But if Anna and her colleagues came upon a solution, they might stop it. What was it she had said over the dinner table? "Everything else has been put aside as we concentrate on this." Of course they were working diligently to suppress the disease. This flu that worked so speedily in its devastation of the human body—the way God had intended it to work.

And if they found a vaccine what then? It would interrupt the cleansing process so carefully put into place. This was a revelation for Earle. The gauzy web had been removed from his eyes and the alternatives were displaying themselves before him.

One of them was that the lab work must be stopped. The agents of Satan even now were at work to prevent the devastation set in motion by the Lord. Earle replaced the Bible and rose from the pew. He made his way to the exit and stepped into the street. His jaw dropped.

The entire avenue was jam-packed with people. Vehicles, horses, and streetcars were at a total standstill. A frozen potpourri of life flashed before his eyes. No: the flash was from a photographer taking a series of stills of the crowd. Had the camera been pointing in Earle's direction upon that last flash? The cameraman was turning, setting up for another photo in another direction. He was up on the back of some sort of carriage where he could peer across the crowd and get a better shot.

Earle moved across the street toward the man. He had to shove people aside to advance. Someone tapped him on the shoulder.

A Winnipeg Police Service constable looked him in the eye. "Take it easy there, mister. No need to be pushing people around. It's not like there's any place to go."

Earle turned an ingratiating grin to the officer. "Oh, I'm sorry. What is it that's happening here?"

"Strike's been called. All these people have walked off the job. 'Bout bloody time too if you ask me."

"Of course. This has been brewing for a long time. I suppose it was only a matter of time."

"Damn right. Best damned thing that could've happened. An' it's not just the industrial workers. It's everyone—civil service, everybody."

"I see, Officer. And where do the police stand in this, if you don't mind?"

The officer grinned a wide-gapped, broad smile. "No I don't mind, mister. We're pretty much behind the strikers to a man. 'Spect we'll walk out with'em in a day or so. Sure hope so anyways."

"But who'll keep law and order? Who'll control the crowds if there's no police?"

"From what I hear, the Committee of One Thousand has that well in hand. They have their own police force. Apparently they don't need us."

Earle felt his heart lighten momentarily. "You don't say. Well I suppose that someone must look after the policing of things. Thank you, Officer. I'll be on my way."

"Hold on just a minute, mister. What's your name anyway?"

Earle felt the familiar prickling of the hairs at the back of his neck. His sweat glands went into immediate action and he could feel the beads under his armpits, staining his shirt. Tiny pebbles burst from the hairline along his forehead. He swiped surreptitiously at them and forced himself to calm.

He smiled again at the officer. "Roger Wilson."

"And what's brought you out to the demonstration, Mr. Wilson? Are you off the job in support of the strike?"

"No, not exactly. I've actually been searching for work for some time now and haven't been lucky. Perhaps with the strike on I can—"

The officer interrupted, "Not a good idea, Wilson. Not without permission from the strike committee. The strikers would see you as a scab and think you were a strike breaker. Wouldn't like it...hurt you...beat up."

Earle could smell the down of singed duck. As he looked up at the talking mouth of the officer, lights began to dance at the corners of his eyes. The world suddenly became much smaller and the police officer much bigger. Earle had to look further and further up to see the officer's face until finally he was looking straight up beneath his chin.

The last thing he remembered hearing before he fell backwards into the street was, "Here now, is something wrong, Wilson?"

***

The first morning of the strike, Kathleen and Al sat in her kitchen and drank coffee. They hadn't slept at all. After Al had dragged her away from the burning Labour Council Building, she remained discombobulated for hours. They hadn't spoken until they'd reached Kathleen's house. Al continued to hold her arm firmly as he steered her through street after street, past clanging fire trucks heading toward the fire.

When at last they were safely stowed inside, he sat her down and poured drinks for each of them. For a long time they sat in the darkness of the living room, sipping at the whiskey and thinking. All kinds of scenarios tumbled through Kathleen's brain. Had anyone been killed? Who was Al really and what was he doing? What if the strike committee got wind of this?

Eventually she felt calmed enough to turn to Al. "I think you'd better tell me what's going on."

"What were you doing out there at that time of night?"

"You said there were things you couldn't tell me. But it was obvious you were deeply involved in the movement somehow." She shook her head at him forlornly. "There's so little I know about you." She paused and thought momentarily, "So I followed you."

He seemed only mildly surprised. "I guess it serves me right for all the secrecy."

She could not see his facial expressions in the dark so she could not tell if he was serious or not. "Yes, it does actually. We've got decisions to make, Al, but we can't do that unless I know the truth. It was you who bombed the Labour Council wasn't it? And I'm guessing it was you who bombed the bank as well? Who do you really work for? What's your part in this?"

He thought for a moment, then plunged forward. "During the war I was a munitions expert for the army. It was my job to blow up things that belonged to the enemy. And I got very good at it. I blew up buildings, munitions dumps, arsenals, bridges, railways—you name it and I took a shot at blowing it up. I started having dreams about blowing things up. I kept having this one particular dream where I'd blow up the Kaiser's bedroom with him in it.

But I was injured, so I was discharged and returned home. Only home wasn't home anymore. There'd been a lot of changes. The old jobs were gone. Nobody was hiring. The vets who'd gone out and fought were ignored, especially the wounded. I visited a hospital to see a pal of mine. It was filled with men who had things missing: arms, legs, faces, private parts. The army was finished with them. Had used them up so didn't want to have anything to do with them. The government who sent them overseas was not willing to take responsibility. These men were in a bureaucratic purgatory.

The economy was a problem too—it had pretty much dissolved after the war. As far as I could see, the whole system was working against us. And I mean everyone, not just the soldiers who'd been demobilized.

So with no possible job and not much in terms of prospects, I ended up back in Minneapolis with my mom and sister. One day a friend and I were downtown, job hunting as usual. I picked up a handbill a guy was handing out; it advertised a meeting of the Communist Party that evening, and since we were there anyway..."

Kathleen was shaken. She finished her drink and in the dark fumbled to pour herself a second. "My God. You're a communist. That means that what the Committee of One Thousand says is true: we have been infiltrated."

Al sounded defensive. "Well, it's like you said yourself. Things have to change. And this is just one more way to change them."

"But not revolution! Don't you see that you're hurting and not helping us? How many people have died because of these bombings, Al? Do you even know?"

"We always take precautions. Nobody has ever died directly. Not that I know of."

Kathleen repeated incredulously, "Not that you know of."

Al persisted and now his voice had a note of growing anger. "The system doesn't work. Capitalism is dying. The bastards who own things are killing it, Kathleen. All the party is doing is pushing it along. Of course people die in this but they'd die anyway, in one of those firetraps they call factories or in one of their Christly foundries where safety is just a joke. They even have safety inspectors who file reports on places they haven't even been inside."

"But you think Communism is better?" Her voice was soft, with a note of hopelessness.

"It's not a question of better or worse. Don't you remember? You were the one who talked about us never asking the right questions of ourselves. The question isn't whether Communism is better. It's what if the state controlled the economic functions of the country? The answer is they could set the rules and make the factories live up to expectations, because the factories would answer to the workers and not to the bosses."

"And you thought I was idealistic and naïve?"

He was shocked. "What do you mean?"

"You thought I was just a little rich girl playing at the game of labour relations. You thought I didn't really understand what was going on in all of this. You told me I had to be careful because there'd be a file on me and—"

Al interrupted. "I was only trying to warn you, to help you out. I was only thinking of your own good."

"My own good! Jesus Christ, Alvin. You blew up my goddamn office!" Suddenly, she saw the irony and laughed. "You tried to help us by blowing us up. But you knew that the Citizen's Committee would get the blame, didn't you? This was supposed to be seen as a retaliation for the bank. It was all to provoke the strike. To get it going. To ensure that it happened. You don't even realize that you didn't have to do it, that the strike would have happened anyway. All your people have done is to ensure that it will be violent. Or is that what the intention was all along?"

Al said nothing. He sat quietly in the dark. He knew she was waiting for him to answer. The next things he said had to be right. It could make all the difference.

Kathleen spoke. "Of course. That's what communists would want—people to start killing each other. Because that's the way revolution happens isn't it? Now the shooting can start and when the smoke clears whoever's left standing takes over."

"You make it sound simple."

"Oh I don't think it's simple at all, Alvin Devons. I don't think it could ever be a simple thing to get people to kill each other. It must be quite complicated in fact. It's something that must be manufactured!"

He opened his mouth to respond but she stopped him. "No. Don't say anything. At least I know where the material for my next column is coming from, whenever I get to write about it. I think I'd better go to bed now. We've got things to talk about come morning."

***

They sat in the daylight staring across the table in the kitchen. The stress on Kathleen's face was readily apparent. A thought brought a slight smile to her face and she said, "All this time they've been warning us to watch for spies planted by the Citizen's Committee. I've been so paranoid about that. I'd never even considered that we might have spies planted by our own side just to make the strike happen."

"I'm no spy, Kathleen. I'm just a guy who's been trying to get a job done. I get orders like everyone else. Just like you do. I try to carry them out."

"Yes, well you'll have to excuse me if I don't quite see it that way. At any rate, I have to go to work. I have to find Bill Ford and find out where we're going to work now that our offices are gone. I'm going to be writing the truth about this, Al. I'm going to be talking about how the Labour Council fire wasn't the work of the Citizen's Committee. I won't bring you personally into it but *I will tell the truth.*"

At last Al said what he'd been waiting to say since the previous night. "The truth doesn't really matter, Kathleen. That's the part you don't understand. The truth is whatever we want it to be. It's what the R.B. Russells of the world want it to be. It's what the Bordens and the Norrises want it to be. It's even what the communists like me want it to be.

You go through your life and your work thinking that the truth is some tangible thing, something you can hold to as if it's a lifeline or a flotation device that can hold you up. But it's not like that. It doesn't work like that. When I went overseas in the war, I thought there was truth too. But I found out differently. What people like you and I call truth is just illusion. It doesn't really exist. Like God or religion or justice. It's just a fairy story. We hold it up so there's something to cling to, but it's impermanent the way we ourselves are. Truth is just fleeting, and worse, it's a whore. Because just when we start to believe in it, to place a value on it, to hold it to us, it runs to someone else's arms."

Kathleen picked up her briefcase and moved to the door. She was just about to leave but stopped and turned back to him. "No. You're wrong. And not only are you wrong, but you must be a really sad and unhappy person. Perhaps you're right when you say that truth doesn't matter, but even that's the case only for you. For others it does matter. It matters to me. I believe it matters to the people I work with and work for. It matters to the people who struggle to make things better than they are, Al. And I bet if you ask her, it matters to your doctor friend you introduced me to. What's her name? Anna.

You're wrong about truth, Al. Hell, it might be the only bloody concrete thing that we have. And if you can't find a way to believe in that then I really feel very badly for you. Because when you really think about it, the people who have made a difference on the planet are the very ones who believed that truth can be seen, touched, talked about, discussed, felt, and even passed on from one of us to another."

***

It was a beautiful morning on May 15 when Kathleen stepped outside. Despite the previous day's stress a stroll down Wellington Crescent always improved her mood. The warm sunshine spilled down on her face and caressed her gently. The stately elms swayed high overhead. An elderly lady worked diligently in the rose garden along her front fence. She worked the soil, turning it up by hand with a small spade. She scooped new black dirt from a basket at her side and spread it about carefully. It hadn't rained lately and the woman poured water from a can carefully onto the roses.

Kathleen flashed a broad smile at her as she walked on by and headed toward the downtown area. As she walked, a brief and odd thought popped into her head. Her period should have started by now. Probably all the stress. Her system was telling her something. Slow down, don't work so hard, pay some attention to yourself.

PART II
MAY 1919

CHAPTER TEN

The snakehead devours its tail. Over time it will consume its entire self. Commercial capitalist ventures and Craft Unionism. Opposite sides of the same coin joined together like demented Janus gods in a search for power and wealth. Capitalism—the fat, overblown, anachronistic head with its hinged jaw opening wider and wider as it slowly and dexterously swallows itself, starting with the tail but inevitably moving on to its own wide-ribbed body.

Craft Unionism—the lean, disparate, multi-veined tail slapping itself from side to side in futility. Raging over its own inability to gain a hold, to steer in a common direction. Reproducing itself by splitting, dividing, reforming. Its dance of mitosis diverting its attention away from the fanged jaws of the oncoming head.

Competition—the big lie foisted upon an unsuspecting public. Rivalry, contest, match—its very definition hinting at its own innate self-immolation capacity.

The children of competition are envy, jealousy, gossip, lies, bullying, loss of esteem, and loss of self-esteem. Its grandfather is discrimination and prejudice. Its grandchildren are greed, self absorption, cheating, and abuse. Its final stand is filicide.

Out of the chaos, the slime, and the miasma is birthed the venture capitalist. It grows to fruition on the rising tide of its own fortune. It climbs upward on the backs of its own workforce. Its grapevine tentacles stretching, grasping, curling, and holding desperately to a small crevice, a cranny, a tiny opening as it cannibalizes its young to ensure continuous progress.

The venture capitalist must have more. It must grow ever larger. Its obesity must overshadow the competition. It has no governing thought process. Consumable is its nature. Feudatory is its law system. It has no life-force except its ever-burgeoning, growing, colossal self. Because it founds itself upon adversarial relationships, gain and loss are its watchwords. Its value system can only be and must only be intolerance, repression, and destruction of its competitors.

Venture capitalism must increase. It must have more. More resources, more money, more authority, more digestion. It must constantly reinvent itself because the competition beast can only drive it onward. Cannot let it rest. Cannot allow it to think. Cannot allow it to reflect.

There can be no counterbalance to it and so it seeks to kill any semblance of a challenge. Even as the venture capitalist has birthed the craft union it must destroy its own child. And the multitude of craft unions, also buying into the great philosophy of competition, begin to eat each other up. They must steal their food from the venture capitalist to continue their own growth. At the same time they must hold their brother and sister unions at bay. Suppressing, impoverishing, annihilating them because they also are the competition.

Competition—the multi-faceted war that dictates that there must be winners and that can only happen if there are losers. Like the futilely religious believer: if my religion is to be right, correct, and true, then by default all others must be wrong. And so it is with competition, the lie that perpetuates the falsity of the value of its own self.

The young believe. They believe. The path to the future can only be navigated by stepping upon those around you. Glory can only be achieved if one is better than the others. Money, riches, fame, fortune are at the behest of becoming superior in strength, speed, agility, intelligence, and performance. Anything less is to fail and in failure to lose and in loss to be relegated to the wayside.

And so the father Capitalism enters into the incestuous, fiduciary marriage with its own child Craft Unionism and continues to produce the children thereof: the competitors. And so is born further tribulation as the competitors engage in sibling rivalry, leading to fratricidal destruction.

The price for such competition cannot be calculated in monetary terms, emotional distress, mental anguish, or family dysfunction.

In Manitoba, by 1911 the money invested in the manufacturing industry rose to a staggering twenty-six million dollars, an increase of more than fivefold in a decade. Competition demanded that investors must receive full value for the money. The machines could not be still.

The machinist operates a four-bit drill. The foreman tells him to operate multiple drills at the same time and never to shut the drills down to remove the metal in safety. Stopping and starting loses too much time. His arm catches in one of the drills when his sleeve slips around one of the bits. Held tightly by the vice-like grip of the unstoppable motor, he is yanked into the drill as it churns its way through the meat of his arm. He never uses the arm again.

Bring in another machinist. Drill the metal pieces. Do not stop. Do not slow down. No idling allowed. The competitor will get an edge on us. Production is all. The machinist owes twelve hours of production time. He owes us. He owes. Owes.

The garment factory is a pernicious building. Overcrowded and poorly ventilated. It used to be a manufacturing plant. Closed in, dirty, grime everywhere. A few bare electric lights hang from the ceiling. Cold, damp, forlorn. Long tables of garments across huge tables. Dirty, gaunt East-European men cutting out garments. Cut fast. Don't stop. Meet the quota. No squandering the material or the time. Here, you! You've injured yourself. Get out of the way, man. Get another cutter in here. You! Why have you stopped? Stop again and I'll fire you.

You women! Keep the sewing machines going. Why are you cough-
ing? If you're ill get out. Someone else will take your place. Don't make
mistakes. If you have to re-sew it costs time and money. Keep up the
quota. You're paid by the piece here. Hurry! Don't stop! The sign on
the wall broadcasts loudly: WE WRAP OUR FUTURE IN EVERY
PACKAGE! So true. So true.
Never mind the rain leaking onto you. Don't let the fabric get wet!
Never mind the cold. Keep going, it'll warm you up. The competition
will get ahead of us.
The investors have to get their money back. The unions cannot
protect you. The Factory Act is just a big joke. There's nobody who
enforces it. You'll have to work overtime. You'll have to work evenings.
You can't work if you're pregnant. Get out! Others are waiting for your
job. It's a competition you know. It's a business. We need more! More
production! More money! More!

***

Kathleen's office moved into the Labour Temple, along with the Labour Movement's various agents and staff. But the Labour Temple could not hold all of them, so some were shuffled off to private homes to meet and work while others crowded into cafes to deliberate upon strategy and organize mass meetings to be held in outdoor parks.

Kathleen had her first column ready by mid-morning of May 16. In it she warned that the Labour Movement had been infiltrated by members of the Communist Party and that a dangerous tightrope had to be walked if a charge of sedition was to be avoided.

She reported that sources close to the action had revealed the bank bombing and the Labour Council bombing had both been the work of communists in an attempt to set one up against the other, to foster fears of revolution in the public mind, and to provoke the police into confrontation with the strikers.

She urged for cooler heads on both parts and responsible actions and counsel from the leadership. Above all, they must not be drawn into military-style encounters that would only result in injury and possible fatalities on both sides.

Good news for the strike: it appeared that a large number of the war veterans were coming out in support. Rallies were being planned and the Veterans Association appeared to be ready to pressure the government about workers' issues.

The column in *The Western Labour News* of this special strike edition also called for the various craft unions to support one another. It was important to remember that on its side the opposition had big money, a high degree of organization, vast resources, and access to military options. The strikers needed solidarity if they were to get their demands met.

After reviewing her column, Bill Ford sat in Kathleen's tiny, new, cubby-hole office in the Labour Temple. The article was troublesome. To some extent, it played into the hands of the Committee of One Thousand. Their propaganda organ, *The Voice*, would take this and run with it. There'd be accusations of Bolshevism. The Committee would try to use it to shut down the strike. Atwater and Julius Archibald would play a merry tune of anti-union dogma and *The Western Labour News* would be the musicians helping them to do so.

The alternative though was even more distasteful. If the infiltration was kept quiet and discovered later by the Committee, things would be so much worse. At least with *The WLN* releasing the distasteful facts, they had an opportunity to control the message.

"You're absolutely certain, Kathleen, of your facts? Your sources on this are solid? There's no doubt about the bombings being the work of communists?"

"I know this from a firsthand source. Someone right on the scene. This isn't something the Committee of One Thousand used to set us up. It's our own problem Bill, and we need to deal with it. Publishing the story is one step in doing that. You know that we're both thinking the same thing: better us than them."

Kathleen studied Bill Ford's face. He still had a long scrape mark down the side of his face. The bottom of his right ear was stitched from where it had torn from his skull for a half-inch at the lobe. The discolouration at the side of his left eye was already beginning to change.

"How are you feeling, Bill?"

"I don't know. I think we should publish. It feels like the right thing to do." He looked up at her abruptly.

There was the slightest smile at the corners of her mouth.

Ford held up his hand to the side of his face. "Oh, you mean physically. I'm okay." He grinned at her broadly. "It's a long time since I've been beaten up. At least with something besides words. I'll recover. Doctor checked me out and said I'm good for a few more beatings yet."

"Things are getting really serious now, Bill. People are starting to get hurt. It could get a lot worse."

"Exactly! And that's why we need to get your column out. So people don't go off half-cocked, spoiling for a fight. The worst thing that can happen is to provoke a violent response from us. It's exactly what the Citizen's Committee wishes."

Kathleen studied the older man. Bill had worked mightily for fair labour laws, for equal pay, and for workers compensation. He was in fact something of a legend in the Labour Movement. He was forever organizing and reorganizing those around him. If he sniffed out any opportunity whatsoever to further the cause of labour he was there. Like a lot of people at the heart of labour, Bill's own people had risen as products of the Industrial Revolution and he never forgot his roots. Never forgot that the working class was an exploited class and non-English speakers suffered even greater exploitation. He'd watched children die simply because of a lack of healthcare. Just basic care that came along with cleanliness, education, a proper diet, and now and then medicine when they became ill.

She knew that Ford saw himself as a missionary in a superbly wealthy land. The life force that kept him going arose from this fight to make things better. Kathleen would never insult him by suggesting that he should back off now that the conflict was rising.

"I just hope that when the column comes out they don't come down and burn us out of the Labour Temple also."

"Oh, not to worry about that. We've people who are paying very close attention now and we'll have protection around the clock. The Committee's goons won't get within blocks of this place."

Bill's face grew very serious and he paused for a long time before he spoke. "Listen, Kathleen. I don't know where you got your information and I don't really need to know. Probably better if I don't. But I am concerned about you placing yourself in danger. There's no need for you to do that. No need at all. If you need out of this, you only have to let me know. I realize it's your job to report. To write the columns. To get the message out. But I don't want you to have to get yourself injured or into some sort of trouble. But if you do—get into any trouble I mean—you can come to me. I'll help out if I can."

"Thank you. I know you'd do that, Bill. I've never doubted it. And I don't want out or need to be out. Whatever's down the road needs to be dealt with. No, I'll see this through. I will."

Ford hesitated again and considered very carefully before proceeding, "You understand do you that we can't win this?"

Kathleen was startled. "What do you mean?"

"This strike, we can't actually win it. In the end, we'll lose and we'll go back to work. It's not actually about winning it or even about losing it, Kathleen. It's about shifting the balance so it works better for us. So that the system works better for us. That's what the communists and socialists don't understand. Capitalism is evil. But that doesn't mean that something else is better. Capitalism doesn't work, but getting rid of it is not an answer. Changing it is a better option, so that down the road things are better for your children and then for your grandchildren. The strike is only a battle. Don't make it more important than it really is."

She reflected on his words, "I guess I'd never thought of it in those terms."

***

On May 17 the typographers struck the three major Winnipeg dailies. *The Manitoba Free Press, The Tribune,* and *The Telegram.* Without them, the newspapers were helpless. To complicate matters and to stoke the fires, the typographers volunteered to help *The Western Labour News* in its daily publication.

The three Winnipeg dailies had always shown a strong anti-union bias and now they were silenced, at least for the time being. The strike committee's power grew immediately with such flexing of their muscles, and when they faced down the city council over what constituted essential services, their ability to control the strike and the strikers became more and more important.

The day after Kathleen's column appeared, the Citizen's Committee of One Thousand struck back like some avenging capitalist angel. Their own paper *The Voice* went on a veritable tirade that the strike committee was riddled with Bolshevik agents and was controlled by those who sought to bring freedom to its knees. And if it took a violent revolution to do that, then the strike was just the first step. There was no doubt. Soon blood would be running in the streets of Winnipeg.

Furthermore, *The Voice* decried the strike as being illegal and therefore negotiating with the strike committee was out of the question. Local, provincial, and federal authorities recognized the owners as the legitimate controls of industry and would never allow a worker-controlled labour force to dictate terms to the industrialists. To do so would be to allow Communism to establish itself as the legitimate government of Manitoba.

If necessary, the military was prepared to take action against the strikers. Already the Citizen's Committee of One Thousand had set up a paramilitary organization, which would step in and assume control of policing, fire-fighting, and public transit. A Home Defense Guard had been established and was ready to take over the post office and the law courts building. Any public facility could appeal to the Home Defense Guard and be assured that strike action would not prevent them from doing their public duty.

Julius Archibald preferred simpler terms. "No Red bastards are coming into my city and dictating what was going to run and what was not."

E.K. Atwater spoke of how it was impossible and implausible that civic authority could ever be ceded to the strike committee and that whatever it took, the strike action would be met with a force intended to destroy it. Nothing less would be permitted.

Commissioner Palmer Stone assured that the Royal North West Mounted Police were already recruiting the necessary men to contain the strike. It was clear to him that last year's strike had been handled softly, but the same mistake would not be repeated. The Mounties had been given their orders and would personally see to it that the federal government's authority would not be challenged again. If the strikers insisted that violence was their course of action, then the response would be indomitable force.

Intelligence had indicated that without question the Winnipeg strike was by its very nature revolutionary and therefore also against the law of the land. Industrial Unionism was not the same as Craft Unionism. It was not just insipid but was demented. It was a kind of psychopathy that, left on its own and untreated, could not help but infect the worker and therefore endanger free enterprise. Best to excise it now in Winnipeg before it was too late.

***

By May 18, Anna was growing ever more alarmed by science's inability to respond to the pace of the influenza. And worse, the medical staff and caregivers were becoming frighteningly depleted in their numbers.

At five in the afternoon, Harold had returned with new samples from the hospitals, including one from Monty Hennessey. Early that morning the doctor had awakened and started coughing. Within an hour, he'd spiked a fever and felt the first signs of congestion in his lungs. Immediately he'd put on a gauze surgical mask and had his wife transport him to King George. Within three hours of his arrival, the cyanotic dark splotches appeared and he knew he was in deep trouble. By four o'clock he had passed away and Harold, having just arrived fifteen minutes earlier, was able to retrieve a specimen.

Harold went to work immediately to centrifuge the samples and prepare them for Anna's observations. Readying herself for work, Anna could not help but reflect on Monty Hennessey. While he'd never been a particularly effective administrator, his role had allowed him to upgrade Winnipeg's previously ineffective public health system. To that extent, his reputation for leadership outweighed that of his abilities to practice medicine. To be blunt, Anna thought Monty should never have been a medical man. He was too removed from his patients. No doubt this was a lack of focus on his part, but it was often interpreted as arrogance.

But Anna knew that it was really fear that motivated Monty. He often felt pressure from all sides and this caused him to dither. Pressure from his bosses forced bad decisions and pressure from the public compounded this. If he felt the department would suffer from negative press, he all but froze. This was why there was no quarantine and no ban on public rallies: Monty Hennessey could not decide which direction to go.

And because he flip-flopped in an attempt to please everyone, it came about that most despised him. Poor Monty, Anna thought. It didn't matter which direction he took in the pandemic, he was going to make someone unhappy. Still, it was troublesome to think of him dying such a horrible death at the King George hospital.

By seven o'clock in the evening, Anna was well into her work when she was surprised by Stanley Parkes's appearance at her side.

"Why Stanley, what brings you out so late? I thought you'd be home with your family by now." Anna bent back over the microscope and peered at the colonies of bacteria before her. "How are Mildred and the children anyway?"

Parkes picked up some of Anna's notes and studied them. "She's gone."

"Gone? Stanley what do you mean gone?" Anna braced herself for the answer.

"I've sent her away. She's taken the children and gone to her mother's in Gimli. I told her she should. That it was no longer safe for them to be here."

"Well for goodness' sake, man. Be careful how you say things. I thought you meant that the flu had got her."

"Oh, sorry. No. I just don't want her to take any chances. Far better to be away. We've removed the children from school and taken them also. I think it best that we don't take any chances."

Anna stared at him for a long time as he studied her notes. Finally he became aware of her gaze and looked at her.

"What?"

"Stanley, don't you find it a bit odd that you sent your wife and family away to apparent safety while the rest of us remain and toil away in the face of this flu?"

He blinked. "I hadn't thought about that. Well we can't just shut down the lab and walk away, Anna. We've a responsibility here, you know."

Anna's voice was soft. "Indeed. But if the rest of us suffer Monty Hennessey's fate—and we easily could—who's going to take our place? Where are the researchers and medical people coming from? Haven't you considered that we should move the whole lab out of the city?"

"That's preposterous, Anna. Why, the expense alone would kill us. It's impractical. How would we get the work done? How could we function? How could Versatile Laboratories be the first to discover a vaccine and become..." Parkes stopped, realizing the vacuousness of the statement he was making.

That feeling of loneliness crept into Anna's brain again. An overriding fear invaded her mind and set itself there like a leaf worm, slowly gnawing away at its food source. Anna had always struggled with feeling inept, not up to the task. Even after all this time and all the years of working diligently, her fear of failure was at times insurmountable.

And who to talk to about such things? Her circle of friends was nil, her acquaintances small in number, her family had long ago ceased to be a part of her life. If she should confess these feelings to Stanley Parkes, he would be appalled and very likely lose confidence in her.

Anna gathered her wits and went back to the microscope. "Yes, well I suppose we must go on. Certainly nothing must stop us from killing this flu before it kills all of us."

Parkes cleared his throat and went back to his officious persona. "Right. I see that you're pursuing a new avenue here, with the pneumococci being a carrier agent."

Anna only shrugged. "There may be some merit in it."

"I'll leave you to your work then." After he'd stepped out, Anna reflected that more and more she had less and less respect for this man.

***

When Earle awoke it was to discover that the strike was five days old. He was in a hospital. His memory was blank. He remembered a police officer and he remembered singed duck and that was all. He looked around: some sort of hospital. He was in a room and there were at least a dozen others in with him. The smell was overpowering.

When he tried to move, he was exhausted and when he opened his mouth to cry out it was only to emit a soft frog-like sound. The dryness in his throat was a desert of choking sand. He laid his aching neck and head back onto a pillow and closed his eyes, wanting the whole scene to just go away. Where was he? How did he get here? Did anyone know where he was? When he opened his eyes again he looked about more closely. The man in the bed on his right looked dreadfully ill. His breathing was just a series of shallow and short intakes and outtakes. Blood ran from his nose and from his mouth and even out his ears. His skin glistened with sweat and he pushed at his bed sheet clumsily, as if it was some huge, heavy, wet blanket straddling him and weighing him down.

His neck, face, hands, and arms were a dark discolouration. Earle realized the man was starving from lack of oxygen. He was choking to death. Earle recognized this. He'd seen it many, many times before, but never as a result of the flu! He was surrounded by people dying from the Spanish influenza.

An orderly came in and went from bed to bed feeling foreheads and throats. He checked the patient charts and looked at their feet. He passed from one to the next. He came to Earle's bed. He examined the chart and lifted the sheet to examine the lower extremities.

Earle croaked, "Don't touch me."

The orderly looked up. "Eh?"

Earle licked at his dry lips. "There's been a mistake. I don't belong here. I don't have the flu. How did I get here? There's been a mistake, I tell you. Who put me here?"

The orderly picked up the chart again at the foot of Earle's bed and examined it more closely. "Mr. Wilson. An ambulance brought you. There was a policeman. Said you collapsed in the street. Thought it must have been the flu. That was six days ago— May 15. We put you in here. But now when I look at you I can't see the typical symptoms. If you'd had the flu you'd have been long since dead. Guess I'd better get a doctor and see if we can't get you moved."

Earle's eyes widened. Six days! My Lord. No wonder he felt this way. He could barely move. And when he did, the muscles ached fiercely. He could feel the effects of dehydration. Six days! He'd never been out this long! He had to get out of here. He had to get back to Mary Jablinka's. They'd think he'd flown the coop. She might have rented his room out by now! Oh God! They might have gone through his room. Discovered the knife! Discovered that he'd gotten rid of Yablonski's box of things.

With a huge effort, Earle tamped down the rising panic in his stomach. With iron tenacity he forced his mind under control in order to examine things calmly. What were the alternatives? Where did he go from here? What logical avenues must he pursue?

First he had to get out of the hospital. It was a deathtrap. It could only be through God's good graces that he'd avoided the influenza while lying in this sea of contagion. And don't touch anything in here: the place must be loaded with flu germs! Find his clothes. Probably in that tiny locker between him and the man on his left. Another flu victim! Not as advanced as the first man he'd noticed, but still well on his way.

The attendant returned with another man. Both were in white smocks and wore the now familiar gauze masks. When the doctor approached, Earle visibly shrank back into his pillow so that the man actually stopped and stood still. "I'm Dr. Arnaud, Mr. Wilson. Harrison here tells me you don't look very flu-like and I have to agree. We're going to take the chance that you're benign at least and move you to a non-flu ward."

"I have to get out of here. It's not flu. I get these blackouts. Sometimes they last for days. Had them before but I always recover." Earle tried to move farther away from them into the bed. The fear he felt was overcoming the weakness from the dehydration and lack of food. "I can't stay in here with these sick people. You have to get me out. I'll be alright once I get some clean water and food. I'll..." He gave up talking. The effort was just too great.

The doctor watched him, not knowing what to think. "I'll have Harrison move you." He went back to Earle's chart for a closer look, took up a pencil attached to it, and wrote. "Things are rather difficult you see. The strike committee, in its wisdom, has deemed that the water pressure cannot rise above thirty pounds. That's only enough to serve the ground floors of all buildings in the city. No water from the second floor up. We have to haul water up by hand. Makes it very difficult to look after people. But we'll see if we can't relocate you. Odd how you didn't get this influenza. Must be some sort of immunity you have. At any rate, Harrison here knows what to do. He'll look after you. You'll have to excuse me if I sound brusque, Wilson. I have to get back to some very ill patients now."

With relief, Earle watched him leave. He turned his attention to Harrison, who began to pack things up in preparation for his move.

CHAPTER ELEVEN

Kathleen sat at her typewriter and wrote:

WESTERN LABOUR NEWS Thursday May 22, 1919

SPECIAL STRIKE EDITION # 4

ACCUSATIONS OF BOLSHEVISM UNFOUNDED. DO NOT FALL INTO THE TRAP.

Once again the Citizen's Committee of One Thousand Capitalists has tried to tie the strike to a Red Scare. Do not be taken in by this. The strike committee in no way supports revolution. It accepts that only a duly elected provincial government (democracy) will be acceptable to Manitobans. Let it be known that the strike committee condemns any sort of violent intervention on either side. Do not carry weapons of any sort. That is exactly the sort of excuse the RNWMP or the so-called "special constables" will use to make arrests.

The strike position has remained unchanged throughout. This strike is about:

1. *The necessity of recognizing organized labour by accepting their right to form unions to represent them.*
2. *The necessity of recognizing that organizations such as the Building Trades Council and the Metal Trades Council are legitimate representatives of their workers.*
3. *The necessity of reinstating all striking workers to their former positions at the end of the strike. No exceptions.*

The spirit of the strikers is unbreakable. Their hopes cannot be set aside. Their aspirations cannot be denied. Their efforts cannot fail. Labour is blazing a new trail. We have not passed this way before. Two years ago such a strike was not possible, but now all must participate if we are to succeed.

It has also come to our attention that the Citizen's Committee of One Thousand has made some outrageous claims. The following examples are drawn from their own meetings:

"Compulsory education is responsible for the present trouble. Because of this, the workers are so intelligent and as fully informed as their employers."

Yet another claim they've made is:

"We can't starve them out. We haven't been able to raise a riot, so we must find some way to create trouble so that we can get the military authorities on the job."

Perhaps their most dastardly move is that of trying to get the moving picture operators to secure and show such pictures as would inflame the public, even though they had to be secured under false titles.

Workers: We know every move they are making. Do not play their game. Keep out of their trap. Do not respond to their bear-baiting tactics. Keep quiet.

THE STRIKE IS ONE WEEK OLD TODAY

SHE IS SURE A LUSTY BABE

No sooner had Kathleen gotten the story ready to go to press than the first striker was arrested for carrying a gun. There was much controversy surrounding the event as to whether it was a set-up by the Committee of One Thousand or an infiltrator planted by communists. Either way, it made Bill Ford an unhappy editor as he perused Kathleen's column.

"No more bylines on your work, Kathleen. It's too dangerous. Better if no one knows who is doing the actual writing."

"You don't think my work will be recognizable even without the byline, Bill?"

"Probably. But there's no point in painting a big target on you. I already worry about problems without making things easier for some of the louts employed by the Committee."

Bill pretended to read Kathleen's article for several minutes. In fact, since the first special edition he'd considered her work so well done that he had little need to give it a read.

"There's something else going on but I'm not sure exactly what it is." Bill waited for her to enquire, but when she remained silent he continued. "Sam Seigalman hasn't been around since the strike started. Nobody's seen him: not at the rallies, not here. No place. So I thought I'd come around and find out if you or maybe Al Devons might know something. I know that he and Al were quite thick."

Kathleen could feel the slow glow of red creeping up her neck and moving into her cheeks. "I haven't seen either one of them for several days now. I was at the rally at Victoria Park two days ago but neither of them was there."

"Kathleen, what do you actually know about Alvin Devons? How did he come to be here? Why is he here? What do you think it is he actually does? I've asked around, but nobody seems to know much about him."

She shuffled uncomfortably. "I don't know much either. I know he's here from Minneapolis. I know that he's been checked out and seems to be legitimate. Beyond that, not a whole lot."

Ford nodded. "Okay. So look, if you should hear anything you let me know alright? I'd just like to know where he stands in all this. I want to know that he's not a spy for the Committee. You take care. Don't let anything sidetrack you." He stood up to leave and glanced at Kathleen with an odd sort of apologetic smile on his face.

"I won't. I always keep my priorities straight." After he was gone, she sat contemplating the visit. Just how suspicious was Bill about her? Had he made a connection between her and Al? And why had she lied to him by telling him that Al had been checked out? She had no idea whether anyone had done a follow-up on him or not.

***

When a group of strikers heard that the Citizen's Committee of One Thousand had demanded the raising of the water pressure to seventy-five pounds, they became enraged. In the first days of the strike, the public fire boxes on the streets were being used to turn in false alarms. This resulted in the newly formed volunteer firefighters from the Committee being roused from their beds to rush into the streets in the middle of the night.

Guards had to be placed at each of these boxes to curtail the false calls. Julius Archibald was confounded that the Committee was being forced to negotiate with the strikers to raise the water pressure to a level where it became a viable firefighting tool.

At a meeting, he pushed through a document which came to be called the Committee Creed. It was a doctrine supported by the Winnipeg City Council stating that they were:

1. *Opposed to sympathetic strikes anywhere that showed support for the general strike.*

2. *Supportive of disallowing unions for any public employees.*

After much arguing, swearing, ranting, and decrying of organized labour, Archibald was finally forced to agree to a third statement that he felt was being placed just to appease the strikers.

3. *The City Council recognizes the right of other workers to form unions.*

Julius picked up a copy of *The Western Labour News* and was infuriated by the wording. "'Every organization but one has voted overwhelmingly in favour of the general strike, and the biggest strike in the history of Winnipeg is well under way. No exceptions are anticipated in this strike. All public utilities will be tied up in order to enforce the principle of collective bargaining.' Bastards! Their mothers are all whores and their fathers are low-life scum. They need to be taught a goddamn good lesson. They need their damn heads knocked together to get some Christly sense into them. If they think that they can do whatever they want with public goddamn utilities that every citizen had a right to then they have another thought coming."

Within an hour, Julius had lined up two dozen specials with billy clubs in hand. They headed for the water building with every intention of taking it by force if necessary. Within a few blocks, they came across the group of angry strikers who were marching in protest over the publication of the Committee Creed.

Benjamin Butler—the leader of the strikers—roared at Archibald, "You men stop! The strike committee has not given any permits for you to be out here. Where are you going? Why are you here?"

Archibald did not break pace for even a moment, "The strike committee can kiss my goddamn white ass. You bastards are not taking over this city and telling citizens what they can and cannot do!" With that, he strode up to Butler and smashed him in the face with a right fist.

Pandemonium ensued. Men clubbed at each other, their frustration and resentment boiling over. A week of tension found release with stones, clubs, fists, bites, curses, kicks, and adrenaline madness.

Julius Archibald found himself hurled to the ground by three strikers and kicked unmercifully. Specials rushed in to rescue him, swinging clubs wildly in a profanity-laced diatribe and smashing indiscriminately into the wad of strikers.

Men cried out in pain. Others who had nothing to do with the two original groups rushed to join in, some as peacemakers but others gleefully throwing punches and jumping on the backs of perceived enemies. Teeth flew out of mouths, tears poured down over broken noses, huge cuts and welts rose on scalps, and blood rolled down into eyes.

A single special constable tried to make his way out of the melee with his hand clasped over his right ear—it was hanging on to the side of his head by a single thread of skin. The special howled in agony as a further gash ripped his cheek open; both his hands became occupied trying to hold a variety of his parts together.

Two specials held a striker face down on the sidewalk and repeatedly hit him on the back, the head, the shoulders, and the buttocks. A third special yelled gleefully and joined in. He ripped at the striker's shirt and pants, trying to pull down the man's breeches so the specials could lash away at his bare bottom.

Blood was flying everywhere. Bones cracked as they broke and joints made a loud popping noise when pulled out of sockets. A man screamed in agony when a knife appeared and sliced through his Achilles tendon. He toppled to the ground, grasping at his now useless foot, and was trampled by a deluge of bodies struggling to get into or out of the riot of screeching males.

Truckloads of police constables, RNWMP on foot and horse, along with a bevy of firefighters sought to restore order. They weighed into the crowd with a vengeance, striking indiscriminately at participants on both sides. Both Henry Hebert and Commissioner Stone personally intervened and led the charge to force the two sides apart. Henry received a good many scrapes and bruises himself but showed why he'd been able to rise through the ranks and come into his position. With no gun on his person but with fists flying and shouting orders for his officers, he slowly gained control over the riotous disorder.

Some just wore themselves down to exhaustion and had to stop fighting. Others sat in the street confused and dazed and looking about at the rolling bodies and tear-stained faces. When Stone and Hebert felt they finally had things satisfactorily under control, they went about arresting some, clasping others into handcuffs, and pushing still others into paddy wagons. Ambulances arrived to begin to carry off the broken and the wounded.

The strikers, easily identifiable by the handkerchiefs tied around one or other of their upper arms, were some of the first to be arrested and the last to be loaded into the ambulances.

Julius Archibald was rescued and transported to a private clinic where his personal physician was called in to attend. That afternoon at the insistence of the hospitals, the clinics, the striking firefighters, and the public health service, the Citizen's Committee of One Thousand, the Mayor's Office, and representatives of the strike committee sat down to negotiate a responsible approach to the water-pressure issue.

Other public utilities were still on hold.

***

Within a week of setting off in search of further types of pneumococci, Anna had discovered a dozen new strains beyond the already known ones. It was anybody's guess as to how many more were possible. There could be hundreds! For Anna, this new information was a critically important discovery. If there were hundreds of pneumococcus bacilli and hundreds of streptococci, then by now she should have come across at least one strain of influenza. But there was nothing! Not a single piece of evidence in any culture that she could point to and claim: "This is the influenza bacillus".

Anna picked up her notebook and entered. "It is very unlikely that the influenza bacillus was itself the cause of the pandemic; there must instead be some sort of permeating agent at work." If this was true, she either had to discover the permeating agent or at least the instrument that would stop the influenza's spread. Now for the first time she felt some glimmer of hope that her work might have a payoff. That she actually could make a difference to the raging death march of the influenza.

It was while she was constructing her thoughts on this and noting them in her diary that she noticed the uncovered petri dish. Harold was getting careless! She'd have to speak to him about this. How long had it sat there? It might have been days!

Anna picked it up and carried it to the incinerator. She placed it inside and closed the door.

There are times when the human mind becomes suspended in its multiplicity of many-faceted processes. There comes a time when a thought becomes frozen and hangs there momentarily, awaiting its birth. If pursued, the birth happens and that singular, focused, minute observation is given a placental feeding and blooms. If set aside, the thought dies and is sloughed off, to escape the imagination and drift into the infinite vastness of the human unconscious.

Anna held the thought. Her movements froze. Her mind tracked to the petri dish. The nub of her concentration focused suddenly on the contents of the dish. Was there something different about it? Something that didn't quite fit?

Anna opened the door and retrieved the sample. She took it back to her bench and placed a sample under the microscope. She turned on the light and peered in. The organisms beneath her eye were readily identifiable. She'd seen this on many occasions before. Staphylococcus. But something had arrested this staphylococcus, stifled it, and prevented its growth. Something had subdued it. It had not developed the way it should have.

She refocused and looked again. This time she concentrated not upon the staphylococcus itself but on the area surrounding it. There was something there. Anna had never seen this in a sample before but she knew what it was. Mould. There was some sort of mould growing in the sample and it was the thing that must have disallowed the production of the staphylococcus.

Anna went back to her notes and recorded her observations. Then she set out to retrieve a sample of the mould. If she could, she would isolate it, introduce it to healthy staphylococci, and see if it would work to restrict its growth. She knew that this could be a very important path in moving toward a possible answer, but she mustn't get ahead of herself. Must not let her growing excitement override her necessity for good science.

First she would have to incubate the mould, then isolate the particular agent that was acting upon the staph, and then...

It was 9:00 P.M. and suddenly Anna felt the bone-weariness that came with fourteen hours of almost nonstop work. She had to quit. Go home. Get some food and sleep so that she could return in the early morning before the strikers were out and about. Already there had been reports of fighting in the streets and people being injured. Avoiding the growing crowds seemed her best method of being able to continue her work without outside obstacles. When she stepped out onto the sidewalk, she saw Roger Wilson waiting for her in a taxi. He motioned for her to get in; a broad friendly smile accompanied his gesture.

"Good evening, Doctor. It's so nice to see you again." He stepped from the taxi as Anna approached. He held open a door for her. "I haven't had the opportunity to apologize to you for having lost you in that horrible crowd of strikers that day. I've been mortified by my actions ever since."

"Why Mr. Wilson, you needn't go through this for me. I'm very capable of making my way back and forth."

"No, Doctor." Wilson climbed in behind her and closed the door brusquely. "If you recall, I made a promise to get you to work and home safely and I'll not renege on that."

"Well thank you, Mr. Wilson. With the long days I've been putting in at work, I've barely had time to see anyone. Not Mary Jablinka or the other tenants for that matter."

"Nor I, Doctor. Sad to say I was called out of town the day after you and I separated. Business has to go on in spite of the strike. People still have to be able to go to work even if the civil service is not on the job. Ought to fire the whole lot of them, starting with the streetcar workers. After all, if the streetcars are not going to run, what's the point in having them? Makes life difficult for people like you, Doctor. Interrupts the important lab work you do."

Anna settled back to enjoy the ride home. She was too tired to focus upon the strikers. "Yes I suppose so, Mr. Wilson. Still, I'm sure the strike didn't happen over nothing. There must be grievances and issues that have prompted this. Surely there are ways to negotiate an end to this."

"Oh, no doubt, Doctor Williams. But I'm afraid that it will come down to more violence and that's why I'll be transporting you from work in the evening. Especially in the evening—a dangerous time you see."

Anna thought of something. "How long have you been waiting for me out here tonight, Mr. Wilson?"

"Not so long. Perhaps an hour. I knew that your hours have been long. I checked with Mrs. Jablinka. She said that you weren't getting home much before ten at night. You must be exhausted, Doctor." Roger's disarming smile appeared out of the darkness. For some reason, Anna felt somewhat disconcerted that Roger Wilson seemed to be paying so much attention to her schedule. He must be a busy man with many, many interests to attend to. His business enterprises must be extensive and if they called him out of Winnipeg for extended periods then he would be hard-pressed to keep the promise he believed he'd made to her.

She was about to comment upon this when something called her mind back to the first day he'd shown up at her lab. He'd been upset to the point of engaging in some sort of histrionics with the secretary. Then they'd stepped outside and he'd tried to get her through the crowd and up closer to a platform where some men were speaking.

And then, a high, whining voice had called out from the crowd, "Earle. I got to talk to ya! I bin' lookin' all over for ya!" It was something like that. Had the man been speaking to them? There was something else, but she could not remember. Something else.

"...as often as I can, Doctor Williams."

"What?" She must have drifted off. She was very sleepy.

He laughed softly. "I said I'll try to make sure I can give you a ride home at least as often as possible."

She drifted again. "Thank you, Mr. Wilson."

***

With management of the dailies pressed into service and recruitment of scabs, the headline across the top of *The Winnipeg Telegram* shouted;

FROM the SIDEWALK They Called Him a Scab and Then Hostile Aliens Trampled Him in the Streets

August 9, 1918, the Eighth Battalion took over a new trench, south of Amiens.

The unit was subjected to a terrific enfilading fire, which threatened to wipe out the entire strength.

There was no artillery support to stop the carnage against which the unit was helpless.

Five men sprang up as one. Each asked that he be allowed to go alone, to give his life in an almost hopeless effort to put the enemy guns out of action.

All five went, but only one reached his objective.

The other four died courageously in their great adventure.

BUT ONE MAN WON THROUGH. SINGLE-HANDED HE SHOT AND BAYONETTED GUN CREW AFTER GUN CREW UNTIL HIS EXCESS OF COURAGE CAUSED THE SURVIVING HUNS TO THROW UP THEIR HANDS IN SURRENDER.

THE WHOLE NEST, ESTIMATED TO CONTAIN 24 MACHINE GUNS, WAS COMPLETELY WIPED OUT AND THE MAN WHO DARED AND WON WALKED BACK TO HIS COMRADES WITH HIS PRISONERS.

For his unparalleled devotion to duty and high courage, this soldier was rightfully honored with the highest award within the gift of his country.

****

This man yesterday afternoon rode down the streets of Winnipeg, once more united with the forces of democracy and sworn to maintain law and order.

FROM THE SIDEWALKS, MOBS HOWLED "SCAB" AT HIM.

THEY TORE HIM FROM HIS HORSE
AND THREE ALIEN ENEMIES TRAMPLED
HIM IN THE STREETS.

The man was Sergeant Fred Coppins, V.C.

Today he lies suffering in Tuxedo hospital,
the victim of a cowardly assault by Austrians.

****

How long will human decency lie dormant in
the face of such occurrences? Appeals to reason
are futile where there is no reason to appeal to.

CITIZEN'S COMMITTEE OF ONE THOUSAND

The representatives in the Labour Temple sat about with copies of *The Manitoba Free Press*, *The Winnipeg Tribune*, and *The Winnipeg Telegram* spread out on the table before them. They pored over the headlines and the columns. The obvious bias came through clearly in all of the dailies. The local press had come down squarely against the strike. The attacks on the labour position were vituperative and endless.

The newspapers were aligned with the capitalists. What else could you expect? It was people like E.K. Atwater, Thomas Bulgar, Julius Archibald, and their ilk who dictated to the newspapers. They were the advertisers. They paid the bills. The advertisers were special. It would be wrong-headed, not to mention downright foolish for the newspaper to get on the wrong side of the issue. The newspaper publishers were not about to engage in economic suicide and certainly not over an issue that was so obviously stained with anti-democracy, pro-communist propaganda.

Bill Ford spoke aloud what many were thinking. "This certainly paints us as the bad guys. I'm sure there's more to this than we're reading about in this so-called story, but who knows?"

Kathleen sipped from her coffee and looked around at the men surrounding the table. "We have to respond to this. If we don't, the public will just take it for granted that this is true. They won't even pay attention to the fact that this is an ad. Fake news bought by the Citizen's Committee of One Thousand."

Sam Siegalman read, "How long will human decency lie dormant?" He shuffled the paper and snorted. "What the hell does that mean anyway? What are they trying to do? What's the point of saying that?"

John Rolufs, one of labour's more active strike leaders, was concentrating heavily upon the newspaper articles. He too, was particularly concerned about the tone and the inflammatory nature of the press release. A paid-for press release.

"Their point is very clear, Sam. It's to stir up hatred. They want to fight the strike in the press as well as in the streets and if they can paint us as a threat to heroes like Fred Coppins, then we must also be a threat to the ordinary man in the street. Right?"

"But what about this 'aliens' crap? It says three aliens pulled him from his horse." Siegalman was becoming more adamant. "How could they know it was aliens? Did the cops catch them? Did they interview them? And what the hell do they mean by 'aliens'?"

Al Devons had been quiet up to this point. Kathleen had not seen him since their last morning together after the bombing of the Labour Council Offices. She noticed he looked tired and worn. He'd not shaved for at least two days and it gave his face a scruffy, haggard look. The fingers of his right hand drummed lightly on the paper set on the desk before him.

"They don't know who it was," he said. "There was a hell of a fight in the streets. People were getting bashed from all over.

We were on our way to the city water station and we ran into the Committee's agents. The fight started and then the police showed up to stop it. They had these military types. They were there for support I guess. Anyway, the Mounted Police and these others attacked us on horseback. Lots of guys got pulled off their horses and hurt. It wasn't just this Coppins fellow. They make it sound like he was the only one."

John Rolufs raised an eyebrow. "You were there, Al?"

"I was there. Got smashed up a bit for it too. Somebody hit me on the back of the head with a club."

Kathleen felt a tightening in her stomach. She wanted to ask if he was alright. As if to answer, Al rubbed the back of his head and grinned. "Knocked me senseless for a while, but my mother always said I didn't have that much sense to begin with."

Bill Ford addressed them. "Okay, we have to try to get word out there on what really happened. Kathleen, you do a front-page column for us so we can combat this a little. Get a more accurate picture from Al here on what happened and print it as a reply to this "ad". We're going to see more of these—count on it. It's another attempt to stir the public up against us. To provoke us into violence so they can arrest us. They'd like nothing better and riots like this just give them their opening."

Al and Kathleen looked across the table at each other.

Sam Siegalman said, "Do you hear what the Committee and the press are calling you guys, John?"

Rolufs looked up with a cocked eyebrow.

"You've now officially been dubbed a loyal member of the 'Red Five'." Siegalman laughed. "That's you and Bob Russell and the others."

John Rolufs shrugged his shoulders, "We're not communists."

"I know," said Sam. "But maybe you should be." There was silence in the rest of the room.

***

Apart from a cut along his eyebrow, a split lip, and a broken-off tooth, Julius Archibald was feeling very fit indeed. Finally some action had been taken against the strike. Finally, Archibald's frustrations with the whole damn thing had found an outlet in the street fight that had dominated the conversation around the city.

And if Julius Archibald was feeling a bit bruised and blood-ied, then others such as Ben Butler were feeling a hell of a lot worse. Julius chuckled. He recalled the look of surprise on the youngster's face when Julius punched him. At least he'd gotten that satisfaction before the bastards had jumped him and the whole thing went out of control. Too bad about Coppins though. Still, it made for good press. The Committee needed more of this sort of thing. It was just the sort of fodder that was most effective against the strikers.

Having been moved to another branch, Archibald liked his new office. He sat behind a large, beautifully made mahogany desk. The leather chair suited him nicely. This office had the advantage of additional windows that looked out onto the tellers and the patrons. He could see what was going on in most of the bank most of the time. He could see who came in and who was going out the front door. He liked that.

That's how he spotted Mayor Ross and Councillor Youngman entering the bank and heading towards his office. Julius thought they might come by so he was not entirely surprised.

His secretary Penny was showing them in and in spite of the swelled lip, he got up smiling and shook hands to greet them. He motioned Ross into one chair and Youngman into another. He sat back in his leather chair and took out a cigar, wincing when it contacted his sore lip.

Ross coughed and cleared his throat. "Julius, as you know I'm not officially a member of the Committee of One

Thousand because I must be seen to be impartial in this dispute. Nevertheless, it's the Committee who's asked Councillor Youngman and me to come to see you."

Archibald looked at him with a somewhat distasteful smile. "Hell, Charles, you're no more damned impartial than I am. And neither are you, Howard. How can anybody be impartial when the whole bloody government is being threatened by this strike?"

Howard Youngman intervened. "That may or may not be true. There's no actual proof that the Reds are at the bottom of this." Youngman sat forward earnestly. He'd removed his porkpie hat and was sitting with elbows resting on his knees. His hands turned the hat round and round. He was not looking directly at Julius. "But whether or not it's true, the City Council does not approve of the street fighting. And we certainly don't think that any member of the Committee of One Thousand should be involved at a...um...personal level."

Julius did not speak for a long time. He leaned back, lit and puffed on the cigar, and looked thoughtfully at the two of them. "I have to tell you gentlemen, I really don't give a good goddamn what the City Council thinks."

"Now Mr. Archibald—" Youngman was about to say more when Ross put a restraining hand on his arm. He stopped twirling his hat and looked at Ross.

Charles Ross was tentative. "Look, Julius. We don't see how rioting in the streets helps anything. What's important here is to get the civil service back to work. We can't operate the city properly without firefighters and police. Without the streetcars, commerce stops. That doesn't help us and it sure doesn't help you. Surely you can see that."

"Oh yes, I see that. And I see a whole lot more. But mostly I see that you boys want to just sit on your asses and let things blow over. But if we do that, this damned strike could go on forever."

Youngman, his face flushed, sputtered, "That's not true Mr. Archibald. Council has been very active. We're trying to negotiate a—"

"Negotiate!" Julius snorted in derision. "Like the newspaper ad says, Youngman. How do you appeal to reason when there isn't any to appeal to?"

Charles Ross once again placed the hand of restraint upon Howard's arm. Archibald glared at them. "You two really don't understand do you? Politicians! Don't you see what's happening here? There can't be any fence-sitting in this struggle. It's either them or it's us. We're either going to have Capitalism, gentlemen, or we're going to have some kind of Russian-style Bolshevik bullshit. And when history writes a chapter on this, boys, then which side do you want to be seen on? Ours or theirs?" The two sat as if they were bad dogs being chastised by their master. "You can't negotiate because communists don't do that. Take a lesson from what's happened in Russia, gents. And don't ever forget that the bank is on your side—and you damn well should be on ours!"

Charles Ross stood up. "This will be in the evening edition of the newspapers, Julius. The city council thought you should know about it ahead of time so that it doesn't catch you or any of the others off guard." He handed a slip of paper to Julius Archibald, who looked at it suspiciously before unfolding it to read.

PROCLAMATION

By virtue of the authority invested in me I do hereby order that all persons do refrain from forming or taking part in any parades or congregating in crowds in or upon any of the streets of the City of Winnipeg, and do hereby request of all law-abiding citizens the full compliance with this proclamation.

Dated at the city of Winnipeg, this 5th day of June, A.D. 1919.

Charles Ross, Mayor.

GOD SAVE THE KING

Julius Archibald read the proclamation a second time and dropped the paper onto his desk. "Well, that's your problem right there, isn't it Charles?"

"What do you mean?" It was Howard Youngman who asked the question.

"The goddamn Reds aren't law-abiding citizens are they now, gents?" Archibald was glaring at them across the desk. "That's your first problem. But your second is that you're trying to undermine the Citizen's Committee of One Thousand. By publishing this proclamation it also means they can't organize countermarches and demonstrations. Isn't that right?"

Youngman twirled his porkpie hat again. "I suppose not."

Archibald puffed on the cigar and grinned. "No but you thought of it didn't you, Charles? You knew that this covered our side as well, didn't you? You knew that you were undercutting the Committee. Right? And taking their power away, right?"

Ross shuffled his feet uncomfortably. "Yes."

"Nice little move but it's not going to work, Charles. You might put things off for a little bit, but that's all this will do. These Reds won't stop meeting and parading, proclamation or no goddamn proclamation. They're in this for the long haul. And so are we, whether we like it or not. So you might as well go back to Council and tell them that. Tell them that Julius Archibald will abide by the law, as always. But also you can tell them that we won't put up with any bullshit from the Red Five. If they organize and march, then we'll have to respond, won't we? It's your civic duty to maintain law and order. It's the city council's duty. But the RNWMP and the soldiers have a duty too, you see. And it's to kick the asses of any goddamn Red sons of bitches that are out on the streets trying to overthrow the duly elected government. And you can count on one thing for sure—they will!"

Charles Ross and Howard Youngman looked at each other. Youngman wanted to say more but the mayor shook his head to silence him. Obviously the meeting was over. Hats in hand, they left the office.

***

After the others had left the meeting, Al and Kathleen sat quietly. Neither spoke as the awkward silence between them built an ever-expanding, rising wall. Three weeks already since the strike had begun and not a single word spoken between them. Where had he been? What had he been doing?

"You look tired, Al. You look like you aren't sleeping."

Al sat silently, waiting.

"Can you talk about what you've been doing?"

He looked. Sat. Waited.

She grew visibly impatient. "I guess this is going to be a very one-sided conversation." When he still said nothing she prompted, "Perhaps we should just talk about the riot then."

"I've been thinking a lot about the last time we were together." He said it softly, hesitating to broach the topic.

"What about it?" She didn't mean to sound flippant, but that's the way it came across. More softly, "That was three weeks ago and I haven't seen you since. Nor have any of the others. I checked."

"I wasn't sure if you'd want to see me. You seemed pretty definite about things that last morning."

"It's easy to see that we have different ways of going about things. The strike committee is committed to non-violence. That won't change no matter what. And they'll do everything they can to disassociate themselves from Communism."

Devons took the time to light a cigarette and to think. He offered one to Kathleen, who refused. He looked up at her and again was taken by those incredible, soft, almond eyes, the high cheekbones, and that remarkable spread of auburn hair. He felt the tug in his loins. She really was a very beautiful woman. He forced himself back to the subject at hand.

"Kathleen, a strike doesn't just happen by itself. And it doesn't just carry itself along on some sort of rising tide. It has to be maintained. It starts off with everyone excited and on board. In the first days, the picketing is loud and noisy. Demonstrations make the strikers feel good. They're confident and powerful; they feel like they can overcome anything. They can win! They can force the enemy into submission.

But it doesn't stay that way. After awhile, it lags. People start to lose interest. Scabs start to do the work. Managers do the floor work and production moves along slowly. After a few weeks, some picketers start to feel the pinch. No incomes, very small amounts—if any—of strike pay. Wives at home. Kids to feed and clothe. Reality starts to batter them in the face. A few sneak across the picket line and go back to work. Some just give up and go away, looking for other work.

Strikers need something to hang on to. They need to see that something is happening. They need to know that their efforts are paying off. If they don't have some hope, the picket line gets very lonely. It takes all they have to get out day after day and continue. My job is to give them that hope. To keep them going. To make sure they know that something is happening."

He stopped. Kathleen said nothing. He ground out the cigarette and sat back. "I don't know if you can understand that, but I hope you can."

"That's why you were at the riot. It was one of those 'things' that was supposed to happen so the strikers could feel progress."

Al grinned. "Actually, the riot was just a lucky break. We didn't start out with the intention to look for a fight. We were going to take over the city water station so we could control the supply. We just happened to meet up with Julius Archibald's bullyboys."

"So a riot is supposed to keep the strike alive? Is that it?"

"I've been in lots of these. I know how they work. If the interest isn't kept up then the whole thing just starts to kind of fizzle away. The boys lose heart. The glue comes unstuck and soon people start turning on each other."

Kathleen shook her head. She was totally nonplussed by this. What had happened to the reasons for the strike? What had happened to the issues? What had happened to fair living wage ideas and job safety and the right to collective bargaining?

She enquired, "So what should we expect next? More bombings? More riots? How about out and out murder?" She found her voice rising and realized that she was having to blink back tears. "I have an idea. Why don't we burn down the homes of the Committee of One Thousand? Or maybe kill off the strike leaders? I'm sure that would get everyone's attention. That should keep them all interested."

Al stood up. "I guess I'd better go. I can see that there's not a lot of point in talking about this."

"Yes. I guess you should."

Al headed for the door but turned back to her. "If you can see your way to it, I'd appreciate your not talking to anyone about us. I mean about the things we've been discussing." He walked out.

Kathleen sat, somewhat bewildered. Was he serious? What did he want her to keep quiet about? That he was a communist? That he planted bombs? That he was engaging actively against the objectives of the strike leaders? That he'd been her lover?

On the verge of tears, she placed her face into her hands and rested it there momentarily. She should go to Bill Ford about this. Why didn't she? What held her back? She didn't owe Al Devons anything. No loyalty. No obligation. They weren't in any kind of serious relationship or anything like that. All she had to do was get up and walk down the hall to Bill's door and tell him, "Hey, there's something you should know." She sat at her desk thinking for a long time.

A thought flitted across her mind then nestled there like some tiny bird settling into its downy nest. A line of furrows crossed her forehead, and her head tilted to one side a bit. The rich, full lips pursed and pouted. The brown, almond eyes flickered a moment.

She was two weeks late with her period. She was never late. Oh good Lord! What if it was true? No! She couldn't think about it. The enormity of this possibility caused her brows to furrow. She started to perspire. Christ. One disaster at a time, please.

CHAPTER TWELVE

On June 10, Mary Jablinka busied herself in her kitchen. The soreness of her arthritis was coming back into her hands and so the work went slowly. Soon the tenants would be descending for breakfast. Most were eating here now. Since the strike, any number of eateries had been forced to close their doors.

Even Alvin Devons might be down for a meal. Mary had seen little of him since the strike began. He'd been home late to sleep a few times she knew, and up again and gone very early in the morning. If he'd gotten a job, she thought, he certainly worked long hours.

In fact, the first to emerge from the night was Anna. Mary became alarmed when she looked at her. Her eyes were ringed darkly and she had lines across her forehead that looked like a permanent scowl.

Mary said, "Good heavens, Doctor. I'm sorry to say but you look a sight. You really are working much too hard. If this continues, you're going to get sick if you aren't already."

Usually Anna tried to avoid conversations about her personal or professional self, but this morning as she drank her coffee, her attempted smile at her landlady faltered. "Yes, it's true. I grow quite weary, Mrs. Jablinka. The research takes so long and the flu moves so quickly."

Mary served up some scrambled eggs and toast. She set salt and pepper shakers on the table. "And you know, there's scarcely a word in the papers about it. Just a few short pieces on the death toll rising and pieces of advice about reducing the risks."

Al Devons and Ike Stavros came in together. Ike carried a reduced version of a daily newspaper under his arm. In his attempt to improve his English he'd taken to struggling with the daily news. He and Al Devons sat side by side at the kitchen table. While Al and Anna talked, Ike opened up the paper over his coffee and set to struggling with the language. He liked the parts with pictures best because it made it that much easier to put this frustrating, cumbersome language into a context.

Al spoke to Anna. "I hope you're able to get back and forth to work more easily now, Doctor."

"Thank you. Yes, in the morning I've been leaving earlier, but thanks now to the mayor's proclamation it's been easier. Not quite such a crowd in the streets."

"And how about the evenings?" Al asked. "I ask because I see that the streetcars are still not running."

"That's a nuisance alright. But I must say, Mr. Wilson is being very kind. Most evenings he fetches me in a taxi and I'm very grateful. I'm so tired that by late evening I don't think I could possibly walk."

Al said, "Wilson?"

At that moment, the man himself appeared and Mary Jablinka glowed as she bustled about to get him coffee and prepare breakfast for them all.

Obviously Wilson had heard Al because as he sat he stated, "Yes, Mr. Devons, can I help you? I believe I heard my name just as I was coming in."

Al stared at him, saying nothing.

Anna said, "I was just telling Mr. Devons about your kindness in picking me up from work in the evening, Mr. Wilson."

"Not at all. Not at all, Doctor. Glad to be of service. Can't have our female lodger out so late alone in the evening. Wouldn't you agree, Mr. Devons? Not safe out in the evenings nowadays, notwithstanding the mayor's proclamation, eh? The streets are still dangerous. No telling whom one might encounter."

Mary set the plates down in front of the men. Her hands were obviously sore again as she had to make individual trips to the stove and retrieve each plate with both hands. She placed more toast in the centre of the table and with considerable effort hoisted the coffee pot and managed to set it on a wooden heat protector in front of Anna.

"Ju see, Meez Ya-blink-a," Ike Stavros said. He clipped off each syllable of Mary's name, trying to get the English version correct.

Mary asked, "What's that, Mr. Stavros?"

Ike pointed at the newspaper with his left index finger. "You see ad. Trucks. Strike. Very bad beezness. Not take care, Meez Ya-blink-a. Buy truck." Ike pointed his left thumb toward his own chest. "Start beezness. Gut verk."

Mary glanced at the ad. "Oh yes, I'm sure you're right, Mr. Stavros. You buy a truck. Start your own business after the strike is finished. You could do well."

Al turned to Ike Stavros. "May I see your newspaper?" He frowned. "What's that ad say, Ike? Can I look?" He held out his hand.

Ike Stavros looked at the outstretched hand, then comprehension lit up his face. "Eh? Jess. Of courz, Meester Devon. Ju look!" Ike handed the newspaper across and pointed out the ad.

GRACE MOTORS LIMITED

STERLING MOTOR TRUCKS CANADIAN
DISTRIBUTORS OF FULTON MOTOR
TRUCKS ATLAS DELIVERY CARS

ARE YOU ORGANIZED TO MEET THE
RUSH OF AFTER-STRIKE BUSINESS?

Enormous stocks of goods must be transported quickly at the conclusion of the strike—retailers throughout the city must have their exhausted stock replenished to meet the consumer demand.

Will the retailer wait till you have the time to deliver his order, or will he order where he knows he can get prompt delivery? Will he allow his customers to go elsewhere for their goods, or will he go elsewhere?

Be Ready for Any Rush Work With a

F u l t o n T r u c k

STANDARD FULTON TRUCK— Stake Side Lorry Body. Their large capacity enables them to carry bigger loads, their speed means quick transportation, and their low cost of operation means bigger profits. Every dollar you pay for a Fulton Truck is represented in actual motorcar value, which will give you better service, lower haulage costs, and bigger cash returns for business.

Al read the entire ad. The blood rushed to his face, making it red. The pulse at his temple throbbed as he clenched his jaws.

He said through his teeth, "Jesus Christ, I can't believe they're doing this."

Mary said, "What?"

Roger Wilson cleared his throat. "Whatever it is, Mr. Devons, I suspect it hardly merits taking the Lord's name in vain at Mrs. Jablinka's table."

Anna sat still, looking at the obvious growing anger in Al Devons.

He peered at the ad again. His lip curled and he snarled, "Goddamn. D'you see what they're doing here? Sons of bitches."

Ike Stavros looked at Al with uncomprehending eyes. "Vaht? Vaht you say, meester? Vaht you tink?"

"They're just blatantly taking advantage of the strike. They're looking at it as a business opportunity for Chrissake! They think it's perfectly alright to use the strike to sell their goddamn trucks."

Roger Wilson spoke up, "I don't see how that matters. There's nothing special or sacred about the strike or the strikers, man. If you ask me, I don't see anything wrong with them making a buck or two out of it if they can."

Al sizzled. He could feel the prickles running down the back of his neck. Sweat beads suddenly broke out along his hairline. His hands formed clenched fists as he stared at Roger.

"What?" Al was incredulous. "What did you say?"

Wilson chewed on his eggs, bit off a small portion of his toast, and munched. "I said I don't see what the big concern is. I—" Too late he finally looked up and got a reading on Devons's body language. He stopped with his coffee in midair. He put it back down.

Al stood up, glaring at the man; his attention focused on the prim little talking mouth. He saw the slight yellow of egg at the corner of the man's lips. He stared at the escaping egg, saw it drop down slightly toward the chin. Al could see nothing else—all of his anger was directed at that tiny egg spot. Everything else was a flare of black and red.

When Al grabbed Roger Wilson by the throat, the toast was still in the back of Roger's mouth. When he lifted him out of the chair, Roger's breath sucked back and the toast lodged there. Al backed the man up to the wall; with his other hand closing on Roger's neck, he lifted him so that Wilson's tiptoes were barely touching the floor.

Wilson's voice was raspy as he attempted to speak. He spluttered and egg and toast crumbs emerged from his mouth, running down his chin and onto Al's hands. Al could not hear the shouts of the women as they yelled frantically for Al to let go. He could not feel the blows on his arms and shoulders as Mary Jablinka's hands landed. The butterfly dusting of her beating fingers screamed with agony as they bounced off him ineffectually.

Ike Stavros was shouting something in his ear but the rushing noise in his head prevented him from hearing the words. Roger Wilson's face turned a deep, deep red then started to move towards a darker hue. It was turning towards purple and would soon be black.

It struck Anna how he began to look like the dying flu victims she'd seen in the hospital. Ike Stavros was prying at Al's hands. He tried to pull the fingers back to get them off Wilson's throat. Roger made a soft, gurgling sound and his body began to go limp. His toes switched about slightly like a cat's tail as they sought some purchase on the floor.

Ike managed to tear one hand away and at the same time he threw his body against Al's side so that the whole group shifted, stumbled, and fell to the floor. Mary Jablinka screeched with all the air her lungs could pump. Al could suddenly hear her and he let his other hand go. He struggled to his feet. The two women swarmed over the limp form of Wilson. Anna moved quickly to clear his airway while Ike Stavros moved in and pounded on the man's back, trying to restart his breathing.

All three worked on him in a frenzy. Al backed out of the room. He grabbed his hat and coat as he shot out the front door of 614 Home Street. He didn't close the door, didn't look back, didn't slow down. He was putting on his hat and coat as he hustled away.

***

Airman Henry Gustafson returned home to Gimli a hero of the war. He was twenty-years old and his plan was to go back to fishing Lake Winnipeg with his father and his grandfather.

In France, Henry had shot down ten enemy planes and was unconfirmed in the destruction of three others. He'd survived the crashing of his own plane into a farmer's field in the early fall of 1918. Badly burned, Henry was removed to a field hospital, where he spent the last months of the war. After the armistice, he was further transferred to a special unit of a hospital in England. By early April of 1919, the doctors felt him well enough to ship home. When Henry boarded the ship, the man bunking next to him, one Seamus Reilly, was fast developing a head cold. His sniffling and sneezing kept Henry awake most of that first night. Henry hoped that he would not catch the cold.

He didn't. But when he arrived in Halifax, he was carrying the Spanish lady virus. It travelled with him from Halifax to Montreal to Toronto to Kenora to Winnipeg. Along with his luggage, he packed it aboard the train to Gimli and took it home with him.

He received a proper hero's welcome. Hundreds turned out at the station to cheer him. He rode through town in a special vehicle decked out for the occasion. A band played and a huge banner welcomed home a native son. Speeches were heard from the Member of Parliament, a representative from the Premier's office, and Gimli Mayor Barclay Sprague.

Particularly memorable for Henry were the numerous extended family members that had shown up for the welcome. A special luncheon was held in the town hall, where there were many hugs and handshakes. His special aunt Mildred Parkes and her children—Stephanie, aged twelve; and Simon, aged eight— were also on hand. The last time he'd seen them, Stephanie was a preschooler and Simon only a baby.

Henry looked upon Mildred as a best friend more than an aunt. His own childhood memories were filled with days of his summer school holidays and visits with Millie. It was Millie who'd taken him to the beach, bought him ice cream, taught him to waltz, and babysat him for the long Gimli evenings when his father was on the lake and his mother at her job in the hospital.

It was Millie who read great stories to him, created fantastic picnic feasts for the two, and told him lies about how strong he was, how smart he was becoming, and what a handsome man he'd soon be.

Henry was and always had been in love with his Aunt Millie.

When at age eighteen Millie had met and married Stanley Parkes, Henry was angry, jealous, and mortified. He'd attended the wedding only at his mother's behest and his father's orders. He was glad he'd been made to go, but not for the reason others thought.

Millie was a radiant angel. Her white dress was stunning. The lace collar that came up over her shoulders and joined at her throat made her long, elegant neck an artwork of curving beauty. Her cheeks were flushed pink; her eyes virtually sparkled with health and life. She was, as far as the young Henry was concerned, by far the most gorgeous creature in the universe.

On the other hand, he neither spoke to Dr. Stanley Parkes nor acknowledged that he was even a part of the wedding ceremony.

Returning from the war with his burn scars, Henry's psyche was greatly damaged, his emotional stability questionable, but his love for his aunt was intact. Henry painfully acknowledged the crowds of people and patiently waded through the photos, the grasping handshakes, and the kisses on the cheeks of the various ladies of the community.

By nightfall when he finally returned to his old room in his father's house, exhaustion was beginning to set in. He poured himself a drink and sat on the edge of the bed. Funny how the room had looked so much bigger in his child mind. It was barely eight by twelve. There was enough room for his single bed, for a small desk, a chair, and his chest of drawers. It was almost exactly the same as the day he'd left. His mother really hadn't changed things much. The family photo still hung on the wall above the desk, and a painting of the Gimli harbor was over the bedstead. He got up, walked to the desk, and pulled open the drawer. He moved aside a few old school books and a primary speller, then took out an old green scribbler. He opened it.

It was still there. The thing he valued most. The photo of him and Millie at the beach. Her standing with her left arm crossed over herself and resting on Henry's left shoulder. Her right arm was behind him and her hand gripped the upper part of his right arm. Henry loved this photo: treasured it.

There were many days overseas when it was this very photo that was front and centre in his mind. Millie's shoulder-length hair somewhat askew in the wind, her eyes peering directly into the camera. The smile on her lips embracing the warm, summer day. People sitting on blankets in the background, children building sand castles.

The knock on the door woke him from his reverie. He placed the photo back into the notebook, set it carefully into the desk drawer, and closed it. When he went to the door and opened it, Millie was standing there, still in the dress she'd worn to the afternoon celebrations.

"I wasn't sure if you'd be asleep yet so I thought I'd take the chance. May I come in?"

"Of course." Henry opened the door wider and stepped back.

Mildred looked about. "Wow, it really hasn't changed at all, has it? Your mom just kind of left things the way they were."

Henry went back and took up his spot on the bed. He picked up his drink. "Would you like some whiskey, Millie? Or are you still a tea-totaler?"

"No thank you. Can't stand the stuff actually." She sat beside him, "What did you think of the big celebration? Imagine. My little Henry a war hero. I think Stephanie's fallen totally in love with you. And Simon can't get the hero worship out of his eyes."

"And what about you, Millie? What do you think?"

She looked at him intently. "Oh, I know you better than your own parents, Henry. I worried all the time you were gone. Everyone thinks you didn't have any fear, but I know that's not true. I'm sure you managed the fighting alright. You'd have been fearful, but you managed it. You always could. It was the burns. When I heard about that, I talked with Stanley. He said you'd have been better off with bullet wounds than burns. He said your chances of living would have been better. I didn't say that to your mom and dad. I didn't write my fears to them. But maybe they knew it anyway."

Henry said nothing. He looked at her. He leaned in as if to kiss her.

She put up her hand and pressed her fingertips to his mouth. "No, you mustn't do that. I'm your aunt, remember. And I'm married. But I do love you. I always will. You'll always be my special Henry. You know that." She pressed her fingertips harder to his lips, then brushed them back and forth across his mouth.

"And now, you need to get some sleep. Tomorrow's a big day—people will want to see you. Be patient and try not to get upset with them. In a week or two, all of this will settle and you'll be able to get on with your life. No doubt you'll meet some nice young lady, just the way you should. You'll fall in love, make babies. That's just the way it's supposed to be." She got up and moved towards the door.

Henry was no longer looking at Mildred. She watched for awhile as the tears welled in his eyes and ran down his cheeks. She brushed them away with her fingertips and finally took a handkerchief from her pocket and dabbed at them. She wiped at his nostrils and at the corners of his mouth. She took his face in her hands and kissed at the tears that rolled down.

She left him and returned to the room she shared with her children. When she was in her nightgown, she went over to their beds and bent over to kiss each goodnight. She watched them for awhile while they slept, breathing evenly. She lightly traced the outline of their eyes, their nostrils, their lips with her fingers. Gently, lovingly, caressing as if she might memorize the very feel of them by doing this.

Her love for them was overpowering. Very nearly all-consuming. Tears welled in her own eyes and she retrieved the handkerchief with which she'd wiped away Henry's tears. She dabbed at her tears. They caused her to sniff and she wiped her nose. She wiped her hands clean with the cloth and climbed into bed.

The small bedside lamp burned innocuously on the table beside her head. She gathered up the book she had been reading and opened it at the bookmark. How many pages to go before she'd be finished this chapter? The pages were stuck together. She licked her fingertips quickly to help her to force the pages apart.

***

E.K. Atwater sat in the plush board-meeting room where he invested so much of his life. He reread the June 16, 1919 copy of *The Winnipeg Telegram.*

THE GREAT CONSPIRACY MUST BE CRUSHED

The man, woman, or newspaper that appeals for "sweet reasonableness" at the present moment and asks us in a mushy spirit to consent to conferences between the Bolsheviks and the citizens who uphold the constitution is not merely a nuisance but a menace.

There can be no such thing as a rightful conference, no such thing as a rightful negotiation, no such thing as a rightful bargain made between Right and Wrong. Wrong must be stamped out absolutely, and forced to admit its impotency before Right can show those who uphold Wrong any consideration whatever.

The present struggle is not between class and class, not between capital and labour, not between employer and employee. It is a direct contest to a finish between Right and Wrong. Right simply cannot compromise and Wrong must be made to submit.

It is nothing short of an outrageous lie, when the coterie of traitors in the Trades and Labour Hall shout through their official organ that this is a fight for the recognition of the right of collective bargaining and for a fair living wage. It is nothing of the kind. It is a deliberate, criminal, and fantastic attempt to make a revolution—an attempt organized by foreigners and British renegades who are a disgrace to their race.

When this small ring of traitors thought for a moment that they were winning in their criminal conspiracy, in an unguarded moment and flushed with seeming success into a candor unnatural to them, they openly revealed their real intentions: to establish Bolshevism in Winnipeg first and throughout Canada eventually.

The spirit of anarchy is not only foreign to the people of this nation, it is both hateful and loathsome to them. They would as soon breed rattlesnakes in their own beds as permit this accursed thing to make its home in this fair land—a thing without morals, without religion, without order, without justice, without honour, without decency, and without brains.

E.K. stopped reading. "Jesus, Julius. Did they let you write this? Sounds like these strike leaders are marching lockstep into hell together."

"I'll take that as a compliment, E.K. But no, unfortunately I didn't write it. However, I must say it's a good example of what one reads when there's fair and objective reporting at work."

"Rattlesnakes! Good God. That's just a bit hyperbolic I'd say." Charles Ross lifted his water glass to drink. The strike was wearing on him. In the month since it started, he'd lost weight. He looked tired and stressed and felt more and more hopeless about a resolution.

Thomas Bulgar watched him in sympathy. "Charles, you have to get the public utilities up and running. The managers and non-strikers are doing their best, but there aren't enough of them. If we try to use replacements it gets really ugly. You saw what happened to Fred Coppins...and there have been more since then."

Youngman, his porkpie hat firmly ensconced in his hands, shook his head. "It's not as easy as that. This newspaper article doesn't help. It just pushes things further apart. Rhetoric doesn't solve our problems. If anything, it just puts more obstacles in the way. Now I have—that is—we, the mayor and council, have worked out a strategy. We intend to go see the labour leaders. Right there in the Labour Temple."

E.K. Atwater frowned slightly. "You mean kind of like facing down the bear in its own den type of thing?"

Charles Ross spoke up. "We think it's better to talk to them than to antagonize them with newspaper articles like this." He gestured toward *The Telegram* in front of him.

Julius snorted and gazed about. "Nothing wrong with the article, Charles. It says exactly what needs to be said. If you ask me, it was a little easygoing." He smiled and tapped the newspaper with an index finger.

Atwater brought them back to the point of the meeting. "Look, none of us thought the strike would go this long. At best we figured a week or two, but some of us are really starting to suffer. The workers who aren't on strike are out with the flu. It's getting so that we can't tell which is the bigger problem. We can't make the flu go away, so that means the strike has to end."

Bulgar jumped in. "E.K.'s exactly right. Nothing's moving. There's almost no action at the C.P. yards and the meat industry is close to a complete shutdown. We figure if the civil service can be made to go back then others will follow. The way to break the strike is one union at a time. Another will follow. Then another."

"They're obviously much better organized than any of us had thought," replied Youngman. "They've been able to maintain discipline and order on the picket line to a greater degree than we figured. They've been provoked to fight a few times, but then they always seem to pull back before the specials can step in."

"D'you all hear about the egg man?" offered the young blond man at the end of the table. The Committee's spy reached into his pocket and pulled a slip of folded paper out. He unfolded it gently.

Atwater said, "The what?"

The young man smiled gently. "Apparently there's this egg farmer just outside the city. Guy named Foster. He delivers thousands of eggs every day to the city cooler. He can't leave them out because they rot. These eggs are for the restaurants and the stores. Anyway, the other day Foster shows up at the cooler with a truckload of eggs. There's strikers at the ice locker. They tell him he can't unload. He has to get permission from the strike committee, so he asks 'Where are they?'

They tell him he has to go all the way down to the Labour Temple and see somebody down there. It takes him an hour to get down there, but when he goes in the person he has to see isn't there, so he has to wait three hours for the guy to show up. All so he can get this little slip of paper."

He dropped the paper onto the table in front of him.

Youngman reached out and plucked it away. He read aloud, "This entitles T.J. Foster to deposit into cold storage, thirty-five cases of fresh eggs." Youngman looked at a seal still attached to the opened letter. "There's a seal on this marked 'Winnipeg Trades and Labour Council' and initials underneath G.G.S."

Archibald sneered. "Jesus Christ. Aren't they just like a regular government agency now? Seals and everything. Goddamn note like that has no authority. Doesn't mean a thing. Seal or no damn seal."

Atwater agreed. "Of course not, but it does point to what we said. Their organization is better than we thought. The strike committee is being listened to and attention is being paid. And we can't let it go on like this."

E.K. eyed the young blond man for some time. Could he be trusted? Was his so-called inside info reliable? They were paying him a lot of money, but what were they really getting for it? Notes and such from the strike committee: nothing that was really very substantial. "Do you have anything else for us?"

"I do," the young man replied easily, "but first I'd like to hear from the mayor. I'm wondering what your plan is for this meeting? Sounds to me like you're planning appeasement. Is that what it's about?"

"Not at all!" Charles leaned forward, alarmed at the suggestion. "No! Nothing like that. I'm going to talk to them. Address them more like it. We have to be adamant about demonstrations. None will be allowed. Demonstrators will be picked up—no exceptions."

The young man raised eyebrows at them. "And how will you do that? I mean, the police have walked out with them. Who's going to do the arresting?"

Youngman intervened. "We have a plan for that. The police force will be dismissed—all of them who refuse to come back to work. We'll hire special police replacements and together with the RNWMP they'll keep order."

Ross added, "And we'll pass an order-in-council. It's already been framed. It'll take a little time though. The attorney general has to bring it forward. It has to be voted on and passed. But it'll take care of sedition and agitators. It'll hurt them where they live. Russell and Ford and Rolufs, people like that. We'll be able to arrest them when the order-in-council passes."

"I don't know," Archibald said. "Seems to me this is taking way too long. Shoulda' had things like this in place a long time ago. We've been going way too easy on the strikers, Charles. I told you before that your damn proclamation could tie our hands and now this. If you'd let the Committee of One Thousand handle things, all this can be settled damn fast. End of strike tomorrow. Guaranteed!"

As much as Atwater was inclined to disagree with Julius most times, his patience with the strikers was beginning to run short. They were losing thousands of dollars every day with no apparent end in sight. Something had to give. They just couldn't let this go on.

He turned to the young man. "What happened to Foster's eggs?"

The young man grinned. "When he went back to the cold-storage locker, the boys had turned them into an omelette."

Archibald said, "Bastards!"

Atwater looked at the blond youngster, weighing things in his mind. Finally he nodded, as if making a decision. "Alright, it's time you stepped up your activities a little. Tonight you'll meet with me and Archibald and Bulgar here. We'll have a new set of instructions for you."

Ross looked confused. "What do you mean? What are you talking about, E.K.?" He shifted in his seat and glanced around the table.

Atwater said, "Doesn't matter, Charles. It doesn't concern you or the council. You're going to have to swear in a new police force. We can't leave the streets to the strikers. You go on with your meeting with the strikers. The Committee of One Thousand will prepare its own agenda to end the strike. We're fast coming to a critical point in this thing. You all need to know though that troops are arriving in the city tonight at Union Station. The 49th Battalion will be at the CNR tonight at 8:00 P.M. There are troops from two other battalions on the way as well. The Empress of Britain will arrive in another day or so. It'll bring in men from the 50th Battalion. This won't go on much longer."

***

Earle had a time of it convincing them not to call in the police. Now a week after Al Devons's attack, his voice was not much more than a hoarse croak, but at least he could make himself understood. It was bad enough that the women had sent Ike Stavros for a doctor, who'd come right away and assured them that Mr. Wilson would survive the attack.

When they'd wanted to call in the police, he'd had to wave his hands frantically. He couldn't speak. The choking had injured the vocal chords and when he tried to talk, a wheezing, whining sound emerged and he had to stop. A pencil and paper were retrieved and he wrote: *No police. No good. Police on strike. None available.*

Anna read the note. "Of course. The police wouldn't be able to help, they're on strike. The new police aren't trained officers. They're just regular citizens. They don't have any training." She looked at Mary Jablinka and then to Roger Wilson. "Still, this man almost killed you. Something like this can't just be left."

Wilson motioned to her to get the pencil and paper back and wrote: *After strike. When police return. We'll report.* He knew full well that by the time the strike was over he'd be gone.

And so Anna Williams had gone back to the lab and Roger Wilson became the victim of Mary Jablinka. For the first days after the attack he'd been too sore to get out of bed. If he tried to shift his head, the stiffness caused his neck and head to throb. He lay on his back in bed while Mary's ministrations were inflicted upon him.

She fed him soup, put hot and cold towels on his injuries, rubbed his shoulders and neck gently with ointment, and continually forced down his throat an assortment of tea, water, coffee, raw milk, juice, and a horrible concoction called wild strawberry.

Roger Wilson came to despise Mary Jablinka. He never saw Anna Williams in these early recuperative days. Each time there was a knock on the door he hoped it was Anna, but then Mary Jablinka's chubby face would peek through the doorway, followed by some repast designed to improve his strength.

He wrote notes to explain that he wasn't sick. Wasn't an invalid. That he didn't need all this. That as soon as the soreness let up, he could be up and around. All to no avail. The food, drinks, and medicine continued to assault him.

By the fourth day he could speak in a soft whisper and insisted on getting out of bed. Mary was downcast. She'd done her job too well and now the patient was way ahead of his recovery schedule.

He had to go out, he said. His business interests were being neglected. The strike was causing intolerable delays. Already he'd lost many thousands of dollars by being bedridden and if he didn't get back to work, who knew what terrible consequences would result.

But even as he was going out the door, Mary was pressing a bottle of elixir into his hand, insisting that he take a spoonful every four-six hours. It was only later that day that he rediscovered it in his pocket and discarded it.

When he finally gained the sidewalk and headed toward the downtown, it gave him time to think. Earle was not going in search of Al Devons. The man meant nothing to him. Besides, he'd not returned to the house and probably never would. No, it wasn't Al Devons that concerned Earle. He needed to return to tent city—that's where the real danger lay.

But he couldn't go looking like this. He'd stand out too much. Dressed in these clothes he'd be remembered. *Oh yeah, officer. I remember a guy bein' here. Well dressed. Looked like he had some dough. Was lookin' fer Hawkshaw he was.*

Or worse yet, some of the scum would jump him because they'd figure he had money. Couldn't trust any of 'em. Vipers and adders. Rejected by society and deserted by God. Living in filth and excrement. And the immigrants were the worst. Lazy pigs who wanted nothing more than to ride on others' hard work.

Earle knew that God would smite them. Would not permit such excretion to live. There must be a cleansing, hopefully starting with Hawkins.

When he finally made it to the downtown, Earle proceeded to Union Station and from the storage shed he recovered his package of clothing. He disappeared into the lower bathroom and emerged fifteen minutes later looking very different. He trudged back into the street toward the fork of the Red and Assiniboine Rivers.

Just before his destination, he stopped short. Tent city was gone! Or at least only the remnants of it remained. Ninety percent of it had burned. Ashes from shacks lay about. Only a very few remaining tents huddled like lost souls on the landscape. A few people were scattered about, but mostly it was deserted. Garbage, broken chairs, benches, and an assortment of bottles and cans were strewn about. Acres and acres of trash. It was like some vengeful force had descended upon it. The tramp city was an apocalyptic painting of destruction.

Earle made his way towards one of the few remaining tents. Two men sat in front of it and eyed him suspiciously. A small fire burned before them. Two open cans of beans nestled up against the fire's heat and bubbled gently.

One of the tramps said, "Ain't got 'nuff fer ya, mister. Wished we had, but we got another inside what needs it more."

Earle shrugged. "Not hungry. What happened here?"

The tramps looked at each other. "You ain't bin round here I guess. Well, first it was the flu. Caught hold here a little while ago. Guys started kinda jus' droppin' in their tracks pretty much. At first we took 'em to hospitals, but then the hospitals said no, can't take no more. We started pilin' 'em up by the river. Had 'em stacked up like cordwood. Course almost right away they started to rot. We tried buryin'em at first. But then this lady from the health department comes along with some police an' says we can't do that. So then we was gonna dump'em in the river, but she says we can't do that either, so all we could do was stack'em up."

The other tramp took two freshly cut red willow sticks and fetched the cans from the fire. He set one in front of himself and one in front of his partner. He retrieved a spoon from under his belt and scooped some beans from his can. He blew on them to cool them before he popped them into his mouth.

"Couple nights after she was here the soldiers come. They pretty much cleaned the rest out. We was a health hazard they said, but I think they was a health hazard to us. They had clubs an' broke some heads. Set fire to the tents an' buildings. Rounded up lots of the guys that were left. Never saw them again. Not the guys an' not the soldiers. Most of the place got burned out. What you see is what's left of us an' that ain't much. Don' know what we'll do. Probably leave I guess in case the soldiers come back."

Earle gazed around again at the destruction and then focused on the tramps. In his husky, rattling voice he asked, "Who's the guy you got inside?"

"Ain't a guy," said the tramp who'd retrieved the beans. "Ol' lady. She was hurt by the soldiers. We found her after they was gone. Broke her arm with a club. She ain't doin' too good."

"You guys know Hawkshaw?"

"Oh sure, everybody knows Hawkshaw. Ain't seen'em though. Lots of people gone."

Earle persisted. "You think he's dead?"

The first tramp shrugged. "Could be. No way of knowin'. Health department come in with a couple big trucks an' horse carts. They took all the bodies away. The flu bodies an' the ones from the raid. Hawkshaw could've been one of 'em. We ain't seen'em." He picked up his beans, which had cooled a little, and dug into them. Neither looked at Earle again. They focused solely on the task of eating.

Earle rose and made his way back through the shambles of tent city. Maybe Hawkshaw was dead. Probably he was, but Earle had grown into a wary and careful man. Even more careful since the attack at the hands of Alvin Devons.

When he'd picked his way to the edge of what was left of tent city and emerged onto the grassy fringe, he looked back. Before him was a wasteland. A smouldering ruins like some ancient Biblical city destroyed by a jealous, raging God. It did Earle's heart good that the cleansing had begun. Now he didn't feel so alone in his work.

In a burning ferocity, tent city and its inhabitants had been scorched from the earth. The influenza had done its work with extraordinary efficiency. It had flicked its death tongue across the camp, sniffing out opportunities to lodge itself into fissures and cracks. It crept from building to tent, its curious tentacles reaching out, searching, and touching with methodical fixation.

It contained no malice, no judgment, no agenda, nor a willingness to choose. Its surreptitious wanderings through camp sought only one objective: to survive, to blossom, to replicate, and to prolong its own span of time. It overcame resistance at the sinus level, crept into the nether regions of the bronchial tract, quietly sidestepped the white corpuscles, leaving a ravaged, ploughed, septic plain of waste as its legacy.

The soldiers too were efficient. They were blunt, abrupt, and viral. Smashing and burning everything before them, they swept through the camp, leaving it incapacitated and sterile. Their clubs reached out to dent heads, break bones, and pound backs and thighs and buttocks.

As swiftly as they cleaned out a tent or a hut it was set afire. The camp grew to bonfire proportions. The flames shot to the sky. Men and women ran about madly to avoid the inferno, the soldiers grimly striking, hitting, crushing, lashing. A fury rose in them. This enemy must be destroyed. There must be no turning away, no going back.

Only a thorough cleansing could set things right! Their preservation was dependent entirely upon the annihilation of this disease, this anarchy, this infection. And so they worked furiously to rid themselves of this illness and to beat back the foe. The flames climbed higher into the night and the ashes dirtied them. The sparks bit their faces and hands.

CHAPTER THIRTEEN

Since her discovery of the mould in the staphylococci, Anna had focused exclusively upon this pursuit. All other considerations had to be swept aside. For her there was no strike. No inconveniences existed. No street riots nor lack of services could take away her attention.

Even the ten days that had passed since Alvin Devons's attack on Wilson were mostly a blur. As upsetting and unsettling as that was, Anna did not let it distract her. She had no time for anyone's concerns except her own. The lab cultures and their results became her life.

On June 19, she peered into the Leitz Wetzlar microscope at yet another culture that Harold had prepared. And, as always, she was overcome by that curious sensation of standing upon the precipice of a vast ocean of microscopic life forms. She observed a curious and somewhat odd phenomenon: a number of the bacilli appeared to have a tiny, hard, cusp-style shell around them, as if for protection. Others, but the same strain of bacillus, contained no such shell. How odd! Why? What could the purpose possibly be? What made them work this way? Then she asked herself the right question: what if the tiny, shell-encrusted bacilli were somehow related to a permeating virus? What then? What would that mean?

Always more questions than answers, but at least it gave her a direction. By now Anna had a considerable amount of both staphylococci and pneumococci available to her. She set up an experiment with pneumococci and discovered the same shell-encrusted covering. She introduced white blood corpuscles and watched them go to work. They rushed about, devouring the bacilli that had no husk. When they tried to attack the husked bacilli, they were totally ineffective.

Anna was amazed. This might have some possibility. If the husk-coated bacilli carried the flu virus or even led to the flu virus living in the human system, then she needed the agent that could combat it. What could destroy the protected bacilli? And why were some of the bacilli wearing this coat of armour and others not? The pneumococci without the shell were not virulent—they were easily captured and destroyed by the body's natural immune response. She needed to focus on the other.

Anna rose from the stool and stretched herself. Her back was very painful. She was working out the kinks and rubbing the lower muscles when the secretary/receptionist Mr. Conners interrupted her. Mary Pownall was here to see her.

When Anna emerged from the lab, Pownall was in the foyer. Obviously it was important, since the interim chief of public health asked to see her privately in her office. Anna led her there, sat at her desk, and was fully attentive.

"We're in trouble, Anna. Really deep trouble. There have been 528 soldiers admitted to hospitals over the last ten days. We're overwhelmed. Ninety percent are influenza. Some doctors are seeing over eighty patients a day. Cadham and Bell are working extraordinarily hard to find some cure, but nothing yet. If we don't come up with something, we'll have to look at a public ban. I don't want to, what with this strike and all, but it might come down to that."

"Why is the strike a consideration, Mary? Surely the strikers would understand a public ban on meetings because of health concerns."

"Perhaps. But before Hennessey died, the Mayor and the Committee of One Thousand were pressuring us. They wanted a ban weeks ago, but to keep the strikers from gathering. They wanted to use it as a political weapon. We were not prepared to do that. Our guidelines don't provide for that."

"And you're here because you think we can help."

Mary Pownall leaned toward Anna as if imploring her. "We need some good news, Anna. Something we can tell people. Something that can make a difference. I'd have gone to Parkes of course, but since he has his own troubles, I thought I'd see you and—"

Anna interrupted. "Troubles? What do you mean troubles?"

Dr. Pownall stopped. She stared at Anna stupidly. Her face flushed. She looked away, then back, waiting for Anna to say something. To acknowledge.

She put her hand to her mouth. "My God! You don't know! How could that happen?"

Anna was becoming alarmed. "You'd better tell me what's going on, Mary."

Pownall became even more flustered. Finally, she blurted, "Millie Parkes is dead. And so are both of the children!"

Anna slumped back in her chair. Her eyes dropped to her desktop. Mail that she hadn't read. Correspondence needing her attention. It popped into her mind that there hadn't been a staff meeting for days. Nobody had said a word to her. How could that be? How could that happen? Not Stanley, McAlister—not even Harold! How could it be? This was frightful! Horrible!

Anna stammered, "My God, Mary. When? How long ago?"

"Two days. Stanley didn't tell me. I learned it from Dr. Bell. I thought you knew. I'm so sorry, Anna. This is awful. If I'd any idea that you weren't aware—"

Anna held up her hand as if to stop her. Was it possible? Was she really so caught up in her work that she could have missed this?

"Where is he? Stanley?"

"In Gimli. The funerals are tomorrow. I don't know what to say to you, Anna. I'm so sorry, I just assumed you'd know. I just—"

"It's alright, it's not your fault. It's not anybody's fault. We've been so busy..." Her voice trailed off. She'd run out of words.

Pownall grimaced. "It's all so crazy. Stupid things are happening. The city has run out of coffins. They can't keep up. Coffin-makers are on the picket lines, if you can imagine. People can't bury their dead. Stanley had to get coffins shipped in so they can have the funerals tomorrow. Anna, sometimes I feel like just giving up. Quitting. Walking away. But how can I do that?" She sat, eyes downcast, shaking her head back and forth. "Funny thing," she continued, "I always thought I wanted Hennessey's job. Thought it would sort of put the icing on my career. Now I'd like to be shed of it. I wish somebody else could make the decisions."

Anna was getting over the initial shock about the Parkes family. "I might have something happening in the lab. I can't promise, but we might be on the edge of a breakthrough. Normally, I'd never say anything like this. Trials have to be conducted, but we might be going in the right direction...finally." She hastened to add, "But it's too soon to tell. You can't say anything in public. I shouldn't even have said what I have."

Mary Pownall looked at her. "I know. You need to be careful. If you say anything and then it doesn't work out. Like poor Bell—it was terrible what happened to him."

"What do you mean?" Anna was beginning to feel like she was the last to be told anything.

"A week ago, he leaked that he might be onto something that could destroy the flu. Things really got out of hand. He was being hounded by everyone. He and Cadham were working together I think. Anyway, when the word got out, different groups started screaming for the vaccination. They were testing the soldiers who started coming into the hospital and somebody leaked that after two vaccines the soldiers were recovering.

I don't even know if the reports are accurate. When no vaccine was forthcoming, the two had to have guards placed on their houses and then they started to get threats. It got so bad they had to get bodyguards if they went anywhere. I thought it was only me losing my mind, but maybe it's the public generally."

"Good Lord," Anna said, a genuinely perplexed look on her face. "I had no idea it was like that. What's going on out there?"

"Fear mostly—a sort of mass craziness I think. And of course the strike doesn't help. There were no city police to protect Bell and Cadham. The Royal Mounted Police had to step in to do it. The strike's losing sympathy. When stories like this circulate, it gets used against them I guess. At any rate, if you've got something promising in your lab you have to be careful what you say in public and how you let info out. Still, it's good to hear that you're positive. It gives me a feeling of hope."

Anna replied, a note of warning in her voice, "Right now this is just between us. I haven't even said anything to Stanley. I shouldn't have said to you what I did."

"My mouth is shut. I know the harm that could happen if I said anything. Will you keep me informed, Anna? I'm not sure how long I can keep on like this?" Her shoulders drooped. She looked beaten. Dr. Mary Pownall was in far deeper than she cared to be and was floundering badly.

"Of course. I will. As quickly as I can inform the staff here... and Stanley. We'll let you know. As soon as we can do something—if we can—we'll tell you."

"Good. Some of the reports I get, you wouldn't believe." Mary Pownall's eyes misted over. Her mind went back to her morning's reading. "People are getting desperate. An Indian woman's husband died. She paddled forty-five miles down a river to get help for her two kids. She had them in her boat. They didn't get there in time. And even if she had, it wouldn't have done any good. People are trying anything. I've had reports of people drinking turpentine because someone said it was a cure. They're ingesting tobacco, drinking raw alcohol. They'd rather try that than die of the flu. I've ordered everyone to wear masks. At least the ones who are still working and not on strike. Telephone operators, bank employees, teachers, and students. The trains that are still running aren't letting people off and then back on. If they get off they have to stay wherever they are. I don't even know if the masks will do anything, but we have to tell them something. Give them some kind of advice. Some hope."

Dr. Pownall rose and moved to the door. "I'm waiting to hear more from people like Bell and Cadham." When she looked at Anna from the doorway, her eyes were far away. Vacant. "I'll wait to hear something from you."

Anna stood and nodded.

Pownall said, "Soon, I hope."

When she closed the door, Anna stood looking for a long time. She thought about Millie Parkes. She'd barely known her actually. They'd rarely interacted—only very short conversations together. Once they'd sat beside each other at a fall supper—a fundraiser Anna remembered—and had talked but it was somewhat stiff and stilted. Anna was no conversationalist.

The children she knew even less. She had been introduced to them once and had spoken with them briefly on a few other occasions. A boy and a girl perhaps? Suddenly Anna realized that she didn't really know Stanley's family at all. For that matter, she didn't really even know Stanley Parkes himself as a husband or a father.

Was Millie in love with him? Did she like it when Stanley touched her? How often did they make love? Did he give her presents? Compliment her? Did they go places together? Did Millie have hobbies? Play cards? And what was her relationship like with her children? Did she play games with them when they were small? What did she teach them? How often was Stanley in their lives?

She wondered if Millie had a friend. What sort of a person would be a friend to Millie? And what kinds of things did friends do together? Anna wondered how one would go about getting a friend. What did a person do to attract a person into being a friend? What would she, Anna, do to obtain a friend? She had no idea.

Anna sat back down. She put her hands down on the desk, placed her forehead on them, and cried. And she didn't know if the tears were for Millie and Stanley, her own exhaustion, or just for the overbearing loneliness that had come over her.

***

Kathleen picked up the morning copy of *The Telegram* sitting on her desk.

IT IS TIME FOR A SHOWDOWN

It is time for a complete showdown between the citizens of Winnipeg and the police. Further temporizing and ignoring painful facts will be weakness of almost a criminal nature.

There is a state of anarchy existing in Winnipeg. There is no attempt to maintain law, to maintain order, or to protect inoffensive citizens from insult and assault.

The police constables are scandalously ignoring their duty. They refuse to interfere when strikers or strike sympathizers form into mobs and openly attempt intimidation. They refuse to interfere when inoffensive and law-abiding citizens are assaulted. They refuse to arrest men making the assaults when those men are pointed out to them by the victims. They openly display their sympathy with one class of citizens and are hostile and indifferent to all other classes of citizens.

This condition is a public scandal and a disgrace that must be wiped out. We must have a police force in which all classes of citizens will have implicit confidence. This means that the present police force, with the exception of the officers must go.

The mayor has sworn in special constables. He will need more. This new force needs to be expanded to such numbers as will enable it completely to protect the peaceable citizens of Winnipeg, completely to protect the industries of Winnipeg, and completely to protect the property of Winnipeg.

If it should be necessary to swear in 5000 or 10,000 men as special constables, there should be no hesitation in employing these numbers.

We simply cannot tolerate bluff, bull-dozing, and brigandage.

There is not one hour of the day when people are not jostled, assaulted and grossly insulted on the streets. Women and children are the chief victims – undoubtedly because they lack the power to defend themselves.

We must look these ugly facts squarely in the face. We might have expected it from the very moment that we permitted the police force to organize into a union. They affiliate with the conspirators against democracy at the Trades and Labour Hall. We should have dealt with this intolerable condition when we first learned of this affiliation. The fact that we overlooked it then, however, merely makes it all the more necessary for us to deal vigorously with it now.

Kathleen looked about the room at the usual assemblage. Grim faces, sleep-deprived, nervous pent-up energy. The length of the strike was wearing them down. Bill Ford in particular looked forlorn and somewhat out of sorts.

Kathleen said, "They're actually calling for the removal of the police force. Would they do that? Fire the entire force?"

Rolufs nodded. "Oh, yes. They can and they will."

Bill Ford offered, "It's not really about whether or not the police are doing the job. They want to make the specials legitimate. As if they are going to be a regular police force. They'll be there to do one thing: break the strike. They're using a law-and-order stance to promote and provoke violence. That's what it's really about."

Kathleen asked unhappily, "Do you think there's anything to this? This part about women and children being assaulted? It's bad enough that these street fights break out among the men. But this—" She raised her hands in a helpless gesture "—this is just so wrong."

Sam Seigalman spoke. "There's probably some truth in it. Some of the boys marching aren't angels. And remember we got troublemakers too. Not real strikers, but plants who stir things up. The Committee of One Thousand sends them. Spies and such. It could be them doing this 'cause it plays so well in the paper."

Al Devons watched the others carefully and finally let his eyes come to rest on Kathleen. "Ross will fire the police force. It's already in the works. They're getting ready for a big fight. That'll be the final showdown. The real one. They've already decided that they'll use force to end the strike. Once they fire the police the specials, some regular soldiers, and the North West Mounted Police will take over. They already have a mandate to kill the strike, no matter what."

Bill Ford let him finish, then asked, "How do you know all this, Al?"

Al thought about this for a long moment before replying. "We have our own spies in their camp. Both sides get to play at that little game."

With a note of bitterness, Kathleen asked, "And what else do *our* spies tell you, Mr. Devons? I'm afraid I haven't been privy to all these inside reports."

Ford looked at Kathleen, then at Al. What was going on here? Why the tension between them? Kathleen was getting angry. Usually objectivity was not an issue with her. She could blow up an issue as well as *The Telegram* any day, but that wasn't her usual way, to push things. Why was she pushing Al Devons?

"We have a newspaper to get out, so we'd better get at it," he suggested. He rose, as if in doing so he'd adjourned the meeting, but Al preempted him.

"I'd like to answer that, actually."

All of them stared at him. Bill Ford sat back down. John Rolufs and Seigalman exchanged glances. Kathleen leaned back in her chair and crossed her arms. They waited.

"Norris won't introduce compulsory collective bargaining no matter how the strike goes. He's not going to use the legislature to support a strike. And it's not just the police being dismissed. There's a plan to order all public employees back to work. If they refuse, they'll be fired too. The ones who return voluntarily will have to sign yellow-dog contracts. They'll start with the telephone operators.

There's a plan to put anti-strike boys into positions of leadership. That'll happen with the police, the military, the new special constables, and the civic employees. Anyone who's not anti-strike can't hold a position of authority. This is all to get ready to crush the strike.

And here's the most important thing: they're cooking up a plan to arrest the strike leaders. There'll be a new law enacted that'll let them deport people who weren't Canadian born but are attached to the strike. No trial for them, no due process, nothing. They'll get shipped back.

They've even gotten a list together of the strike leaders they say are committing treason. And by the way, Bill. You're on that list."

Ford's face went white. He took time to compose himself then glanced round. His mouth set in a firm line. He nodded. "Well, I guess I can't say I'm surprised entirely. We all knew things had to come to a head eventually."

John Rolufs broke in, "You're really in touch with what's happening, Al. Obviously your spies are getting the job done. The intelligence you've gathered is helpful."

Al looked around at all of them. "We need a plan of action. If we don't come up with something, we're going to get knocked around. They're gaining the upper hand on us in the newspapers and in the organizing. We still have control of the streets, but with the police force losing their jobs all that could change."

Kathleen pointed out, "Charles Ross is going to address the strikers today. They've moved the meeting from the Labour Temple to Victoria Park—too many people I guess. I think we should hear what he has to say."

Seigalman spoke up. "Perhaps." He hooked his thumbs into his suspenders and ran them up and down. "But if I know Charlie, it's going to be one of his political talks. A whole lot of words said with a whole lot of nothing behind them."

"You could be right." Kathleen picked up her notepad and gathered her thoughts. "Still, we might learn some more about what they plan. Especially if we get to ask some questions and can pin him down."

Bill Ford agreed. "You attend this rally then, Kathleen. But don't go alone. Make sure all of you that you're protecting yourself and each other. If there's action at the meeting try to stay clear of it. If the specials are patrolling, they'll be spoiling for a fight. Don't let yourselves be provoked."

When they arrived at Victoria Park, a throng of people in the thousands packed a huge, open grass area. A temporary stage had been set up as the focal point. Many of the top labour leaders were in attendance that day, including four of the Red Five. Kathleen recognized Bob Russell, A.A. Heaps, Fred Dixon, and R.E. Bray. Bill Ford was back at the Labour Temple trying to get *The Western Labour News* ready for publication.

Kathleen sensed a change. There was no aura of festivity about this meeting. Howard Spack was not out hawking pen knives. No food vendors appeared, nor was there any sign of a band or even a scrap of frivolity in evidence. The crowd was dour and moody: waiting, tense, nervous, like condemned prisoners whose multiple-prorogued deaths had finally arrived.

Kathleen, Al, and Sam Seigalman made their way closer to the stage as unobtrusively as possible. Kathleen needed to hear better so that she could take notes and get questions and answers.

Fred Dixon stepped forward and held both hands high to get the crowd's attention. "Alright now! You all know that Mayor Charles Ross has asked to address everyone today. I want us to listen to what he has to say."

A low rumble went through the mass so that he had to hold his hands up again to quiet them.

"I know, I know. None of us is happy that the strike has dragged on this long. The mayor's not happy about it either. That's why he's here today. He didn't have to come. Nothing compelled him to do so. He's here of his own volition because he says he wants to help end the strike. That's his primary and only concern. We're all suffering from the fact that civil services aren't back to normal yet. It's hard for everyone, so let's at least hear the man out."

Charles Ross stepped out from the men at the back of the stage. Even before he'd arrived he was nervous. Ross was used to crowds, had spoken on hundreds of occasions to gatherings. Indeed, public speaking required talent, grace, timing, voice and body control, and enthusiasm, all of which Charles had in abundance.

But he'd never spoken before in this kind of setting. Charles liked to think he could best anyone in a public forum and indeed had often reduced political opponents to tatters in a controlled, rules-bounded, and contained environment. But this—this was something different.

The mayor knew he was not particularly popular with this group. This could not be scripted. He needed to be careful to strike the correct tone, to avoid stirring people up. But like many fine public speakers, Ross was plagued by self-doubt. Having one- or two-hundred sets of expectant, smiling eyes upon you is not the same thing as ten-thousand dark, wary, mistrustful faces standing and awaiting your every word.

Ross used an old public speaking trick to steel himself and to slow his racing pulse. Not a single person in the crowd realized what he was doing. As he prepared to talk, he took a moment and placed both hands over his solar plexus, with the thumbs forming the base of a triangle just underneath the sternum. His index fingers joined to form the top of the reverse triangle at his belly button. He pushed with both hands against the solar plexus while the muscles of his stomach pushed back. He did this twice as he looked out across the faces. After each, he inhaled deeply and breathed out as long as he could.

The resulting action released a stream of energy into his blood, which served to relieve the tension and stress of standing before the crowd.

"My friends," he began, "I come here today to ask how I can help. To find out what it is you need from me as your mayor and what it is you need from your council to induce an end to this strike.

I think we can all agree that this has gone on for too long. It is of utmost importance that city services resume normal activities. We need to be able to ensure that streetcars run, that electricity is on, and that water services are provided properly. The fire department needs to be able to know that they can do their jobs. Again I think we can agree that our city and our lives need to return to normal. Delivery of services and goods has been too long delayed and too often stopped altogether.

Your city council, in its wisdom, has seen fit to pass a resolution that would require the return of the power utilities, the streetcars, and the firefighters, so that...so that..."

Ross lost his train of thought. What was it he had planned to say? Where had his mind shifted?

A man shouted out from the crowd, "So that business can go on as usual!"

Ross nodded in agreement. "Yes, that's right. So that..." Once again his mind blanked.

Again the voice from the crowd. "So that Archibald, Bulgar, and E.K. Atwater can continue to make money while they sit on their big fat asses." A roar of laughter followed this.

Ross's face grew red but he forced himself under control. "No! No. That's not what I meant. This is about safety for everyone. There's only a volunteer fire brigade now and the new police force can't handle everything. There has to be training."

R.E. Bray asked, "Mayor Ross, it's being said that city council has fired the entire police force because they were too sympathetic to the strikers."

Ross shook his head. "No, that's not right." He could feel the sweat gathering now. "There's a police commission. They're the ones who decided what to do about—"

"But they acted with the blessing of you and the council. Isn't that right?" Bray insisted.

Ross did not respond.

Bray pressed on. "And isn't it also true, mayor, that in this same resolution you're speaking of, it also states—" He opened a piece of paper and read aloud, "—Whereas with a view to preserving law and order and to protect the citizens of Winnipeg in carrying on their business, an adequate force of citizen constabulary has been organized."

Ross said, "Well yes, of course. There has to be law and order after all."

Bray flashed a grin. "Oh don't get me wrong, Mayor. I'm all for law and order. So are they." He motioned with his hand to include the rest of the labour leaders on the stage. "And so are they!" He motioned again to include the thousands of onlookers.

Ross shrugged. He said nothing.

Bray pressed his point. "I just don't see why it has to come from a damn bunch of bully boys hired by the Committee of a Thousand. Who hires the new police, Mayor Ross? Is it you? Is it the Police Commission? How many pro-strikers are among the new police recruits? Do you know?" Bray stopped. Waited. Silence. He waited longer.

Finally Ross responded, "To my knowledge, none."

"That's what I thought. Your new police force is entirely anti-strikers, is it not?" Bray waved off an attempt by Ross to respond. "Never mind. I have a different question. Will you lift the ban on parades and marches in the city?"

Ross shook his head. "I can't do that. It'd be against the riot act. I'd be acting in bad faith if I rescinded the order. It's difficult enough now with tensions so strong. But as you know, a few days ago I asked Major Scott, the army pastor, to act as a negotiator between the two sides."

Bray stopped him. "Yes, that's true. And we have a lot of respect for Pastor Scott. In the very first meeting, he tried to point out to the employers that it was their own mistrust of the unions that had caused the strike. But the Committee of One Thousand didn't like to hear that. Funny thing about the pastor, Mayor Ross. After that suggestion, he found himself transferred to Quebec."

"Well, he shouldn't have said that. He should have remained neutral, like me." Again Ross showed a broad smile and a laugh erupted from the crowd. Ross turned to them. "I want to assure you that I am partial to neither side in this strike. My only concern is that the citizens of Winnipeg are spared needless suffering."

Bray shouted and swept his arm across the large gathering. "Are these people not all citizens of Winnipeg, Mayor Ross?"

Ross looked startled and nodded assent.

Bray roared, "What about their needless suffering?"

The crowd began to come alive. They shouted and several fists were raised. Suddenly a crowd of four-hundred specials appeared from seemingly out of nowhere. They brandished clubs and baseball bats. Not a police uniform among them. They wore suits, ties, and a variety of hats, from round boleros to Stetsons to Panama styles.

Immediately the tension in the strikers rose sharply. The speakers could no longer be heard. Bray jumped off the stage, followed by Heaps and Dixon. They pressed their way through the throng towards the small hill on which the special constables planted themselves. The strikers booed the specials and cursed them unmercifully. As if by magic, eggs appeared and were hurled into the midst of the special constables.

This caused a response to erupt and Bray, Heaps, and Dixon were thrust aside. The specials marched down the hill and weighed into the strikers. Batons and bats flew as men scrambled to get out of the way.

Ross remained on the stage, vainly attempting to gain the attention of both sides. For a few moments he waved his hat, shouted, and moved back and forth along the front of the stage. He appealed for quiet and attention. Finally, in despair he placed his hat back on his head and stood, hands on hips. He wagged his head back and forth helplessly, staring at the melee that had erupted at the base of the hill.

The shouting and the screaming flared as the two sides pressed for advantage. A number of the strikers had come to the rally prepared. Weapons appeared, including billy clubs and knives. A bevy of short iron pipes made their appearance as the strikers forced themselves upon the specials.

If one striker fell, another took his place as they clawed, pounded, thrust, and jabbed against the constables. The specials, recognizing just how outnumbered they were, retreated towards the hilltop and formed a tight knot to defend themselves.

Kathleen and Al, having moved to the stage area, now found themselves at the back of the riot. Al tried to make himself heard over the roar, yelling in her ear that they'd better get out. This was going to get a lot worse in a very short time. He took Kathleen's hand and they pressed against the horde of men who were surging forward toward the hill where the specials swung their clubs and cursed at the strikers. They lashed out indiscriminately, breaking arms and smashing heads.

Al shouldered his way through the oncoming angry faces until he found them pressed right up against the stage. Here, he ducked under the structure and followed the maze-like cross-pieces to the far side. Behind it there was room to move about and breathe. They headed towards the parking lot, passing many men running in the opposite direction. When Kathleen looked up, she found herself in step with Charles Ross, also making his way towards the parking lot.

Kathleen pulled Al up short and nodded towards the mayor. She stepped up and tapped him on the shoulder, wanting to ask a question. When Charles Ross turned, Kathleen was taken aback.

Tears rolled down the man's cheeks. His bloodless face was a ghostly white. His eyes tried to focus upon her but could not. Clearly the man was shaken to the core.

Kathleen felt terrible. The strike had done something to Charles Ross. It had changed him in some basic and palpable way. His strained features were contorted, stretched, and limp.

Kathleen put a hand out. "Are you alright, Mr. Mayor?"

Finally Ross looked at her, realizing that someone had addressed him. The words she said crept into his conscious thinking. He looked at her, at Al, then back toward the stage, and across the field to the ever-growing furor that was spreading like a galloping stampede.

He looked at the two of them again. "No," he said, his voice husky and sad. "No. I guess I'm not. I tried to...I wanted to tell them that..." His words trailed away. Once again he was blank.

CHAPTER FOURTEEN

"I warned him," said Julius Archibald. "I told him that going and talking to those dumb bastards wasn't going to work. He had to go and try though. And what happens? Starts a goddamn big riot, that's what! How in the hell is that supposed to help anything?" The hypocrisy went unchallenged.

Major Lyle, newly appointed commander of the Citizen's Constabulary, replied, "Well in fact the mayor may have inadvertently done us quite a favour. Lately it's become more and more difficult to press things forward. Now we have reasons to focus on the strike leaders. They were at the forefront of this confrontation."

Thomas Bulgar broke in. "It seems to me, Major, that your specials got bested in this one. From what I've heard and read, the strikers defeated them handily."

Lyle looked belligerent. "There were at least ten-thousand men in Victoria Park. I had a little over three hundred. I thought we did damn well considering!"

Atwater intervened. "Doesn't matter who did what to whom, gentlemen." He was not happy with the choice of Lyle to command the new force. The man was a hothead and prone to make rash decisions such as this one to confront the strikers in the park.

Atwater continued, "We'll make sure you have what you need, Major. We're purchasing horses and equipping your men with supplies. We've ordered several gross of new bats. You'll have two thousand more men by the end of the week. General Ketchen is recruiting some of the veterans. If we get enough of them we'll be a substantial force. We'll pay them six dollars a day. That's twice as much as the allowance the government is giving them. They'll jump at the chance for that kind of money."

This was Senator Robinson's second visit to the city. Sent by the federal government to bring an end to the strike, he was painfully aware of Pastor Scott's failed attempts at conciliation and had no interest in following him to Quebec. The strike was going to end and the military build-up to prepare for that was well underway. Still, Robinson was not unsympathetic to the strikers' cause. There were many things in Canada that needed some fixing.

"We don't want things to get too out of hand. People have already been hurt. Let's see if we can avoid people being killed. I'm also concerned about some other things. My department has received reports that the strike is being financed by Bolsheviks in the U.S. I have a report that says $24,000 in U.S. currency has crossed the border and been brought into Winnipeg."

Commissioner Stone nodded. "Yes, we have the same reports. Also, there's been a sympathetic strike in Vancouver. We believe this whole revolution is starting to spread. It's growing and we need to take steps to prevent this."

Archibald agreed. "Exactly. We have to teach these goddamn bohunks a lesson. They think they can come to Winnipeg an' do anything they damn well like. We got a few surprises for them."

Atwater said nothing. He was gazing at Julius with keen interest. How on earth had the man ever become a successful banker? He was uncouth, unfriendly, abrupt, and discourteous. His butchery of the English language was surpassed only by his ability to articulate profanity. Yet the man handled millions in transactions. Some of the wealthiest Winnipeg families were associated with his bank. He was more like an uneducated, rapacious bully than a businessman, and yet people were attracted to him. His ability to run a strong organization was legendary even as far as Toronto. But he was so bloody despicable.

Before Atwater could speak, Senator Robinson intervened. "The government is busy taking care of our problems, Mr. Archibald. These aliens will be deported. The House of Commons believes the strike to be a fully developed attempt at anarchy. The general consensus is that the strike-leaders are trying to create revolution. The amendment to the immigration act will allow for the deportation of anyone not born in Canada."

There was a good deal of thumping of hands on the oak table and smiles all around.

Atwater held up a hand and called for quiet. "Wait a minute. Doesn't that include a number of the strike leaders? People like Russell were born in Scotland, I believe. Isn't that right?"

"Correct," said Robinson. "That's part of the point, you see. We can get to them. We have a mechanism in place."

Thomas Bulgar sat up straight and frowned. "I think I see your point, E.K. Arresting and deporting aliens is one thing. But many of these people are from the British Isles, Senator. My people are from England, as is the case for many around this table. Commissioner Stone, weren't you born in England?"

Stone nodded. "Yes, I was. If we arrest the leaders under this act, they wouldn't get a trial. They'd be deported without due process. That's very heavy-handed. I don't like it and I don't think the general public would support it."

"Nor I," said Atwater.

"I get your point. I understand," Robinson said. "It is heavy-handed, but this strike is causing havoc. If it spreads to the railroad, the entire country could be shut down. If our railway system stops then Canada stops, it's as simple as that." The senator allowed a minute for the implications of this to sink in around the table. "The government is not prepared to allow that."

Thomas Bulgar stared at Robinson. "But deportations of this type, man. Good God! It's unheard of. If we can deport Britons, then pretty much anybody in Canada could be deported."

Senator Robinson argued, "I have to tell you, gentlemen. This decision-making is being taken out of your hands. Out of the hands of the local government and the Norris government. The cabinet has given me the authority to keep the railways running, and I will. If I have to arrest every last strike leader to do it, then that's what will happen. We have an internment camp set up in Ontario. The strike leaders will be detained there until deportation can be arranged."

Atwater blanched. Even he had not foreseen this. This was martial law. The feds were prepared to circumvent the democratic laws of the nation. Good Lord! He'd agreed to the use of the military to break the strike. Had even made arrangements for General Ketchen's troops. But this! This was a whole new development, and a dangerous one.

Julius Archibald, on the other hand, saw no problem with the government's approach. "About damned time too. What the hell took so long? Major Lyle's men may have lost the skirmish in the park but that's only one battle. Things will heat up again!"

"Indeed!" exclaimed Robinson. "That's exactly the way the government sees it. That's why General Ketchen's militia ranks have been filled to capacity, including reserves. They are fully equipped with rifles, horses, and Lewis machine guns. We'll institute raids on the Labour Temple and any other offices the strike leaders use. All materials therein will be confiscated, including anything related to *The Western Labour News*."

Atwater protested, "But you can't deport British citizens. Senator, the Canadian government needs to look at this again. There must be trials for sedition. Arbitrary deportation of Canadian citizens cannot be permitted. We cannot support that!"

Robinson shrugged. "We're beyond all that, Mr. Atwater. It's all been decided. This strike will end and it will end very shortly. The warrants for the arrest of the strike leaders have been issued. The RNWMP will conduct raids and apprehend them."

Lyle stood up. "Good enough, then. The special constabulary is prepared to act in support of the RNWMP as we've been ordered. The men have been training hard. I understand that the militia has also been ordered to support. We'll be ready for them I assure you. There will be no doubt as to who is in charge when it's all said and done."

Lyle and Stone got up to leave with Senator Robinson. They paused at the door. Robinson looked back at them. "I don't have to remind you that anything we've discussed stays in this room. Confidentiality is important here. We don't want anyone flying the coop on us, right?"

When they had gone, the remainder looked around at each other. E.K. Atwater and Thomas Bulgar looked glum. Julius Archibald lit up one of his very large Cuban cigars and sat back.

The young blond man sat quietly, his hands folded in his lap as he contemplated the events of the meeting. He knew E.K. Atwater was watching him intently. Suspiciously.

Atwater finally asked, "Did you know about this?"

The young man's gaze held him. He nodded.

"Why didn't you say something to us? Seems to me that's the kind of information we pay you for."

The youngster chewed his lip thoughtfully for a moment. "Well, it's like the man said. This has been taken out of your hands. How could it have made any difference for you to know?"

Julius Archibald puffed and snorted in derision.

***

After Earle had returned to Union Station and had once again become Roger Wilson, his first task was to begin the preparations for the fulfillment of his God pact. As surely as sin's stealthy hand reached out to pluck the minds of men and women, he knew that the day of reckoning was on the horizon. All signs pointed to it. The scourge of tent city was one of them. The deadlines of the flu racing across the world only served to convince him further. The festering sore of the strike added to his certainty.

What more did anyone need to see? Fleeting images of a battleground flitted through Earle's brain. Smoke and smouldering ruins on a plain of death. Dead bodies as far as one could look. Rats feasting upon human carcasses. Rusted-out tanks and military vehicles lay about. Machine guns, rifles, bayonets clutched in skeletal hands of the not-so-long-ago living.

Flags tattered and drooping. Lying in the mud, shorn of pride and meaning. A half-burned copy of the Holy Bible lay, partly buried under a battered and dented soldier's helmet.

Far off in the distance, the remains of once-proud buildings. Castles half-blown apart, their turrets askew and ready to tumble. Huge crater holes blown into the earth and filled with mud and bodies.

And over there, humans hanging from gallows, staked out on crosses, burning at the stake and being thrown into mass burning pits.

And there in the midst of it He sat on a high backless stool. The Prince of Darkness Himself. Amazing. He looked so human. A pale white face, triumphant. Part smile, part-grimace. A long black robe clothed His body from head to ankle. His feet were bare and His taloned toes clutched at a rung at the base of the stool.

In one hand He clutched the short broadsword of the Roman soldier. A shiny, clean, beautiful sword with a carved steel handle tipped by a death's head emblem. In His other hand a scroll. The rolled-up paper had words written upon it: DECLARATION OF WAR.

But it was those monstrous black wings tucked behind His head and shoulders! They curved upwards and out in their folded, resting position. They framed the face and neck perfectly. The muscular structure was prominent even under the raven feathers.

"Beast," said Earle aloud, "I recognize You for what You are and for who You are. But You shall not tempt me. For I am the *Light* and the *Way*."

"I beg your pardon. Are you alright?"

"What?" Roger was jarred into the moment.

"Oh, sorry," the waitress said. "I thought you said something to me, Mr. Wilson. Can I get you more coffee?"

He shook his head, returning to the present. "I guess I was daydreaming. Yes. Please. I'd love coffee and a piece of that wonderful pie your cook specializes in. What's it called again?"

She smiled at him. Roger Wilson always left a substantial tip at her table. "Triple berry. The cook's using her canned stock from last year. Nothing coming in by rail now, what with the strike and all."

Roger flashed a smile. "Of course, dear. The strike. A very difficult time for everyone. Still, one must press on with one's duty."

She returned the smile. "I suppose." What an odd man. He came out with the strangest things. "I'll get your pie." She cleaned away his dinner plate and disappeared into the back.

Wilson looked out the window and across the street at the Versatile Medical Laboratories building. Inside, Anna Williams would be toiling away at her microscope and searching for a solution to kill the influenza. Even now she might be making progress. That fine brain would be poring over the minute details of her investigation. She'd have dozens of experiments going at once. There'd be no telling when, by hard work or happenstance, she would land upon a cure.

And what then? God's Great Plan would be foiled. The most important day on the planet would be postponed. Alternate arrangements would have to be made. A fall-back plan would need to be devised. But surely the time was now; it could not be otherwise! He must not allow this to happen. Now he knew why it was Winnipeg he had gravitated towards. It was his destiny to meet Anna and to—

A man was sitting in a booth close to the restaurant door. The waitress had stopped to talk to him. She held Roger's serving of triple berry pie in one hand as she conferred with customers. Roger almost didn't look a second time.

When he did, he recognized the symptoms immediately. This man had the flu. She'd been enquiring about how he was feeling. Roger could see the flash of heated brightness in the man's eyes. He was sweating and mopped at his brow with a handkerchief. His face had a gaunt, worried look and a pallor had cast itself upon his skin.

Roger got out of his booth and moved closer for a better view. Not too close! The man covered his mouth with the handkerchief and coughed once, furiously. When he did, his face strained with redness. And weren't those spots? Wasn't that the beginning of dark splotches starting to form?

Roger shouted, "Don't touch him!"

Both the waitress and the young man looked up, incomprehension on their faces. Then the girl brightened, smiled, and indicated the man with an extended hand. "Mr. Wilson, this is my brother Gil. He's only recently returned from overseas. He was—"

Roger Wilson said very loudly as he pointed, "He's got the flu. He's dying."

The waitress frowned. "No, Mr. Wilson. He has trouble with his lungs. Emphysema, the doctors say."

Wilson looked at her, confused. "What? Didn't you say he's home from the war? Discharged?"

"No—he couldn't get into the army, Mr. Wilson. His lungs are too bad. He was overseas I said. In the Mediterranean. For his health." The young man held the handkerchief over his mouth and coughed again. His face turned red and splotchy as he sought to gain some air and force it into his lungs. The waitress patted him on the shoulder and rubbed his back as she encouraged him to breathe.

Wilson's own face reddened. "I'm sorry, I was so sure that you..." He went back to his table and retrieved his coat. He fumbled in his pockets for several bills and placed the money on the table. He put on his coat clumsily and with a good deal of effort as he pushed his way past them and towards the exit.

Once outside, he strode very quickly down the sidewalk. He didn't look back. He knew he would never again return to the bar and grille. He had seen this young man before. Where? He cast his mind back to the Satanic figure of his earlier imagining. Yes! That was it! The brother looked almost exactly like the Prince Himself.

***

Kathleen read The Telegram advertisement with a growing distaste. In spite of the terrible writing, the lack of clarity and the abysmal structure the central meaning was very obvious.

MAKE CANADA SAFE FOR CANADIANS

The proposition that the Strike Committee should supply the executives of the Veterans' Associations with exact particulars about the part which the alien members of the unions played in bringing about the general strike, and to indicate how they proposed to assist in ridding the community of alien enemies, has not been accepted.

It is not likely to be. The reasons for its non-acceptance are indicated by the following excerpts from the official strike literature.

ALIENS AS BROTHERS

The Calgary Convention declared "That the interests of all members of the international working class being identical, that this body of the workers recognize no alien but the capitalist."

It is further declared that "To us workmen no worker can be an alien so far as we are concerned. Our alien insofar as we are concerned is the Master class."

Strike Committee Undertakes to Speak for Aliens

From The Strike Bulletin, No. 1, May 17

The Strike Committee feels that such requests as the following are not helpful:

G. W.V.A. (WINNIPEG BRANCH)

From information received, the executive committee of this association is satisfied that certain elements of the population (chiefly enemy alien) are ready, should an opportune occasion arise, to take advantage of the existing state of unrest to indulge in the destruction of property for purposes of pillage and loot, consequently all comrades, who are ready and willing at any time to do their share in maintaining the public peace and safety, are requested to leave their names and addresses in the Secretary's office, and in the event of any disorder arising, all comrades are asked to assemble as quickly as possible at the club rooms of the association. —JOHN O. NEWTON, Vice President

The Strike Committee is in a position to inform Mr. Newton that his fears are wholly without warrant. No enemy alien will commit any untoward act.

Strike Committee Advises Alien Members

From The Strike Bulletin, No. 2, May 30

ALIENS, CARRY YOUR CARDS

we appeal to all aliens to carry their cards under all circumstances

THE ALIEN

IS ON HIS WAY!

- With the formation of the Returned Soldiers' Loyalist Association yesterday, began the movement which will speedily clear Canada of the undesirable alien and land him back in the bilgewaters of European Civilization from whence he sprung and in which he properly belongs.
- The men who are back of this task have devoted one to four of the best years of their lives to "making the world safe for democracy".
- Now they have a new job: "making Canada safe for Canadians". And Canada can bank on their carrying on to a finish.
- These are the men who were characterized by undesirable alien Duncan as ignoramuses presumably because

they refused to follow the lead of men like Ford, Dixon, etc. who took advantage of every public appearance to urge that we at home desert our soldiers at the front and leave them to perish miserably alone and unsupported.

- Thanks to these "ignoramuses," the people of Winnipeg, for the first time since the strike began, can go about their affairs with the reasonable assurance that they will not be molested or annoyed.
- MR. EMPLOYER, these men are officially pledging themselves to preserve law and order and to protect your life and property. Do not fail in turn to do your part, without stint of limit. There are sufficient positions vacated by striking aliens to provide immediate employment for our returned men. If there is unemployment in our midst, it must be the undesirable alien and not our own returned soldiers who walk the streets.

Choose Between the Soldiers Who Are Protecting You

and the

Aliens Who Have Threatened You

CITIZEN'S COMMITTEE OF ONE THOUSAND

It was true then. Everything Al had told them about coming events. There would be deportations. No trials. No way for the strike leaders to seek reparation, let alone redemption.

The Committee of One Thousand would force the issue. They'd choose the time and the place for a showdown. The Great War Veterans' Association was being morphed into an organ to support the anti-strike committee.

The strikers and those sympathetic to them were under a barrage of propaganda in all the daily newspapers. *The Western Labour News* could not compete with this. No matter how many hours of work Kathleen and the others put in, their voice was small in comparison. A mouse peeking out from under a lion's paw.

Ford was right too. There had never been hope for a labour victory. It had never been about that. All the picketing, the marches, demonstrations, the speeches. Was it so obvious to the strike leaders as well? Did Bob Russell and Fred Dixon see it the same way? Had they known from the start that the whole thing was fruitless?

After seeing the look on Charles Ross's face at Victoria Park, Kathleen was coming to some awakenings and to some conclusions. The strike was not going to be allowed to go on. But at the same time, it was not going to be allowed to die any kind of a natural death. It was going to be crude, bloody, and horrifyingly destructive. People were going to die. It had already been decided.

There would be no honourable truce. There would be no grand signing of a peace treaty that recognized the legitimacy of the unions and their right to collective bargaining.

Kathleen smiled an embarrassed little grin. She'd been so naïve about it all. She'd actually come into it thinking that she and people like her could make a difference. That reason would be recognized, condoned, and even applauded.

But nobody wanted reasonable compromise. That was a fool's pursuit. The whole process was set up to be conflict-based. Even if labour won the strike, things wouldn't change much. Down the road awaited more strikes, increased conflicts, and an enforced surrender of ideals and values.

The really sad thing was, it didn't really matter if the employers won. The same destiny awaited them. More desperate and dangerous workplaces, more suppression of wages and workers, increased mistrust, a rise in industrial sabotage, family poverty, family violence, and family destruction.

The immigrant population was to be scapegoated. They would become the burnt offering on the altar of the great economic god called Capitalism.

All religions required sacrificial lambs and this one was no different. Jews, Balkans, Russians, Ukrainians—it didn't really matter. If you were East European, it was a guaranteed passport to be shipped "back to the bilgewaters of European Civilization from whence they sprung".

Soon. Very soon she knew there would be a reckoning. It was the golden promise of the capitalist-worker relationship. An accounting. A great leveling. And as always in such calculations, the detritus must be winnowed and gleaned.

And so it must be. Kathleen too would be a particle of collateral damage. The pestle of authority would grind against the mortar of law and those caught between would become the dust. And like dust, they would be blown about by the uncompromising wind of the so-called Master class. They would ride momentarily on that wind, then gradually float, settle, and disappear.

***

The previous evening, Anna had injected a set of lab mice with the non-husked living pneumococci. Another set she'd injected with dead pneumococci that still had the husks intact. As she expected, both sets of mice were alive this morning. The non-husked live cells had been merely devoured by the immune system. The dead husked cells were not virulent.

In a third group, she injected a combination of living non-husked cells and dead husked cells. This group was dead.

Anna was astounded. How could it be? If the first two sets were alive, then the third set had to be alive also. It hit her with a flash—there was only one way this could be. The non-husked had to have acquired husks sometime between last night and this morning. Such an acquisition would make them deadly to the mice! It had to be! Nothing else made sense.

Quickly, Anna had Harold prepare three more sets of mice for the combination injection. If they died then she had something to work on. Even if she couldn't find the acquisition process, she might be enabled to prompt immunity.

She prepared samples from the dead mice for centrifuge. She repressed with great force the excitement she felt arising from her stomach and moving towards her heart.

Some sort of change had been undergone. She was almost positive of it, but what it was she could not say and finding out could take months or even years. She did not have that kind of time. Whatever the change was, she had to find the element that would effectively prevent it. If she could do that, she would have the answer that was so badly needed. Stanley would be ecstatic. Mary Pownall would be relieved. She, McAlister, and Johnstone would go to work on finding the solution.

Then the image of Millie and the children popped into her head. She hadn't seen Stanley since he'd lost his family. He'd spent most of his time in Gimli. She didn't know when he'd return to the lab. He needed to come in. She had to report on her findings. If she could get Stanley to push the other researchers towards this new development, then the answer might be discovered more quickly.

Anna set her experiments aside and went in search of McAlister and Johnstone. When she found them they were hard at work, hunched over microscopes and making notes, totally unaware that she'd entered the room.

"Do the two of you realize we haven't had a staff meeting for weeks?"

The startled pair looked up. In all the time they'd worked for Versatile, Anna had never before entered their lab. Somehow, a silent boundary had grown up between their lab and hers, and between the two of them and Anna. McAlister conceded a grudging respect for her, but that was as far as it went.

Johnstone did not even try to disguise his feelings. By walking in here, Anna had crossed the line. A woman in a bacteriology setting was just not acceptable. Too many changes happening in this century and too quickly. With barely concealed animosity, he offered, "We were just talking about that earlier actually. Haven't you seen anything of Parkes?" He spat it out more as an accusation than a question.

"No, I thought maybe the two of you had. That's why I came down here. We should have a meeting. There are things to discuss. But he needs to be here for it."

McAlister looked at Anna. "What sorts of things, Dr. Williams?"

She almost blurted forth about her discovery. The words were on her tongue, but then she swallowed them quickly. No, this was not the time or place. Stanley Parkes had to know first. Besides, Anna was aware of Johnstone's only slightly covered feelings towards her. She could not allow them an opportunity to put her into an embarrassing position. She needed their help, but it had to come from Stanley Parkes. It was the only way she could avoid being undermined.

She chose to ignore the question. "Do either of you know if he's been into the office since ...his loss?" she finished weakly.

McAlister answered, "I think he was in one day but only for a short while to talk with the secretary. We don't know when or if he's coming back fulltime. This has been shattering for him. I didn't actually talk with him, but I can't even imagine that he'll be here anytime soon."

Anna was getting frustrated. "Yes I know, but I...I really need to—" Suddenly, she turned and walked out.

McAlister and Johnstone stood looking after her momentarily and then at each other. Johnstone shrugged and turned back to his microscope.

Rather than go back to her lab, Anna walked past the receptionist and out the door. She was embarrassed and anxious. She must have appeared to them to be abrupt and uncaring. Not that she cared about their opinions in particular, but she didn't want to appear empty of feelings about Stanley Parkes's tragic turn of events.

Anna turned south on Fort Street and ambled along, trying to gather her thoughts into some sort of logical pattern. Should she try to get word to Stanley? Was it possible to send a telegram? And if she did, where would she send it? Could he be contacted by telephone? Not all homes had such things by any means—were there phones in Gimli? Anna had no idea. She realized that since she'd come to Winnipeg to work, she hadn't left the city for any reason. Her world was very small indeed. It had narrowed down to a tiny group and a very small set of circumstances. There was no macro world for Anna. A microcosm—that's what she lived. And a peculiarly miniature one it was too. It was an atom of a life, really. When had other parts of her deserted? What happened to the girl who wanted to know everything, from internal combustion engines to the microbial life forms inside a slide of culture?

Her life hadn't always been reduced like this. Or had it? Hadn't there been a time when the company of others had been a prerequisite? Hadn't there been a time—twenty years ago perhaps—when the thought of a man coming into her life had been a longing? Something that she thought of as—

"You know Earley?"

Jarred from her thoughts, Anna stared upon the most diminutive, forlorn-looking creature she'd ever seen. The hunched gnome figure could have walked straight out of a Dickens novel.

His cap sat askew upon his head. It, like everything else about him, appeared dirty. His shirt, which at one time was probably white, was scuffed and torn. Part of it was tucked into the waistband of an equally dirty pair of pants. Suspenders held the pants up, but Anna could see that at the front on one side the clip was missing and the suspender had been tied through a loop in the pants. The oddest thing though was that he had on a new pair of leather boots. The laces were new and the boots still had shine upon them. It had been days since the man had shaved and even from a distance Anna could smell the ripe, pungent odor coming off him.

If not for the fact that she was on the street in broad daylight with people all about Anna might have been afraid, even though the man was considerably smaller than she and had difficulty with one of his legs.

He stood off from her, not blocking her path exactly. He nervously stepped back and forth. "You know Earley, huh? I guess you know Earley."

"What?"

"I see'd you. You an' him. I see'd you awhile ago."

Anna was about to protest when suddenly a voice in her head shouted, "Earle! Earle! I need ta talk to ya. The cops been nosin' aroun'." Anna looked at the little figure. His eyes were dancing back and forth and glinting, recessed deeply beneath bushy brows. The sun was making them a little watery and red beneath the lower lids. There was nothing to fear in this tiny man.

"You were trying to talk to us on the day of the strike. When the street was full of people. Roger said he didn't know you and then..." She cast back to that day, trying to reconstruct the events as they'd happened. There had been the crowd—so many people, so much noise. She and Roger trying to get through the crowd. He'd pushed someone out of the way, someone calling out to him. And then they'd become separated. And then Al Devons and a young lady...

"What's early?" Anna asked. "Or who's early? And early for what?"

The gnome was looking at her confused, as if she must be stupid or something. He shuffled back and forth from one foot to another. He studied her, frustrated.

"Earle. He's Earle."

"Earle? Do you mean Mr. Wilson? Are you talking about Roger Wilson? The man who was with me that day?"

The gnome nodded his head vigorously and his feet never stopped shuffling, as if ready to run at any moment. "He's Earle."

"His name is Earle?"

The little man nodded his head in excitement. "Earle Nelson. Ya gotta watch! I know he's lookin' fer me. They tol' me at camp. I bin watchin'. I'm smarter than he thinks. I bin watchin' him an' you."

Anna was growing alarmed. "What do you mean watching me? Why are you watching me? Who are you?"

"Hawkshaw!" The man looked about and then behind him, as if searching. "He don't come aroun' now. It's in the evening, when he thinks nobody's lookin'." The man who called himself Hawkshaw grinned and displayed several gaps in his mouth. "He's lookin' fer me an' I know why. He don't see me but I see him. I follow him all the time. That's how I stay safe ya see!"

Anna shook her head, wondering if she shouldn't just excuse herself and leave the man to babble. "No, I'm afraid I don't. And I don't know you, but you seem to know me. How is that?"

"Cause I bin followin' Earle. I see him. I know he lives with you. I see him at night when he picks ya up. I'm watchin'."

"But why? Why are you watching us?"

Hawkshaw looked about again nervously. He looked across the street. He gazed over his shoulder behind him. He looked past Anna down the street. "Ya won't tell Earle, eh? Ya won't say nothin'?"

"To Roger, you mean?" The man was gazing at her and her own nerves were getting more high-strung. "Alright, I won't say anything. Now what do you want?"

"Ya shouldn't let him pick ya up. I know why Earle's lookin' fer me. Cause I know about 'im. An' I know about the guys in the river. An' tent city. An' all that. Earley's bad. He's lookin' fer me an' I know why. An' he'll hurt ya."

Anna felt a streak of fear move through her, but it wasn't because of this little man. In her mind she was seeing the charming, smiling face of Roger Wilson.

The gnome continued. "Ya won't tell' im eh? Ya won't say I talked to ya eh? Don't say anythin' 'bout Hawkshaw!"

Anna looked at him more closely. Clearly he was very frightened. His feet hadn't stopped moving since he'd first spoken to Anna.

"Alright, I won't. I think you better tell me more, Mr. Hawkshaw."

"Can't. Not now. I'll come back. 'Bin waitin' fer ya to come out when he's not here. Didn' think ya ever would. You come out tomorrow. Noon. I'll watch fer ya. He's never aroun' then."

Any fear that Anna might have had of him eased away. "Alright." She nodded at him and then turned back toward the lab.

"Miss."

She turned back to the drab little figure.

"Don't let him pick ya up no more. He's bad, Earle. He'll hurt ya."

He turned and scuttled away down the street. Anna watched him momentarily before she started back toward the lab.

CHAPTER FIFTEEN

"They'll be out this afternoon," Al explained. "But one of the conditions of their bail is that they won't participate in the strike."

"I still can't believe this happened." Kathleen shook her head, "Raiding their homes like that, and in the middle of the night. And why take them all the way out to Stony Mountain?"

Siegalman shrugged. "It makes it that much more difficult to get to them. The road out there is in terrible shape. The whole intention was for them to never get bail. The government actually thought they could hold them indefinitely with no bail. But once we got the lawyers and bail bondsmen out there, there was nothing they could do. They figured to deport them and sidestep a trial, but they forgot Canada's still a democracy even if Winnipeg's not."

Kathleen's hand unconsciously dropped to her stomach and rested there as she looked at Al. "How much is the bail and who's paying it?"

"Two thousand for each." Al grinned at her. "It was quite a procession. We had twelve or thirteen cars heading out to Stoney. Between the lawyers, the bondsmen, and strikers, it took that many to hold us all. There must have been fifty of us at the door to the pen. Andrews and Murray got the chief warden out of bed we were there so early."

Seigalman chimed in, "Lawyers are no respecters of a person's sleep." He guffawed. "We were quite a show outside the gate. Nobody went anywhere until Russell, Ford, Bray, Heaps, Armstrong, and Rolufs shook the hand of every person there."

"What about the others? There were more arrests than just these six!" Kathleen was staring at them, prodding for information for her next *Labour News* issue.

"That's going to be a little more difficult," Al responded. "The specials made sure they'd picked up foreign-born strikers. They pinpointed them specifically. We're working on getting them bail too, but they'll face deportation. Lot quicker an' they don't have to have expensive trials."

"What will this mean for the strike?" Kathleen wondered.

Sam Seigalman shrugged. "Not much really. The strike will go on. These are just the leaders and it hurts us a bit, but the strike's bigger than them. Bigger than anybody. It's got a life of its own now. They might jail hundreds of us and it won't matter. There'll be others who just step in and take their place."

Kathleen looked at him inquiringly. "The Committee of One Thousand must have thought of that."

It was Al who nodded his head in response. "You're right—they have. And that's why things will happen real quick now."

"What do you mean?"

"The Committee of One Thousand has decided to push the strike to an end." Al looked grim. "They have everything in place, it's just a question of getting the timing down and the place. It can't be avoided. Positions have been staked out now and neither side will back away. We can't afford to and the bosses won't. But that's alright. It was always going to come down to this."

Seigalman reminded them, "There's a call for a mass rally tomorrow at Portage and Main. It's to protest against the arrests. We'll have to be careful. There's talk of tryin' to bait the new cops into arresting a whole bunch. Tyin' up the legal system with an overload of cases."

Kathleen said, "You know, there really wasn't a reason to arrest Bray or Bill Ford. These are warnings. By arresting Bray, they want to get at the vets and keep them in line. Same idea with Bill. Arrest him and maybe *The Western Labour News* will shut up. They want to close us up."

Seigalman added, "Ottawa's jumped into it too. They're passing an amendment. Conviction for sedition is being raised from two to twenty years. They're setting it all up. They're getting ready."

Kathleen looked at Sam. "I don't understand why they're starting to push back so hard now. Most services have been returned. Milk, bread, ice—it's at least being delivered on an irregular basis. Really, it's just the streetcars that are still down."

Al offered an explanation. "Because now they feel they can win. The arrests have given them confidence they can push us around. With Russell and the others not participating, it's the moderates like Wes Whitmore who are the new leaders. And moderates aren't good in strikes. They give in too easily. But watch out, don't kid yourselves. The Committee of a Thousand wants blood from us. They intend to get it and they will."

Seigalman nodded in support. "Yeah, Ross's talking about proclamations again. No parades. Ketchen will use that against us. The parade tomorrow's supposed to be silent. That's how we're trying to get around Ross's law, but how do you keep ten or twenty-thousand people quiet?" Sam paused and thought this over for a moment. "No, there'll be trouble. It'll happen. For sure."

Kathleen picked up a sheet of clean paper and loaded it into her typewriter. She began to write her next column as a warning to strikers. She titled it: Truth and Justice Victims of the Strike.

***

During the afternoon of Friday, June 20, Earle killed Mary Jablinka. It had been so easy—too easy really. She barely made a sound. Didn't put up much of a struggle even. She didn't even know it was him.

Hours after he'd left, Earle had obtained a taxi and returned to 614 Home Street. He knew the routine of the house well now. Mary would be alone. Friday was always busy for Mary. It was on this day that she did laundry for the tenants. Beds stripped, fresh-laundered sheets and pillow cases, towels and face cloths were changed. Mary did a quick dusting and wipe-down of the rooms.

After these chores were done came the afternoon laundry, which took up several hours. Hand-washing sheets and towels on a glass and wood scrub board was a tiresome task. Handwringing the washing and then out on the backyard line if it was a nice day.

When Earle stepped out of the taxi and made his way round the back of the house, the laundry was white and gleaming, dancing and snapping in the warm breeze. He used the back steps to enter the house, opening the door gently and closing it noiselessly. He stepped from the kitchen to the hallway and to the tiny laundry room. Mary used a small pail to empty the contents of the galvanized square washtubs. She lifted the full pail and poured it into the laundry sink. It was slow and painstaking.

Earle crept to his room. He removed his hat, jacket, and tie and placed them carefully over the back of the single chair in his room. From his desk drawer he retrieved a leather belt. He looped this round and round his left fingers, then closed his hand upon it. No blood—blood meant lots of cleaning up. He opened the door and moved back to the hallway and on to the laundry room.

Mary Jablinka was emptying the final pails of water from the rinse tub. She'd already finished the first tub, wiped it clean, and stacked it behind the door. There wouldn't be much for Earle to do later—finish cleaning the second tub and take in the clean laundry.

When he wrapped the belt around her neck from behind, she gasped and reached with both hands as he knew she would. She wanted to turn her head to look, but in the vice-like grip she could not. When he lifted her so that her toes danced lightly on the floor, she was completely helpless. He held her up like that for a long time. Finally he jammed her face-first against the wall so that he had better leverage and because his arms were tired. He held her perched like that, arms at her sides, for several more minutes until he was certain she no longer could be alive. When he let go, she dropped to the floor in a heap.

Earle removed the belt and set it aside on the shelf. He checked Mary for signs of life. Satisfied, he dragged her by the wrists, out of the room, down the hallway, and into her own bedroom. He hauled her to the bed and pushed her underneath it. He tucked her back against the wall and positioned the bedspread so it was just inches off the floor.

He closed the bedroom door and returned to the laundry room, where he drained off the remainder of the tub, wiped it dry, and placed it with the other. He took a laundry basket and went outside. Everything seemed close to dry—didn't take long in this wind. He removed each item and folded it carefully before placing it into the hamper. He set the pins into a small basket attached to the step. He was unhurried and casual, humming to himself as he worked to help out the landlady.

When he'd returned the clean items to the laundry room, Earle went back to Mary Jablinka's room for a detailed inspection. Very carefully and deliberately he went through the drawers of the sideboard. He pulled it out from the wall and checked behind it. He felt along beneath the drawers.

He opened the beautiful music box on top of the dresser and smiled when it gave a little tinkle of sound. He removed several pieces of jewelry and pocketed them. Most of it was junk and costume jewelry. There was one ring with a small diamond set in it.

But there had to be cash somewhere. Mary Jablinka was one of those old-fashioned, old world types. He would be surprised if she even used a bank. Even if she did, that meant nothing. She kept a store of cash on hand somewhere.

He went to the built-in closet, the only one of its type in the house. On the top shelf he spied it. A small, square white case finished with genuine leather and with a small handle on top. Earle took this back to his own room. It had a small, flimsy lock which he snapped open easily with the knife he retrieved from under his mattress.

When he opened it he found a red silk lining covering the box and the lid. The box was stuffed full of papers: letters, electricity bills, a few bonds, a will. All these he set aside. When he had the box empty, he looked at it more carefully. He measured the outside of it with a span of his hands from thumb tip to middle-finger tip. He knew he could span at least nine inches with his hand, so the outside of the box was at least ten inches deep. When he spanned the inside it was only eight inches. He grinned broadly. God bless you, Mary Jablinka—a false bottom! He tugged gently at a corner of the bottom and it lifted away.

Here it was then. He lifted the stash of money from the case. Only after he'd replaced the bottom and the papers and returned the case to its proper place did he go back and count the money. Over eight-hundred dollars! Very good, Mary. She'd been thrifty; frugal even. Her mistrust of the banks had paid off nicely. Earle pocketed the money.

This intense day had made him tired. He lay back on his bed, stretched mightily, and yawned. He closed his eyes and Hawkshaw popped into his mind. He must really find him—and soon. Anna Williams ran across the screen of his brain. He must deal with Anna. She could not be allowed to stand in the way. Her work was dangerous. So very dangerous.

He grew drowsy. Auntie Lillian visited him. She held a copy of the Good Book. She opened it and beckoned to him. *What does it mean Earley? What does it mean?* He slept.

***

When Anna returned to the lab the mice were all dead. This threw her into such a frenzy of work that she forgot completely about Hawkshaw and Roger Wilson.

But now she needed a new starting point and where to begin? She possibly could get McAlister and Johnstone working on proteins and carbohydrates, but she would need Parkes on side for that to happen. She could work on acids. There had to be some substance and it could be an acid that enabled transformation of the influenza cell. Allowed it to move from being non-husked to becoming husked. This was amazing! It was an actual changing of a life form, possibly at its most basic level. And if this was indeed the case, then it had to be something that was happening at the genetic level.

But the mice had been alive as little as twelve hours previous. Was it possible? Could the cells have changed in such a short time? Anna could not dispute what her eyes and brain were telling her. If the virus had killed the mice this quickly, then no wonder some human victims perished so readily.

When she arrived, Harold had already prepared samples he'd retained from the mice while they lived. Anna peered into her microscope. What was it that must be happening at the cellular level to allow this transition? Was it some sort of strange hybridization at work? *The neuraminidase was busy breaking up the sialic acid on the surface of healthy cells. It was through this breaking-up process that the flu cell was allowed access to the healthy cell and it was in here that the transforming agent worked. If the neuraminidase stopped slicing up the sialic acid, it would prevent the entry of the change agent into a healthy cell. The cell's own protection system would trap the flu cell and either destroy it or at least render it harmless.*

Anna had Harold set new experiments with the mice. As in her previous test, she injected one group with the combination of living non-husked bacilli and dead husked bacilli. If everything held true, this group would be dead. It was at this point that she decided to attempt something new. She injected another group of mice with the deadly strain of pneumococci developed in the lab.

She then took the combination non-husked living and husked dead and heated them until all the pneumococci were dead. She injected the new serum into the ill mice. As she set these experiments aside she went on to perform several others, including some with the little known and much ignored deoxyribonucleic acid that had been isolated at least sixty years ago.

She was deep into one of these experiments when something nudged the memory function in her brain. She swept it away as she would a spider's line on a walking path. Five minutes later it returned and crept across her mind with little pinprick sensations. She looked up from the microscope as if to pay more attention to the sharp needles marching across the folded matter of her brain.

That Hawkins person! She was supposed to meet him! She glanced at the clock. Two P.M. already—they were supposed to meet at noon.

Anna grabbed her coat and headed towards the door. When she was on the sidewalk she headed south, looking about for him. She would have walked right by if he hadn't put out a hand to restrain her.

My goodness! What a transformation was Anna's first thought. Hawkshaw was cleaned up. Or at least what passed for it. A game attempt at shaving had left a few bloodspots on the lower part of his neck. And he hadn't got all the whiskers; a few straggling clumps had escaped and held fast up beside the ears.

His pants were almost clean as was the shirt. Why, he must even have taken a bath, for the most noticeable thing was the absence of the smell. Now his shiny new shoes did not stand out nearly as much.

Anna remarked, "Why Mr. Hawkshaw, I'd never have recognized you! You look so different when you're so...clean."

Hawkins grinned from ear to ear. "Part of my new disguise. Earley'll be lookin' for the old Hawkshaw. That's how he always saw me. He never see'd the cleaned up me. I don't think he'd know who I was long as I kept my mouth shut."

"I'm sorry I'm late. I was working very hard and didn't even notice—"

"S'alright. We need to talk, like I said." Hawkshaw looked about, checking every person within his view. "But not out here. Too dangerous. We got to go somewhere's else. You choose. That way you'll know that you're safe."

Anna smiled slightly. She did not in the least feel endangered by this man. "Alright, let's go to the café just across from my workplace. It's one of the few still open. It's public, but we can probably get a quiet booth. You look like you could use a meal. I'll buy."

Hawkshaw fell into step with her. He continually looked about as they moved toward the restaurant. Once he stopped abruptly and peered at a figure down the block standing beneath a store canopy. This caused Anna to stop and stare also. Satisfied, they moved on and crossed the street to the bar and grille.

***

When Al Devons sat in on the meeting of the Committee of One Thousand to make his report, a new person was in attendance. The editor from *The Winnipeg Telegram* had never before attended any meeting when Al had been present. Like all the dailies, the ownership of *The Telegram* was in the hands of a staunch free enterpriser. The morning's edition of the paper was filled with front-page news that decried the demands of the strike committee and supported the position of the RNWMP and the newly installed city police.

The RNWMP were upset about being tagged with the moniker of yellow dogs. They had been given orders to clear the streets if any attempt was made at marching or parading. Even gathering in groups was considered out of the question. The soldiers who supported the strikers' efforts were just as determined that the silent march would go forward.

Devons decided to start the report with the news that would be the most galling. He stood up and looked around at the assemblage, ran his fingers through his blond hair, and rapped his knuckles on the table. "Okay, so now you have your answer. The strike will not be shut down just because the authorities are arresting the leaders and threatening retaliation. In fact, you've made things worse. Now there have been more resolutions passed. One requires that the attempts to run the streetcars cease within twenty-four hours. The other is that the Committee of One Thousand gets out of the Board of Trade Building. Also a twenty-four hour deadline."

"The strike committee can go to hell," barked Julius Archibald, who sat and glared around the table as if to challenge others to disagree.

It was Commissioner Stone who took up the challenge. "We're at a critical point here. Obviously things are coming to a head, but we need to handle this properly or people are going to get hurt or even killed. That's not what we want! We need to end the strike. But not at any cost, Mr. Archibald. We'll control any marches or parades. What we don't need is you or the specials in there stirring things up. Ketchen's not happy about this either. He wants to use regular enlisted men and the Mounted Police. Together we can take care of it."

Thomas Bulgar stepped into it. "Commissioner Stone, the 'specials' as you call them are the city police now. They've been duly hired to protect the city and its citizens. They have to be on the scene."

Stone's face was grim. "You can call them what you want—they're a bunch of thugs. Most of them are incompetent. Without the strike, only a very few of them would ever be accepted into the police force. The whole lot should be dismissed out of hand."

Charles Ross held up a hand to silence the man. "Now hold on. Bulgar is right. No matter what you or anybody thinks, Commissioner, the specials are now regular police and they have a part to play here."

Al brought the attention back to him. "If you use the specials in this, there's going to be a goddamn riot. Don't fool yourselves. This isn't a time to make stupid mistakes. The strikers can put up with the presence of the RNWMP and even with Ketchen's soldiers, but using specials on them is just a provocation. Unless of course, that's your intention."

Julius Archibald curled a lip at Al Devons and glared across the table. "Sometimes I wonder exactly whose side you're on here. You're supposed to be working for us, but you sound to me like one of them. We pay you a good salary but it always seems like you're feeding us a line of shit. Union shit! Do you really think this is about this strike? Goddamnit man, this is about future strikes and about future negotiations. We have to smash this union business forever. And if that takes strikers dying, then I for one am willing to pay that kind of a price!"

Al looked at him, disgusted. "What makes you think it'll just be strikers, Archibald? Seems to me like you're the one who doesn't understand. You could kill a hundred strikers and it won't make a speck of fly shit of a difference to anything. A year from now, two years from now, hell ten years from now you men or your successors will sit down and bargain collectively, but you're too damn shortsighted to see that. In fact, your pushing them into a fight won't slow that down—it'll speed it up."

No one responded. All looked around at each other. E.K. Atwater, Bulgar, Stone, and the news editor Simcoe had decided the strike would end the way they wanted it to. Nothing less.

Al cleared his throat and continued. "As for that salary you pay me, Archibald. You can take it and stuff it in your ass. I don't need it and I sure as hell don't want it. You're spoilin' for a fight and you're not going to let it go until you get one. Well, you will. Put the specials on the street and you'll get what you're looking for. And I hope they kick your ass good and proper."

Al picked up his hat from the table and covered his blond hair. He pushed back his chair and stalked out. He was smiling, happy in the fact that he'd done a good job for the American Communist Party. There'd be a fight just like they'd wanted. It was the only way a revolution could happen. Bloodshed is what it took and Al Devons would be there to help it along.

It wouldn't be long now. He should see Kathleen and explain some things to her. Make sure she stayed off the streets and out of harm's way. Maybe he owed her an apology, but he'd come here with a job to do and he'd done it.

In the history of the class system, nothing had ever changed without resorting to violence. There had not been a single time since humans first walked upon the planet where a revolutionary struggle had been won without lives being lost.

It had been Al's job to see that the Citizen's Committee of One Thousand was pushed to action and thanks to Julius Archibald he'd succeeded. There were always the Archibalds. All agents like Al had to do was find them and promote and provoke their squinty-eyed view of the way things would be. Soon the tension would boil over, the war would erupt, and his people would be ready to step in and fill the gap.

*　*　*

When Anna returned to her lab experiments, she didn't know what to deal with first. The set of mice injected with the combination formula were dead, as expected. The virus was particularly powerful and had worked its way through their systems with astounding speed. The genetic adaptation—if it was indeed that—had been worked with such rapidity as to be unbelievable.

The second set of mice, injected with the dead virus, was alive and healthy. She had drawn blood samples and sent them with Harold for preparation. She was waiting for him to centrifuge them.

And what of this Hawkins/Hawkshaw fellow? If what he'd told her was true, then the monstrosity who called himself Roger Wilson was a dangerous predator: a homicidal mind which could not be left to chance.

At first Anna had urged Hawkshaw to go to the police with his information. Surely they would listen and act. He had only grinned at her naiveté. He pointed out the obvious. There were no police—not any real ones at any rate. Of course, the entire force had been dismissed and only this group of untrained amateurs was present.

"You could go to the Mounted Police with this. They'd be able to do something."

Hawkshaw's feet hadn't stopped, even though he'd been sitting in the booth across from Anna for well over an hour. "Can't," he whined, "I helped Earle I tole you. Helped him put those two guys inna river."

She nodded. "And if you told them that you'd be charged." Anna had no reason to doubt this man's story, but still it all seemed so unreal. So crazy.

She realized now why Hawkins had come to her: there was nobody else. He couldn't hide from Roger Wilson forever. Sooner or later the man would find him. It was inevitable. The only way Hawkshaw could be certain of his own safety was to make sure Roger was in jail or dead. And he hoped Anna would be able to do that for him. The frightened little man was grasping at straws.

So it wasn't about protecting Anna, although he'd given her the warning to not let "Earley pick ya up".

"Anyways," he continued, "with all this strike stuff goin' on, no police 're gonna take the time or the word of someone like me. They got bigger an' more important things to do. If another tramp from tent city dies it's nothin' to them. They bin tryin' to clean that place out anyways."

She could see his point. Hawkins would make a poor witness and an even worse informant. Even if he was believed, that was no guarantee they'd catch Roger or even bother to try. Anna thought back to the day when she, Mary Jablinka, and Stavros had forced Al Devons to relinquish his hold on Roger's throat. If only they'd just let things alone.

Al Devons! That's who she needed to talk to about all this.

Harold interrupted her thoughts when he delivered the prepared samples from the mice. She slid one of them under the microscope, turned on the light, and peered through the lens. There it was! The immunity booster had created a highly efficient response. Both the non-husked and husked bacilli had been destroyed. The mouse trachea with its thousands of epithelial cells was healthy and robust. Anna could combat the flu even if she didn't know the precise details of how and why. She looked away from the microscope, stunned beyond belief. She could do it. She had done it! Parkes and Pownall needed to know about this and right away. Clinical trials had to begin.

She slid from her working stool after making several notations in her research log. She had to see Parkes. She glanced at the clock: quitting time. If he'd returned to work, no one had told her. She headed down the hallway toward his office. She gave a sharp rap on the door.

"He's not here." It was McAlister, behind her. "Still hasn't been in. Nobody knows when, or if he'll be back. Connors hasn't been able to reach him. The work's piling up. Back orders aren't arriving. I know he's grieving, and I don't want to sound callous," he was putting on his coat, preparing to leave for the day, "but really, we need him here. I wish he'd get back to work. Good night, Anna."

There was a complete contrasting silence with McAlister having stepped out. It was strange; Anna had never noticed before how quiet it was in the lab. She did something she couldn't recall ever doing before: she followed McAlister's footsteps out and snapped the lock shut on the door.

Anna returned to the lab. What was she to do now? She needed Parkes here. She could tell McAlister and Johnstone, but that would gain her little. Perhaps worse than little. She was not popular with her male colleagues and she knew it. McAlister tolerated her, but Johnstone was worse. For no apparent reason he hated her. Anna could feel it. If he could, she knew that he'd get rid of her. They had no reason to cooperate. None.

It had to come from Parkes. When he saw her results, he could order them to the research. They'd need to get volunteers. There'd have to be a control group. They'd have to run a series of concurrent trials to triple-check the results. There was no time to waste. Anna found herself growing weary, then slightly frustrated, and finally it turned into full-blown fury. Damn them! Why the hell did it have to be like this? Why couldn't they just accept that she was a good researcher? Gifted even! And where the hell was Stanley? Damn him and his goddamn selfish grieving! And damn Millie for dying now! And those damn kids; they could... The image of Andrew popped into her mind.

Andrew. Lying there with blood and mucus pouring from him. With his splotched skin a darkening hue of black. With his lungs filling up and his restricted breathing causing his chest to rise and fall with each struggle.

She didn't have weeks or months. She didn't have time for Stanley to return, or to work to coerce her colleagues to get them on her side. There was no time. No time.

She slid open a drawer on the right side of her table where she kept a considerable number of vials and dispensers. She removed a small box and from the box a syringe.

She pushed her sleeve up and exposed the muscle of her upper arm, above the elbow. Next she obtained a sample of the combination husked and non-husked vaccine. She heated it and slid it under the microscope to double-check that all the viral cells had died. She transferred the mixture into the syringe. There was no other way; she had to know, had to believe that she was correct. That she could kill this virus. She inserted the tip of the syringe and pushed the plunger.

She felt tired. Very, very tired. All she wanted was to go home and sleep. Sleep for days if she could. She turned out the lab lights, retrieved her coat, and headed to the door. That was when she remembered Hawkshaw. Anna stood at the door for a moment. She turned and went into Stanley Parkes's office. He had a window that looked out onto the front street. She could see across Fort and to the bar and grille. She gazed about carefully and was about to turn away when she spotted him. It was Roger Wilson alright, but with different clothing and there was no cab in sight.

Anna left the office and went back into the lobby. She double-checked the lock on the door. No lobby lights on. The window curtains were pulled. No one could see in. She went over to the small couch in the waiting room and sat down gingerly, then carefully lay down full length. She covered herself with her coat and brought the collar up around her neck. She was so tired. She closed her eyes and drifted off.

PART III
June 1919

CHAPTER SIXTEEN

Travellers Pledge Support

That this Grand Council representing the Commercial Travelling men of the three western provinces of Manitoba, Saskatchewan, and Alberta are fully impressed with the importance and significance of the labour trouble recently developed in Western Canadian cities. And particularly in the City of Winnipeg and realize that the situation has now developed until it is a matter of Dominion-wide concern. The principle of the workers using the strike weapon in their own defense is generally conceded, but the issues related to the Winnipeg situation threaten the life of the state and the stability of our representative institutions. We respectfully urge that the federal government immediately make power to denaturalize all undesirable naturalized aliens and to deport every undesirable other than Canadian born who advocates the overthrow of constituted authority in Canada. And we further pledge our support to the authorities in maintaining law and order in every part of Canada, so that this country may surmount the trying circumstances brought about by the Great War with fortitude—in order that we may return to normal conditions at the earliest possible moment.

Winnipeg Telegram

June 1919

Characterizing the Influenza Disease

Occasionally it is advised to have a patient roentgenographed. Leukopenia should be carefully observed as transient albuminuria is frequent in influenza patients. New measurements through urine analysis and through Wasserman reaction allow the tracking of antibodies. Such tracking indicates the presence of foreign bodies which can then be excised through treatment. It is through a dedication to action based on knowledge that the presence of the deadly bacillus can be annihilated.

The culprit for this infection lies in germ theory. Sputum studies, blood cultures, and urine examinations should be made mandatory. Pneumococcus, staphylococcus, streptococcus, and bacillus influenza must be sought out and eradicated, for upon them rides a host of ills which threatens our existence.

The scourge of the agent causing influenza must be exposed and isolated. It is only in such an unveiling of the mystery of this disease, this microbial world of infection, that we can combat the intransigent force and render it useless and therefore harmless.

Pandemics must never be allowed to go unchallenged. If our thinking on this remains limited and short of optimal then our very survival as a species becomes compromised. Such a virus is parasitic and like all parasites can be identified, measured, treated, and destroyed.

We need to unravel the causes of this disease so that our ultimate goal of extinguishment becomes achievable. It is in our genuine interests as thinking humans to disallow extraneous bodies into our systems. It is only through such vigilant processes that we can triumph over such threats to our health and be restored to our previous status.

Medical/Scientific/Social Perceptions of Influenza

1918/1919 Pandemic Responses

***

The silent parade was scheduled for Saturday, June 21. When Charles Ross arose that morning, he had a sick, empty feeling in his stomach. He was unwell and had felt so for some weeks now. At first he put it down to the general strike and the stress of the ongoing debate surrounding it.

The labour councillors at city hall were a group of bulldogs. Stuart and Simpson were especially problematic. Anything that they perceived as anti-labour or anti-strike turned into a major harangue by one or both of them. At the last meeting, council was to vote for a 75,000 dollar special allotment to pay the new police force.

Stuart and Simpson prolonged the meeting well into the night with a filibuster that reduced the local political government to an act of folly. Tempers flared on all sides, with Fowler firing back volleys against the strikers and labour leaders. Charles had been afraid that the meeting would itself turn into a riot.

When Stuart called the specials an imitation police force, Sparling was vehement in his reaction. He denounced Stuart and Simpson and even Mayor Ross for insulting the police this way. These were men who'd fought bravely for King and Country. Sparling shouted that they deserved better than to be called names by a couple of labour's bitch pups.

Finally, Charles had had to entertain a motion to adjourn the meeting with very little business having been accomplished. Damn strike. Giving him ulcers, perhaps worse.

When he walked into the Royal Alexandra at 10:00 A.M. he was still not feeling very healthy and was anxious about the wisdom of even holding the get-together. But Senator Robinson had insisted upon it. Apparently, they must try one more time to meet with labour leaders to attempt a resolution. Why, thought Charles? What could it possibly accomplish except more disquiet, more threats? When he entered the meeting room, he was greeted by Commissioner Stone, Andrews, the city's lawyer, and Deputy Minister of Justice Keith Kennedy. The Senator had pulled in some of the influential power wielders.

The meeting room had a huge table with at least fifteen large wooden chairs. Someone had had the foresight to order coffee and snacks, though Ross didn't feel that his stomach could tolerate either.

Across the table were some new faces Charles didn't recognize: members of the soldier-strikers. Since the arrest and jailing of the labour leaders, this new cohort had risen to fill the gap and now had to be dealt with—but how? Charles was disconcerted to see Al Devons sitting with them. What on earth could he have to do with this?

Senator Robinson opened the meeting. "Alright gentlemen, we all know why we are here. We're going into our sixth week of this situation and it needs to come to an end. You all know our position. We think we understand yours, but we feel like we're approaching a period of trouble. Things are getting somewhat out of hand. The strike committee no longer seems to have the hold it did on the strikers. We're having many incidents of threats and intimidation. Women and children are not safe to walk on the streets. What will it take to end this?"

For a long time there was silence in the room. A gentle voice from a soft-spoken veteran soldier finally responded. "Well Senator, I guess the strike itself is easy enough to end. You all know our demands. They aren't particularly onerous. They never were. We still need the owners to agree to our original conditions. They have to recognize and bargain with the unions. They have to accept the trades' councils as legitimate. All strikers get to go back to work. No exceptions."

Keith Kennedy interjected, "That's easy to say, but I think we're well past any of that happening, don't you?"

The soft voice answered, "You should not make the mistake of thinking that because you've jailed the strike leaders you've broken our backs. You may be talking to different people now but the demands have not changed or gone away. We're ready to return to work, but only when our conditions are met."

Al Devons spoke up. "Mayor Ross, we need you to rescind your proclamation against marches and parades."

Ross knew this was coming. Had, in fact, prepared himself for it. Balefully he shook his head. "No, there can be no such thing. We've been more than patient about this strike but now the decisions have been made. There can be no parades, silent or otherwise, and if it happens it will be dealt with directly and forcefully if necessary." Ross felt his stomach lurch involuntarily as he said this.

Again the soft voice, "You should not make the mistake of thinking we will respond to threats, Mr. Mayor. The people you see before you are all veteran soldiers. All saw action in France in the Great War. You should understand that threats cannot frighten us, nor can your imitation police force, nor the RNWMP, nor the soldiers under Ketchen's command. We see your plan for what it is: a heavy-handed attempt to break the strike by force. You should not underestimate us, Mayor Ross. Six weeks of strikes are nothing. We are prepared to go on for six more if necessary—or six months."

A man sitting beside Al Devons insisted, "Take the streetcars off the streets. You've got many of them back to work. Too many of them! They're the cause of a lot of the anger out there."

Again Ross shook his head resolutely, though he was not feeling so inside. "We will not. The streetcars, insofar as we can do so, will continue to run. The city needs them. They will run whether the strike committee says so or not."

Al Devons interjected again. "Then you provoke us deliberately." He leaned forward in his chair, touched the coffee cup in front of him, and ran a fingertip thoughtfully around the rim. "You have no intention of ending the strike by negotiation. This whole meeting is a sham, a ploy to get us together in the same room. Do you have police outside waiting to arrest us?"

Robinson shook his head vehemently. "No! Not at all! We come here in good faith. We want to negotiate. But you also need to understand that the strike is hurting the economy, and not just locally. The government can't just let things go on as they are. This strike has to end, and soon!" The senator sat back, realizing he'd spoken in an almost pleading tone. He could feel the redness creeping up his neck and into his face.

"The parade will go ahead as scheduled, Senator. As you can see from the Mayor's response, we have little hope of the city or the Citizen's Committee of One Thousand becoming more responsive to us. From the start, they've tried to turn the strike into a revolution. They've tried to turn it to violence so they could undermine everything. They want to turn the dogs loose on us. To destroy us if possible. They're bent on destruction."

Ross shook his head. "Not so! I've tried everything to settle this peacefully, but the strikers won't see reason. We don't believe it's the majority of strikers. It's the Bolsheviks. They're running the show and they're not going to accept negotiations. They want it all: to overthrow democracy and defeat the government. We won't let that happen, not under any circumstances. If you parade, there'll be consequences. We'll try to stop you peacefully." Ross could feel the acid in his stomach eating away. "But don't be under any illusions. We'll take whatever measures we have to."

The soft voice said, "We're all too aware of that. You've made it clear with the arrests that happened this past week. No doubt there will be more. But there won't be more without a fight. You should not think that we are without the means to defend ourselves. We do not recognize that the specials have any authority over us just because the city has hired them, Mayor Ross. And you, Commissioner, should not mistake our avoidance of conflict with the RNWMP as acquiescence. If you turn them loose on us, we can and will mount an appropriate response. The same thing goes for Ketchen's armed forces. We're well aware of their access to rifles and machineguns, but we've faced those things before and doubtless will face them again.

We don't want this kind of conflict, but neither will we run from it." His voice dropped even lower and Charles saw that Kennedy and Stone were leaning closer to hear his words. He had engaged them. Charles allowed himself a slight smile—the youngster would make a damn fine politician one day. Charles himself was leaning, trying to catch the remainder of the soft words that spilled out like droplets of water just prior to the cloudburst.

"It seems that you cannot leave us to better ourselves. I saw men dying from gangrene poisoning during the war and that's what you people remind me of. First you wound us and then you begin to consume us. I wonder why it has to be like that? It must be some flaw in our thinking, I guess. Whatever it is, it makes it dangerous for everyone. Our children cannot grow and learn and achieve unless we can pull and tear every last bit of sustenance away from you. And you don't seem to believe that yours can aspire to their rightful places except by standing on our backs and shoulders.

A curious house it is that we've built. A house should be a kind of a living thing, I think. But ours is not. My father told me that the Bible says that a house divided against itself cannot stand. And I guess it's so.

We've failed our children, you see. All of us sitting around this table have. You have failed yours and we have failed ours. The sad irony is that it didn't have to be this way. We're actually a lot closer to being the same than we are to being different, but we can't acknowledge it. What is it that we all want when we really look at it closely? Safety, warmth, full bellies, homes, family—the right to as good a life as our children can possibly have. That's what I want. That's what every person on this side of the table wants. The really strange thing is that you desire the very same things for your children.

But here's the difference. This morning we all on this side of the table walked to get to this meeting to demand these things of you. And you all drove your bright shiny cars to this same meeting to deny us and our children the very things you have. And to keep us from getting them, you're obligated to destroy us. You don't have a choice. You think you do, but you really don't. To live, you must kill us just as surely as we must kill other things so that we and our children might live."

Deep in his bowels, Charles Ross felt a roiling and a turning over. His acrid stomach was threatening to revolt. Somewhere deep in the churn of his thinking, the butter paddle agitated the arcane and unfathomable truth that it was all a futile struggle leading to nothing.

***

Kathleen was still in a furious state when she went into the street at 1 P.M. on June 21. She could feel the electricity in the air. She was on her way downtown with her new publication prior to the silent march scheduled for the afternoon. This would become the basis for a feature article on how the state subjugated the press during the strike.

At least it would become the basis of the story if and when *The Western Labour News* could publish again. Earlier in the morning, Kathleen had opened her mail to discover a letter from the Justice Department. Even now, hours later, she was still shaking from its effects. She'd had to read it three times as she tried to grasp the implications.

Winnipeg, June 21, 1919

Gentlemen,

Certain articles of *The Winnipeg Western Labour News Special Strike Edition* have contained objectionable matter that is seditious, inflammatory, and inciting to riot and this publication must be discontinued. No more issues of this publication must be printed or circulated.

Alfred J. Andrews

Agent, Department of Justice

They were trying to shut them down! No warning, nothing. Just a blatant order to close the presses. No fair play about this. No indication that this was coming. How, in a democracy with such deep British roots, could it happen that anyone could arbitrarily close the press? Obviously free speech had disappeared.

Bad enough that Bill Ford and the others had been arrested and imprisoned, but this! It was too much.

She'd summoned Sam Seigalman to her office to show him the letter. She was shaking with rage and brandishing the letter in her hand as she shouted, "They can't do this to us. It's illegal. Goddamn Andrews! Who the hell does he think he is? We need Murray in, Sam. He got the strike leaders out on bail. He must be able to do something about this piece of nonsense."

Seigalman rubbed his forehead and said unhappily, "I'll see him this morning and show it to him. But that's not the only thing that's happened. They arrested Woodsworth too."

"What?"

"Yeah, just an hour ago. He and Dixon were on their way to the McLaren Hotel. The new strike committee holds their meetings there. A couple of detectives stopped them. Had a warrant for J.S.'s arrest."

"But why? What's going on? Have they lost their minds?"

"It's just part of the strategy. First Bill and now Woodsworth. Once he took over as editor for us he was doomed. Anything that supports the strike will be suppressed. That includes us."

"But what about the silent march this afternoon?"

Sam shrugged. "Same thing. It's all a part of their plan to finish off the strike. Silence everyone and we cease to function. It's what the Committee of One Thousand wants. It's what Ross wants and now it's what the government is going to do."

Kathleen was silent for a moment as she took this in. They were at a crossroads, that much was clear. It was about the only thing that was clear in all this. She came to a decision.

"We can't just shut up and do nothing, Sam. We can't just give in and let these people walk on our graves. If the paper has to stop publication then we'll do it another way. This order doesn't say anything about broadsheets."

Sam Seigalman looked at her and cocked an eye. "You're going to publish a broadsheet?"

Kathleen smiled for the first time that day. "And distribute it—and not under the banner of *The Western Labour News!*" She picked up a clean sheet of paper and inserted it into her typewriter.

She rapped out the headline: The Latest Desperate Trick of Tyrants. The first paragraph was the letter that had been received from Andrews. The second was a condemnation of the arrest of J.S. Woodsworth. Then she went on.

> The illegal closing down of *The Western Labour News* is an infringement on the freedom of the press. We will not surrender this lightly. Even now, as these words are being written a

plan is being formulated by our legal department to combat this menace to free speech.

No doubt the Citizen's Committee of One
Thousand is behind this blatant attempt to
close the voice of the Labour Movement. We
will not be silenced.

Imagine the astonished looks on their faces
when they read this. Their curious and dreadful
attempt to quiet *The Western Labour News* has
not had the result they desired. They may have
closed one channel of truth, but many others
will open up just as one leak in a dam leads to
many more.

They can lock up Bill Ford and
J.S.Woodsworth, but they can't keep truth in
jail. It will out itself. These opponents of labour
will stop at nothing. It is clear that a plot has
risen to destroy the strike by any means. This, in
spite of the fact that the strikers have remained
peaceful and calm in the face of baiting by
the other side. These reprehensible tactics
on the part of the opposition only strengthen
our resolve.

Apparently, free speech has become verboten
in Winnipeg. Rest assured, that the meetings
held on the outskirts of the city have generated
huge attendances as well as cash deposits to
support the strike.

We must all continue to sacrifice so that the
weeks of strike will not be in vain. The eyes of

the labour world are upon Winnipeg to see how we will respond to this goading on the part of our enemies. Here's one way we can demonstrate that Winnipeg's Labour Movement can and will stand up for itself.

We must defend all who have been arrested. Our idea is to create a defense fund. Make no mistake: Andrews and the Manitoba Justice Department intend to prosecute and jail our leaders, even if they have to contrive a boatload of circumstantial evidence. The only crime that Russell, Heaps, Woodsworth, et.al. have committed is to dare to stand up to crushing oppression.

If you believe in fundamental British equality and justice (as we do), then you can do your part by supporting our efforts to free our comrades.

An account for this fund has been opened at the Home Bank of Canada. Cheques can be made payable to the fund or to Secretary James Law, Rm. 11 at the Labour Temple.

ON TO VICTORY!

Within half an hour, Kathleen had the article written. She marched from her office with it to the Bracken Publishing Company and contracted them to publish five-thousand copies. She requested the first run of 250 be ready by one P.M. She wrote a cheque on her own account to pay the costs.

***

Anna had been watching the clock endlessly. At 10 A.M. she checked herself for symptoms. She felt healthy. No headache, no side effects from the inoculation, her pulse was strong, and her breathing was normal. Was it possible that the serum was working, building antibodies, and preparing the body to wage a war against an invasion of flu virus?

Perhaps Stanley Parkes would come in to work today. Perhaps she'd have to share after all with McAlister and Johnstone. That would put her at great risk, however, in terms of her profession. What laboratory anywhere in the world would employ a bacteriologist who'd injected herself? And worse yet, it would make it exceedingly difficult for women to enter the field in the future. Her actions would be put down to typical female hysteria and she'd be used as a good example of why science and females could never be reconciled.

No, she couldn't tell the others. Parkes would have to know. They'd publish and of course he'd get the credit. Well, it wasn't like it hadn't happened before.

But before she did anything, she needed to go home, bathe, rest, and get a good meal and a change of clothes. She'd come back in the afternoon hoping to catch Stanley Parkes.

Before she stepped out, Anna again went to Parkes's office, peered past the curtain, and studied the street. No sign of Roger Wilson anywhere, but she did see Hawkins. If he was about waiting for her, then she was fairly confident that Wilson was nowhere around.

Fort Street was unusually busy for a Saturday morning and when she finally made her way through the traffic, Hawkshaw approached.

"He ain't aroun' here. I know that fer sure. But I lost 'im. Don't know where he is. I don't like that, missus."

"He waited for me last night, so I didn't come out. I stayed all night in the lab just to be safe."

Hawkshaw shuffled his feet back and forth and cast his eyes up and down the sidewalk. "He'll keep comin' back 'til he finds ya. Wish't I knew where he was. This ain't no good."

"Mr. Hawkins, I'm going to my apartment on Home Street. I'd greatly appreciate it if you'd escort me. I'll get a cab for us. I'd feel better if you were with me."

Hawkshaw looked at her. She thought he could protect her from Earle? Strange woman. He looked down at his new shiny shoes and nodded.

As soon as they pulled up in front of the house, Anna had a sense of foreboding. Something was not right. She insisted that Hawkshaw get out of the cab and accompany her. The curtains were closed – that was unusual – Mary always had the curtains open in the morning to let in the daylight. They bypassed the wide verandah steps that led up to the front door and opted to move alongside the house towards the backyard.

Hawkins was nervous and fidgety and Anna was starting to catch it from him. She reached out and grasped his arm to calm him before they entered the house. He looked at her helplessly and shrugged his skinny shoulders. His eyes were quite wide and for the first time Anna saw the wrinkles at the corners and noticed the silver in his day-old whiskers. He was older than she'd thought.

There was total silence in the house when she opened the door and entered. Hawkshaw stayed close to her back. He blinked several times as he let his eyes adjust to the darkened interior. Both stood for a long time, listening for any sound.

Nothing. It was a void. The kitchen sparkled with cleanliness. The dining room was in order. They crept down the hallway, looked into the laundry room. All was in order. Anna kept Hawkshaw close by as she checked her own room and any others that were not locked.

Anna was about to dismiss her fears and send Hawkins along when she decided to check Mary's room. She could see nothing out of order. The bed was made, bureau drawers were closed, the closet was shut. She made Hawkshaw check it to ensure no one was inside.

What was it that was bothering her? Something was not quite right. Though Anna had never been in this room, there was something odd, out of place maybe.

But no, it wasn't here. Somewhere else then. Silently Anna began to retrace her steps. She went to the kitchen and inspected it very carefully, then back to the dining room, but nothing there either.

She was back in the laundry room when it struck her. The laundry was in the basket. Mary would never go away without putting the laundry away in the cabinets where it belonged. The woman operated like a clock and her schedule was unchanging. Saturdays were Mary's best opportunity to clean. The tenants rarely were around. Ike Stavros would be at a weekend job, Al had not been around at all and very little seen of Roger Wilson since his emancipation from the landlady. Anna would be at work—always at work. Mary would clean in the morning and shop to replenish house stocks in the afternoon. And no matter how much her hands might have pained her, that laundry would have been put away. At any rate she should still be here, cleaning.

She was about to leave the room when she spied the belt. It lay curled like a snake on the shelf over the laundry tub. Anna had seen this shiny buckle before. Somewhere. She picked it off the shelf and let it unfurl from the buckle down. A large belt. A man's.

"It's Earley's." Hawkshaw speaking startled her. "I seen it before."

"But why is it in the laundry room instead of in his room?"

"Don't know." Hawkshaw shrugged. "He must've fergot it."

Anna looked at him. "He was in here. He put it down and then forgot about it." She lifted a set of keys off the wall beside the laundry door. "Go check Earle's room, Hawkshaw. It's up the stairs. First door on your right. It's probably locked and I doubt he's there, but be careful."

He took the keys from her and reluctantly ascended the stairs. At the top, he stopped and looked sorrowfully down at her. She waved her hand to motion him to go on.

She returned to Mary's room. Where could she have gone? Again Anna inspected the room carefully. Something still bothered her. Then she knew what it was. The bedspread. Whenever Mary changed Anna's bedding, she always changed the bedspread, and the bed was always made in a specific way. The sheets, both lower and upper, would be tucked carefully under the mattress. The upper part of the bed sheet would be turned down like a flap. Over this would go the pillow and blanket. Finally, the bedspread would be placed and always the same way. Mary would never leave a bedspread so close to the floor. It was always six inches from the edge to the floor. Anna was sure she could have measured it and found it to be exactly the same every time.

She advanced to the bed and dropped to one knee. She took up the spread in one hand and folded it back to rest on top of the bed. She bent down and peered into the dimly lit underside.

When she screamed, Hawkshaw nearly jumped through the ceiling. He crashed down the stairs, knife in hand. When he reached Mary's bedroom he saw Anna on her knees, frantically pulling at something under the bed as if trying to dislodge it. He looked around the room for Earle, gripping the hunting knife tightly and forcing himself not to turn and run. Anna continued desperately to claw at the thing under the bed until a hand, an arm, and a head emerged.

When Hawkshaw touched her shoulder, she screeched and struck out at him. He retreated and stared at her, then at the body of the dead woman. "Earley," he said. "It's Earley. We gotta get out'a here, missus. We gotta go."

Anna's hands covered her mouth. She physically forced herself to stop shrieking and to adopt a semblance of composure.

"Oh my God, Mary. I'm so sorry. You must have been so frightened! Oh God! Look at the marks on your neck! He must've..." Somewhere she'd dropped the belt. She thought back to the laundry room. That's why the belt was there. Anna sat back on her haunches and she let the tears flow. They ran down her cheeks and her chin and dropped onto her dress.

Hawkshaw was trying to help her up to get her to leave the room. He was clucking and whispering and soothing. He held that enormous knife in his hand. Anna looked at it in horror and allowed herself to be guided out of the bedroom and to the kitchen.

He placed Anna on a chair at the table and got her some water in a glass. He sat on a chair to her right and when she appeared to be able to listen, he said, "We can't stay here. He'll be lookin' fer me an' probly fer you too. That's why he's bin hangin' aroun' yer workplace at night. She bin dead fer awhile I think. If he was watchin' yer place las' night, then already he killed her. We ain't safe. We gotta do somethin'. Run away maybe."

Anna shook her head. "We can't run away. I can't anyway. But maybe you should. It'd be better for you to be away from the city. I can't. I have to stay here. I have to go back to my office. Something very important you see. I'll call the police—they'll arrest him."

Hawkshaw shook his head vigorously. "Uh-un! Not Earle. They won't find him. An' who knows when they'll even start lookin'. It's the strike, missus. They ain't got no time an' they ain't got no manpower. I tol' ya. This lady dyin' it's nothin' to them. An' Earle won't wait. He'll look 'til he finds us."

Anna took a drink of water, then another. She thought for a long time. "Still, we have to report it. We'll go back to my lab for now. It's the safest place. I'll telephone in to the police from there. I wish we could warn Al Devons and Ike, but I wouldn't even begin to know where to find either of them."

Hawkshaw could sit still no longer. He prowled about the kitchen, looking out the windows and scanning as far as he could see. He disappeared into the dining room and then emerged, looking more and more agitated.

Anna looked at him and nodded. "You're right of course. We can't stay here just waiting. We should go." She went to her own room and gathered a change of clothes, a towel, and some toiletries. She stuffed them into a cloth bag and grabbed her purse. She locked the door to Mary's room, although she didn't know why. Something told her that the poor woman would have liked some privacy.

CHAPTER SEVENTEEN

On Main Street across from city hall, a crowd was growing to prepare for the silent march. Charles Ross stood inside and looked out over the increasing thousands who plugged up the sidewalks and were beginning to choke off the traffic.

His sour stomach had grown more unruly with the arrival of the soldier-strikers, who began taking up positions on either side of the city building. When the new police chief had called earlier to inform him of the gathering, he left the meeting at the Royal Alexandra and headed to his office. In his heart though he knew that going to city hall to confront the strikers would be just as useless as the meeting had been. Forces beyond the mayor's control had been set in motion and it was well beyond his authority and his capacity to change the day's agenda.

Therefore he was not entirely surprised when he walked into city hall to find E.K. Atwater, Julius Archibald, and Thomas Bulgar awaiting him. He sighed and resigned himself to the bleak prospect of the next few hours.

When Julius Archibald opened his mouth to speak, Ross held up a hand and precluded him. "I know! I know! The proclamation has been ignored. The gathering is illegal. We'll deal with it."

For once, Julius snapped his mouth shut and said nothing. Charles thought that it was the only time that he'd been able to shut the man up.

Atwater said, "What will you do now?"

"What else can I do? I'll read them the riot act and try to get them to disperse. I'll order them off the streets—but they won't go."

Thomas Bulgar was obviously nervous. The sight of thousands of men lining the streets and so obviously willing to fight had been overwhelming to him.

"Perhaps they will," he offered hopefully. But when Ross stared at him, he looked away.

"You people have started something here for which others will end up paying. I hope that when the day's over there will be a lesson learned."

Archibald puffed. "Damn right there will be, Charles. And those bastards out there will be the ones learning it!"

Charles Ross turned on him and snarled. "You thickheaded ape, Julius. I'm tired of your damned bullying and shoving people around. You didn't hear a bloody thing Devons was trying to tell you, did you?" He could hear his voice rising and he squared himself around and leaned in toward Archibald. "Don't you understand what's happening here today? Can't you get it into that skull of yours? This is only the beginning! It's not the end of the strike, just the start! You can't see that there'll be more strikes. More problems. More walkouts. More anger and hatred. And it's not because of them." He pointed with his outstretched arm toward the ever-increasing crowd.

Charles could feel a growing vitriol. Julius Archibald was staring at him, open-mouthed. Ross's voice was growing very loud. Others around them were becoming attentive, listening.

"Things have to change, man! I have to change and you men have to as well!" He smiled ever so briefly. "Sure as hell you have to change, Julius. Oh, we'll put an end to this little demonstration today alright. But they'll be back—in a month or a year or two. And no doubt we'll repeat the whole damn exercise until finally somebody wakes up and sees that we're not living in the 1800s any longer and that for prosperity to happen it has to happen for everyone."

He stopped for a moment and stared at Atwater and Bulgar and Archibald in turn. His voice softened and he grinned a bittersweet smile. "Don't you realize what it is that you fear? The old way is dying and you're the ones going through the death throes. We'll win this little fight today, but we'll lose it in the future. Your children and your grandchildren, they'll look back on this and shake their heads in disbelief that we could have been so stupid."

The three stood and looked at him. Archibald was red in the face but remained silent. The staff and the press waited.

Charles said, "Now, if you gentlemen will excuse me, I have to go outside. I've some business to attend to."

When he stepped outside, Charles was taken aback at the crowd. Every available space was filled with a body. As far as he could look down each side of the street it was jam packed. But the thing that was most eerie, really haunting, was the total silence. Not a single word spoken, no vehicle sounds, no horses clopping loudly. When a flock of pigeons took air close by, it was shocking to be able to hear their wings beating on the air. He couldn't recall ever hearing the sound before. For minutes he stood on the marble steps and gazed about.

Then Charles reached inside the breast pocket of his jacket and extracted a sheet of paper. He unfolded it, then looked around again through the crowd. So many grim, silent faces.

He read, "Our Sovereign Lord the King chargeth and commandeth all persons being assembled, immediately to disperse themselves and peaceably to depart to their habitations, or to their lawful business, upon the pains contained in the act made in the first year of King George, for preventing tumults and riotous assemblies. God save the King!"

Not a sound. No jeers or boos or whistles. Not a person moved. The pigeons lifted again and flapped about over the heads of the assembly.

He folded up the paper and replaced it. He took out a second sheet. "I'm going to read you the proclamation that was printed in the newspapers, but I'm doing this as a reminder. You need to understand that this is a special warning. We will not go back on our decision that there are to be no parades."

He unfolded the new paper. For the first time, he noticed that his hands were shaking. He clutched the paper tightly.

"The Riot Act has been read and remains in full force and effect in Winnipeg.

Riotous assembly of crowds, riotous attack on persons or property, riotous damaging of property are indictable offences and all persons guilty of same are liable to imprisonment.

Assembling in crowds, congregating, and standing on the streets is dangerous and you do so at your own risk. Such a gathering is a direct challenge to constituted authority and will be promptly and vigorously suppressed and this proclamation strictly enforced.

Citizens—all lawlessness and intimidation must cease.

> Those of you who wish to return to your work can do so without fear of molestation and if you are in the slightest way interfered with or intimidated, notify at once the Mayor or Chief of Police and the offenders will be traced down by the Royal North West Mounted Police and the city police."

His voice faltered and cracked when he added, "If it takes years to do so." Charles could feel his mouth getting dry. Standing in front of and reading the proclamation to twenty thousand or more faces was not the same as having it published in the dailies. Perhaps this part was a mistake. Perhaps just the reading of the act would have been enough.

He tried to clear his throat and throw more emphasis into his voice.

> "Any foreigners who make any threats of any kind or in any way intimidate or worry would-be workers in the slightest degree can expect immediate deportation to Russia, or wherever you came from. We intend to purge the city of any lawless elements and prosecute to the full rigor of the law. On the other hand, all law-abiding citizens can feel free to go about their business in the full realization that British law will protect them to the limit. No further open-air meetings either, in parks, streets, or public places, will be permitted until further notice."

Charles's hands dropped down. They felt very heavy from holding up the paper. The acid reflux of his stomach battered like a nightstick on a victim's head.

He gazed over the silence and stillness. He finished the epistle in a low voice that didn't sound at all like his own. "Winnipeg, June 21, 1919. God save the King."

Later on, he would not remember for sure if it was at that precise moment that the devil paid his visit. Did he hear the shots then or was it later on? Was that the time when the first streetcar arrived or was that after a while? What possessed that streetcar driver to move into the crowd just then? Was the man mad?

Charles remembered the high-pitched squeal of the steel wheels on track. For a time it was the only thing anyone could hear. He remembered that suddenly he could not hear the pigeons anymore. He could see the streetcar off to his right. The driver was edging forward into the crowd.

That's when he remembered sensing the change in the crowd. He remembered thinking that he should go down there and order the driver to halt and to not move the car. He watched as the car crept along and the men began to surround it. Very slowly the car continued. It nuzzled the men away from the front of it. It thrust them aside as gently as a mother might move an ambling youngster out of her way.

What the hell was the man doing? Someone was going to be injured. He watched as, incredibly, the car moved its way along the tracks, down Main Street, and past Bannatyne. Moments later, a second car started up and began to move its way forward. What the hell? Had they planned this? It was deliberate provocation.

Charles was about to wade into the crowd and prevent the streetcar from further movement, but that's when the response began to assert itself. At first it was just a man crying out. Then it was a small group. Someone pitched an object through one of the windows. Three men ascended the roof of the car and yanked the electric pulley from the overhead grid, rendering the car useless. The crowd surged on each side of the streetcar and began to rock it back and forth. They pushed and pulled mightily, but the effort to overturn it failed. Frustrated, dozens of strikers boarded the car and began to tear apart the inside. The driver was cast into the street to fend for himself. Seats were ripped apart, windows smashed, and the crowd outside continued its vain attempt to throw the car over onto its side. From somewhere, a can of kerosene made its way onto the car. Someone began splashing the liquid about and others shouted to those inside to clear the car. When a lighted torch was thrown into the car, the crackling of spreading fire soon drowned out the surrounding shouting. The men closest to the car pushed and yelled at those behind to get back and make room. Black smoke billowed into the sky and flames roared up and down the inside of the car.

Charles was too late. He turned his back on the rising tumult, mounted the steps, and went inside. He glared at Atwater, Archibald, and Bulgar. "Well, Julius, looks like you're going to have your fight after all. Just remember at the end of the day that this is what you wanted."

He turned away and headed for his office. First he had to telephone Commissioner Stone and get the Royal North West Mounted Police into action. He knew that already they'd be at Portage Avenue and ready to go. Then he had to get down to Fort Osborne Barracks and sign the papers that would set Brigadier-General Ketchen and his troops to quell the riot and support the civil authority. The "specials" who had become the new city police force were already in the streets—armed and mounted. Charles Ross wondered whether or not, even with all this firepower the rioters could be contained. There were at least enough of them he thought to defeat his forces easily.

***

When Kathleen saw the numbers on the street it was mind-numbing. Her copies of her broadsheet were not even close to being enough. The 250 copies she carried with her were microscopic in proportion to the crowd, and even the 4,750 being printed could not make a dent. Still, she knew she had to try.

She had no hope that she would get anywhere close to Portage and Main, so she retreated to Fort Street, thinking it was just possible she'd see Al. This was where they'd listened to the speakers down at Broadway. Although there were many people on the street, she could move about at least and start delivering her broadsheet.

That's what she was doing when Anna Williams took her by the arm. "You're Miss Johns, aren't you? Mr. Devons's friend? Aren't you the reporter?"

Kathleen smiled at her. "Yes, but perhaps not for much longer, Doctor. It seems that the authorities have seen fit to close down *The Western Labour News*. Would you like one of these?" She proffered a copy to Anna, who took it but did not glance at it. Kathleen became aware of the nervous little man hopping from one foot to another behind Anna Williams.

"Oh, I'm sorry," Anna said. "Everything's so upside down right now. I need to talk to someone and there doesn't seem to be anybody..." Her voice trailed off. "I was hoping you'd be able to connect me with Al Devons. It's very, very important that I speak with him...it's about Roger Wilson."

Kathleen looked at her, confused. She glanced over Anna's shoulder at the man behind her, whose eyes were red, his grizzled beard bedraggled and patchy. He looked an unlikely companion for Dr. Williams.

"Who?" Kathleen asked.

"It's Earley," the little man said.

"I beg your pardon."

Anna explained. "The man I thought of as Roger Wilson. Apparently his real name is Earle Nelson and he..." Anna paused, looking frustrated and helpless. "Oh, this is going to take so much explaining, Miss Johns. I was hoping to see Al because, well you see, back at the boarding house one day he and Mr. Wilson... Mr. Nelson..." She stopped, totally frustrated. She stamped her foot on the sidewalk in anger and looked as if she might start to cry out of plain bafflement.

Kathleen reached out and took her forearm. "Whatever it is I'm sure it can be dealt with, Doctor. I think we better go into The Bar and Grille and you can fill me in. Obviously this is causing you a huge amount of distress."

Anna shook her head. "No not there. Too public. He might come in and see us. Is there someplace else? How about my office? It's right down the street. Much safer. And Mr. Hawkins should come with us. There's things he knows and can fill you in a bit more."

They retreated to the Versatile Medical Laboratory and ensconced themselves in Anna's office. Connors, the secretary, gave them an odd look when they passed by his desk but he said nothing.

It was Kathleen who closed the door and plunked herself down in a chair adjacent to Anna's desk. Hawkshaw stood on the other side, his feet in a constant shuffling motion. Kathleen gave it a few moments, then said, "Okay. Now tell me. What's all this Wilson/Nelson stuff?"

Between the two of them it took forty-five minutes to get out everything they knew. Hawkshaw filled in what he knew about the Earle Nelson of tent city while Anna told the story of Roger Wilson at Mary's boardinghouse. Kathleen listened in horror as both described the discovery of Mary Jablinka's body.

"My God!" she exclaimed. "The man has to be insane."

"Perhaps," Anna responded. Her hands had been working nervous patterns in her lap all the time she'd been revealing what she knew. "But nevertheless, we're in danger—I mean myself and Mr. Hawkins. You see now why I needed so badly to speak with Al Devons."

Kathleen nodded. She was thinking about Al's hands around the throat of Roger Wilson, choking the man's life away. And then she recalled those same hands upon her. So gentle, awakening and then arousing her. Her cheeks turned a slight pink when she realized Anna was looking at her curiously.

She said, "I agree with Mr. Hawkins. There's little point in going to the police with this right now, but at the same time we can't just leave your landlady there. After you two leave, I'll phone in the report of her body and have someone sent down there to investigate. There's little hope that we'll be able to find Al Devons today. Probably he's somewhere in this crowd downtown if he's still around at all, so that doesn't help us much."

Anna said, "I'm so sorry to bring you into this. That was never my intention. You could end up in danger also."

Kathleen gave a short laugh. "Dr. Williams, just getting up in the morning is dangerous for me right now. Just passing out those broadsheets I gave you is a danger. Believe me, this doesn't add a whole lot of danger to my life. I've already had death threats."

Anna looked at her in alarm, and Kathleen smiled to calm her. "It's just a part of the work I do. You can't take such things too seriously or you'd never get anything done. Now let's talk about what we should do next. Obviously you can't go back to your boardinghouse, Doctor, so you'll have to come stay with me." She stopped and became more aware of Hawkshaw standing off to one side. She gazed at him awhile before deciding. "You too, Mr. Hawkins. If you're at my place then we don't have to worry about Nelson finding you and forcing you to tell where Doctor Williams is located."

Kathleen's very practical mind took over and searched every avenue of possibility. Safety came first, then some way of dealing with this monster. Some plan, perhaps tomorrow or the next day, and they'd have a better chance of bringing Al into this.

Anna blurted, "But I have to be able to be here. The work I'm doing right now is important. More than that, it's critical. It has to do with the Spanish flu. I've been working on a vaccine and I have to—" Suddenly, she snapped her mouth shut, as if she'd already said too much.

There was momentary silence. Kathleen and Hawkshaw exchanged glances. They waited but Anna had retreated and volunteered nothing more about her work.

Finally, Kathleen said, "There's one thing I'm really curious about. You said that Nelson waited for you in the evenings to come out of work and would escort you home. Why do you think he was doing that?"

Anna was dumbfounded. "He said it was because it wasn't safe for me to be out at night so he would come fetch me home."

Again Kathleen and Hawkshaw met eyes and this time a glint of humor passed between. Anna saw this and looked confused, then realized the irony in what she'd said. "Oh, I see. I guess I was not very safe after all."

Kathleen smiled at her. "You're a very, very attractive woman Anna."

"What?"

"Quite pretty as a matter of fact." Kathleen looked from Anna to Hawkshaw. "Don't you think so, Mr. Hawkins?"

He nodded vigorously.

Anna looked at Kathleen. "I don't understand. I don't know what you mean. What an odd thing to say."

"That's the real reason." Kathleen ventured, "He's attracted to you."

Hawkshaw's hand came up and covered his mouth as he nodded his head in agreement. The rhythm of the shuffling of his feet notched up.

Anna's face turned a blaze of red. She felt frozen to her chair. She looked back and forth between the two of them and finally blurted, "That's preposterous. I never ever gave him any reason to think that I had any interest in—"

Kathleen shrugged. "He might be a monster, but he's also a man. He doesn't need a reason. You're attractive to him and he wants you."

***

Al Devons and Sam Seigalman watched as the remainder of the kerosene burned off inside the streetcar. Huge plumes of black smoke circled in the downtown air as numerous men moved, attempting again to topple the car.

Seigalman tapped Al on the shoulder and nodded his head toward events across the street. Al glanced up at the specials who were making their way towards them carrying bats and clubs.

Seigalman said, "Ya see that guy out front? The tall one in the Stetson wearin' that purple armband?"

Al nodded.

Seigalman went on, "He's one of the bastards was in the office the day they come in an' bust us up. I remember him 'cause he was swingin' that club about real good. Thought he was gonna take my head off."

Al said, "Ok. We'll give the son of a bitch some of his own and see how he likes it. Ya got your gun?" He felt for his own in the waistband of his pants. "Use it if you have to. Don't let yourself get hurt for nothing!"

The specials moved down the west side of Main Street. Periodically a group of them would stop and confront the crowd. Verbal accusations and denouncements could be heard. A special would reach into the crowd and prod a chest with the fat end of the club. The receiver would brush away the bat or grasp hold and wrestle with the man holding it.

Al and Sam calmly watched the specials moving towards them where they stood next to the smoldering, tilted streetcar.

"You men! You get back from that car. You've no right to be here. Get the hell back or by Christ we'll break your heads." When they were closer to the car, the strikers closed ranks around them and fists began to fly. A few specials went down when they became isolated from the larger group.

The Royal North West Mounted Police moved out on horses from their location on Portage Avenue and headed down Main towards the streetcar altercation. They moved slowly, pushing the crowd back as they maneuvered into a line and forced their way through in a plodding fashion.

"Get back! Move off the street!"

"Goddamn bastards. Sons of bitches!"

"Break it up! Get away! Move on!"

"We're not scared of you pricks."

Small missiles came hurling out of the crowd. One caught an officer in the cheek and split it wide open. He was thrown from his horse, but the other Mounted Police closed ranks and kept moving. Police on foot behind picked the constable up and protected him as he was removed to an ambulance.

When a striker in the crowd jumped into the street and attempted to unhorse a rider, the officer simply wheeled the animal about, knocking the man down, then calmly walked the horse over him. There was a loud shriek when the horse's back foot stomped on his ankle and broke it.

Al moved past several dust-ups, searching for a purple armband. He spotted the tall man who was intent on bludgeoning a youngster with his club. He wielded it with such ferocity that Devons had no doubt he intended to kill his victim. He removed the Colt from the waistband of his pants and gripped the handle tightly. He forced his way past two men and just as the special raised his club for another blow, Al pressed the barrel against the man's temple.

"You try to hit him again and I'll blow your goddamn head off!"

The man froze with his club hand high over his head.

"Drop the club, you bastard!"

The man did so. Around them, men pushed and shoved against each other and against the specials. Al took a moment to glance at the young man, whose face was a bloody pulp. Two men picked him up and tried to move him away from the crowd to safety.

Sam Seigalman made his way up beside Al. Without a word, he cocked his arm back and smashed a fist to the man's jaw. The special dropped and Al found himself holding a gun pointing at nothing. Seigalman reached down and pulled the man to his knees. He had his hands wrapped in the man's shirt collar and was shaking him viciously. Al put the pistol barrel between the man's eyes and cocked the hammer.

"I don't see one goddamn good reason for you to be alive."

When the horse hit him, Al didn't know what it was. In a moment, everything went black and he found himself face down in the street.

An officer was shouting, "They've got guns! Watch out! They have guns! Draw your weapons!"

Al was still holding the pistol, but now his head hurt and his left shoulder felt like it had been wrenched from the socket. For sure some of the muscles were torn. He had the presence of mind to un-cock the gun and thrust it under his shirt. When he'd struggled to his feet and looked around, he could not see Sam or the special anywhere. The RNWMP horse that had run him down had already moved past as the entire line of police continued their plodding way down Main.

Commissioner Stone was barking into the telephone. "Charles! Where the hell is Ketchen? He was supposed to be here already. I tell you my members are outnumbered badly and now I've had a report that the strikers have guns."

He listened, nodding his head at the phone while Thomas Bulgar, Julius Archibald, and E.K. Atwater stood looking at him. Stone continued nodding at the phone as if it could articulate an answer to his inquiry. Finally he hung up and turned back to the others.

"What'd he say?" demanded Bulgar.

"Supposedly, Ketchen's on his way with trucks and machine guns."

Archibald exploded. "What the hell's Charles doin' still down at the barracks? He needs to get back here and take charge."

Stone looked at him. "There's not really much for him to do here. He won't be in charge anyway. He signed the order to call in the military. They'll take over now. It'll depend upon what they decide."

E.K. had moved to the window and said, "Your men have reached James Street, Commissioner. This must be the slowest charge in their history."

"They aren't supposed to charge, damnit. They're here to control the crowd and to support Ketchen's men if they ever show up."

Bulgar was looking out the window. "Who are the riders in khaki, Commissioner? Why are they with your men?"

"Some of the returned vets. They aren't supposed to be there. They were told to stay away. That we'd handle it."

"Well, they fill out your ranks a bit. Maybe it's good they're here," Bulgar stated.

"No. They aren't trained. Not in this sort of thing. They'll only add to the problem. I'd better go out and see if I can get them off the street."

E.K. Atwater said, "You'd probably be better off staying here, Commissioner. I'm not sure how you could accomplish anything other than raising the tension level out there."

Stone picked up his hat and placed it on his head. "Until Ketchen gets here, I'm the officer in charge. My men are out there and they're in grave danger. I will not stand here and do nothing. They need help and direction and I'm going outside to do that." He opened the door and plunged down the steps, wading into the crowd. He pushed and shoved people aside as he headed towards William Avenue, where the Mounted Police were reforming and preparing to head back down Main Street.

Inspector Mead shouted at his men, ordering them to form a new line and to prepare for a second "charge". He ordered that handguns be taken out in a state of readiness. There were guns in the crowd. They'd been seen and if the crowd started firing, they were to shoot back.

It took him some time to make himself heard and to get his men into order. By now the shouts and cries from the strikers rang in the air about his ears. A brick grazed his chin and took enough of a nick out of it to draw blood. Mead wheeled his horse about and, removing his own pistol from its holster, shouted, "Shoot! Shoot them!"

A volley of shots screamed into the crowd. A striker yelled, "Don't be afraid! They're just blanks! They want to scare us."

The man beside him clutched at his chest and wobbled and teetered about. A bright red spot appeared on the front of his shirt and began to grow. Momentarily, he stood gazing at his own chest in wonder. Then he clutched at the hole as if to stifle the bleeding. He dropped to his knees in the street and looked about in wild disbelief.

More shots pounded the crowd and a riotous disorder resulted. Men scrambled to get out of the line of fire. Mead charged forward with his men following. The strikers fell back and panicked. They were desperate to get out from under the onslaught of horses. Hundreds jumped to get into the alleyways and off the street.

From inside city hall, E.K. could see the arrival of fresh specials. They rushed from the Rupert Street Police Station and weighed into the crowd on Main Street. The police swung clubs arbitrarily, cursing the strikers and pounding them on heads, shoulders, and arms. The strikers were forced into a retreat to the sidewalks and to the side streets.

Julius Archibald guffawed. "I wonder if the sons of bitches feel like going back to work now."

Thomas Bulgar looked at him. His own face was a ghostly white and he was shaking his head as he gazed across the melee.

"My Christ," whispered E.K. Atwater. "They're firing on them."

Several men were lying in the street either wounded by the gunfire or from being knocked down by the charging horses. The foot police walking behind the Mounted Police were busy arresting them and loading them into paddy wagons or ambulances as required.

The crowds who had maneuvered themselves to the alleys and side streets were busy making their way out the other end when they encountered the special police, who had cordoned off those exits and entrapped them. Packed into the alleys with no escape, the strikers were pounded on mercilessly by the clubbing specials. A few tried to respond with bricks, stones, and anything at hand. Chaos and destruction reigned.

Meads's mounted officers pressed the crowd back with the horses. When they reached the burned-out streetcar, one of the horses hit the bumper and tumbled down. The rider was thrown over the horse's head and plunged awkwardly into the street.

For a moment, he lay splayed out, arms and legs spread helplessly. Suddenly, he sat up and looked about at the crowd surrounding him. His pistol lay on the street and he scrambled to get his hand on it when a boot crunched down on his fingers. He screeched in pain and tried to extricate his fingers. The last thing he remembered before his world went black was the gigantic fist that smashed down upon the side of his face. The resulting explosion of his teeth coming loose rendered an end to further participation in quelling the riot.

More shouting was heard and the crowd broke up and fled toward the relative safety of the sidewalk. The street patrol police rushed in to rescue the fallen officer. They packed him off on a stretcher and loaded him into an ambulance.

The horse had broken its leg. One officer held its reins tightly while a second pointed a pistol at its head and pulled the trigger. It shuddered momentarily and its three good legs kicked as it convulsed into death.

Having witnessed all this from his position on the city hall steps, Thomas Bulgar stood and wagged his great head back and forth. Tears flowed from his eyes and down his cheeks. It had all gone beyond his comprehension. Winnipeggers shooting at Winnipeggers. Civil servants crushing employees. Humans bent on destroying each other.

In the wild confusion that followed the second charge down Main Street, Earle Nelson felt himself hard-pressed to escape the alleyway he'd been forced into. With the specials swinging their bats and clubs, he'd twice had to dance out of the way. After being pitched and buffeted back and forth, he'd found himself on the wrong side of the police line.

He'd known it was a mistake to let himself become side-tracked like this. When he'd left the boarding house, he had only three tasks that remained unfinished before he could leave this abominable city. The first was simple. He'd returned to the shed behind Union Station, where he retrieved the money from the stashed suitcase. Everything else was left behind.

The second item of business was Hawkshaw. But that whole thing was becoming way too complicated. He'd scoured the areas in search of him from the favoured barfly haunts such as the Kicking Horse to the New Jerusalem shacks and shanties of the North End. The man was either dead—which was Earle's hope—or he had fled the city, which was almost as good.

At any rate, he was prepared to put Hawkshaw aside. But Anna Williams was a moral obligation. Under no circumstances could she be permitted to interfere with God's grand plan for this Sodom of the prairies. Yea, had ever such a quantum amount of evil crept through such a tiny population of the world as existed in this vile pit, planted at the confluence of two rivers?

Surely when the horsemen of the apocalypse thundered through these streets and dispatched the citizenry with an inundation of influenza and swords, there would be an accompanying heavenly host singing glory to God in the highest.

And so when Earle came out of the Union Station and looked north down Main Street, he realized that the day was at hand. He'd slowly made his way down to the front of city hall, where he'd heard Mayor Ross read the riot act. From there he'd seen the attack on the streetcar and the fire that resulted.

When the red-coated Mounties made their first, slow foray through the crowd, Earle had made his way to William Avenue. When they charged back toward Portage Avenue with guns drawn, Earle had fallen in step with some of the specials, who were menacing the crowds with clubs and threats.

When the gunshots exploded and the panic ensued, he'd found himself pushed into the alley with hundreds of others. He had to get out, to make it known that he was not on the side of the horde and that he was not of the Godless communists and aliens who were the general flotsam of the damned.

He'd managed to push his way to the right side of the alley and close to where it emerged into the street. Here, special police shouted and thrust, punched and kicked at the people they could reach.

A brick hurled by a striker hit a special almost directly in front of Earle. The man went down like a felled tree, his club landing beside him. Earle ducked down, forced his way past two men, and crawled until he reached the downed officer. He searched about for the club and when he retrieved it, he emerged behind the line of specials and made his way down the street. He brandished the club high overhead and raised his other hand in a fist, which he shook at the strikers jammed behind the human barriers.

"Enemies of God!" he screeched. "Betrayers of the truth! Polacks, Ukrainians, Jews! Bloody hypocrites and deniers of Christ! Today you pay! God curses you into hell! Filthy pigs! This is the day of reckoning! Of atonement!"

Earle waded into a line of specials and began to wield his bat heftily. The first head he crunched dropped a man at his feet. He was replaced by a small child and a woman, whose arms were flung about the child protectively. She looked at Earle, stared into the madness in his eyes, and tried to fall back into the crowd with the child. She could not. She was trapped, help-less before a man who had no resemblance to anything human.

"Whore! Slut! Yet another damned Eloise Jacobs with a pup of hell!" He raised the club and brought it down. The woman disappeared. The child was gone. In their place, Earle looked upon the face of Al Devons.

The shouted voice insisted its way into his raging brain. "Goddamn you, Wilson! You bastard! I knew you were a plant by the cops. I knew it! You son of a bitch! Out here clubbing women and kids!" Devons took the pistol from the inside of his shirt; he was standing almost directly in front of Earle now, pointing the gun at his forehead.

When the shot rang out, it caught Al two inches over his right eye. For a second, he just stood there with a startled look on his face. Then he crumpled and fell. He was dead before Sam Seigalman caught him and lowered him gently to the street.

Mead shouted, "I said get back man!"

Earle, standing with his club held high, frozen in the spot where Al Devons had fallen, realized that Mead was yelling at him.

"Get back and give me room I say." He plunged his horse forward past Earle and fired again into the crowd. Earle heaved himself to the side and back so as to avoid being run over by the horse. He'd dropped his club in the rush and was now looking about to retrieve it. He glanced behind him to witness a most amazing sight.

Four of the Mounted Police sat astride their horses in the middle of Main Street. They were all in a line facing Earle. With grins on their faces they joked, laughed, and conversed. Two of them had their pistols out and twirled them about on the forefingers of their right hands, western style. A photographer was standing in front of them, his camera set up on a tripod as he adjusted the lens. He encouraged the men to continue their antics as he focused and then flashed their picture.

It was time for Earle to go. When he turned to do so, he saw another sight that struck him as odd. The military had arrived. Troops in cars poured down Main Street. Hundreds of men in full uniform and carrying rifles stationed themselves at every intersection. Gripping their rifles, they took possession of the street. Several cars with machine-guns mounted ran back and forth in support of the troops. The men who manned the guns scanned them across the crowds, leaving no doubt that they had been ordered to shoot as necessary. Earle turned away and headed toward Fort Street.

***

It was almost a full day since Anna had injected herself with the vaccine. She had no physical symptoms. She felt strong and healthy. There were no negative reactions. Her arm was a little sore, but there were no other aches or pains. Nothing indicated that the vaccine was anything but safe. She was clear of any physical deficits.

However, her brain was not free from confusion. The conversation with Kathleen had unhinged her a bit. And not so much because of the woman's forthrightness as by her acumen and assessment skills. Anna? The object of a man's sexual desires? What a strange and complicated world it was.

In her youth she'd been somewhat adventurous, but she could never have viewed herself as a sexual creature. That was for others. She could take apart an internal combustion engine if not put it entirely back together again. As a young lady, she'd flown and the thrill and the wonder of it could still be conjured in her mind.

When she was a child, she'd enjoyed horseback riding and even hunting. She'd shot a bear once and her grandfather even showed her how to skin it out and prepare some for cooking.

But sex! Both the comprehension and the act of it were beyond her. It wasn't that she was cold to it and it wasn't that she didn't like males. It had just never ever occurred to her that she might be missing something.

Anna just wasn't good at relationships. She knew that and accepted it. She didn't ever know what to say or how to approach the other person. She was somewhat more comfortable she realized with females than with males. But even at that she could not recall a single friendship that had any impact on her.

When Kathleen had spoken so plainly about Roger Wilson and what he wanted, Anna had gone through an array of emotions from repulsion to anger and then to fear and finally an extraordinary dread that such a creature should become fascinated with her.

As in all things that came into her life, her studious mind began to turn this idea over and over in her head. She had to take it out, examine it, and look at its various sides and angles. To measure it, weigh it, poke and prod at it with question after question and to analyze the component parts. Having little experience with this part of the human world made it difficult to quantify and qualify: two things she was very used to doing.

This new knowledge must be important, but in what ways? And how does one use such information? How does one make sense of it? And if one could make sense of it, what was its practical or theoretical application? How was a person to take this information and synthesize it in order to make some new use of it?

And what exactly does it mean to say he wants you? Besides the obvious, that is. Did it mean that he simply wanted to have sex with her? Did it mean an emotional attachment? She shuddered at the thought that he might consider them like-minded.

"Anna?"

Her mind snapped back to attention. Kathleen had said something to her.

"What? I'm sorry, I wasn't paying attention. I was thinking about what you said."

"I said I'm going to go pick up the rest of my broadsheets from the publisher. I'll take Hawkins with me. We'll distribute them and then come back here to get you then we'll all go to my house together. I live down on Wellington. We'll work out something for a safety plan in case we need it. It's possible that Earle Nelson's already left the city.

Anna nodded. "Alright, though I think we need Al Devons in on this. It seems to me we need more than just the three of us."

Kathleen hesitated then agreed. "Yes. If I see him, I'll invite him to the house and we can tell him everything we know. Perhaps that will make a difference."

CHAPTER EIGHTEEN

After supper that night, Anna and Kathleen sat in the living room, drinking wine. Anna had complained earlier that she needed to go back to Versatile to work, but Kathleen had pointed out that part of the safety plan was to avoid getting caught alone.

She never did see Al in her wanderings, but she managed to make her way down to Portage and Main and witnessed the aftermath of the Saturday blood bath. Wounded men were still sitting about waiting for ambulances or police wagons to take them away.

The streets looked like bombs had exploded. Everywhere there was blood, sticks, stones, cans, and bottles. A dead horse lay in the middle of the street. Kathleen stood, mouth open at the sight of a tilted, smoldering streetcar.

Even as she stood, a few pamphlets left in her hand, a parade of RNWMP, army troops and vehicles, and special city police paraded back and forth, indicating by their presence that they were fully in charge.

A young man on a horse stopped beside her. "Miss, it'd be best if you cleared off the street. This here's a military operation now and our orders are to make sure the streets are clear and no more gatherings or parades."

Kathleen gazed about and shook her head at the carnage. "My God. There must have been people killed."

"Couple for sure," replied the rider. "Could've been more, but nobody knows any numbers yet. Lots of people injured—mostly strikers, but we lost a few too. What's that you got in your hand there, Miss?"

She was heartbroken and sickened at the sights and smells. "Nothing really. I guess it doesn't matter now." She moved off down the street, intending to make her way back to Anna's workplace. She'd sent Hawkshaw out with some of the broadsheets and hadn't seen him again. She wasn't worried—he'd obviously been taking care of himself for a long time.

It was only later that she'd got a full picture of the day. Apparently there'd been three or four charges by the police (depending upon whom you chose to believe). The final charge Kathleen understood was more for a show of force. A few pockets of resistance remained but they were quickly dealt with by the RNWMP. She heard a report of a pumping plant employee being saved by Ketchen's troops. Apparently the luckless man had found himself the target of about two-dozen strikers intent upon taking their frustrations out on someone. One of Ketchen's machine gunners fired a spray of bullets overtop the men and they scattered quickly, leaving the badly wounded soul lying in the street. Such stories would haunt the press for weeks no doubt and paint a black picture of the strike. Somehow, Kathleen realized, they would have to combat that viewpoint.

***

Julius Archibald sat in Charles Ross's office and lit up a cigar in celebration. Others sat around the table also but were mostly quiet. Commissioner Stone, Thomas Bulgar, E.K. Atwater, the news editor Simcoe, the new Winnipeg Chief of Police Chris Newton, and the city solicitor Andrews were all present. Charles still felt his churning stomach and he wondered if he'd ever be able to eat again.

"That pretty much takes care of the strike," Archibald puffed mightily. There was nothing quite so pleasant as a good cigar. "But we'll have to keep the pressure on, at least for a few days. Until we know that the goddamn Bolsheviks are finished for good."

"We will," Stone offered. "Ketchen and I have complete control of the streets. There'll be no repeat of today. We pretty much have them on the run."

The city police chief was looking at him, wondering how and why he and his men had not been included in that statement.

"We need some sort of plan for the next few days and weeks," E.K. Atwater said, though his voice sounded weary and he had a look of dread about him. "Some kind of ordered approach to this so that people can return to work and lives can get back to normal."

Julius Archibald looked around at the gathering. "I think we can leave that up to the Committee of One Thousand. Some things definitely have to go into place though. Strikers should be fired or at the very least have to sign agreements. No more unions and no more striking. If they don't sign, no work. We need to keep a list of the leaders. No employer should rehire them. And anybody who does return to work loses benefits and seniority. That's just the price they'll have to pay to keep their jobs. What do you think, Charles?"

Ross seemed to awaken as from a dream. He looked about until his eyes lighted upon Julius Archibald. When he spoke, his voice was flat and without any emphasis. "I don't give a damn what you do, Julius." He struggled to his feet and when he finally did attain them, his demeanour shifted. "As far as I'm concerned, you can go to hell. That goes for all of you. This is a real black eye for us. It's no victory if that's what you think. I know you want things to be black and white here, but down the road that's not how it will be viewed. You want to be seen as the good guys who ended the strike and saved the city. But in just a few years people will see you as tyrants who spent their time fear-mongering and who used hatred and intolerance to gain the upper hand. And if you use the strategies that Julius has been suggesting, you'll live to see your names associated with foolishness and nonsensical thinking. Because if you kick a man to death when he's down and out, that's what people pay attention to and that's what they remember."

For a moment he seemed to lose heart and faltered. He sat back down and gazed around and most of them avoided his eyes. He lighted upon the editor of *The Free Press*. "And how do you think you'll be remembered in this, Simcoe? You believe that you'll be seen as leading the charge in the great victory over Bolshevism, don't you? I can see the headlines shouting even now: Arrest Dangerous Aliens, No Bail for Red Agitators, Bolshevists Started Bloody Riots. Your newspaper will be screaming for trials, bloodletting to appease the capitalist cause, preservation of democracy. But democracy was never in danger here, Simcoe. These men. These strikers, just a bunch of poor, sad ignorant bastards trying to make a difference. You aren't saving anything. And neither am I! Did you see the women and children in the crowds? Do you seriously think that people who were trying to overthrow the government would invite their wives and kids along to march with them? How's your newspaper going to explain that?"

His voice took on an even more gloomy, somber tone. "And how will my grandchildren and their children remember me? As the mayor of the city when Winnipeggers fought in the streets and killed each other. As the mayor who set loose police and army units and so-called upholders of the law upon a group of silent protestors. No doubt they'll read it proudly as my eulogy. And who will stand up to defend Charles Ross's name at his funeral? Will it be you, E.K.?"

Atwater said nothing. He looked away.

"How about you, Tom?"

Bulgar folded his hands in his lap and looked down.

"No? I thought perhaps...maybe you, Julius?"

Archibald shrugged then ground his cigar out in an ashtray. He looked at Charles, then growled and gazed across the room and out the window.

Charles pushed back his chair and struggled to his feet once more. He started toward the door. "No. After all's been said about this and written about it in the future, I'm afraid we'll be seen as tiny and small-minded people. We might think that we started out to do the right thing, and maybe we did, but when we beat those people today...when we clubbed them to their knees, when we ran over them with our horses and when we killed them... We lost our claim, we gave up our—we have no right to say..." His voice trailed off. He took his hat and coat from off the rack. He opened the door and walked out and closed it very softly behind him.

***

Anna let her wineglass be refilled by Kathleen. In her entire life she couldn't remember drinking two glasses of wine back to back. She smiled to herself, thinking that alcohol, like many other aspects of her life, had been overlooked—something she just hadn't bothered about and had little knowledge of regarding either its pleasantries or its potential for problems.

Kathleen had been describing what she'd seen downtown. "I don't know why I hadn't foreseen this. I should have guessed how it would turn violent, how people would be injured... and killed."

"I don't see how you could. And supposing you had known? How would that have changed things?"

"I might have done things differently. I might have made a better attempt to...to..."

"Exactly. It would have changed nothing. These events were set in motion long ago, just as so many others are. Neither Kathleen Johns nor anyone else has the capacity to manage all those events and change things."

"I suppose that's true. Anyway, enough of plowing this unfruitful ground. We still haven't talked about this whole Earle Nelson fiasco or whatever his name is. How will we handle this? And when I say 'we,' Anna, I mean you and me. I don't think we can depend on Hawkins, even if he does return."

"That's true. Poor man, though I was happy to have him with me when we found Mary Jablinka." Anna waited to see if Kathleen offered anything. When she didn't, Anna said, "I have to assume that you were serious when you said that this man wanted to have sex—with me."

Kathleen took a drink of wine and nodded her head vigorously, giving a rueful snort. "Oh yes! Very serious. It's at least one good reason for his hanging about."

"I have to tell you that I would not even begin to have a vague idea about how someone would ... how a person goes about..."

Kathleen smiled at her. "Having sex?"

"No. No, that's not what I mean. Of course I know about copulation. I know about reproduction. It's the other things, the things that go along with that. All the other...?"

"The other what?"

Anna's face was beginning to redden. "Well for instance, how does a female go about getting a man to....?"

"To have sex with her?"

"Uh, yes. I mean obviously one does not just walk up to a male and say—"

Kathleen laughed. "Actually, with many males that would probably work very well." Then she grew serious. "I know you're not planning to have sex with this Nelson, so we need a different approach and it has to be as safe as we can make it." Kathleen thought for a moment. "How would you feel about having a gun? Or a knife?"

Anna shook her head vigorously. "Absolutely not. I'd end up shooting myself, and never could I shoot someone. Not even Roger Wilson."

Kathleen saw the foolishness of her suggestion right away. "No, of course not—neither of those is an option and not really all that safe."

Neither spoke for a long time until Anna finally prompted, "You were going to talk about..."

"Oh right, about attracting males." Kathleen cocked her head to one side and looked at Anna questioningly, wondering who Anna was thinking about.

"Well, it depends a lot upon the man actually. There are some who are shy about sex believe it or not. Especially if they are not experienced with it. Let's see, how can I explain this? You need to make yourself accessible for one thing."

"Accessible?"

"Right. That's because a man needs to know that if he approaches he won't be rejected. Rejection's a very big thing for men. They feel like it demeans them. That they aren't bull males. Sometimes it even takes away their ability to perform."

Kathleen stopped. Anna's face had turned a deep scarlet and she looked as if she would jump out of her skin.

Kathleen laid a hand on Anna's arm. "Oh dear, I'm not helping much at all am I? Making things way too complicated. The truth is it's such a natural act that you really don't need to do a whole lot. Especially a woman as smart-looking as you are." Kathleen wondered what Anna's life had been like–how it must have unfolded with such simplicity. "Let me start over," Kathleen said. "Come into my bedroom. Bring your wine. We'll start with the hair and then some makeup. And the dress! Has to be something that really shows off that chest." A broad smile crossed Kathleen's face. She was starting to cope with the events that were Bloody Saturday. They both needed some distraction and what better way to gain that than by spending time developing friendship.

***

On Sunday morning, June 22, Dr. Stanley Parkes finally returned to his office. The choice of coming in on Sunday was deliberate. He felt like he'd slowly awakened from a terrible dream. Where had the time gone? In his immense grieving, he'd given not a thought to the Versatile Medical Laboratories or to the denizens who worked so competently under his steerage.

Truth to tell, he was embarrassed. So deeply engrossed was he in his personal losses that the daily plight of his workforce and his business had been cast aside. At first, his despair was so great that he thought he would never return. The grind of triple funeral arrangements, the demands of extended family, and the derangement of his mind were so overwhelming that he pulled a blanket of obscurity over himself and refused to participate.

Finally, it was his brother who'd had enough. The previous day at 9:00 A.M. he'd thrust himself into Stanley's room, threw open the curtains, lifted the window, and propped it with a stick.

"Alright," he said, "enough of this. Time to get back to work and start patching up the holes. We all hurt from this, Stanley, but that doesn't mean we get to just quit. I'm going out on the boat later today. You can either come with me and get some fish smell on you or you can go back to work in the city."

Stanley was still squinting to adjust his eyes to the sudden overflow of light. His brother seemed intent on continuing. "But by Christ it's going to be one or the other. Krystyna says if you're let to you'll just lie around here and mope so it's time to get off yer arse and get some things done."

Stanley tried to wipe the sleep from his eyes, "That's what I've always loved about you, Wilbur. The way you beat around the bush and never come to a point."

His older brother was tall and rangy. Life on the fishing boats had made him a hard and muscular man. Stanley was not exactly afraid of him, but his respect was prodigious. As boys, Wilbur—four years older and quick to temper—had never protected Stanley from life's hurts and apparently he was not about to start now.

"You can tell Krystyna that I'm on my way down, brother. How you managed to attract such a couth, thoughtful, pleasant, and industrious lady to be your wife I'll never know. You must have lied to her."

Wilbur snorted. "I did indeed. I told her I had the biggest cock in Manitoba." He walked over and picked Stanley's clothes from off the back of the chair where they'd been carefully draped the night before. He examined the excellent quality of the fabric and took the time to rub his rough fingers up and down the lapel of the jacket. He took the white silk shirt, bunched it in his hand, and placed it over his nose.

He sniffed it. "Still clean," he pronounced. He tossed the clothing into a pile on top of his brother. "Why, maybe one day I'll catch enough fish to get me a suit like that. And maybe one day the price of fish will actually pay me for my work. What d'you think, little brother?"

Stanley held the clothes in a pile in both arms. "I think you haven't changed a bit since we were children."

"Change? Change? A highly overrated thing I'd say. I think if I was supposed to change Krystyna would've told me about it by now." He rubbed his hand along his ear much the way a cat would, trying to wash itself.

"Yes. Well." Stanley struggled from the bed and peeled the long nightgown off. "I believe she probably sees the hopelessness of that as well."

His brother grinned and headed towards the door.

Stanley stopped him. "Wilbur?"

The older man turned back.

Stanley's eyes, for the first time since his loss, contained something of a sparkle. "You know, we grew up together. We went through childhood together. I don't remember you as having a particularly large cock."

Wilbur held a hand up at the side of his mouth and whispered as if in confidentiality, "Yes, let's just keep that between us, alright? No need for Krystyna to know."

Stanley sat at his office desk and smiled at the memory. He looked at the stack of correspondence and frowned as he waded into the pile.

***

Having spent more time with Kathleen than she'd intended and then accepting her as an escort to Versatile, Anna was determined to work on Sunday. Kathleen refused to leave until Anna was safely inside and they'd arranged for Kathleen to return in the afternoon. Kathleen remained outside the door until she heard the lock click and she'd tested it. When Anna discovered Stanley Parkes in his office she was taken completely by surprise.

The first shock was his appearance. He was thin and looked tired. He'd dropped an alarming amount of weight so that his cheeks were gaunt and the caste of his skin was a sallow white. To Anna he looked smaller, something akin to a child sitting behind a very large, outsized desk.

But if she was shocked to see him, he was totally bewildered by her. He knew it was Anna, but a very different Anna from when he'd last seen her. For one thing, her hair was hanging down and glistened with life. And was that a ribbon she had tied in it?

Her dress was bright, colourful, and set off her figure wonderfully. He suddenly realized he was staring at her breasts and that she was aware he was doing so. He forced his gaze to her face and she reddened and faltered momentarily as she stood in his office door.

While she still looked tired from overwork as she almost always did, her face glowed with good health and something he'd never noticed before. She had dimples. From the day he'd hired her, Parkes had always been vaguely aware of Anna's attractions, but not like this. This was a change of significant proportions.

"We were wondering when you'd be back. I'm so sorry, Stanley. What a terrible time you've been going through. What will you do now? Do you know?"

He was still trying to get over the physical changes. Did she have something on her lips?

"For now I thought I'd better try to catch up on this backlog." He waved his hand to indicate the stack of mail atop his desk. He gazed at her again. "You look wonderful, Anna." A long gap of silence grew then and threatened to engulf them completely until Stanley bridged it by saying, "How does your work go?"

With that he unleashed a torrent of information from her, so much so that he was forced to interrupt her and sit her down in front of his desk so that he might listen to everything and try to grasp some of it. As he listened, he felt a curious change coming to him. Her description of her research findings lit a small spark in his belly and turned his mind outward and away from his inner self. As he cogitated about her report, a multiplicity of possibilities began to arise and he sorted the options into specific categories and detailed each.

His brain began to stir. In his absence, Anna's work had bounded way ahead. There'd been nothing to curtail it: no obstacles placed in her way, no rendering down of her immense capacity to search, uncover, decipher, and reach conclusions about a myriad of intelligence. It was the very thing he was incapable of doing himself.

When she was finished telling everything (minus the part about the self-inoculation) it was a full hour later and Anna still had more to say. But at that point Stanley Parkes held up a hand to stop her. His brain was becoming too full and his information processing in danger of overload.

"So, are you planning on continuing work this afternoon?"

"Yes, of course. I was going to work Saturday but this whole unfortunate strike thing changed my plans. I'm just hoping I haven't left Harold's samples too long. I really should get right to it."

"I understand. Anna, this is incredible. If your findings stand up under rigorous testing in the field then I see no reason why we would not contract for production. This is very exciting. No word of this to anyone! Let me break it to McAlister and the others. They won't be entirely pleased about having to redirect their research." He dropped off suddenly and seemed to go into a dreamy state. He became so deep in thought that Anna seemed to have disappeared.

She thought that if she got up and walked out at this moment he would not even be aware of it. She watched as a series of facial expressions presented themselves, from a curious and self-satisfied part-smile, to wrinkle-browed confusion, to raised eyebrows in doubt. Just before he spoke, Anna felt sure she could see patterns of dollar signs floating in an aura about him.

"Anna, there's one thing. If you did happen to be incorrect about the data and your observations...."

"But I'm not wrong. As sure as I'm sitting here talking to you I'm just as sure about what I've found. We can save lives, Stanley, hundreds and thousands of them. There's nothing to prevent us unless we take too long to get a vaccine out there."

"Alright. I accept that you're accurate in this. I'll have McAlister and Johnstone and a few others run blind checks and see what happens."

"I should go to work now." She stood up.

"Yes, absolutely. Oh Anna, this is amazing! This will make such a difference to Versatile. It will be the making of our lab and of...your reputation as a scientist."

Why did she feel that that last part was not what he had started out to say? She wondered—did he see the irony that, even as she was discovering a possible vaccine, he had been in the middle of losing his own family?

***

After leaving Anna at work Kathleen returned home. For her, Sunday brought some quiet relief from the rapidly circling wheel her life had become. She realized that the previous day's grisly work was the end of the strike. Probably it was the end of her job as well, although in terms of making a living that meant nothing to her.

But not so for thousands of others. The bosses would demand retribution. Someone would have to pay and she understood that it would be at a much heavier cost than what she herself would pay. What would the families of the immigrant workers do? What would be the final tally for people like R.B. Russell, Bill Ford, and Fred Dixon?

And what had been gained at the end? Had they made even a tiny inroad into what was happening for the workers in this city? In some ways it had all been so damned futile. What was it that Bill Ford had said to her? "We can't win the strike. It's not about whether or not we win it. We're just trying to make a difference here. We can win in the long run, but not here. Not today and not with this strike." It had been something like that. He knew, but he still went through with it. Amazing. What did the struggle mean to him? What did it mean to her?

Sitting at her kitchen table and drinking coffee, she thought about what to do with this Sunday. Since she employed a lady to do the housecleaning, there wasn't a lot to do there. She didn't grow a garden, so nothing there. She did not cultivate flowers either, but maybe she should try. Was it too late in the year already to plant?

In her mind she went back over the plans for dealing with Roger Wilson. Clearly, Anna could not be alone—that was paramount. She was not entirely satisfied because it depended upon her locating Al and making sure she got to Versatile Laboratories. She'd wanted to tell Anna's boss. Had been very insistent about it. But when Anna explained about his being absent because of the loss of his family, it seemed hopeless even to try that approach. And the police would be useless. Kathleen had to find Alvin and the two of them would show up at Anna's workplace early, just in case Roger Wilson was also there waiting for her.

With the three of them present, there was no way that Roger Wilson would make a contact. It was obvious from his pattern of behavior that he'd only initiate things when it was safe for him to do so.

So who was Anna dressing up for then? Kathleen had hinted and even cajoled during their evening of preparations, but she could not budge her. Dr. Anna Williams was a very private person and that was not going to change.

Perhaps it didn't matter. Maybe there was no man. In an odd way, maybe Anna was only doing it for herself. Hadn't Kathleen gone through the same thing: wanting to look better, to dress up, to be pretty, or at least more attractive? For Kathleen it had happened in her teens and early twenties. For Anna it was happening now. She was running the possibilities over in her mind when she glanced out the window and saw Sam Seigalman's rotund body coming up her walkway. She got up to meet him at the door.

"Sam! Good Lord! What happened to you?"

Seigalman was beaten up. A huge lump had grown up over his left eye. Dried blood had formed down his face and neck and had run inside a red-soaked collar. His shirt was torn and ragged as were his pants. He was covered in dirt and grime as well as small white bumps from mosquito bites. These he scratched at incessantly.

His eyes were red and unfocussed and when Kathleen looked at his hands there appeared to be a large human bite mark along the edge below his little finger. One of the flaps at the base of an ear had become detached and had bled profusely, although now it seemed to be staunched. Kathleen thought it should be stitched closed.

"I got caught up in yesterday's riot," he managed. He was exhausted and Kathleen drew him inside and placed him at her kitchen table. "Christly specials! They were beating on us with bats. Wouldn't stop. And the cops rode us down with horses and shot people." He stopped for a moment and his eyes glazed over as he thought back. His right hand came up and covered his face and she realized that he was trying very hard not to cry.

"When I finally got away I had no place to go. Cops were arresting us. There must be sixty or seventy people in jail.

Maybe a hundred. Not sure. I couldn't go home. I knew they'd come for me there. Same as at the Labour Temple. I stayed in a ditch last night, then this morning I came looking for you. I knew you lived on Wellington but not exactly where. Had to ask directions."

Kathleen stopped him. "Okay, enough talk for now. First thing we need to do is get you cleaned up and get some food into you. Then some sleep. After that we can talk about things."

He was staring at her so hard. A sense of dread crept into her voice. "What's happened?"

He blurted it out. "Alvin Devons is dead. A North West Mounted Police shot him during the riot."

For a second she said nothing. Just stood there and took it in. Then, in a stunned silence she pulled up a chair and sat beside Sam. She took his wounded hand in both of hers and placed it in her lap. For a long time both sat there and said nothing.

Kathleen spoke very softly, "I guess we might have expected something like this. I guess maybe he knew it too. It's just that... when it actually takes place it's so... I don't know...unnatural."

"I thought I should come and let you know. I didn't want you to read it in the press or something like that. I'm not sure what to do now. With everyone in jail and the strike probably finished. Anyway, I didn't know what to do or where to go. So I came here."

"It's good that you did. Where is he? I need to go see him."

"I took him to the city morgue. Didn't really know what else to do, but I couldn't leave him just lying there in the street. They just shot him! There was a lot of fighting. They charged us on horses and then this cop appeared and just shot..."

Kathleen squeezed his hand slightly and said, "Alright. It's okay. We'll deal with it, Sam. You both knew what you were into. You were aware that the consequences could be huge. Alvin knew it too."

Sam looked at her, startled momentarily. His mouth opened into question marks directed at her.

She answered, "Yes. I know about who he was and why he came to be sent here. I don't know all the details because he didn't tell them, but I know you're both communists and I'm guessing you were also a part of making sure that things got done. Don't worry, Sam. Your secrets are safe with me. I won't be writing about them."

Seigalman retreated into silence. He waited while Kathleen cleaned up his cuts and bathed the wounds on his face and neck. He winced when she touched the large bump over his eye.

Kathleen continued, "You have nothing to fear from anything I'll do or say. It's just that it all seems to be such a big waste now. People get injured, arrested, and even killed. And for what? What strange creatures we are, Sam. Caught up in an overblown sense that what we are doing is of any consequence. What are you fighting for? And what was Alvin fighting for? The bosses have the money and so they have the power. We want the power and we fight like hyenas to get some of it.

And when you think about it, how much would things change if we did gain some power? Would we be any better off? Would we be any more considerate of others than they've been with us? We might think we would be different from the E.K. Atwaters and Thomas Bulgars of the world, but is that really the case?"

Finally, the tears arrived and began to flow down her cheeks. "I know we like to think that we'd be better. That we'd treat the workers differently, but I really wonder if the union itself wouldn't become just another form of bondage?"

He closed his eyes and let her gentle fingers minister to the wounds.

"And now, Mr. Sam Seigalman, you'll eat some breakfast and sleep. And when you awake you and I will go downtown so I can see Alvin and tell him some things he needs to know."

***

Earle Nelson was certain that he had the flu. It was that cursed hospital. Terrible luck to end up there. Shortly after leaving he'd developed a cough and then the sniffling started. As his temperature rose and his joints began to ache, his diagnosis was confirmed.

Fear hammered in his heart. He recalled the flu victims in the hospital with their black, strangulated looks. What must it be like to live those horrid, pain-filled final moments?

Wasn't it enough that he had to avoid police and soldiers? Now he had this to deal with as well. But he would find a way. Earle reached up and swiped away the sweat forming on his forehead. His eyes darted up and down the street.

He found himself having to be very careful. While the strike might have ended, everyone remained on high alert. Day and night the streets were filled with city police, specials, and the RNWMP. Groups and individuals were being challenged constantly. Slowly, people were returning to the downtown during the daylight hours, but for many it was onerous and tense.

When the telephone operators tried to go back to work they discovered that many of their jobs had been filled. The fired police who tried to return to work had to sign the Committee of One Thousand's pledge form. They lost seniority and privileges. Every officer had to reapply for his job and each had to swear allegiance and to never participate in union activities.

The raids on the union leaders' homes continued. James Grant found himself in jail on a charge of sedition. The local gossip was that province-wide searches for strike leaders were ongoing and it was this kind of thing that made Earle nervous.

He could not afford to be caught up in a dragnet operation. Especially now, when he was on the dawn of striking such a blow for the angels of goodness.

All this was running through his mind when he stood on the sidewalk across from the Versatile Medical Laboratories. It was the second day of summer and the evening light in Winnipeg stretched on forever. Already Earle could see the half-full moon and it was still fully daylight. The day's temperature began its slow decline toward nightfall. Earle noted that a murder of crows had taken up residence in the trees on the property across the street. They seemed to glare at him with an understanding based upon mutual inclusion. A very intelligent bird, the crow. And perhaps the only one in the bird world possessed of a malignant and vengeful spirit.

That's when he saw Hawkshaw and stepped back into the shadow of the building. He watched carefully as the man moved up the street, casting glances about and taking note of every face in the vicinity. The diminutive elf drew close to where Earle was standing so that the latter dropped a hand to his belt and felt for the knife inside the waistband of his pants.

The prey was almost directly in front of him. Suddenly Hawkshaw turned and headed straight across the street. He gained the curb on the far side and trundled up the worn path that led to the front step of Versatile Laboratories. Here he paused, looked about, casting his eyes into the various shadows and nooks and crannies on both sides of the street. He tried the door and then knocked. Curtains were pulled back on a window. A moment later the door opened and Hawkshaw disappeared inside.

The hackles at the back of Earle's neck raised and bristled. He forced himself to be calm and to not rush across the street. So Hawkshaw knew Anna Williams. How on earth had that happened? How could they possibly have come to meet? Earle turned the scenarios over and over in his mind, until finally he decided that it really did not matter. Whatever had gone wrong could be fixed and very soon would be. After five minutes, Hawkins had not come back out. After ten minutes Earle was beginning to get a stress-related headache. After fifteen minutes, and just when he was almost compelled to enter the lab, the door opened and both Hawkshaw and Anna Williams stepped out under the door's canopy.

Both stared up and down the street and peered deeply into the shadows around the buildings. At the same time they continued in conversation as Hawkshaw maintained his little dance on the doorstep.

There was no doubt now in Earle's mind. They were looking for him and they were talking about him. Anna said something to Hawkshaw and the man's hand dropped involuntarily to the inside of his coat towards his hip. He was carrying his knife, then! Of course he was. Earle would have to watch for that.

Then Anna turned and went back inside and Hawkins made his way from the veranda and headed straight toward him. When he reached the sidewalk on the opposite side of Fort, he turned toward Broadway and shuffled along, still glancing about. Earle stepped out to follow him.

He knew he did not have long. In a short time Hawkins would turn to look back, simply because he always did. Earle dropped back and let several people get between the two of them. Then, as so often happened, good fortune fell to Earle. Or, as he thought of it, Hawkshaw was guided into an alleyway by a heavenly force.

In the alley, where the sunlight could not penetrate and the shadows concealed the rummaging rats, Hawkins crept along. He felt more comfortable here, could not be seen so easily. Darkness was the natural ally of the itinerant.

"Hello, Hawkshaw. I've been looking for you."

Hawkins froze. He could feel the chill of Earle Nelson creep into his spine and then into his brain. Suddenly, he needed very badly to relieve himself. Then his mind began its thaw and he looked up and down the alley. The entrance he'd come into was a lot closer, but it meant getting past Earle. It was at least three times the distance to get back onto the street in the other direction.

"I wouldn't if I was you," Earle said. "I doubt that you'd make it. What do you think?"

Hawkshaw licked his lips. Once again he glanced up and down the alley and then gave a helpless shrug of his shoulders. His head dropped in dejection. He stared into the dirt at his feet and noticed that for a time at least they'd ceased to shuffle.

"Give me your knife, Hawkshaw." Earle held out his hand and when the knife was not forthcoming he snapped his fingers with impatience. Slowly Hawkins reached into his belt and withdrew the weapon. He held it out for Earle, who smiled and took it blade first into his hand. Hawkins released the handle as though he was letting go of his life.

"Now, before I kill you, you're going to tell me everything about you and Dr. Anna Williams. You'll tell me how you know her, why you know her, why you were in her lab, and everything that she knows."

Hawkshaw said nothing in return but he nodded his head up and down. Now that he'd come to this, the fear was leaving him. Instead he felt tired and worn. He wanted to lie down and sleep. His most profound feeling was to disappear. To shrug off the very heavy blanket of life that he'd wrapped himself in for so long.

"Come over here and sit on this crate and tell me all."

He moved to where Earle was pointing. He looked about the alleyway. Garbage was piled high everywhere. There had still not been any pickups since the strike. A great mound of rotting food sat in back of a grocery store. Broken wooden crates lay piled one atop the other. He could smell both feces and urine and hoped it was not his own. Hawkshaw sat down wearily, folding himself down onto the crate. He caught the glint of his own knife blade just a short distance to his left.

When Hawkshaw was finished talking, Earle knew that Anna's knowledge of him was complete. Well, at least now all pretense was gone. When he confronted her he would not have to be Wilson. He would not dissemble.

"You can close your eyes if it will make things any easier." Hawkins did so. He tensed a little and gripped his knees with his hands. He held his breath.

"What the hell's going on in here?"

Earle's head shot up at the two specials on horseback. He turned to face them and when he did, Hawkshaw fired himself off the crate and rabbited off down the alley. He didn't look back, never slowed, neither glanced left nor right. Before Earle looked back at the empty crate, Hawkshaw was out on the street, around the corner, and gone.

The specials were advancing their horses at a walk down the alley. Earle turned away from them and thrust the knife onto the pile of rotting food. He unbuttoned his trousers and posed as if he'd been relieving himself in the alleyway. He felt hot and miserable. The sweat trickled down the back of his neck. He forced a smile over his shoulder at the special police. "Evening officers, and a fine one it is too!"

One of the specials demanded, "What are you doing? And where'd the other guy go?"

"Uh, what other guy would that be, officer?"

The other special glared down at him. "Don't get wise with us or we'll run you in."

"You payin' that guy?" the first special asked.

At first Earle was lost, then slowly nodded an understanding. "Something like that."

"If we didn't already have the jails full, we'd throw a pervert like you behind bars. Now get the hell out of this alley and off the streets. There's a curfew still on. We see you out again an' we'll beat the hell out of you. Now get goin'!"

"Of course, officers." He flashed the Wilson smile. He turned and made his way quickly in the direction Hawkshaw had taken.

CHAPTER NINETEEN

As it turned out, Sam Seigalman slept for only two hours. When he awoke, he found Kathleen sitting in her living room and reading back copies of *The Winnipeg Telegram*. Sam knew the paper well. Of the three dailies, it had come out most strongly against the strike.

Sam picked up one of the copies and stared at the front page. Funny how he'd never before noticed the icon at the top nor the legend, which proclaimed *The Telegram* as "Western Canada's Greatest Newspaper". Above this there issued a banner with the words COMMERCE, INDUSTRY, PRUDENCE in block letters. Yes, in its motto the paper had spelled out its socio-economic and political stripes. No wonder it had sought to crucify the strikers and to portray the leaders as diehard communists.

Sam studied the stamp representing the newspaper. Clearly planted between the words *Winnipeg* and *Telegram* was a shield on top of which stood a bison. Below the bison but placed at the top of the shield was a locomotive pulling a car. The bottom two thirds of the shield was taken up with what appeared to be three sheaves of wheat standing on end.

From either side of the shield sprouted long stalks of grain apparently bent over to the side as if from some unseen prairie wind. In behind the shield there appeared an arcing line with small hair-like projections sticking out. At first Sam thought it to be a rising or setting sun, but then he looked more closely. No, they were tiny little people figures, barely discernible, and they were joined hand in hand in a line. Solidarity. He smiled ruefully. Yes, it was all there, wasn't it?

"What does yours say?" he asked.

Kathleen read, "The attempt to make a Bolshevist revolution has failed. The strike is officially called off. It has terminated, as was inevitable from the first that it must terminate, once the true citizens of Winnipeg grasped the significance of the dastardly attack that was made upon them and their liberties.

The strike has been a miserable failure. It has resulted in not the slightest gain on any point for any man that engineered it or for any dupe who participated in it. On the contrary, it has caused an enormous loss to every citizen whether directly interested in the strike or not.

The fomenters of the revolution are now mostly either under indictment awaiting trial on one of the gravest charges in the calendar, or they are fugitives from justice.

Not only have the leaders in this comic opera revolution got themselves into serious trouble with the authorities, they have also completely destroyed themselves as far as any future influence that they might hope to have with the working men of this city is concerned. There is not a man, woman, or child who has not suffered during six long weeks the privations of hunger and inconvenience of a score of kinds and who is destined to suffer privations without number during the next year in consequence of these weeks of idleness, but will be prepared to curse the name of every strike leader who brought misfortune down upon the heads of misguided victims."

When she finished, Sam said, "Interesting how they think that they actually speak for everyone."

Kathleen added, "And not a single word about the fact that people lost their lives. It's as if they'd never existed. And they actually believe this tripe they're writing. They don't understand, they really don't. They actually think that the workers will come out against the strike leaders. No wonder we can't make any progress."

Sam shook his head. "I guess it's true that the victors get to write the history."

"Yes. However dishonourable it might be."

***

When Charles Ross sat down with the heads of the Committee of One Thousand, he knew that it would be for the last time. Whether they wanted it or not it was going to be the last time. If nothing else, he recognized that his stomach was not going to allow him to go on like this. Neither was his wife nor his family for that matter. Charles looked old and he felt old. There was a creaking in his limbs that he hadn't noticed before and his fingers hurt like hell. In the last couple of days, pain had flared intermittently and he wondered if he wasn't getting an attack of arthritis. He remembered that his father had suffered from it. He was only partly listening as Thomas Bulgar (also not looking well) recited a police report on the last few days from the new police chief.

As the name Alvin Devons was read, Charles's attention was brought back to matters at hand. "Devons. He the young man you guys employed to spy on the unions?"

E.K. Atwater responded, "Yes. Turns out though he wasn't just working for us. He was a member of the Communist Party in the U.S.A. They sent him across the border to try to bolster the revolution. To make sure it got started. He was the one doing the bombings."

Charles allowed a bittersweet smile. "So the Committee employed a communist to spy on a bunch of Bolsheviks?"

"Something like that," E.K. nodded. "Course, we had no idea he'd been sent here. I still don't know who hired him—any of you know anything about this?" He cast a look about the rest of the room.

"Don't matter," Julius Archibald offered. "He's dead now and we're probably better off for it."

Charles asked, "And what of the other guy?"

Brown replied, "Died in hospital. Infection. Gangrene I think they said. What happens now, Charles?"

Ross shrugged and a gloom enveloped him. "Andrews tells me there'll have to be trials. What a hullaballoo that'll be. It'll turn out to be nothing but an opportunity for the union leaders to get their agenda moved forward. I can see it already. Russell, Heaps, Ford shouting their cause from the rooftop of the court-house. They'll come out of this heroes and we'll be the villains. This is just the kind of thing I meant when I said we'd lost even though we won."

Thomas Bulgar nodded. "I agree. What'd we accomplish? Ran a few aliens to ground and shipped them out. But they're nothing but scapegoats. We've got a hundred people in jail and now what're we supposed to do with them? All we've done is split our city into warring camps and it'll take one hell of a long time for the wounds to heal."

"We defeated a revolution," Archibald chimed. "Says so right here in the newspaper." He stabbed at the headline of *The Manitoba Free Press* with a forefinger.

Bulgar smirked. "If that was a revolution, Julius, then it had to be the shortest and least bloody one in history. No, I don't think we're going to be able to prop this up as a revolution no matter how hard the press tries. Just a sad little skirmish in a sad little town and I have to say, conducted for the most part by sad little people. And by the way, this is my resignation from the Committee of One Thousand sad little men."

Thomas Bulgar arose from his seat and made his way around the table to Charles Ross. He held out his hand, which Charles took and shook vigorously. Bulgar said, "Charles. You're too good a man for politics. It's time you thought about getting out so you don't have to associate with the likes of us." He turned and walked out.

For a long time no one spoke. Finally the deputy mayor cleared his throat and picked up a sheet of paper. He said, "Dr. Pownell has told us to get ready for a bump with the flu epidemic. She says we'll probably have to suspend public meetings, gatherings, and maybe even the schools. The hospitals are full. There's no more room. She wants to issue an edict to shut down theatres and halls as well. She doesn't want crowds gathering anyplace because they just pass the flu on to each other. Seems to me that we're kind of closing the barn door here after the horse has already escaped."

Charles Ross laughed. "Oh yes. I guess we've never done that before, have we?"

***

By ten P.M. Earle felt that finally it was safe for him to move. The streets had grown quiet. In the last hour he'd seen only a few people about and twice they'd been evening patrols of the new city police force. Darkness such as it was had finally arrived, shops had closed up, and Henry's Bar & Grille had pulled the blinds and locked the door.

Though he'd lost Hawkshaw, he couldn't be upset entirely about it. As soon as he'd emerged from the alley he knew he was not going to see him again. The man would not let himself be taken a second time. As a result Earle did not even bother searching for him. Instead, he'd retreated to the hiding spot across from Versatile Laboratories to ensure that Anna Williams did not leave without his knowledge. He was there at nine P.M. when a man he didn't know emerged and stood momentarily at the top of the stairs. Immaculately dressed, the man looked at his arms and legs and reached down to give them a quick brushing with the back of his hand. When he stood upright again, he placed an expensive fedora on his head before proceeding down the steps and onto the street. He turned down Fort Street at a casual walk and headed toward Broadway. Since then no one else had come out.

A few times a wracking cough had plagued Earle and he could feel a gathering phlegm in the back of his throat. His desire for Anna Williams was changing to a fear of the Spanish Lady's visitation.

When he could see no one on either side, Earle moved into the open and crossed the street. On the opposite sidewalk he stopped again and checked the street. No one. He went up the stairs and tried the front door. It was unlocked. He opened it quietly and let himself in. The foyer was empty. The secretary's desk was clear, with only a pen, a bottle of ink, and a large blotter sitting atop it. A dim overhead foyer light glowed softly.

The door to an office was open and he moved silently to it. When he entered, the office was empty and a clutter of papers lay atop the desk. He advanced to it and glanced at a notepad on the pile.

Anna,

Got tired so I went home. Don't work all night please! I will set up a meeting tomorrow for us with McAlister and Johnstone. Thank you for your concern about me and especially

for your superb work these last few weeks. I
realize how important this is for you.

Please make sure you lock up when you leave.

Stanley

Earle slowly and quietly removed the note and crumpled it. He
placed it in his pocket, then took the time to glance through the
remaining correspondence. All business. Nothing else as personal as the note, but when he was finished with Anna he'd take
the time to have a closer look. He needed to make sure now that
she'd left nothing about Roger Wilson, especially in light of the
fact that she obviously had such an extensive knowledge about
him. Time for that later. He moved from her office and towards
the door that led to the labs. When he opened it, he saw a very
long hallway and he had to pass a number of doors as he made
his way to where a light shone through a doorway window.

When he peeked in, Anna was sitting at a desk before a
microscope. At least he presumed it was Anna. The figure was
three-quarters turned away from him and writing in a notebook.
But surely this wasn't Anna from the boardinghouse. This
woman's dress was bright and colorful, even under the antiseptic lab coat. And the hair was very different—combed differently
with some sort of brooch or pin in it, and a ribbon.

As he watched, Anna stood up and turned to her left,
moving to another desk. While the lab coat was closed, there
was no mistaking the prominent breasts. Earle was also able to
note the makeup and the lipstick. And she wore earrings! Had
he never noticed this before? She was indeed very lovely. He
reached down with his right hand and touched the crumpled
note in his pocket. The picture of Eloise Jacobs flashed in his
mind momentarily. Then he felt that urge to cough rising in the
back of his throat. Earle opened the door and stepped inside.
He thought to startle her, to throw her off stride. He expected

to see a look of fear come over her and for her to cringe and fall back and perhaps to seek an avenue of escape.

If she was surprised, she showed little evidence of it. Was that a fleeting indication of fear when she first looked up?

"Hello, Dr. Williams. I take it you're not entirely surprised by my suddenly showing up?"

But she was surprised! Al and Kathleen were not here yet. They should have been. Kathleen said she would not be late. In her work, Anna had almost forgotten about the rendezvous. Anna tamped down the first sprouting of fear rising in her chest. She turned to the microscope to escape his gaze. She tried to make her voice sound assured. "No, not entirely surprised. You did say that you'd chauffeur me home as often as possible."

"Yes, I did say that." His tone was flat. No emotion. Controlled.

She continued to be turned away from him, pretending to look down the microscope. "And of course, you've always been punctual and...and most reliable." She could feel the uneasiness creeping up toward her brain. Her body tensed.

Nelson coughed. "Yes, you seem to have come to know me well. I wonder how that can be?" He advanced further into the room.

It took an effort, but she made herself glance back at him. Where was Kathleen? Why wasn't she here yet? Was she still searching for Al Devons? "You're not so much an enigma as you might think, Mr. Wilson. Perhaps none of us is." She stood and turned.

"What do you mean?"

Anna knew she needed more time. Why weren't they here? Did Kathleen really not have any intention of showing up? She glanced past his shoulder and towards the door. She'd never get past him. She broke into speech. "I've always found it difficult to understand people. I mean people, generally. But now that

I've given it some thought, it's not so complicated really. After all, we're all motivated by the same kinds of things aren't we?"

His eyes closed. He seemed to rock a bit unsteadily and that's when she noticed the sweat along his hairline.

"I mean we all need something and we all want something. We need food and water and..." He swayed, seemed to slump.

"Mr. Wilson, are you not well??"

Earle's eyes shot open and Anna could see plainly that in fact he was quite ill.

"I have the influenza, Anna."

"I...I'm..."

"Enough pretending. You know all about me, don't you?"

Anna dropped her hands to her sides and stared at the floor. She nodded ever so slightly. "Yes, I know who you are. I know what you've done."

Again his tone was flat. He took a handkerchief from his pocket and mopped at his forehead. "I have the influenza, Anna, and if God wills it I will die. Even though, in his master plan—" He stopped, swayed as he coughed violently into the handkerchief, and examined the phlegm he'd expectorated. "—But before I do...but before...I have to make sure..."

A thought popped into her head. "I can save you!"

Earle gaped at her. "What? What are you talking about? This flu is a death sentence."

She nodded vigorously. "I know. But I've been working for months. I've developed a vaccine. It can help you get well." Her mind worked furiously. What did he know? How much? A vaccine couldn't help after the fact, but did Earle Nelson know it? Could she make him believe?

His eyes gleamed, "You can what, Doctor?"

"I can create the vaccine right here in the lab. I have every-thing we need. It won't take me long."

He moved closer. Grimly, he stood only inches away and leaned into her as if to read her thoughts. She forced her eyes to return the stare.

"Let me help you, Earle." Softly. No desperation in her voice. A simple factual statement.

"God does indeed work mysteriously." Earle smiled at her. "He has sent me an angel of life. He has spared me to continue his wondrous work." For a long time he engaged her eyes and through the rising tumult of fear she almost looked away.

He commanded, "Do what you must do."

Anna worked quickly and efficiently. She removed the previously prepared centrifuged pneumococci sample. She injected the deadly combination of living non-husked bacilli and dead husked bacilli into the test tube and ensured that the mixture was ripe for growth at the ideal temperature. She repeated exactly the same process with a second vial. The entire samples were prepared in a few critical minutes.

CHAPTER TWENTY

Having discovered that Alvin's body had already been moved to Carson's Funeral Home because the City Morgue was overrun, Kathleen and Sam made their way there. Kathleen spent hours with Alvin, going over and over in her mind everything that she needed to say.

As Kathleen sat beside Al's coffin, she felt it just was not him. She was struck by how much the human body was only a shell. With the life gone from it, the spark had been removed. Those elements that had made him human, now bereft of a living space had left a macabre, synthetic, valueless shell. The body of a person was like a house from which every stick of furniture was removed.

The glint of humour or the glow of sadness in the eyes. The regular breathing when at rest in a sound sleep. An habitual movement of a hand or a peculiar gait of walk. The great sigh of reminiscence or the furrowed brow of an invading memory. These were the things that made us unique, or fascinating, or attractive, or diabolical. The body simply was superfluous. And wasn't that odd, considering how much living time was spent assessing each other's physical structure?

At the time Kathleen perceived that the body of Alvin Devons lay before her, she possessed the thought that in no way was this Alvin Devons. The real Alvin had run his hands across her, cradled her breasts, and gently sucked the nipples hard. His tongue had touched every crease and fold of her flesh. His arms and legs had enveloped her, wound about her, gripped her thighs and hips, and his erect penis had thrust so slowly and...

It was not often Kathleen blushed, but now she looked about surreptitiously to check that nobody else was in the room with her. Such thoughts. And then she smiled to herself because she realized that if he could know them he'd be having a gentle laugh about it.

And she knew that she possessed the best part of him. He would always linger there in her mind whenever she'd be doing ordinary things as her life progressed. Making a bed. Cleaning up after a meal. Writing a feature story. And suddenly he'd be there; having been uncalled and unsought he'd just show up, smiling and touching. She was astounded to discover that this is where we all really exist, in each other's minds. Was all the rest an illusion? The real creation?

Kathleen thought about the baby. It was a worry. How would she handle this? The people at her workplace would not be prepared to accept a single mother with a child. Even Anna had not been able to be receptive totally when Kathleen had disclosed her situation. Members of her own family would not be ready to accept this. What did other women do? She thought of termination but rejected it. Not because she had moral objections, but because it was the only connection left with Al Devons. This seed must be allowed to grow, to continue, to persevere.

She thought of orphanages but rejected that idea also. She could take far better care of a child than an orphanage could ever do. No, their child would need to be nurtured, educated, supported. He must come to understand that in some way, his father had tried to make things better.

She didn't touch Al. Didn't have to. It didn't matter. She only said, "I'll take care of our child. He will have family and love. He'll not want for anything. I'll tell him about you. That's all I can do."

***

J.T. Hawkins had no idea what he should do and so, for the time being, he just stood and shuffled. He'd watched Earle cross the street, ascend the stairs, and let himself into Versatile Laboratories. But his fear was so great that he was nearly immobile.

Earley would kill Anna Williams. That much was certain and he'd kill Hawkshaw too if he showed himself. No doubt of that. He felt for his new knife as if to reassure himself and looked about in the very spot where Nelson had stood not twenty minutes earlier.

Something was different for Earley though. Something was wrong. Hawkshaw couldn't put his finger on it exactly but there were things he noticed. Earley wasn't checkin' round and lookin' back the way he usually did. Hawkins had been following him for hours and he'd never seen him stop so often or move so slowly. And he kept coughin' and blowin' his nose. At first it looked like he was going to have one of his seizures. But no! It wasn't that! Somethin' else then. Twice Earle had leaned up against buildings like he was all out of breath.

But maybe he was fakin' too. Maybe he knew Hawkshaw would be watching and was trying to draw him close, where he'd have a chance of gettin' hold of him. And then...

Hawkins shivered in spite of the warm evening. He couldn't just leave and let Anna Williams be murdered. He should walk away, but he couldn't. In the darkness he shifted back and forth from foot to foot and waited.

***

Anna's hands shook so that she had to force herself to be calm. She worked slowly but steadily after Roger Wilson had gone back to her office. It was not like she could have escaped. To do that she had to pass by him. She was trapped and they both knew it.

She prepared a serum. The combination husked and non-husked bacilli were in a healthy, growth-friendly environment. She heated the solution and placed some under a microscope slide in order to check that it could provide a healthy boost to the immune system. When she was ready, she transferred the solution to a syringe.

The man she knew as Wilson sat at her desk, facing the open door so he could see her if she tried to leave. At the same time, he thumbed through a stack of correspondence on her desktop. He searched for something out of the ordinary: notes she might have kept about him, letters to police or other authorities, incoming documents that might be suspicious.

As he searched he continued to feel miserable. He was getting chills now and there were definite aches in his muscles. He put his hand to his forehead and held it to check for a temperature. His skin was starting to hurt and his throat itched. He kept feeling as if he wanted to spit out from deep in his throat, but when he tried to, nothing happened.

Two or three times he opened letters that looked odd but when he glanced through they offered nothing. He gleaned the pile and when nothing exceptional showed, he went to Anna's file case and opened it. For such a busy person he was surprised at how little the cabinet contained. He glanced through quickly and lifted out ten files which he took back to the desk. It was a slow, painstaking business but he had to be sure.

***

Hawkshaw despaired that he could do anything to help Anna. He was about to cross the street to see if he could peek through a window when he heard the horses. He recognized, even in the dark, that these were two of the special constables he'd heard about. Nobody else would be out at this time of night—not on horses. These two were out, checking the streets to enforce the curfew.

If he was going to do something it had to be now. This was his best chance. Maybe the only one he would get. He bent down and felt around in the dark until his hand found a good-sized rock. He pulled the knife from his belt and held it in his left hand.

He stepped into the street in front of the two, who were so intent on their conversation that at first they didn't see him.

Hawkins, in as loud and threatening a sound as he could muster, brandished the knife in the air. "C'mon you two yellow bastards! You think you're tough 'cause you beat up on a bunch of tramps? C'mon you two! I'll slit both you sons a bitches before you can even—" He reared back and threw the rock, hitting one horse between the eyes. The animal startled and lifted its front feet to paw the air.

The special slid down its back and landed on the street. For a moment he sat there, stunned and quiet and wondering what had just happened.

Who was this tiny, horrible little man standing in the street and waving a knife? His partner recovered more quickly and plunged his horse forward. Hawkshaw turned and ran. He raced to the sidewalk and up the stairs of Versatile Laboratories. When he reached the door, he began pounding on it and yelling. "Open the door! Open the goddamn door! We know you're in there. Nelson! Open the damn door and come out. You murderous bastard. Come out!" Hawkshaw continued to pound and kick at the door. He kept at it right up to when the special constable caught up to him and wrapped a huge arm around his neck.

***

At the very first pounding on the door, Earle moved into action. He jumped from the chair and headed towards Anna's lab. At the same time his mind began to crystallize into a plan as it always did. When he burst into her workroom, Anna was capping a syringe, which she quickly slipped into the pocket of her lab coat.

Earle crossed the room in a few strides and grasped her wrist. He yanked her closer to him. "Not a word now. No shouting. Don't struggle, Anna. We have to leave right now." He pulled her into the hallway and towards the rear of the building.

Al and Kathleen had finally arrived then. Thank God! But she needed to slow this man down. Give them a chance to get inside the building.

She pulled up short. "Wait, Roger. There are some things I need. If you just let me get them I can still help you. I won't have to make the vaccine here. You can still get it."

"No!" He snarled into her face. "No time. That's cops out there. We have to go now!" When he yanked her this time it was so violent she could feel the muscles begin to tear. Pain shot through her arm and into her shoulder. She couldn't hold back. She had to move along with him.

At the back door Earle pulled a knife and forced Anna in front of him. "Open the door—slide the bolt back and open it. Do as I tell you now! Quick!"

With her good left arm, Anna forced the bolt. The door hadn't been opened for a long time and she had to work the bolt loose. Finally it gave way. She turned the doorknob and pushed.

There was no one outside. Momentarily, Anna was frustrated and then angry. Where were they? Why didn't they come help her? What was wrong with them?

Earle forced her down the back stairs. His intention was to use the back alley, but in the darkness he tripped and let go of Anna to break his fall. She darted away and ran alongside the building toward the roaring voices she heard at the front. When she reached the sound, she stopped because two horses stood at the bottom of the steps. What on earth?! Why were horses standing there and chewing at the grass? Then she saw the commotion on the steps and heard the shouting and cursing as two men tried to subdue a third. It was Hawkins! What was happening?

At that moment, Nelson grabbed her sore arm again and pulled her toward the street. She opened her mouth. She was going to scream. And that's when Earle hit her. The pain was excruciating. It bounced around inside her head until she thought she'd faint. But now he was tugging her, pulling her out onto the sidewalk and down the street.

Under a streetlamp he stopped to look back at the struggle that had now moved down the stairs and into the path of the horses. In the light, Anna had a chance to gulp down some air. She felt like she would vomit and was trying to pull away even though her arm was on fire. Roger Wilson was not looking at her. His eyes were intent upon the struggle in front of the horses. His grip was crushing the bones in her wrist.

She thought he'd look panicked. Out of control. But no, his eyes were calm and observant. Flitting from the men to the stamping horses to the street and finally to Anna. "Now, we're going to walk. But quickly. Don't try to run. Don't look back at them. Walk with me, Anna. You're going to tell me where we have to go and what we need to do to get that vaccine." They turned and headed up the street together.

For a short distance they walked quietly, but for Earle it was with a firm resolve. "God has laid out his plan for me, Anna. I'm to be his commander-in-chief for the greatest battle ever to be fought. And imagine, you are to be the instrument of my resurrection. You'll bring me back from the dead. It's through you that I shall be blessed to aid in my Lord's enterprise."

Once more Anna felt like she would scream. The gripping fear rose up and she willed herself to force it down.

"What do you mean? What are you talking about? What enterprise?"

He stopped and stared at her as if she was a dumb beast. "Why, the influenza of course. It's a plague, Anna. It's been sent from above. Don't you see the good work that's being done? The annihilation of the sinner is at hand. There will be rejoicing."

Anna's eyes were wide with fear. She realized she was facing total and absolute madness. There was nothing to prevent this monstrous mind from continuing its path of destruction. The only thing she could think now was that she must escape.

When the horse stomped on the constable's hand, it finally gave Hawkshaw the opening he needed. As the man screamed and his partner moved to his rescue, Hawkins shot out from under the brawl and into the street. His immediate concern was the pursuit of Anna and Earle.

He raced away and at the same time searched frantically for his knife. He'd lost it somewhere in the tumult. Now what would he do? Without it there was no way of stopping Earley. He couldn't see them yet in the street and he began to shout, hoping Anna would hear him and answer.

He ran out of breath quickly and had to stop. With great ragged intakes he bent over and placed his hands just above his knees. He forced the air into his lungs and gulped loudly. He compelled himself to breathe steadily until he felt he could stand upright again.

When he did so he could hear shouting behind and looked back at the specials, who were now pursuing him on foot. Ahead he squinted into the light offered by the streetlamps. That was them. They'd stopped. Earley was towering over Anna. He'd let go of her wrist but had her turned toward him and clasped her by her upper arms. He was yelling something, shouting into her face, but Hawkshaw couldn't hear. The specials were rapidly closing up behind him.

Anna raised her hands and feebly tried to fend him off. Her resistance was depleting sharply as he shook her and her head snapped about like a flag in a breeze.

He was screaming at her. "You have to tell me! What do we need for the vaccine? Where can you prepare it? Is there somewhere besides your lab? Tell me, Anna!"

Finally, she managed to wrench her good arm loose. She tried to step away, to regain balance. To make herself think of what to do! She looked about in a frantic bid for help. Then she looked back at her tormentor and she watched in horror as a human mind convulsed, wrenched itself into a knot, and in the throes of desolation broke upon the night and cried its agony aloud.

> *"And when thou art spoiled what wilt thou do?*
> *Though thou clothest thyself with crimson, though thou*
> *Deckest thee with ornaments of gold, though thou*
> *Rentest thy face with painting, in vain shalt thou*
> *Make thyself fair; thy lovers will despise thee,*
> *They will seek thy life."*

Anna was croaking out something. She had reached into her lab coat pocket and withdrew the syringe. Hopelessly, she was trying to impinge upon his brain. She held the vaccine up so he could see. "I have this. I can help. Let me help before it's too late. Do you hear me, Earle?"

But he could hear nothing except Aunt Lillian. He watched in wild-eyed wonder as she held the book and motioned at him in a menacing way and continued her questions unmercifully. "Do you hear me, Earley? Earley, do you hear? Do you hear the verse? Do you understand? Do you know what it means? Earley? Do you know what it means?"

"Yes, Aunt Lillian!" Earle reached out and smashed her across her left ear with a powerful right hand. He reached down with his left as if in a motion to help her up but instead seized her throat and brought her to her feet. He thrust his face into hers as she danced before him, her feet several inches off the ground.

He roared, "Give me that! Give me!!" He was shaking her like a doll and her body flopped about, devoid of control. Desperately, she held up the syringe to his eyes and tried to get him to see it. Her painful left hand sought to pry his fingers loose. The starvation for oxygen was causing her to slip towards unconsciousness. In a huge effort, Anna flung the container into the street. Earle's eyes followed its arc as it sped through the night, hit the sidewalk, and continued to roll away from him.

He dropped Anna, who crumpled to her knees and fought to breathe. Earle lunged towards the street and fell. The syringe continued to roll. He crawled toward it on his hands and knees. Anna tried to move into the darkness.

Earle reached for the vial and a large boot crushed down on it.

"Alright, you bastard. I warned you once that if we saw you again we'd beat the hell out of you. And a goddamn dope fiend too. You son of a bitch!"

Earle's arm stretched out. "No! No! I need it! Don't break it! You don't understand! I'm sick! I'm sick! Please don't do this to me." At the end, his voice dropped off to a hoarse whisper.

Suddenly the smell of singed duck down wafted to his nostrils. He prostrated himself in the street and stretched out a hand, trying to reach the life-saving vial. He looked past his hand, past the boot crunching the life from the syringe. The last thing he saw was a new pair of shoes. They were dancing about as if the owner had no control over the feet contained within.

***

They sat in the living room of Kathleen's home on Wellington Crescent. Monday morning had dawned beautifully and the air had not yet started to acquire the heat. Later, Kathleen thought, it would become sticky with the humidity and if there was no breeze everyone would be hot and uncomfortable.

She studied the marks on Anna's neck and though they looked horrific with dark patches of bruised and damaged skin, she felt reassured when the doctor said there did not appear to be lasting damage. Who could know, really? Right now Anna moved her head gingerly and pretty much had to turn her whole body when she wanted to look about.

Anna didn't remember much. She had no idea the police had arrived until much later, when she was at the hospital. She had a faint memory of someone helping her to her feet. Must have been Hawkshaw. And then Kathleen being there and then this Seigalman person and them bundling her into a cab.

And Kathleen had brought her here while the two men stayed behind with the police. She must have been in shock after that. Her jaw ached and the upper part of it close to the ear was swollen and had a small laceration. She knew Kathleen had also taken her to the hospital but recalled nothing of the details.

"Kathleen?"

"What?"

"Shouldn't we go to the police? To explain...to tell them about Earle. To tell them about the murders."

"He's dead, Anna. Nothing we know or say can change things. It won't make a difference."

"Perhaps not. But he didn't die from the flu, I'm almost sure of that."

"How do you know?"

Anna tried to move her head but the pain brought her up short and she grimaced. "I guess I don't for sure. But he wasn't the same as the others in the hospital. When I was there the symptoms were different. It just wasn't the same thing."

Kathleen smiled. "Well, I guess Earle Nelson just died from contracting a real bad cold."

Anna looked at her strangely.

Kathleen took both their cups and refilled them. When she came back, she sat directly in front of Anna so that the woman would not have to move that painful-looking neck.

Kathleen took her hands gently. "Look, I don't really know what to tell you except to say that the police won't believe us. In fact, they have no idea you were even there. Oh, they know somebody was there but they don't know it was you. Hawkins and Sam Seigalman were with him. They were with him all evening. They'd been drinking together down at tent city. Just the three of them. They were on their way downtown when the argument broke out. Hawkshaw and Sam wanted to take Earle to a hospital because he'd started showing the flu symptoms and it scared the hell out of them. That's what was happening when the police showed up. Sam had gone to look for help from the police and Hawkshaw was arguing when Earle knocked him down. And let's consider something else. If we decide it's important to go to the police to set the record straight, then we have to think about what happens with Mr. Hawkins. Is it really a good idea to drag him into this?"

Anna gazed directly into Kathleen's eyes. "How did Roger Wilson die then?"

Kathleen hesitated only momentarily. "I don't really know. He was already dead when Sam and I got there. As for you, you were with me. I picked you up just after your boss left for the evening. That would have been about nine. You told me so yourself, that he'd been there. What's his name? Parkes. So you were with me all the rest of the evening. I'll swear to it. And they'll believe me if it comes down to that. And what are you going to tell them, Anna? Some fantastical story about how Earle was following you? And about how he came to get the flu? And about how you were going to give him a vaccine? Really, Doctor, who's going to listen to all that?"

"What about these marks, Kathleen? All over my neck and my face?" She touched her jaw line and winced at the pain.

"What marks? I don't see any marks. And certainly, by the time you recover from the flu at my house, no one else will see marks either. Dr. Parkes already knows how ill you are, but I've assured him you're getting the best private nursing care available. And of course, no one can see you because right now you might be contagious. Who knows when you'll be able to see people?"

Anna cocked an eye and tried to shake her head but it hurt too much. Instead she asked, "What will you do now?"

"Do? What do you mean?"

"Well, the strike's over. Your newspaper has been shut down. And of course you're...there's the baby. What will you do?"

Kathleen pondered this for some time. "Well, let me see. There's a lady in Minneapolis who has no idea she's going to be a grandmother and a girl who doesn't know she's going to be an aunt. They deserve to know this so I'll be making a trip. A child needs family so that if Mrs. Devons shows up with a baby why they'll be very pleased."

"What about your work? The dailies will never hire you. Not someone who supported the strike the way you did."

"As a matter of fact I wouldn't work for one of the dailies under any circumstances. Seigalman was telling me there's going to be a new labour newspaper. They may have been able to shut down *The Western Labour News* but that doesn't have anything to do with *The Western Star*. Later today, when you're resting and giving that poor neck a break, I'm having my typewriter brought round from the Labour Temple. I've been asked to write the first feature article for the new paper and I've been turning over in my little brain exactly what I might say. But never mind that. What will you do, Dr. Anna Williams?"

Anna was startled. What, in fact, would she do? Parkes was aware that she was on to something at the lab. She'd have to see that work through. It was an obligation. But what then? Other than Versatile Medical Laboratories, she did not really have commitments here. Perhaps it was time to look elsewhere.

"In New York there's a hospital. In fact it's an institute. The Rockefeller. I know the Director. His name is Rufus Cole. I believe that the work he's doing will revolutionize medicine and especially the way we work with patients. He's been trying to get me to come down there for some time now. I think perhaps it's time I had a talk with him."

Kathleen got up and walked to Anna. She reached out and touched the hair gently and let her fingers trail lightly down the woman's sore jaw line. "You're still very tired. I think you need to lie down and see if you can get some rest. When my typewriter gets here its noise will probably wake you. We'll talk some more then."

***

Anna had been sleeping for three hours when the typewriter arrived. As soon as Kathleen started, Anna was awake. She stretched and tried to stifle a yawn, threatening her still-aching jaw. She listened for a good fifteen minutes to the clack-clacking rhythm. It was satisfying and somehow reassuring to hear the keys slapping on paper.

When Anna left the bedroom, Kathleen was leaning over the machine, her hands flying across the keys, pausing as she thought, then flying across them again as the thought leaped onto the paper. Anna walked to where Kathleen sat, pouring out the words of the article.

Anna put a hand on each shoulder and returned the smile that flashed up at her. She leaned over and read:

> The Winnipeg daily newspapers are reporting the death of the general strike. They should not confuse that with the death of the Labour Movement. The unions live on and will live on long after the demise of this city's dailies.
>
> Newspapers like *The Telegram* would have their readers believe that nothing was gained by the strike. Not so. History will determine that much was gained. Indeed let it be recorded that the strike was the birth of change in Canada, where the shift from absolute power vested in the employers began to loosen its hold upon serfdom to make way for the rise of fairness, labour rights, safety on the job, and most of all, recompense for one's work.
>
> Contrary to what the Committee of One Thousand and their supporters would purport, the Right to Collective Bargaining was very much on trial here as was a fair living wage

and preventing discrimination against strikers. These are much in danger as a result of the so-called victory over the workers.

Indeed, the very fact that the employers and the press think of the strike in terms of victory and defeat speaks to the heart of the labour trouble in our city and in our country. This sets us up in adversarial positions and as such there can be no commonality that aims to raise the standard of living for all.

And now we have the threats against our leaders. Blood has been shed in the streets, but apparently that's not enough for the fear-mongers. They want even more blood and so someone will have to pay a price. Why not Russell, Woodsworth, Ford, Heaps, and Dixon? After all, these promoters of revolution must be taught lessons, like schoolchildren who have run amok! The fact that these men stood courageously in the face of threatened prosecution, intimidation, and prison will be forgotten conveniently.

The Telegram cries out that the defeat of the strike is a great victory for democracy. This is nonsense of the vilest sort. Democracy was never in danger in this strike and the issue never was about the state of democracy in this dominion.

Fifty-two years ago, when our forbearers saw fit to give birth to a nation called Canada, they perceived it to mean liberty, justice, freedom, and acceptance. Ask yourselves: is it liberty when we condemn our workers to jobs where their very lives are put at risk? Is it justice when labour leaders can have their homes invaded in the middle of the night and be summarily packed off to prisons? Is it freedom when our own city fathers deny us the right fundamental to all countries that would call themselves free states: the right to public dissent? And what of acceptance? Is it not so that your own fathers and grandfathers and even generations before them arrived at places like Pier 21 expecting to be embraced by their new country?

And what do we do today? We arrest non-Canadian-born humans in secret pogroms. We impose a vengeance upon them by tagging them as aliens. We spirit them out of the country under the cover of darkness to return them to their "Bolshevik" homeland.

No. The end of the strike is no great victory for democracy. It's a step backward as we march collectively into the mists of time. Once again we will have to witness the forced impotence of the working poor, the starvation enforced by a class society, and the imposition of the crucifying doctrines of Capitalism upon our people.

NOTES

While much of the factual data from the manuscript can be found on multiple sites I am indebted particularly to John M. Barry for his remarkable documentation in "The Great Influenza, The Epic Story of the Deadliest Plague in History".

The information on wages and costs of living for the painter can be found in Ken Osborne's book "R.B. Russell and the Labour Movement".

The poem beginning 'Bread by permission of the likes of Ed Parnell' was published by the Western Labour News in 1920. Reference to it is from Doug Smith's book "Let Us Rise! An Illustrated History of the Manitoba Labour Movement".

The signs carried by the strikers and the anti-strikers are accurate and can be found in many places which refer to the history of that event.

The newspaper advertisements and commentaries are accurate and can be found in the dailies that existed in Winnipeg in 1919.

Other sources that were of help were "Immigration Canada – Origins and Options" by Iain R. Munro, and "United We Stand, A History of Winnipeg's Civic Workers" by Jim Pringle.

I'd like to recognize the staff at Manitoba Archives and Hudson Bay Archives who always go out of their way to be of service.

I'd be remiss if I did not thank the good folks at FriesenPress whose painstaking attention to detail, suggestions, commentaries and encouragement brought The Silent March to publication.

My apologies if I've neglected any sources.

AUTHOR'S NOTE

As much as possible I tried to honour the accuracy of the dates, times, buildings etc. in order to maintain the integrity of the events surrounding the strike. In that regard many of the names on both sides of the issue are the actual people who participated in the strike of that summer. At times I've used actual statements voiced by participants on both sides of the strike.

Likewise, a number of the stories and events that found their way into the book are not of my creation but can be found in a variety of historical records. Specifically they are: the Howard Spack story, the Foster egg story, the Fred Coppins story, the Dr. Mary Crawford story, the Fred Keeley story and the story of the police officers twirling their pistols western style on the day which came to be known as Bloody Saturday. Again, I used these to provide an authentic framework for the events prior to and during the strike.

Earle Nelson's infamous and destructive path wreaked havoc upon the American and Canadian Midwest but at a later time period.

Other characters, events and situations are fictitious.

Thanks to...

A book like this does not get written without some help from others. In particular I need to thank Margaret who helped in the early going with the research. Bruce also spent time reading a draft and researching Winnipeg downtown in the first decades of the 20th century. Janet assisted with her computer skills and the creative Catherine did the art work for the cover for which I am grateful. A special thanks to Stephanie who helped get the science terminology correct and Peter Bretscher at University of Saskatchewan who gave great advice about immunology. I hope I haven't strayed too far from the facts (as they were known in 1919).